VALKYRIE'S SONG

Wolfsangel
Fenrir
Lord of Slaughter

Also by M.D. Lachlan from Gollancz

Wolfsangel
Fenrir
Lord of Slaughter

VALKYRIE'S SONG

M.D. LACHLAN

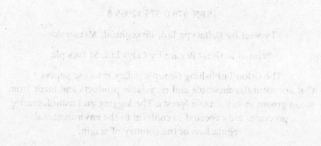

The right of M.D. Lachlan to be identified as the author
of this work has been asserted by him in accordance with
the Copyright, Designs and Patents Act 1988.

First published in Great Britain in 2015 by
Gollancz
An imprint of the Orion Publishing Group
Carmelite House, 50 Victoria Embankment
London EC4Y 0DZ
An Hachette UK Company

This edition published in 2016 by
Gollancz

1 3 5 7 9 10 8 6 4 2

A CIP catalogue record for this book
is available from the British Library

ISBN 978 0 575 12965 8

Typeset by Deltatype Ltd, Birkenhead, Merseyside

Printed in Great Britain by Clays Ltd, St Ives plc

The Orion Publishing Group's policy is to use papers
that are natural, renewable and recyclable products and made from
wood grown in sustainable forests. The logging and manufacturing
processes are expected to conform to the environmental
regulations of the country of origin.

www.orionbooks.co.uk
www.gollancz.co.uk
www.mdlachlan.com

To dead friends.
Too many, too soon.

'In his anger at the English barons, William commanded that all crops and herds, chattels and foods should be burned to ashes, so that the whole of the North be stripped of all means of survival. So terrible a famine fell upon the people, that more than 100,000 young and old starved to death. My writings have often praised William, but for this act I can only condemn him.'

ORDERIC VITALIS

'I have persecuted its native inhabitants beyond all reason. Whether gentle or simple, I have cruelly oppressed them; many I unjustly inherited; Innumerable multitudes, especially in the county of York, perished through me by famine or the sword.'

WILLIAM THE CONQUEROR

1 The Harrying of the North

It was winter, and the land bloomed with murder. From the shoulder of the frost-stained fell she could see the burning had reached the near villages. Four fingers of smoke clawed at the pale blue sky. The brittle evening was hazy and in her mouth was the taste of other fires, now spent. On another night she might have mistaken the distant screams for the cries of gulls, blown inland from a sea she had never seen.

She had asked about the sea but her grandfather, who had come over from Denmark with Canute and had been a great traveller, said it was a dirty big grey thing that killed people; a serpent that cast its coils around the world, and best avoided by those who had any sense. The Norman invaders, the killers down in the valley, came from over the sea, but it was a different sea to the one her northern ancestors had travelled.

The Normans worked with a terrible industry. From dawn she'd seen them moving in, raising plumes of smoke from the villages like black banners in their wake. Tola had to run if she wanted to live. She had no choice.

She was cold to the bone but she could feel the killers' effort even at that distance. She imagined herself among those columns of men; her arm warmed by the toil of slaughter, her body glad of the heat of the animal beneath her and the fire of destruction about her. For an instant she felt herself inside the thoughts of a Norman soldier, one real or imagined so sharp he may as well have been real. He felt not entirely warlike but a fussy, particular man. He would see that Old Nothgyth's apple tree was felled and split to the root, her pigs slaughtered and their blood turned into the hard soil, lest it freeze on the earth and the people creep back to suck at it in their starvation. The

3

axes blunted easily on frozen wood and frozen soil and it was an effort keeping them sharp.

He would see the fields salted from the bulging carts that followed the column, the well fouled with pitch and the corpses of Nothgyth's sons. He knew the salting was only a gesture but it was worth doing – the rebels needed to believe that their land had been laid waste for a thousand years. When the house was fired and everything she owned along with it, he would lead his men away, turning back at the gallop after a short while to catch her digging at the grain she had buried. He knew all the tricks. Only then would he leave her, standing close by her burning home taking the last warmth she would ever know before she died. He had to hurry away. The scene would be repeated one more time before the end of the day. It had been played out nineteen times already. Sometimes he would leave a survivor to spread the fear for a while before the cold took them. Sometimes he would not. There was no reason in who lived and who died. It was a matter of feel, he'd tell his men.

She heard an echo of words in the man's mind. If they had been spoken to her face she would not have understood them but in the cavern of her head they took on meaning. She saw a stern-faced man, bald at the front of his head, strong-armed, pot-bellied. 'No one alive from York to Durham.' That was the whole world.

She came back to herself and gazed out over the wide land. White everywhere, like the little woollen blanket the travelling fool had put over the coins at the summer fair. When he'd removed it the coins were gone. The world was changing, hiding itself to emerge anew. When it did, there would be no place for her.

How many soldiers? She didn't know her numbers but she had never seen such a host – not even at the market day at Blackdale. More people than she had ever seen, more than she could ever have imagined seeing. They had come upon the dale at an easy pace, walking their steaming horses through the wide snows. One column from the north, another from the south and a third from the sea. It was not a net, nor even an encirclement. The attackers were indifferent to whether their prey stayed and died or fled to the hills. Death by fire or death by cold; death either way.

'Yes,' she said, though no question had been asked. The man who stood beside her was to have been her husband. Hals. He had not been a rich man, though he had a little land and kept a few sheep. She was a poor woman, pretty enough to marry better, her mother said. A man with five or six hides might have considered her. She hadn't wanted a man with five or six hides. Hals would do. Tola, so sensitive she could put herself into the mind of a Norman across a valley, knew Hals was a good man and she understood him.

She shivered deeply. 'We can't stay on the hill all night,' she said.

Hals hugged her and she sensed the question in him. 'What can we do?' He was of the Danish line too, his father coming over with Canute to farm, so Hals would more naturally trust a woman's opinion than an Englishman of older heritage might.

'Wait and see if they move through. Then go down. To whatever's left.'

She saw that he feared they would come back.

'They'll go everywhere,' she said. 'It's a hunt to them. What man doesn't love to hunt?'

He gestured behind him. Nine standing stones circled the hilltop. The local people called them the nine ladies. They were said to protect the valley. They offered scant help now.

When she was girl, wandering up on the fell on a sunny morning, they had spoken to her. The weather up there could not be trusted, and in the afternoon a grey mist had come down so quickly it was as if the day had closed its eyes. She had found herself among the standing stones then. They'd given her a start at first, as she'd thought they were people standing watching her in the mist. She'd realised they were just stones with her next breath. She'd wandered among them, trying to get her bearings. The last stone slewed at an angle, pointing along Blackbed Scar and out to the boggy top. There was a quick route down from there and she knew it well. The mist was cold on her nose and lips, the shawl tight about her as she stepped along the broad arc of the Scar and out onto the sodden earth of the top.

The going was harder than she'd thought. There had been little rain but the bog had held its water. She was soaked within twenty paces, about to turn around, when she'd seen him under the surface. The hanged god, his skin blackened from its long soaking, the frayed noose at his neck, one eye ruined and eaten, the other half-open, looking at her. She looked across the Scar and saw the nine standing stones, no longer stones but eight fierce women, staring across the valley, spears in their hands and shields at their side. Where was the ninth?

She saw a vision of a great battle in the north – Danes camped around a river surprised by an onrushing horde of Englishmen screaming over the brow of a hill, a scrambled defence, no armour, no helms, as the English king led his men against them.

And then, from a strange country of chalky soil, the other men came; those she now knew to be Normans with their tear-drop shields, their shaved heads. The English king rode south to meet them, his weary warriors at his side, and from every shire and every village men ran to meet him to join and refresh his army, though they might have walked or not bothered at all.

Even Tola knew that the Norman king was done for. She sensed his feeling for his ships; it was a familiar one that she felt largely from the young – one of need and resentment. The king could not go far from the ships. If he was beaten he needed a way home. He had ravaged the land, so he needed to resupply. This man, with the pot belly and the strong arm, was walking a ledge above a crag. He felt vulnerable, arrogant, belligerent and exhilarated. He had come too late in the year.

He feared winter, feared being king of only the wasteland he had created, his army coughing, rotting and dying beneath its tents. There was a lurch in the pit of her stomach, a vision of two ravens flying against a stormcloud sunset. The English king would not listen to counsel. His mind sank into the blood mire. He would give the Norman king his battle. She knew that the man in the peaty water was a god and he had entered the mind of the English king to drive him on to death and to a place in stories to last a thousand years.

She fell into the mire and through the god's mind to a burning city where gigantic beings, half shadow, fought in the ruins. One shadow was a wolf, another the noose god, battling forever under a cold sun. Then the god had turned his eye towards her and she had seen bright shining things, symbols that expressed everything – how a baby grows to be an adult and a calf to become a cow; how the sea pushes against the land and the land pushes back. More light than she had ever known was all around her. After that it was dark.

Her brother had found her, half dead in the water, and carried her down to the farm.

Her brother. Where was he in this burning land? He had gone with a party of men to face the Normans, to ambush them as they rode through the woods. It had given her the pause she needed to run to the fell. He was dead now. She could feel the hounds dragging him down, their weight more awful than their teeth; hear the swift and certain stride of the Norman soldier coming through the woods towards him, the punch of the dagger into his ribs.

She used the cold against her emotions, locking them in under ice, under the will to survive.

'The ladies never offered me help,' she said to Hals.

He hugged her tighter, his arms shaking with the cold. The last rays of the sun warmed them from the rim of the hills. They'd have to move again soon and keep moving throughout the night if they weren't to freeze where they stood.

Hals had ice in his beard. There was no wind yet, no rain.

7

Even without them she knew they couldn't spend the night still in the open.

Hals' eyes were full of tears. He was a strong man and she had never seen him cry. She knew he wanted her to ask the ladies.

'It is against God's law. The priest told us that.'

He drew his knife.

'That too is against God's law.'

'Orm at Ing End took that way out,' Hals said.

He was trembling, with fear and cold, with misery.

'His father was a northern man. He should have fought.' She pulled her cloak around her. 'You couldn't kill me, Hals.'

He offered her the knife. 'You do it,' he said. 'You are stronger than me. Kill me and then yourself.'

She turned her eyes away. Out over the valley, a silver half-moon lit the smoke, the dying light rendering the land grey but for the red sun in the west. Away by Alfred's house a flame sprang up. The Normans were burning again. Surely soon they would stop, if only to secure shelter for themselves.

A flash from down in the valley – someone holding up a bright sword that caught the light of the burning house. A cry, bounding towards them from far away. Had the warriors seen them?

'Do you remember the rhymes Nana used to tell? About the end of the world?

Surt fares from the south with the scourge of branches,
The sun of the battle-gods shone from his sword.
The crags are sundered, the giant-women sink,
The dead throng Hel-way, and heaven is cloven.'

She crossed herself. 'This is the end of the world. Christ must come,' she said.

'So where is he?' said Hals.

A group of six riders broke away from the burning farm towards the hill, small as mice in the distance. Tola looked at

Hals' knife, so sharp, so clean. It had caught the sun, she was sure, and given them away.

They couldn't run. The Normans were burning on the south of the dale too. They might make the woods but it was a scant hope. There was no other option.

'I'll go to the gods,' she said.

Tola walked along the ridge of the Scar to the stones. She knew in her gut the key to what she sought. Pain. Denial.

'Keep moving, Hals,' said Tola. 'Either run down or stay with me but keep moving. You'll die if you don't.'

It didn't take someone of Tola's sensitivities to see the question on Hals' face. 'And you?'

'Death had his chance with me before here. He won't harm me now.'

She took off her shawl and laid it down, took off her skirt and her tunic, and stood among the stones in only her underhose and her shirt.

Hals paced the line of stones back and forth, his breath steaming about him. They'd made their decision, he wasn't about to go back on it now.

Later, Tola would know there was a point of transition in invoking the gods where you went from willing them to appear to willing them to stay away. Colder than she had ever been, human and vulnerable, she stood – warm flesh among the frozen stones. She knew who she sought. The people still had their stories and their faith. They called to Jesus on a Sunday and, if Jesus did not come, they left their offerings and their carvings for the elves and the gods. There was a charm and she spoke it for want of knowing really what to do.

'Ladies of the Dale, watchers by night and day
Hear me singing your furious song.'

There was nothing that had not been there before, only the shouts of the Norman soldiers in the dale, the pacing of Hals along the line of stones.

'Hear me singing your furious song.'

She said it again and again and its meaning started to slip.

9

Furious song. Furious singer. The old words for that phrase came to her. Woden. Odin, as Hal's family called him. Death in his hood, death in his noose, in the waters of the mire, his nails black, his skin leather. Hals kept pacing the line. She felt his anxiety as if it was her own, a lurch in her belly, a need to shit. The feeling faded, her body grew colder.

How long had she been there? Always. She was a stone, watching the valley. Her sisters were beside her, looking down, their dark wings stretching to the sky.

She heard a name she recognised. Waelcyrian – Valkyries, as her father would have called them.

'*Choosers of the slain. Dark ones, overseeing the land.*'

She had a sensation of flight, of great wings beating at the sky; wings or shadows, she could not tell. She heard the call of ravens, felt the rush of cold air.

Hals shook her. He was trying to tell her the enemy was coming.

The half-moon was big and bright but there was now a low fog on the hill. She was above it, looking down, the heads of the riders emerging as if they swam through a lake. She saw the bodies of the horses moving through the fog like dark fish through a silty sea, the spears of the riders before them.

'What is to be given?' One of the strange women spoke, her voice rattling like earth onto a coffin.

'I have nothing to give!'

'Then you must want nothing.'

'Help me vanquish those I hate.'

'The price is high.'

'I will pay it.'

She was on the ground and in the air at the same time. A rider gave a cry and said something in his strange speech. He'd seen them. He turned towards her, his sword free.

He said something else and she heard delight in his voice. He was pleased to find a young woman.

Moonshadows were on the fog and the shadows were the wings of gigantic birds, or something like birds. A dark shape swept past her and she threw up a hand to protect her face. The rider slid down from his horse in an easy movement. His hand was at her throat but it was as if she was watching herself in a dream.

He tore away her tunic and pushed her backwards.

A woman's face loomed from the mist, a death mask, her skin like pitch, golden hair falling in a braid to a noose at the neck. On her arm was a shield, in her hand a fireblack spear and at her back were wings like those of a gigantic raven but made of moonlight and shadows. She screamed one word – 'Odin!' – and Tola knew that name meant death.

The spear was a shadow, thrusting forward to take the Norman at the throat. The man fell backwards onto the frosty ground and the woman followed him, drawing a sharp black knife. She seized the man's hair and, in a swipe, beheaded him. She passed up the head to Tola and it seemed to the girl a marvellous gift, like a flower. Still she was above the fray in most of her mind, looking down, cradling the severed head to her breast.

Figures condensed from the fog and then were gone, only to reform again – women, some flying on great black wings, others descending on horses of fog and shadow.

The Normans thrashed with their swords in the murk, like beaters trying to drive ducks into the paths of slings and arrows. She saw one man lifted straight from his saddle, flying up into the swirling air. The voices of the Normans were urgent, those of the horses panicked and shrill. A horseman cried out as his horse stuttered backwards and reared, falling. Another slashed about him as if the air itself was his enemy. He too fell, though she did not see what had struck him.

Wings were everywhere about her, like the beating of a mighty storm on a door. Horses screeched, men cursed and the women who swooped around her screamed their war cries.

'Woden, Odin, Grimnir.' The names sounded inside her like the wind bawling in the hills and she knew their meaning. 'Fury, Madness. Death.'

On the ground a woman held up her spear and cried out in exultation as her horse gorged itself on the body of a fallen Norman.

Tola cried out for Hals but she could not see him. Only two Normans were left now. One had seen her and his horse charged the arc of the hillside. She had come back to herself and was no longer in the air but in front of those stamping hooves, a frightened and defenceless woman, the fog about her waist. Then the rider was dead, two arrows protruding from his back. From along the ridge she saw a man, no more than a shape in the mist. He wore a bearskin on his head as some of her father's people had done in war, hoping to take on the characteristics of the animal.

The horse careened on, dragging the rider by the stirrup. It caught her a glancing blow. She spun around, falling back hard on the cold earth. The bear man ran towards her. Above him the dreadful women moved in the fog like embers caught in a swirl of smoke.

Then they rose up above the fog, wings beating, horses breathing a frantic rhythm, looking down on her and the bear as if readying for a charge.

From across the valley came a howl, a long tether of sound that tugged her head around to face it. In the howl was the sound of terrible grief, of mothers screaming as they were torn from their children, of fathers watching their families butchered, of old women by the burning ruins of their home.

'The wolf is in the hills,' a dead sister spoke. 'Gift for gift. Your enemies are dead.'

The women, with their peat-black faces, their nooses, their horses, their wings and their spears were submerged by the mist and Hals' arms were around her but his body was limp, a red wound on his breast. Tola held him and wept at the price she had paid for the sisters' help.

2 The Slaughter Beast

He had run when his daughter by his mistress had died. She was fifty years old, a high lady of the Byzantine court who had lived a good life and shown him the pleasure of sitting in an olive grove under the sun, watching his grandsons wrestle, answering his granddaughter's million questions about the world. Little dark Theodora was the one who had been most curious that her grandfather looked younger than her mother. She had visited him at his small hill farm weekly – often she was the only human he saw from one month to the next. He had told her, in the end.

'I'm immortal, I think. Or rather, I don't get older.'

'Could you die if you were run over by a cart?'

'I think so.'

'Best look out for carts, then.'

He'd watched her grow from a child. His daughter died and he had seen the grey hair among the black of Theodora's curls and realised he could not stay any longer.

'How are you feeling?' Theodora had asked him, by her mother's grave.

'I feel as though I am death,' he said.

'There are many men who spend days with potions and ancient books trying to gain what you have got. Never to die.'

'I think I can die.'

'How?'

'I feel mortal. I feel . . .' He looked for the word. 'Vulnerable.'

'You think too much of the future,' said Theodora.

'It seems vast. And it seems empty. What shall I do, Theodora?'

He squeezed her hand and put it to his lips. She smelled as she had used to smell as a child, of the bitter oil rubbed into her hair to counter attacks of the lice. She had been putting it on her own children, no doubt.

'What do you want to do?'

'I don't know.'

'You have robbed death and he will have his compensation from you.'

'Weregild.'

'What?'

'My father was a northerner. A Varangian of Norway. If a man kills another he must pay money to his family. Perhaps death wants gold for life.'

'If it was only gold you could pay it. Will you not see my children? They might bring joy back to you.'

'I will not see them.'

'Then you have made your decision to leave the world,' said Theodora.

He remembered Beatrice – mother to Célene. She had never stood for sentimentality either.

Most of the time, Beatrice was a fleeting presence in his mind. She wouldn't sit still to be looked at. Only when he told Theodora about her, how he had met her when they were both Normans – she a lord's daughter, he a monk brought in to tend her in a fever – did she live again in his mind.

Beatrice had pretended to be ill for weeks in order that he could keep visiting her. What had they talked about? He'd forgotten. He remembered only her voice, its timbre and tone. Not what she said and the shifting light in the little cell where she lay, the chaperone dozing by the scented fire. For this. For this. Anything.

'I would have liked to have known her.'

'And she you.'

He'd never told Theodora how he had fought the old mad gods of his fathers by the World Well in the catacombs beneath Constantinople where the Norns sit spinning the destiny of all men, or how Beatrice had given her life in bargain for his. It was a deal he had never wanted her to make. He'd never said, either, how he'd travelled through the catacombs of his mind to free the great wolf that the gods had bound and how it had set upon the gods. Had they died? He didn't know but the wolf had put its eye on him, mingled its soul with his, and from that moment Loys had never aged, never changed.

He could feel the wolf inside him, watching him. He had chained it down and subdued it. Around his neck he wore a stone – part of the magic rock called Scream to which the wolf had been fettered. If he took the stone off then the world crackled and spat with sounds in registers he had never heard as a human. Smells no human had ever smelled burst upon him – meat-deep, berry-rich, smells that did not evoke memories like the bitter oil on Theodora's fingers but that were of the now, only themselves, and opened the gate in the garden of his mind to wild places, to hunger as deep as love. He knew then that without the stone the wolf would claim him and he would be no more than an animal. It was time to let the claim be made.

Suicide, by his Christian code, was unthinkable. By the law of the old gods he had seen at the well, it was the path of a coward and thus contemptible. But to live as a wolf, to anchor oneself to the present as an animal is anchored, would be possible and, as an animal, he might die. To seek danger was the noble path of the Christian saint and of the pagan warrior.

He kissed Theodora for the last time and then he ran from the south and Constantinople, up through the forests of the Dneiper, past the Ever-Violent Rapids that promised death, through the bandit lands that promised death, waiting for winter with its promise of death.

He had lived because he wouldn't let him die – the god, the pale traveller, the one who called himself Loki. Loys didn't know if the god existed or was just the product of a brain fever. The Pechenegs of the Dneiper had captured Loys by the Laughing Rapids but they had been afraid of him, even as they stripped him and tied him, ready to throw him down into

15

the raging waters as a sacrifice. They were an intuitive people. Had they sensed he was marked by the gods?

They'd taken the stone he wore on a thong at his neck – the little triangular pebble with its wolfshead etching. Even as they cut it free he felt the world change subtly. The men who tied and bound him, haggled over his few clothes, his fine sword and his good shoes, were no longer quite people. They weren't even enemies or threats. He was curious about their movements in the way a cat is curious about the movements of a spider. The Pechenegs were scared of him – the three who tied him would not even show their faces but wore their blank-eyed war masks whose impassive silver features were terrifying to him. After they cut away the stone, the rooms of his mind's mansion fell in and he saw the world only in broad categories. Living and dead. Food and not food. Enemy and bird.

'We kill you, devil' said a warrior, in corroded Greek.

Loys heard the fear in his voice. How did they know what he was?

'Yes,' said Loys.

Loys tumbled into the waters, felt their mighty weight shoving him down, saw the green of the riverbank, the black of the rocks in that jumbling, breathless churn.

He did not die. Instead peace came down on him and the waters stilled. He looked up from them at a smooth black rock, slick under the moonlight. On the rock sat an extraordinary figure – an impossibly tall man with a shock of red hair. He was naked, save for a white feather cloak, and his face was torn and bloody, his teeth visible through his cheek.

'See what you did?' He gestured to his face.

'I did nothing but try to protect those I loved.'

'That's every murderer's excuse,' said the man. No, not a man. A god. Loys could remember his name, if only he could clear his head. He had met him before.

'I committed no murder.'

'You are murder, Fenrisulfr.'

'Don't call me that.'

'You are the wolf, the wolf who killed King Death at the twilight of the gods. But now the king is gone. And you want him back, don't you, Fenrisulfr? You want him to live again.'

'He is not gone. I see death all around.'

'Funny that,' said the god.

'What do you mean?'

Loki – that was the god's name. He was a liar, Loys remembered, but not a malevolent one. He had helped him.

'You need to die. A new age is being born but it cannot come to be until the fates have their final sacrifice.'

'What sacrifice?'

'You. You were supposed to die after you killed Odin but you cheated destiny.'

'Then kill me.'

'I would if I could, but I can't.'

'Who can?'

'You are death. You can.'

'Then let me die here.'

'Not so easy. You can die here but you will be reborn. I was thinking of something more permanent. Your total and abiding extinction. Forever. Then the world can heal. Look down into the waters.'

Loys did and it seemed to him that he was both sitting on the rock under the cold metal moon and in the water at the same time, his vision flashing between the dark and the light.

'The dark is appealing, isn't it? Less confusing. Less demanding.'

'Will you let me die here?'

'I can't let you die anywhere. You're the killer, Fenrisulfr, you need to work out how to die for yourself. I wouldn't have thought it was too difficult.'

'How do I die?'

'I don't know. Follow your nose.'

The god gestured to the bank and the waters raged again. Loys splashed, gulped, thrashed for air. In the tumult and the

17

panic he felt his humanity wash away like dirt in a flood. He was an animal, fighting for survival. His arms had come free of the bonds and he reached out, his hand catching on stone, steadying him against the flow. The night bristled with sensations – he heard the scratching of insects in the leaf mould, the soft wings of the bats who hunted them in the dark, the muffled flight of the owls that hunted the bats.

He smelled decay and death in its rich glory – the browning leaves, the body of a fox, the autumn growth of mushroom and spore. It was as if his life before had been lived under the influence of some deadening drug and now he saw the world as it truly was. He'd felt this way before, when the wolf had looked at him when he had freed it to face the old gods. He was strong and he was certain. He pulled himself from the waters. The rapids' roar was like a dim echo of the roar he felt inside himself.

Two of the Pechenegs saw him and one fitted an arrow to his squat little bow, sending it unseen through the night. Loys didn't have to think, he just ducked and the arrow snicked through the air above his head. He ran forward, bounding from rock to rock. Two more bowmen fitted arrows, other warriors found swords and axes but it was too late. He was gone, into the dark of the trees.

He heard the Pechenegs arguing, their voices full of panic. Clearly some wanted to chase him, some to hold their position, keep watch and wait for the dawn. He was itching to kill but he crouched low and listened.

The Pechenegs' breaths sawed at the dark. They were terrified. He could smell the sweat of fear and, though they could not see him, he could see their panicked movements. Every quick turn of the head, every stiff, uncertain step forward spoke a single word to him: 'Prey'. A man, silhouetted against the camp fire, struggled to tie on his metal facemask, his fingers unwilling to obey the commands of his fearful mind.

Reason lay before Loys like a book on a table that he could pick up or ignore. His more insistent instincts were like fresh baked bread to a starving man. He could not put them from his mind.

The Pecheneg secured his facemask and Loys killed him, tearing past to strike him to the floor and disappear into the woods again. Uproar in the Pecheneg camp, warriors firing arrows blind into the dark. Already they were aiming in the wrong direction.

Loys circled the camp, loping around, looking for a weakness in the circle, attention directed the wrong way, imaginary noises causing a man to point and jabber. He struck again. There were twenty men but none of them saw him coming. He leapt upon one, breaking his neck from the rear. A sword fell towards him but he stepped under the blow, driving his head into the man's midriff, sending him sprawling.

All the men were around him now, spears and swords pointed, axes poised. Their fear smelled as strong as a Constantinople sewer. Their little dances back and forth as they summoned the courage to strike and then lost it again were oddly fascinating.

'You should go. I will be a bane to you,' he said, but his voice was not his own. His words were crunched, minced and chewed from his mouth. His tongue felt heavy, made of wood.

A warrior in a blank-faced mask spoke. 'Dora Lukelos.' Wolf skin.

The words triggered something inside Loys. He threw back his head and howled. The sound was a ribbon stretching out through time, something connecting him to everything he had been, to two brothers who had fought and died for the gods' protection, to a wild man of the woods, to a prince leading a war band, to a scholar coming frightened to the greatest city on earth. All the Pechenegs ran. The bodies were at his feet, sizzling in their succulent aromas. He was still human. He would not give in to hunger but his resolve could not last long. He bent to look for his wolfstone. Nowhere. The fleeing Pechenegs must still have it.

He set off after them through the trees.

19

3 Child of Blood

In the north, where emerald seams the night skies and dawn rises with the colour of cooling steel, Célene waited. She kept her fire on the cold island rock, offering amber flames to the silver moon, her white spear leaking the ruby blood of fish, whales and seals, turning pearly blubber to the jasper light of the candles that she made.

Her mind was wide and full of colour, green sea, grey sky patching with white; the sun tracking out her days, the moon her months, the cold and heat her years. In the long days of summer she was warm but autumn chilled her and winter froze her blood to ice. When the berries grew and the leaves fell she fattened like a bear, eating and eating, fish and whale fat, nuts when she could get them. When the snow fell there was no thought beyond survival – she burrowed into the earth of the cave, fur-wrapped, nurturing the fire, managing the stored fuel, offering prayers for the return of the sun.

She prayed to Jesus as she had been brought up to do but it was not Jesus who drew her to the island, nor Jesus she felt beneath the earth. A thumb's depth down, the ground was cold, even at midsummer. The god was down there, buried, his magic corpse sucking all heat from the land. The life on the island was abundant, though, the trees rich in fruit, and she believed it to be because their roots fed on the body of a god.

The dream lands were hers to wander and in them she chose to walk with her Aunt Hawis in the stories she had told her as a girl in Normandy. Sometimes she stole rings from sleeping dragons, at others she was Hawis herself, the floor seeming to fall away beneath her feet as Loys – who had run away with her sister – walked in with his little girl in the merchant's house at Beauvais. The ladies had been on pilgrimage south to the cathedral at Paris and the duke – a man closer to his horse than to God – had not come with them.

Hawis had thought she would die when she'd seen Loys, she really had. Célene asked about her father but Hawis said he was like two people. The one who had stolen away with the duke's daughter had been kind and funny, a little chubby from the monk's good life. The man who returned was spare and lean, serious, with eyes that seemed like – Hawis had thought for years how to describe them and, one day, hit on it – eyes like those of an animal, peering out from beneath his brow as if from some set or den.

'You can have no place here,' Aunt Alice had said.

'No,' said Loys. 'But she might. I am walking a hard road; it's no place for a child.'

Aunt Alice had at first said it was impossible to take her, that the duke would not have her. He would beat them all for even entertaining the idea. Hawis had stretched out her arms and the child came running to her. Alice really had cried then. 'Just like her mother,' she'd said.

Loys said that they should keep Célene with them on their tour of the country. He would talk to the duke.

'Then I will not see you again,' said Alice.

'No,' said Loys. 'You won't.'

The news came from Rouen a week later. The duke was dead. His horse had been spooked while hunting and he'd been found with his neck broken in a stream. Hawis had to regard that as fortune. She had hated the duke and was glad he was gone. The idea that Loys had killed him was impossible. A scholar could not take on a man at arms like Duke Richard and live.

That was the story Célene had been told. That was the story she knew, all she knew of herself. She'd been shipwrecked on the island at fifteen years old, going east as a bride to a Swedish king. She had not wanted to go and sometimes felt she had called the storm herself, emptied a void in her heart into which the storm had poured.

It had felt right to be on the island. She learned to survive, her mind widening and the magic that lay sleeping inside her growing.

Men came to the island. At first she did not know if they were dreams or if they were real. They came after she had been on the rock a long time, dragging their ship up the beach to repair it. A plague was among them and she was not sure if she was the plague. They couldn't see her, though they complained that the island was full of sounds, that the air was weak and the breathing hard. They all died, in a goggle-eyed fever, all twenty of them − boys and old men, warriors and three women. The dog kept her company for a while and she fed it sea bird and fish but it too eventually grew grey at the muzzle and died.

She kept the human corpses fresh, burying them in the cold earth beneath the warm topsoil, seeds that sprouted ghosts. In life the men had not seen her. In death, they sat by her fire, sang their songs and told their tales, and watched her as she slept. Busla was a goodwife escaping poor soil and famine. She had come from the north seeking the fertile south, in one of three ships that rowed out with the morning sun at their backs.

A storm had separated them and cracked their mast and they had lost their way.

'Is this Hel?' she asked Célene. 'Is this the kingdom of those who do not die in battle? Are you the goddess?'

'I am not a goddess.'

'You speak to the dead.'

'I came here as a living woman. I am a living woman.'

'Half your face is burned. That is what they say of Hel.'

'I slept too long by the fire,' said Célene. The pain did not bother her any more. It had ceased a long time ago.

'I would leave this lonely place,' said the woman. 'Can you be content here, no man to warm your bed, no children to brighten your days?'

'I cannot think of being anywhere else. How might it be

done? I am near to the god here, comfortable on his bones.'

'Then bring the god with you, raise him from death. You are the gatekeeper of death, I think. You can let him go.'

Célene thought for a long time about how the god might be freed. She dug at the earth with her fingers, looking for his bones; she ate worms and crawling things, trying to taste his blood on which they might have fed; she part-buried herself as best she could, digging down with a dead man's axe and piling the soil back over her, lying vacant-eyed, staring at the stars.

She felt a rune within her and she sang its long song. The rune was Ansuz, Odin's rune, and the god's magic and madness hummed within it like a struck gong. The other runes might come, she thought, but a great spell would need to be woven. It would take the endurance of years.

'Why am I here?'

The rune answered. 'To tell the story again. To pay the price to the Norns. You are the angel at Christ's tomb, rolling away the stone. You are his servant. Valkyrie. Sister Death.'

Ghost-accompanied, star-chilled and moon-minded, she sang a story, the one the god told, of two lovers sacrificed to the grim ladies of fate who sit at the World Well, sacrificed in eternal time, again and again, so the god might live. The song spun out over the gull-tormented sea to Constantinople and to England, to Norway and Normandy, where those with the ears to hear might hear it and begin to dance to its tune.

23

4 The Wildman

Tola held Hals' body in her arms, swallowing down the pain. The horse had caught her only a glancing blow but all the wind had gone from her and her ribs were agony.

'Get up, my love, get up!'

In death he no longer brought to her mind a sensation of a summer breeze, of the still air beneath an oak, heat in the nostrils, of cool stream water on the hand or the buzz of sunlit meadows. He was like the stones now, like the grass; things without a signature, things that were entirely and only themselves. She had killed him, she was sure, struck a bargain for her own life and sacrificed his.

She saw the wildman coming through the mist, the long bow in his hand, the bear's head staring blankly forward. He knelt above her and she thought he would kill her. She was so cold she was almost glad.

She had no weapon, nor any way of fighting him.

He put one of the Normans' cloaks about her and spoke not in Norman but in Norse.

She understood a good deal of the language, picked up from her father.

'Horse,' he said. 'You must be warm.'

'Man. My man,' she said in the same language.

'Dead,' he said. 'In battle. Valkyrie took him. Waelcyrge. Good. He's with the gods now.'

'Not with the gods,' she said. 'He must be buried and blessed.'

The wildman pointed to the mire.

'A door,' he said. 'To the gods. Let me.'

'The god in there is not the god of Christ.'

'In there, the mire, the gods,' said the wildman.

Tola thought it fitting to send Hals that way. His family were of the north, still left out bread for the elves and called Freya to make the fields bountiful, as they called on Christ to heal them and protect them. He could go that way.

'Yes.'

The wildman carried the body to the edge of the mire. He was just visible through the mist as he laid the body down. She tried to stand to follow him but her ribs were broken, she was sure, and it was agony to move.

He held up his hand and she held up hers in reply. He made the sign of the cross over Hals, said, 'Go to the warrior's halls,' and rolled Hals' body into the water.

He returned in a short while.

'Go now,' he said.

Any certainty she ever had about her life left her. She thought of the first men and women of the dale, of their children growing to become parents, their children too, of how the Danes had come – fighting at first but quickly settling, the rhythm of life and death unaltered. All that had gone. Death had made his camp here and there would be no more life, no babies with their rose-petal breath, no harvest, nothing.

That moment was a mire to her, sucking at her feet, holding her down. She wondered how she would ever move on from it. Surely all the doings of the world must stop now? Surely no new dawn could rise now? She turned to the man.

'You are death.'

'No,' he said. 'Not me. Death comes. Not death.'

'Why am I alive?' She was recovering from her trance and the cold was hitting her so her jaw chattered as she spoke.

She didn't understand every word of his reply but she understood enough of it.

'The women of the hill. Valkyrie. Waelcyrge. The Dead Sisters.'

Tola crossed herself. Hals was dead. Her brothers were dead. Everyone she knew from the farmsteads and villages was dead or about to die. Only she remained. She knew very well none of this was her fault but, looking at the standing stones and the odd northerner with his heavy, dark presence, she couldn't but help feel that it was.

'I will die here soon,' she said, struggling to find the Norse words.

'Yes. You must live. I need you.'

'For what?'

'Vengeance. Their blood for our blood.'

'I cannot fight.'

'Valkyrie, Waelcyrge. You help. You are a volva.' He stabbed a finger towards her. 'Witch.'

She tried to see if she could trust him, staring into his eyes, listening to the echoes of his thoughts that sounded in his breathing, shaped the way he held his face. She found nothing, just raw fear inside him.

'I'll find a horse,' he said.

She was convulsing with the cold now, despite the cloak. The wildman too was shivering. He went to the body of a fallen warrior and took his cloak, wrapping himself in it. He went on through the mist and came back with another, putting that on top of the one he had already given her.

'We go,' he said.

'Where?'

'Not here.'

'Fire,' said Tola.

'Fire. Yes. And vengeance.'

She looked down to where she guessed the valley was, under the mist. 'Back?'

He didn't seem to understand what she meant. 'Down,' he said.

'I have the courage to die.'

'Then die well, not cold. Die for the land.'

Her mind widened, spreading out across the frozen hilltop, down through the mist to the burning farms. The valley was full of men seething with violent intent. She felt all their bubbling animosities, their complaints and dissatisfaction with their leaders. *Not another farm to burn. I am tired and need to rest by the fire. Why must we campaign in winter? These people are poor, there's little profit in it. We should be allowed to take slaves. The Bastard owes us that.*

She hated them more than if they had been enthusiastic butchers.

'Magic has a price,' she said.

'What have you to pay?'

'Nothing.'

'Then what can the fates charge you?'

'Nothing.'

'Have your revenge. First, live. Warmth is the first step.'

Her feet were numb, her body shaking, she had scarcely any feeling in her hands.

The future had appeared in the shape of this man who had come bringing death and kindness. He was a Norseman, so perhaps he was used to surviving. After the great battle, where Harold threw the Danes back into the sea, the Norsemen who hadn't regained their ships or been slaughtered roamed the land in bands. They were lucky to survive. The people bore them a great deal of ill will, no matter that half the English were only two or three generations out of the longships themselves.

He supported her and led her across the broad plateau. She saw the severed head of a Norman warrior at her feet as she walked on, heard the fretting of a riderless horse somewhere in the mist. The wildman quickly found it and helped her to mount. She cried out as her body pressed against the horse's but she managed to make the saddle.

She hugged at the horse's mane for its warmth but then had to sit up as the man led it on. Every step seemed to break her ribs anew.

As they descended the hill, they came out of the mist, which sat like a hat on the summit. The fires were still burning all across the dale. It was as if the autumn bonfires they lit to mark the end of summer had blazed again, but so many more.

The old tradition said that the sun would not return if the fires were not lit. Now it was as if the people of the dale feared the sun would never, ever return and had burned everything they could in a bid to entice it back. There would be no more sun here or, if it shone, no one would be there to see it.

'This is the end of the world,' she said. A word came into her mind from a story her grandfather had told. 'Ragnarok.' The twilight of the gods.

'Yes,' said the man. 'Maybe always now.'

Her brother, Hals, Nan Johanna. All the people of the dale. Bone fires, she'd heard the autumn fires called, though no one was ever so stupid to burn something as valuable as a bone that could be made into a soup or fashioned into a blade. There would be bones in these fires, though. Human and animal – dogs, cats, the cattle the Normans had no use for. The emotions that drifted up from the valley were overwhelming. Exultation, fear, anger, sadness, delight and despair. Her head felt as if it had a great stone resting within it. She looked out on the burning night of frost, of stars and flame.

'I will fashion your bones into blades,' she said. 'They will pay for all this.' She searched for a word. 'Beauty,' she said in her own language. The word surprised her. She saw no beauty in destruction.

'Fire,' said the man. 'Then their blood for our blood'.

5 Cursed By God

'What if she recovers?'

'She will not recover.' Lady Styliane was irritated by the Viking's questioning. Travelling by camel was not her first choice but here, in the great red desert of the Rub al Khalid, there was no other way. The heat was intolerable and she sweated heavily beneath her desert robes. Her guardsmen, northerners, had it worse. They were big, pale men who flushed like lobsters and were tormented by the scarcity of water.

During the day, of course, it had been impossible to move and they had sweltered beneath their tents. Now it was dusk, the sun an angry red eye glaring out over the land, firing the dunes but leaving the plains beyond a metal blue. It was as if the sun was a hammer and the land the anvil on which it fell. They were the metal beaten upon it. The camp prepared to move, glad the wind that had nailed them to the spot for four days had died. The Arabs folded the tents away in no time, the Varangians eyeing the camels nervously.

The captive had not stirred. She was a young woman of around sixteen, blank-eyed, dry-browed and sweatless in her bonds.

Myskia, the big Varangian, bent over her as they prepared to go. He had been the worst in the sandstorm, moaning and crying out to whichever gods would listen to him, which were none.

'You did this to her?'

'She did it to herself.' It wasn't Styliane who answered but Freydis – a nimble, neat little warrior who, on close inspection, revealed herself to be a woman. She was of average size for a Roman of Constantinople but small for her own people, the Varangians. She was Styliane's personal bodyguard – her company more pleasing than that of the men. She had been in the lady's service a long time and Styliane had come to depend on her.

Freydis was baked brown by the sun, her thin blond hair poking from under her headscarf. Her nose had been punched to a clay splodge and a scar disfigured her right cheek.

Styliane had spent long nights with her in the gardens of the great palace, the moon shimmering above them as the streets released the heat of the day.

They had shared a lot, though Styliane kept her affection for the warrior secret. It would not do to be seen to dote so on a servant.

Freydis had told Styliane her story. The Varangians had met Freydis when they had taken her longboat in the northern seas. Of course, they had tried to rape her 'as a matter of principle, believe me we didn't want to,' Myskia had joked, but she killed one of their number – boldly, by taking the sword of one of her fallen comrades. They had been impressed and made a gift of her attacker's weapons and armour to her. She, a pragmatist, had asked to join them and, since she could fight as well as a man, they let her. In Styliane's experience the northerners were almost unique in judging people chiefly by their actions, rather than their sex. A woman could prove herself manly or a man womanly.

Did Freydis stand in Styliane's life for a man in other ways? Sometimes. Even in the longest life it is difficult to remain indifferent to everyone you meet. And besides, love has its uses. Her brother had taught her that.

'And the girl's rune?' Myskia sounded worried.

'Still inside her. She had only one,' said Styliane.

'Pray that Odin, master of magic, keeps it there,' said Myskia, crossing himself.

'Odin is dead.' She had watched him die all those years ago when her mind had cascaded down through the stars to where the gods dwell and she had watched as he was torn by the wolf.

'I'm a Christian anyway,' said Myskia. 'But he isn't so dead that you're sure he'll stay that way, is he, ma'am?'

'Don't talk that way to the seer,' said Freydis.

Myskia shot her a glance. If she had been a man he would have had to answer her rebuke with a challenge but he let it go.

Styliane sensed Myskia's soul, a hot, tormented thing. He was nervous and ashamed of his nerves, covering them up with the bravado of talking to a famous seer disrespectfully. She made allowances. The heat bothered him terribly, mottling his skin and kindling his temper. It was necessary to travel with such men. He was a prodigious killer, the best of the Varangians, battle bold and quick to anger. One blessing of the extreme heat was that the Varangians were too exhausted to fight with each other or with anyone else. She kept him close to her, for such men were like sharp knives, best handled carefully.

Styliane kept her gaze on him, unwavering, but she said nothing. He crossed himself again, bowed and said 'Odin protect us. Jesus too. And you, ma'am.' He tapped his sword as if reassuring himself it hadn't melted and lifted the young woman up to put her across a camel's back. So much cargo.

Styliane would turn north for Baghdad as soon as she had killed the girl. She longed to sit in the shade of the flower garden at the palace of the Caliph, to sip sweet sharbat chilled with ice from the northern mountains. The drinking glasses were made according to the secret formula of the Kitab al-Durra al-Maknuna. It was true what they said – the glass hid its colour from the sun, leaving the liquid within seemingly suspended in space. Nothing hid its colour from the sun in the desert, its fierce gaze brightening any colour to a dazzle.

They mounted, she helped up by one of her Varangians. The Arabs would not go near a foreign lady, fearing offence to the giant northerners. Then the Varangians themselves mounted – spurning the help of the Arabs. None of the tribesman laughed at their efforts to climb aboard, though a boy had to turn his face away. No one wanted to antagonise these odd blond warriors with their long axes and big swords.

The procession moved on through the channels among the vast dunes, some as big as mountains. The Varangians sat unsteadily on the camels, swaying as if drunk, comically dignified.

The sun fell behind the dunes and the red land turned blue. You could not say it was dark; the stars themselves were a desert, nearly as numerous as sand grains, the sweating moon looking down, its face wavering in the heat haze. Was the moon as bare as this land? Did moonmen suffer in such heat?

The unconscious girl moaned on the back of the saddle. It wouldn't be long before she was beyond all pain. She had come to Styliane, as Styliane knew she would come, looking to kill her. Styliane was preparing to leave for Baghdad anyway; talk of her unageing appearance had grown too much again. The last time she had gone to Baghdad as her own granddaughter. She would do so again, sixty years after she had left.

She took with her ten selected Varangians, oath-bound to keep her secret of immortality: that within her dwelled a fragment of a god's mind, four magical symbols that expressed and controlled the fundamental nature of the world – runes. It was tempting to allow one to grow in her thoughts. The symbols were of the northern land and all brought a chill. One moaned like the wind in the hills, one stamped and blew like a bull, still another came with the silence of ice caves, the dead air of crevasses in glaciers she had never seen. A fourth boomed and swelled like the ocean, a dirty green, cold sea – not the bright water of the Bosphorus or the Sea of Mamara. It filled her mouth with the taste of salt and made her shiver however hot the day.

She would not call them yet. She had needed to summon all four to defeat the girl on the camel and she still felt unhinged by the experience. The runes flared compassion inside her, making her regret the death of the girl, though Styliane knew the girl needed to die so she might live. She spat. To put a foreigner's life before her own. That was a rare madness. She was an aristocrat of Constantinople, born to rule. Her life was more valuable than other people's. The order of men on earth reflected the divine will.

They tramped all night through the heat.

'We will be met?' said Freydis. Her eyes met Styliane's and the lady took comfort from the warrior's concern for her.

'Yes. They are awaiting us eagerly,' said Styliane.

She felt the well before she saw it, as if her daily thoughts were just robes she put on and the presence of the well a wind that nagged at them. It was out here. Mimir's well, where the god Odin had traded his eye for insight. She did not fear it. She had been to the World Well where the Norns sat spinning the fates of men, the well that was all wells. Mimir's well was present there too, as all the wells of wisdom were, but she would not risk a second visit. She had emerged from the earth there once and had no certainty of being able to again. She knew it was foolish to talk of a magic well 'being' anywhere in the realm of men. They were vast things that existed in the realm of the gods. Mimir's well appeared in the desert, it might appear in the snow fields or forests too. This manifestation was the nearest she could find to Baghdad.

'There are three roads that meet there, Shaddad?' Her Arabic was perfect. She'd spent a long time in Baghdad sixty years before, would spend as long again when the business here was done.

'Yes, lady, as I told you before.' The little man looked like a Constantinople street deceiver, over-keen to do a deal. Styliane cursed herself for betraying her nervousness.

She tapped three times on her thigh, a blessing from her goddess, Hecate – lady of the dead, lady of the crossroads, lady of the moon. Of this burnt ash moon? In the days before the Norse god had entered her mind she had been a sorceress. The goddess had always come as a shimmering, cool presence, like the moon on water. Was Hecate here? Was she anywhere? Or were the gods all one – Hecate with her three faces and mastery of magic, goddess of death; Odin, king of enchanters, god of death, Christ, who cast out the demons and came back from the dead, king of death.

'They will be there?'

'Yes. I have said. Praise to God.'

This man did not mean that. He was not an Islamist, though he pretended to be so. He followed an earlier faith – a worshipper of the star called Sirius. Was everything linked? Hecate was attended by dogs, as Styliane was now attended by worshippers of the dog star. She recalled her Homer:

Sirius rises late in the dark, liquid sky
On summer nights, star of stars;
Orion's Dog they call it, brightest
Of all, but an evil portent, bringing heat
And fevers to suffering humanity.

Very apt. Her guide was a member of the tribe of .. Ād, cursed by God, so the Arabs said. Only a man like this would make such a deal. Two nights of such travel and her Varangians were sweating.

Myskia came to her side.

'I wish this was not necessary, Volva.' He gave her the old Norse title of 'seer'.

'The Varangian guard owes its exalted position in the emperor's service to me, to the sacrifices I have made, to the runes I carry. It is necessary if you wish that to continue.'

'If Odin could return ...'

'The god chose death. How else can a god die? Would you presume to resurrect him? Honour the god's will, Varangian.'

'Yes, Volva.'

She could feel the well strongly now, a current that drew in all her thoughts. She found it hard to think of anything else. The travellers rounded the purple bulk of a vast dune. There under dark, flat-topped mountains was the oasis, a begrudging smear of water among the rocks and the sand. Ten tents were pitched next to it, goats running free – no need to tether animals that had too much sense to leave the water.

Styliane felt her mind shift, like liquid in a tipped glass. She could see the water for what it was but, at the same time, it spun with stars, the moon at its centre. The wells were a gateway between worlds for those who could see it. Was Odin dead? Of course he was. She had seen him, torn by the wolf. He could not be there waiting for her and, if he was, she was part of him because of the runes within her. She remembered the noose at his neck: the suicidal god, endlessly dying in his incarnations on earth. He would not hesitate to kill her. No, he was dead, though death for gods was not like death for others.

'Lady.' It was Freydis. The camel had knelt; she was offering to help her down.

She took her bodyguard's hand and dismounted.

The tribesmen were already running ahead to the camp, greeting its guards.

Shaddad bowed. 'We have a tent with our women if you would rest after your journey.'

'No,' said Styliane. 'We'll do it now. I will rest the day after and leave the next night.'

'It is customary for us to speak to our brothers for longer than that.'

'It is customary for me to leave when I have worked the magic of the gods.' She pointed up to Sirius, bright eye of the dog constellation. 'It will still be looking down on you when you return. We do a serious thing here, Shaddad, and the sooner it is a memory to us all the better.'

The little man nodded. Was he afraid? She couldn't tell any more, the runes pulling at her thoughts, turning them always towards the well.

'I will fetch the child.'

'Don't. I must prepare.'

'When then?'

'At my signal. I need to go to the water. Can you make sure your people allow it?'

'They will allow it.'

Styliane went to the water as if dragged. This was the place. A muddy puddle, really, no more; the moonlight thick with insects. But she saw it as it really was, a chasm deep with stars.

'What will happen?' said Freydis.

'The girl will be offered to the waters and her rune torn from her. The baby of the .. Ād will receive it. You carry her in. It is a girl child and the Arabs will not suffer to let a man touch her.'

Her attacker – the girl – had come to her in her chambers at the palace, bribing her passage in by way of the kitchens, no doubt. The assassin had thought to surprise her but Styliane had heard her coming, or rather, heard the moaning of the rune she bore inside her. The rune had granted the girl insight and she knew that by killing Styliane she could become a god, or take a step on her way to that destiny. There were twenty-four runes in all creation. When all the runes inhabited one body, Odin came to earth. Or rather, Odin was the twenty-four in one body; he came to being. Once, his birth in the realm of men had been inevitable. Now, not so. She had seen him die under the teeth of the wolf. Was he dead everywhere? And if he was, would he stay dead? If she strove to keep him in the grave then perhaps he would remain there.

Styliane put her hand into the water and kept it there. She could feel the connections to the other mystical wells, from the cold currents of Hvergelmir in the ice lands to Urðarbrunnr, the well of wyrd, into which she had fallen beneath Constantinople. She felt too the icy currents of the first rivers that flowed from those wells, the cold sparks that fired life onto the earth. They were threads connecting her to the three grim women who sat spinning the fates of all men at the centre of creation.

There was so much magic in that well for those who were prepared to pay the price of denial and pain to take it. She was not one of them. She had given as much as she was willing to give two lifetimes before.

Once she would have invoked ritual, called on the names of

the three-faced goddess of darkness and the dead, called her Cthonia and Bellona of the Battles; drunk bitter potions. Now none of that was necessary. Rather she just stopped suppressing the runes, let them grow inside her mind with their hollow light of grey skies, their animal stink, their sighing and their chiming.

It was hard here to keep them where they needed to be. The well was a vortex, sucking at them, and her hands stretched out as if she could pull the symbols back from its brink. They were hers and she would not let them go but she felt the well's need for sacrifice, for blood.

She sat for a long time deciding what to do. The tribesmen could not move her from the midday sun, so they built a shelter over her as she sat watching the waters. Should the child be immersed? What felt right? Magic was such a thing of instinct not something that could be learned in books like men said, not true magic like this. She asked the goddess Hecate for help, a prayer born of instinct, and for a time fancied she could hear the howling of dogs. She felt as though she walked on the rocks of great rapids and could be swept into foaming waters in a moment's loss of concentration.

She expected to see him, the dead god, sitting by the water's edge; his bog-black body lean and lithe, the madness burning in his one good eye. Nothing. Her mind fell through the sand to dry graves where she lay among the bones of the dead, where her mouth filled with dust and her thoughts too. She needed to cling to the question: what to do? The rune in the unconscious girl could not be allowed to unite with hers. She had four runes. Five would edge her nearer to twenty-four – the number that meant she would cease to be Styliane and become Odin.

'Djinn?'

Shaddad was speaking. She could not reply. She thought that perhaps she was in the water, drowning, looking up at him through a shimmering veil of liquid.

'You must drink. You have not drunk for a day. You will die here like that.'

37

Three women came to the edge of the water and sat down. Were they tribeswomen? Perhaps. She found it hard to focus on them. They had distaffs in their hands and began to spin, a weft of stars that fell tangling through the pool. She picked up one of the threads and she saw that it was wound around something down in the spangled darkness. She tugged on the thread, feeling it snag. She kept pulling and pulling. The effort was immense; she was dragging an enormous weight up from the bottom of the pool. She could see a massive black body snared in the bonds of stars. She knew who it was – the wolf – but she kept pulling.

Its head reared above the water, its great jaws dripping, its dead eyes on her. The runes around her shrieked and clamoured. She felt the connection between herself and it, knew that she had been shown their destinies were linked. It was looking for something, its nose twitched at the air, its tongue flicked as if trying to take taste from it.

'What are you looking for?' said Styliane.

'Death,' said the wolf.

Styliane saw a vision – a foreign land under flame, warships pouring in across a grey sea towards a cold shore, men sweating in their armour, unsure of the reception they would receive. And then a girl standing amid destruction in a white land.

'Who?' said Styliane. She had not expected this. She had hoped the well would show her the way to take the rune from the girl and plant it inside the infant.

'Death,' said the wolf. 'My death.'

'Do not seek her,' said Styliane. 'If you die, the Norns' broken story is over. The time of magic will be gone. I will die too.'

She knew the man that the wolf had been was godly and she tried to appeal to his better feelings. But the wolf was heedless. It plunged into the water, the starry ropes snagging around Styliane's hands, snagging her as she desperately tried to unravel them. They were pulling her under, pulling her down to death.

The runes were screaming around her in ever widening orbits, fleeing her. It was time.

'Now!' she said.

Freydis splashed forward through the water. She had the baby with her in her arms. Two Varangians dragged the unconscious girl between them.

'Drown her?'

'Drown her.'

They plunged the girl's head into the water and held it. Her rune expressed itself in her – a spear flying across a blue sky. The wind was like a fist, knocking Styliane down. Still she strove to untangle herself from the coils of stars. It was all right. The rune would not come near her when her own runes fled for fear of the wolf.

The baby screamed. Freydis collapsed to her knees in the water and then fell backwards, the baby on top of her. The young woman was dead, the runes returned and Styliane shook free of the coils. Styliane lost consciousness, as if the ink of the sky had leaked into her mind.

When she awoke, the tribe was gone. Only her guards and their camels remained.

'Success?' said Styliane.

'Success.' said Myskia.

'Where is Freydis?'

'Gone,' said Myska. 'She went with the .. Ād.'

'Why?'

Myska shrugged. 'No point asking. She's gone. A pity. She was a strong warrior.'

Styliane cast down her eyes. It would not do to be seen to cry over the loss of a servant. What had Freydis seen at the well?

6   For Love

Freydis could only travel so far with the tribe. They did not understand a woman alone. The tribesmen would not tolerate her for long. She had to spend time with the women, at the back of the column, and could only speak to Shaddad through his wives. Freydis was not Styliane. She had no riches or magical gifts for which custom might be ignored for a moment. She ate only what the men left. It was enough and she did not feel hungry.

In the water of the well, as she'd held the little girl, something very odd had happened to her. She heard chiming and rain, a cool breeze sprang up. The rune hung in the air, whispering its name in a rush like the passing of an arrow – Tiwaz, the spear, bright as a star. It seemed vastly attractive to Freydis and she lifted her hand to take it, forgetting that she was supposed to hold up the baby for it to enter.

The rune flew through her mind like a raid, screaming and howling. In an instant she relived all the battles she'd been in since she had left her home in Hordaland. She smelled the burning of the monastery, felt the crunch of the beach pebbles underfoot, the rushing, flashing sensations of the fight, everything fast and slow simultaneously. Her hand ached as if weary from the sword, her body buzzed as if slammed and battered by the frenzied defenders. The rune was all these things and it was a longship too, a spear through the surf cutting out around the bay, heavy with treasure.

The rune took root inside her and she felt its shining tendrils coiling around her heart, singing and chiming and spear-rattling, shield-bashing. It came with cries of torment, of exultation, of elation at battles won and dejection at battles lost. She knew what had happened – the Volva had explained the true nature of magic to her.

Styliane had lived a long time and had no one to confide in. In Freydis, silent and thoughtful, raised in the traditions of the old gods but believing in Christ, she found someone she could speak to. Freydis was her closest servant and never doubted her mistress's magical gifts nor the truth of what she said. Odin was dead and must never live again to threaten the Christ god. If he did, Styliane would die and the people would fall to his worship, bringing destruction, evil and, eventually, damnation to the world.

But now, a fragment of the god inside her, she did not know what to think. She knew only that the girl who had come carrying the rune to kill Styliane had been a great danger to her mistress and was now dead. Since she had no desire to be either of those things herself, she had fled with the tribe. The Varangians had not been sad to see her go. Styliane would pay them as a unit when she returned to Baghdad. With Freydis gone, there was one less warrior taking a share of the pot.

In the shade of the evening's camp, when it was cool enough to cook and to talk, she sipped a little water and looked out over the blue desert. She let the rune come to the forefront of her mind. It was not a restful presence at all but brimmed with a fitful aggression. Men were like that on the eve of battle. Freydis had never known such a feeling. She had taken up the sword because the men of her farms were always at sea, raiding. This left their women vulnerable to opportunistic raids by other Vikings. It was natural and necessary for women to know the use of arms and she had proven the best of her kinswomen at it – fast and accurate and, above all, dauntless. It frightened Freydis to face an armed man – it would frighten anyone who wasn't mad or drugged – but her fear never stiffened her arm, nor slowed her swing. Rather it strengthened her. She had killed three men in her life before she had joined the Varangians – one on her own farm, backed by her dogs. Then she had killed her brother when he had returned from his raid with a poison wound. He had told her to do it and she had, holding a blanket over his face to smother him. The third was the man who tried to rape her when her longship was attacked. Freydis had no future on the hard stony ground of her farm, unsupported by her brother's raiding, the sheep thin and sickly. She was headed to Ireland with a family of her neighbours. They'd hit trouble near Orkney when a boatload of violent men on their way east had attacked them. She'd thought her life was over then and it freed her of all restraint. The man who attacked her had laughed when she picked up her friend's sword. She cut his head half off with it and he didn't find it so funny.

The violent men had respected her and called her 'shield-maiden'. She went with them to Constantinople. She remembered seeing the city for the first time, vast and white in the autumn sun. When Styliane had told her the gods were dead she had believed it. Mankind had surpassed their achievements, built a monument to itself in stone and marble.

In the desert camp, she took out her little cross and studied it. Christ had hung there when his father demanded his blood. Odin – all father – had hung on a tree too, for wisdom. The path to paradise was suffering, there was no question of that.

The tribesmen made a fire to cook with and the smell of roasting goat seeped over the hot ground to the sweltering canopy where she lay. They were celebrating the rune going into the child. She remembered what Styliane had said – that the girl was the ideal candidate to receive the rune. She was a baby, so it would be many years before the magic flowered in her and snared her mind in its roots. She was a member of a tribe that was shunned by its countrymen and who kept away from all contact and civilisation. More than this, women were only so much chattel to the.. Ād, expected to do nothing beyond serve men and raise children. She would know nothing of the world, have no experience of how to travel outside her desert home. Eventually, though, the rune would shape her mind to seek its fellows, to become the god again by murdering Styliane.

Freydis traced the shape of the rune in her mind. It was

an arrow, flying against a clear blue sky. The rune said its name. Tiwaz – the symbol of the sky god Tyr, lord of battles, binder of the Fenris Wolf whose destiny it was to kill the gods on their final day. The arrow wanted blood – Styliane's, she could feel it. Well, it wouldn't have it.

That lady had given her so much. Money, yes, and a trusted position within the guard. But more than that, she'd given her companionship. Freydis had escorted her everywhere. She remembered down by the Galata Bridge, the moon on the Bosphorus, the city's domes seeming to smoke with the fires driving off the autumn chill. Styliane had confessed to Freydis there how long she had lived, what she had seen in that city and in Baghdad. She had lived for many lives, won her magic with pain and grief in the well of all the worlds that sat below their Constantinople, the world city.

It had never occurred to Freydis to disbelieve her. The lady was too grand, too noble, to bother lying to a servant. And besides, Freydis knew it to be true. Styliane was not like other people. Her beauty was like that of the city itself – ancient, deepened by time.

Styliane valued Freydis as someone simple and direct, unswayed by the currents of politics that eddied and swirled through the empire's court. She told her stories she had heard at the court of Baghdad – one of a prince who went mad with love for a girl whose tribe forbade her to see him.

Freydis remembered the beautiful words about a boy lit up by love. 'As a ray of light penetrates the water, so the jewel of love shone through the veil of his body,' and about a girl 'caught between the water of her tears and the fire of her love'. By Styliane's side, Freydis was a thing transformed, a medium like glass or diamond, through which love might shine and attain its full beauty.

She remembered most what Styliane had told her the boy had written in his letters to his lover.

'For how long then do you want to deceive yourself? For how long will you refuse to see yourself as you are and as you will be? Each grain of sand takes its own length and breadth as the measure of the world; yet beside a mountain range it is as nothing. You yourself are the grain of sand; you are your own prisoner.'

No one she had ever met had spoken to her like that. The people from her farms were of the earth, regarding the earth; their conversation limited to the privations of their existence and as much gossip as could be mustered between eight farmsteads. Styliane was of the stars, talking of gods and goddesses, of magic and love. Freydis loved Styliane and would die for her; she'd known that within a month of working for her. Now she must live for her, keep the thing inside her quiet, away from her mistress. Her rune would seek Styliane's runes. She could not allow it to succeed in its quest.

She needed to put as much distance between her and Styliane as possible. Freydis's tears had dried up years before yet she felt close to weeping at that thought. But Freydis had lived a life of hard choices. She would do what needed to be done.

The heat told her where to go – to the cold. She needed to feel it in her bones again. She'd return home, buy back her farm with the plunder she had won in the east, and live for as long as she could, knowing that she would see Styliane again at least once before she died. She would need to call on the lady, or the lady on her, to ensure the rune did not ensnare its sisters. The ritual at the well would be repeated but it would be Freydis drowned in the water.

The men finished with the goat and it was the women's turn to eat. She wished these people could be hurried but she knew they could not, not under that sun. She'd go back with the .. Ad to the edge of the Empty Quarter, then strike for Jeddah. From there she could take a boat north on the Red Sea, strike overland for Alexandria and on to Constantinople; pick up her pay and plunder and head up the Dneiper to Novgorod to find a trading boat home. Surviving that journey as a lone woman would be a challenge but her face was so weathered, her nose so broken and her shape so angular she could pass for a man. People rarely looked beyond the sword and the shield anyway. Still, a man would find it hard enough.

She stood and went to eat. She didn't like these tribesmen of ..Ād, particularly the hard little man who seemed to be their leader. She could see by his eyes that he disapproved of her warrior's dress, of the sword at her side. She'd be glad to be gone. Something inside her shuddered. The rune. A great longing sprang up in her, a desire to stand with Styliane in the umber light of Hagia Sophia again, feeling the presence of Christ, the hanged god, floating in the air. The lady, and the runes inside her, must be awake. She crossed herself and prayed.

'Let me live, for her, and die for her. Grant me the strength to stay away.'

She looked down into the bowl of goat's bones and picked one up to gnaw at the remaining meat.

7 Mask of Fear

'What is your name?' Tola asked the wildman.

'Ithamar.'

'You are from the past the woods?'

Tola knew only the few farms on which she had been raised. 'Past the woods' was her term for anything beyond a day's walk from her house. The man led her horse down the hill. He could not ride, he said, but she could sit on the horse, take in its warmth and rest. The Normans had food with them and she'd eaten as much as she could of the bread and ham. She was wrapped in two of the Normans' fine cloaks. If they found her with them, she was dead. It didn't matter, she was dead anyway. Hals was dead. She could hardly take it in and allowed her mind to be consumed by her bare need for survival.

'I am of the woods.'

'A wildman?'

'A man of the woods.'

'A wildman.'

'So what should we call you, girl? You who pull demons from the air to save you?'

'Those ladies are the protectors of the dale. They would come to the help of anyone who knew how to ask.'

'And what do we call those who know how to ask?'

'I don't know.'

'Have a think,' he said. 'Until you think of the word "witch"'.

She felt his fear of her, as strong as that of a bird in a snare at the approach of a hunter. Why fear her, of all people, in this burning land, this ruin?

They dropped off the side of the fell. The clouds were thick and there was no moon but the fires of the farms cast some light and told her where they were. To the right, Nan Elswite's; above that Hunfrith the weaver and his family; to the left, Winfrith the cooper; and below them Aylmer's farm. All burning, a constellation of terror marked out in the dark.

'Where are we going?'

'To the woods first, and then from there we'll have a ponder,' said the wildman. 'I have people who would speak to you.'

'Who?'

'The lords who would throw the invader from our lands.'

'What can lords want with me?'

'You saw what you called on the hill. They want that.'

Again, fear. It came off him like the smoke from the burning houses. She let her mind wander away from her.

'I want to go to my farm.'

They had all fled when news of the riders' approach had reached them. Her brothers went to the woods to set an ambush and her mother bid Tola and Hals run on without her. She could not feel her out there in the darkness – no scent of mint and soil, no warmth or comfort. She knew she was dead. Yet still she needed to see.

'Your farm is gone.'

'I want to go.'

'Not with me and my horse,' said Ithamar.

'Then on my own.'

She slid down from the horse.

'Or my cloaks.'

He spoke harshly but the fear was still there. When she allowed herself to sense someone's feelings or attitudes she saw them as images or sensations. In front of this man, she sensed herself. To him she was the shape moving at the edge of the firelight, the night noise that is neither owl nor fox, the thing unremembered from a dream that leaves you only with the sweat and your thumping heart to remind you of its presence.

'I will take the cloaks,' she said. 'You may keep the horse.'

She walked on down the dark hillside.

'Get back on the horse,' he said. 'I will take you to your farm.'

It was three hours in the darkness to get to where they needed to be. The Normans on one farm had found some ale it seemed, because they were singing, drunk. A girl screamed over the song, a desperate wail like the trumpet that heralds the end of the world. Then she was quiet. Tola did not want to think about who it was, though she knew the cooper's girl Eldreda lived on that farm. Her friend.

'A bad business,' whispered Ithamar.

It was. Tola kept her feelings locked down tight. She could not think on what was happening or she would go mad.

They kept silent around the farms. The horse's hooves were not loud on the wet earth.

The Normans would have heard the battle on the hilltop, even if they couldn't see it, and would be expecting their men down soon.

They found the little lane between the fields that led up to her house.

'They have gone,' said Ithamar.

'How do you know?' Her voice was low.

'They've burned the house to nothing. It would be mad to do that if they were staying. They'd want to sleep in it and shelter their animals.'

They trod carefully down the lane, she dismounting in case the fire picked out her shape and the Normans saw her on the horse. She was wearing a Norman cloak but she knew no Norman carried himself as poorly in the saddle as she did, especially with her broken ribs.

The firelight was low by the time they arrived at her house. No Normans were there but everything had been smashed, to the smallest detail. The body of Lar the dog lay in the yard, an ugly wound in his side. Tola had cut him free but he was old and had preferred to lie before the house instead of run with them. They couldn't make him move and hadn't had time to drag the dog across the fields. He had a good bark on him but was a sweet old thing. He would have greeted the intruders wagging his tail.

They moved around the back of the farm, keeping low. Ithamar warned her that as the farm was on a hill they would be easy to spot, black against the red, by any watching Normans. She picked up something from the floor. The ashen remains of a knife. It had been her mother's, made all of wood, though the handle had survived the fire. She took it. One day, she would come back with men and make one of them push it through a Norman's heart.

She looked at the outline of the house, broken in, her mind providing its shape, true and whole. The house had sunk a little at one end and that outline was home to her, a beautiful slow collapse that they always vowed to fix in the summer but somehow never had by the autumn. The flames were low now, little dancing ghosts where her mother had sat, her brothers, friends, around a fire, sometimes long after sunset.

'That is past,' said Ithamar, his face gaunt in the firelight. 'Burned now. Only future.'

'The past is a blade in my hands,' said Tola. 'Forged anew and stronger by the fires the Normans lit.'

'Fine words for country girl.' Again the wave of fear from him.

You can lead me to men who would avenge this?'

'Yes.'

She let her mind wander the land. Only drunkenness, hatred, wariness. There were no living kinsmen in the dale. She couldn't even find the girl who had been screaming.

'My mother is dead, my brothers too. Death has served me, now I will serve death.'

Ithamar looked into the flames.

'We should cook the dog,' he said.

8 A Senseless Rescue

Loys touched the stone at his neck as he moved with his Norman companions through the burning farm. The horse underneath him felt skittish and frightened. It was not a war-horse like those ridden by the Norman warriors around him, and the screams of the dying men and animals set its flesh quivering.

He turned his eyes from what he saw – all the degradation and slaughter of war, yet this was no war. It was a massacre, the like of which he had never seen before. The Norman conquerors were putting their mark on the land, teaching the English the cost of rebellion.

His belly trembled, his bones felt rotten and his flesh old. Human then – disgusted, vulnerable among this carnage, the wolf locked away inside him. He tried to stop himself feeling good about that. It had cost him a lot to regain such control.

A gritty wind sprang up and he covered his face with his scarf. He remembered his Bible:

> 'Have you entered the treasury of snow,
> Or have you seen the treasury of hail,
> Which God has reserved for the time of trouble,
> For the day of battle and war?'

A gut-churning squeal from his right; a pig gushed blood into the snow. They threw its carcass onto the fire of the farmhouse. There was a glut of plunder in this land, too much to carry, so the Normans destroyed everything. Even the bet-ter men among them grinned at how wealthy they felt: 'So rich we used fine robes for kindling,' they'd tell people later. There was a joy in waste. A confirmation. They had two carts, heaving with what they had robbed from the farms – grain sacks mainly, some spades, metalwork, even a bed. These were not rich people they robbed. They did not bother to drive the pigs or cattle – they were moving too quickly and there were no markets nearby. Not any more.

He touched his stone again and kicked his horse on. Was she here? Or was she already dead, the girl from the vision?

In the Dneiper Woods he'd fled north after he'd killed the Pechenegs and found the wolf stone. He needed to go quickly, quicker than any horse, so he had not put on the stone. He ran hard, though to nothing. Through the vast woods towards Kiev he went, running with the wolf packs beside the roaring Dneiper, hunting like a man with his bow, eating like a wolf – the meat raw, still as warm as when it had lived. As a man he risked bandits and ambush but with the wolf unfettered inside him, he could slip through the trees as softly as the shadow of a stoat, unseen but seeing.

His mind was a cave as he ran, full only of moonlight and sunlight, of the voice of the waters and the song of the woods. When he stopped, he forced himself to wear the stone again in case he gave in completely to the wolf. So by night the memories of his humanity came flooding back.

There had been a woman, Beatrice. He saw her now only in glimpses – her bone-blond hair, her smile, her body naked beside him in the bed in the little inn beside the water when they'd first come to Constantinople. It had all changed there, in the catacombs beneath the city. A century before? More? Time was a parchment left out to the rain, its meaning smudged.

He had buried his sword, thrown away his clothes and lived in the great forests with only his wolf brothers for company. Their bodies warmed him by night and their cries filled his mind by day. Beatrice was a memory, a shade who seemed to watch him through the trees, her eyes reproachful. 'You are not a wolf,' she seemed to say.

'Then what am I?'

'A man.'

'You gave me life. Can you give me death?'

'If you can find me.'

The other woman had found him in the woods and he'd thought she had come to kill him. No, she had come to make him live. The symbols danced around her, silver, some like darting fish, some moving with the sound of the rain, others chuckling or fluttering by like a tumble of sparrows' wings. He raised his head and, in her sight, he knew it was the head of a great wolf. The symbols around her shrieked and tumbled as he settled his gaze upon her. She was not there. She was somewhere else. In a desert, mind blown with magic before a mystic well.

She had summoned him to her presence, called forth the vision of Beatrice and with it the certain knowledge his wife had been reborn, to offer him the chance of release from life.

He'd seen the girl, seen the ships, in the visions Styliane had conjured. They moved him to action and when William had attacked England he'd been with him, looking not for plunder but for a young woman who might offer him death.

If he was to find Beatrice he needed to think, doing most of his travelling with the stone suppressing the wolf in his breast. That made him vulnerable, easy as a man to kill. So he needed to travel the land with companions – the Norman invaders.

The woman, Styliane, fled from death. They were bound by a magical pact formed under the gaze of dying gods who would not let him die the death he needed – a final ending, never to be reborn. But first he had to find the girl – the lady of fate. Styliane was a powerful seer, a holder of the runes, and she had seen what he had seen. If the lady could find the girl she would kill her if she could. Death to Loys was death to Styliane too, their fates were linked, and the great lady could not allow that.

In the burning, plundered north, he took the wolfstone from around his neck, put it into his purse. As long as it didn't touch him it would not affect him. Immediately his senses were keener, as if he had instantly emerged from a heavy cold. He tasted the air, cold iron and smoke; sharp fear seeping from every animal stall, every byre. He tapped his tongue to his palate. In a day or a week he'd gain the magical sense to lead him to her. Could he look at her? She had something inside her – a sound, a shape – that called to him. A rune, but one made of darkness where the others were made of light. It had been in Beatrice, and before her in others. Would she be like his wife? He hoped not.

More screaming. They were killing again. This time he went over to look – a stir of curiosity in him edging out his revulsion. A rush; the thumping of feet. A boy of maybe thirteen tore from the burning house, dashing for the fields. The Normans watched him, expressionless, unmoving. The kid wasn't equipped for the weather – just a shirt and trousers and a split shoe that flapped like a snapping mouth as he ran.

At the start of the day the men might have charged him down. Now, out of pity for the horses, they let him go. The animals were weary with chasing.

Loys felt the flicker of an instinct to pursue. As a wolf, the sight of that uneven gait and the smell of the boy's panic would have been a great lure to him. But he was human. He wanted the boy to be all right. He wanted it all to be all right. Why this one? Why select one pebble from a beach above any other? Why? In the flood tide of murder that had engulfed that land, reasons were swept away. Why save him? Loys envied the dead, free from the mire of sensation and loss. Perhaps the boy reminded him of a child he'd known – a son he'd watched grow old and die.

'We need someone to cook and make the camp for us tonight,' said Loys.

The knight in charge of the men, Robert Giroie, shook his head.

'We'll head to the next farm and stay there for the night. The farmers can cook and tend to us and we'll slaughter them before turning in, save any funny stuff at night.'

'He might be a smith. Worth saving.'

'What makes you say that?'

'The forge.'

'He'll need hammers. I'm not letting him wander about with those.'

'I'll take them.'

'You've too soft a heart, foreigner.'

The men called Loys 'foreigner' because he had come from the east, showing many eastern manners. The style of his dress was eastern, too – his loose-fitting trousers, his curved sword and turban. He had presented himself with gifts at the court of Duke William and been accepted. He had quickly conformed to the style of the court, though he'd kept his curved sword. His manner of speech too was strange – archaic, using many words that only the oldest people knew. And of course, he had not had a part in the invasion. Many of the men regarded him lightly.

'I am a practical man.'

'As you please. If you want to flog your horse catching him, go ahead. And stop fiddling with that pebble. You drive me mad with your heathen habits.'

Loys realised he was stroking the cord of the wolfstone. He returned it to his purse, then kicked his horse forward and headed out into the wild countryside beyond the farm. The boy was making for a line of woods a good three miles away. Loys could not yet sense the boy's desperation like the smell of roasting meat on the breeze as he would were he a wolf, but he didn't have to. The boy howled as he ran on with that flapping, beating shoe.

The horse was difficult to control – the stone that suppressed his wolf nature also made it possible for animals to bear his presence. Another week without it and he would have to walk. A week after that and he might run all day, fleeing his hunger, finding it waiting for him at every turn, behind every tree.

The boy's breath was reedy and high, like an ill-made flute; the horse's hooves beneath it like an accompanying drum.

Loys knew the boy wouldn't understand him, so when he spoke he did so for his own benefit.

'There's enough harm here. Come back. You'll die in the cold. Come back.'

The boy's shoe tore away on the hard ground; he stumbled, fell and stood again. Loys brought the horse around him to cut off his path but the boy dodged, nipping around the animal and running once more. A great cheer went up from Giroie's band.

'Try an old woman, foreigner, you're not up to the lad.'

Loys turned the horse. It was like trying to ride a dog. It writhed and bucked under him. He had never been much of a horseman and when the animal stumbled and lurched it spat him from the saddle. He hit the hard earth, all the wind going out of him, the heel of his hand smashing down to break his fall. Another cheer from Giroie's men, this time ecstatic. Whoops of laughter came bounding across the cold field. He stood. He'd broken his sword hand, he was sure. Never mind. There would be time to see to that.

He chased on by foot and a Norman wag shouted 'Follow my goose!' after him, the name of a child's game. Another ten steps and the boy stumbled again, falling to the ground sobbing. Loys knew what was required of him – kill the boy. That was the only way to reclaim any respect at all with his companions. He would not do it. His father had been a Norseman and he knew the English language was similar to Norse.

'Friend,' he said. 'Protector. I have seen enough hurt.'

The boy's breathing was violent, each inhalation nearly lifting him from the earth.

'Come on.'

Loys bent to him and put an arm to his back but the boy rolled. He had a knife! Loys recoiled but the boy stabbed into his chest. He was wearing no mail but he turned and his thick gambeson took most of the force of the blow. The wolf skulking inside Loys came snarling into his mind. He struck the knife away and caught the boy by the throat, his lips drawing back from his teeth, ready to bite.

55

No! Not that! He threw the boy down and stepped back. The boy got up and ran again. The cries and catcalls of the men across the meadow came to him like the screaming of gulls behind a ship.

He was chasing the boy, fast, his instincts triggered by the violence. No! Loys stopped, forced himself to find the stone in his pouch. This was too fast; he could not go to a place where the human faded and the wolf ruled. He couldn't open the purse with his broken hand so he fumbled for it with his left. He finally had it and he tied it about his neck in a loose knot as best he could, pressing the cold stone to his skin. Immediately his hand hurt more, he breathed harder but the will to tear and bite the boy had gone. Two riders broke from the group at a trot.

'If you can't do it we will, foreigner!'

He ran hard now, desperate to reach the boy before the horsemen. The boy could not outpace him, exhausted from running so far, only one shoe on his foot against a man in good boots who had not run a fifth of the distance. Loys grabbed him and dragged him down. Now the boy was not even struggling. Loys took him in his arms, holding him, his body hot from the chase.

'I had a child like you,' said Loys. 'I couldn't save him. But I have saved you.'

The horsemen drew up. One – a big man called Stephen – drew a sword.

'Are you going to fuck him? You look like you are.'

Loys returned his gaze. 'We will have a servant for tonight,' he said.

'Well put him to work,' said the horseman. 'Guillame will be back from his excursion up the hill soon and I want the pick of the meat before that fat bastard gets his teeth into it.'

Loys looked towards the great hill that loomed over the dale. Cloud had dropped onto the top. Was that why the farmers had run there, because they knew the fog would descend at that time of day? Guillame would be lucky if he didn't fall off the side, along with his men.

56

The cold woke Tola. Her house had stopped burning and now did not even smoke. The predawn pinked the sky and Ithamar shouldered his pack. The clouds that had rolled in the night before were still there, purple as bruises, full of snow, ready to drop. The light revealed no more to eat than the fire had – the Normans had been thorough. Tola was not hungry. They had skinned and roasted Lar the night before. She did not let herself think about the meat. She was hungry and had to survive, that was all.

They had not spoken during the night. She had nothing words could say, there in the ruins of her home. Ithamar, if she had been able to marshal her thoughts to think about him, would have been a mystery to her. Fear was the only thing she felt from him and scarcely even that. He seemed to reflect her own self to her. Somewhere up on the hills a wolf was howling, its voice the key to a trove of nightmares. It was that sound that knifed through her heart when she tried to read Ithamar but it came from her, not from him.

'Will they come?' said Ithamar.

'They might go anywhere,' said Tola. 'They don't know the land and could come upon us by accident. You came for me. Where are you taking me?'

'I want to go to York,' said Ithamar. 'The seer who found you is there.'

Lost in thoughts of her family and of Hals, she had not questioned him on that. Her father had spoken of Volva – wise women who could see the future, find a thief, or curse a pig to barrenness. He was a Dane and such women had once been famous among his people. She had asked him if she, who could certainly know a thief by sensing his creaking, sneaking heart, might be one. 'Perhaps,' he'd said. Her father had died fighting the Dane Hardrada two years before at Fulford Gate under Earl Morcar. King Harold had come and driven the northerners back into the sea, but too late to save her father.

'There are such people? Seers?'

'You raised an army from the stones on that hill,' said Ithamar. 'You should know.'

'Are you one?'

'I follow the old gods. I follow Woden, who makes bountiful our fields and slays our enemies, but I am not a seer. Magic is women's work, or that of the gods. I know a few tricks but no more.'

She drew the cloak about her.

'Where, then?'

'There is a band of us at Grey Horse Cave. We need to get there and then move on to York.'

'Why not go directly?'

'Other men need to come there and we can't make it alone. There are men at the cave who know good ways to the city, who will keep us from the Normans. We should leave the horse now the day is clearer.'

'Why?'

'Too easily seen,' said Ithamar. 'We need to go on foot.'

She touched her ribs. Would they be better or worse out of the saddle? She would soon find out.

They cut loose the horse and struck south, a bitter wind at their backs. The horse followed them and Ithamar had to drive it off with stones. They had to be very careful about being seen, though they could not go up onto the fells. The weather became too bad – the wind hurling sleet at their backs, pushing them on as if impatient with their progress.

It hurt her to breathe and walk but it hurt to stop and freeze. She went on, afraid to stop to sleep because of the cold.

They travelled out of the valley, further than Tola had ever been. Strange hills were all about her, looming grey out of white. The ice wind made her head ache and the sleet had forced its way through both her cloaks, making a damp patch across her shoulders. At one point, where paths crossed, they saw a great many horses had passed – Normans at their ravages, no doubt.

'We will die if we stop,' said Tola.

'Yes.'

'But can we have a fire?'

'We have nothing to make a fire with.'

They walked all morning and then most of the afternoon. In the evening they saw a farm – no more than a hut and a few fields. The Normans had not got to it yet.

'Will it be safe?' said Tola.

Ithamar didn't speak, just strode towards it. It was obvious the hut would be safer than staying outside in the open.

They descended the wide valley. It was snowing properly and the wind was blowing hard. They came to the hut. There were no animals around, not so much as a chicken. Ithamar knocked on the door. No answer. He shoved the door. It would not budge.

'We need to get in,' he said.

He climbed up on to the low turf roof and cut into the packed earth with his knife. He had made two cuts before he gave a great 'hey!' and jumped back. A spear had emerged through the turf, narrowly missing his leg.

Tola shouted at the door. 'It's not the Normans, sir, just two travellers looking for shelter.'

'Get out! Do you think me mad? No one travels in this season.' It was the voice of an old man.

'We are burned out by the Normans ourselves. Please grant us shelter, all our family has been killed.'

'Then you're bad luck. Go away.'

Ithamar thumped the door. 'Old man, open, or I'll open it myself.'

'Then you shall have a spear's greeting.'

Ithamar shoulder-charged the door. It bent under his assault but did not give. As it bulged Tola saw a glimpse of rocks behind it. The man had barricaded himself in.

'Don't make me break the door!' shouted Ithamar. 'It will be a colder night for us all if I do.'

'Get away!' The voice inside was hysterical, full of wolf howls, of the cries of lost lambs, of the anguish of the people of the dale trapped inside their burning farmhouses.

'Please be calm, sir, we only want shelter. The Normans are far from here!'

There was a scraping from inside. He was removing the rocks. Ithamar signalled for Tola to step to the side of the door. He did so himself.

A bang. The door was open and the man flew out, spear first.

Ithamar drew his axe. 'Accept what we say. We are friends!'

The man was old, thin and tiny, his eyes wild. He was almost comical; he reminded Tola of an indignant little bird. He fixed his spear on Ithamar and charged again. Ithamar side-stepped the attack and smashed the butt of his axe into the man's face, sending him reeling backwards.

The old man did not drop the spear and was not finished. He charged again and this time Ithamar knocked the weapon aside and engulfed the man with his arm, taking him to the floor. The old man had all the strength of frenzy and wriggled free. From somewhere he produced a knife and stabbed into Ithamar's arm. The wildman cried out and now it was his turn for frenzy. He smashed his fist into the old man's face, again, again, again. Then he was upright, stamping down on him. It was a while before he had finished, and when he had, the old man was dead, his mouth gaping open, deformed so far that it looked as though he was pulling a face for a child's amusement.

Tola said nothing. It was just a horror among horrors, a white sheep on a snowy landscape. She looked down at the body. It did not even seem human – just a bundle of rags. The hand still clung to the knife.

60

'I had no choice,' said Ithamar. He removed the knife and took up the spear.

'No,' said Tola.

'Here,' he said. 'Take these weapons. Do you know how to use them?'

'No.'

'Best not bother with the spear, then. Keep the knife hidden and wait until the Norman is close. They'll almost certainly try to rape you so that will be your chance. Stab hard and well into unprotected flesh.'

'That will not save me if there are many.'

'No. But it will kill one of them.'

She went inside the hut. There was wood and kindling but the man had not risked a fire. There was nothing in the way of comfort there and the bed was just a stack of blankets and skins. A cup was on the table, the rim bitten. The old man's terror had killed him. A braver man might have welcomed them in and been glad of the company and protection.

Ithamar joined her, the old man's clothes in his hands.

'Can you tell if they are coming?' he said.

'The whole land seethes with hatred and fear. It is difficult.'

'Will they come tonight? Can you tell?'

'Maybe. If they are near. I cannot tell.'

'Then we'll have a fire. Leave the corpse at the door and the Normans may think their kinsmen are within.'

'There would be horses here. And they would not pass by in this weather but come within for shelter.'

'Nothing can be ideal here. We'll die from cold if we don't have a fire. We'll wait until full dark. They won't see the smoke. Thor has sent us a good cloudhead and the night will be black.' He spoke haltingly, as if any word took warmth with it as it left his body.

Ithamar saw to his wound. It was not deep but it was bloody and she saw how he pressed it with the old man's shirt for a while, put leaves upon it and finally tied it. She would need those skills soon if she was to have any measure of revenge.

61

There was a little food in the hut – some gritty bread and cured meat. Had the man lived alone here? Not possible – there must be other farms nearby. She could sense no one. Perhaps they had fled, leaving this stubborn fool to die by the hands of his kinsmen.

They lit a candle and both sat close in its tallow stink, holding their hands around it. Ithamar's hands were raw where he had beaten the man.

'I had to do that. I had no choice. These are hard times and we must look after ourselves.'

'He cut you. He brought it on himself,' said Tola.

Did she mean it? It didn't matter if she did. The cold land, full of enemies, meant only the most basic things could be seen to. The man had died not because of his hostility but because it would have been too difficult, too cold, to solve the problem he presented.

The dark filled the hut so Ithamar lit the fire and drove it out.

He took off his coat, shirt and trousers and set them to dry.

'You should dry your clothes,' he said.

She removed the cloaks and set them down but only turned her back to the fire to dry her dress.

'The shift will not dry beneath that,' said Ithamar. 'You should remove the dress.'

'You are neither my husband nor my father, sir, so I decline to be naked before you.'

'I am not so wild as to fall upon the first pair of tits I see.'

'I'll keep my dress on.'

When her back was quite hot, she turned again to the fire. She could not enjoy it, however much it warmed away the ice of the day. The fire of the hearth was the same fire that had burned her home, the fire that cooked the same as the fire that killed.

Something was out there, among the valleys. Not the murderous Normans, nor the frightened farmers. This was a dark and heavy presence, an ending of things. It crept through the ice black night towards her.

Ithamar was restless. She knew what was on his mind and needed no insight to say what it was.

'Will you lie with me?' he said.

'No.' There was no lust in him, just the wolf call of fear. That was surprising.

'I have saved you.'

'I will not lie with you. My family is dead. The man who should be my husband is dead. I am hunted in my own land, frozen and dirty. I will not lie with you, man of fear.'

'If you use that knife on me,' he said, 'you will die here. You rely on me. So you stab me and I die and you die. You stab me and I do not die, you die.' Still he didn't come close but his eyes owned her.

'You have troubled yourself greatly to find me. I do not think you will kill me. And if you get me back to whoever wants me, I will tell them of anything that happens between us, good or bad. If it is bad then I will demand I am revenged before I consent to anything they might ask.'

'You are a troublesome girl.'

'I will be no trouble to you, if you are no trouble to me.'

After that he was quiet.

She watched the firelight and tried to stay awake to keep her mind on the land about her. But that flesh-hungry thing, slinking through the hills, made her mind retreat to the hearth. They let the fire burn out and slept at its side.

Before dawn she awoke and shook Ithamar to rouse him.

'There are Normans near here,' she said. 'We need to go.'

Outside, the day was bitter but they had no choice but to take to the hills, dodging columns of riders.

A snow storm came in and they spent a day locked to the side of a small overhang. The wildman knew how to keep a fire going from the sparsest of materials – digging a pit and then angling a hole into its side, the wind feeding the smoke. They would have died without it. She did let him near her then – she had to, for warmth, but the cold had frozen the lust out of him.

When the wind dropped it was time to move. Ithamar knew the way, reading the bends and folds of the land before pointing and saying 'there'.

She ate snow in the pink dawn. The whole country was white now, save for the scars of the fires the Normans had raised. What were they burning? Surely there weren't farms enough to feed their appetite for slaughter.

At first they came down the mountain and then they came to a huge hill, white shading to purple under the labouring sun.

'Now we climb again,' said Ithamar.

She was glad of the effort, it warmed her, but they were terribly exposed to the wind as they went up. It lay on her back like a troll from a story; cold-skinned, life-sapping, as if it were feeding on her, turning her slowly to stone.

The riders passed them by halfway through the second morning, two hundred paces below. There were ten of them and they had seen Tola and Ithamar. They didn't chase nor even threaten the pair but they stopped. They were in a steep ravine, a pale cliff like the dirty tooth of a giant between them. The horsemen talked, pointing, and she could see they were debating what to do. She felt no animosity from them, merely a workmanlike attitude. It would be a chore to climb the hill.

'We should run,' said Ithamar. His breath was heavy.

'There's no running,' said Tola. 'Our fate is spun. It ends here or it doesn't.'

The Normans looked up and then one held up his hand. For an instant she couldn't work out what he was doing. Then she realised. He was waving to them, as a hunter might wave to a deer he sees on the hillside, knowing it is too far away for his dogs to catch. She put up her hand without thinking and waved back. The sinuous, wolfy rune inside her writhed and with it a feeling, not a thought, that they were bound in a pact as old as the earth; hunter and hunted, acting out roles set by the Fates at the beginning of time. She disgusted herself. These men were killers. She had no bond with them, gave them no respect and, should she get the chance, would extend them no mercy.

She knew why he waved – he expected her to die. She wouldn't die.

They came upon the cave after two days' walk. Her feet were swollen in blisters from the wet and the cold, and she had no feeling in her hands or arms. The wildman was useful to her as they travelled but his fear never relented, never dropped. It was like a veil and she could see nothing of him beyond it. It covered the land of his mind like a snowfall.

They climbed higher than she had even been before. The wind was a vindictive spirit, never leaving them, never tiring, becoming ever angrier that it couldn't blow them down. She could not stop shaking. The man beside her was a mute, all his concentration taken up by just keeping moving forward, not becoming another stone among stones.

At times she thought she would die. She fell twice but he made her go on. To stop moving for a moment was to stop moving forever. In the frozen agony, she thought she saw death stalking behind her, loping along, his soft wolf tread slow but relentless.

A sentry saw them coming from a long way off and the men were out in force to greet her by the time they arrived, armed with pitchforks and clubs – not a sword among them.

These, she could see, were masterless men – their manners rough and their faces lean and sharp. They looked the sort who hunted the woods and roads, waiting for people to rob.

'Ithamar!' The voice was only just audible on the iron wind. Men came running down the stony slope towards them – a ragged band of five or six, while the others remained where they were, watchful.

The biggest of them spoke – a tough, dense-limbed, stooping little man who seemed to have been physically squashed down by his troubles. She felt fear from him too, but not as complete as that from Ithamar. There was a vinegary taste

65

beneath it, one of ashes and resentment, greed too. Was he going to fight the Normans? His presence felt like a marsh in the woods – indifferent to whether it drowned a conqueror or one of the vanquished.

'This is the girl?'

'Yes.'

The little man looked at her like a farmer might look at a horse at market, as if scanning her for signs of any imperfection.

'We all get a slice of this.' A man spoke in an accent she didn't recognise. A foreigner?

'Them of us who puts the work in, southerner of Bradford,' said the little man. 'Get her inside, Ithamar. We can't stay here.'

They ran back along a scree slope – running to fight the cold, not for fear of being seen; no Norman was going to hunt the high passes in that weather.

The cave was more like a well, a round blackness on the white hillside that smoked like the mouth of a dragon. They dropped into it, scrambling down on their backsides until they reached a flat floor. From there they ducked under a low overhang into the cave itself.

The fire was like a rebirth, offering comfort beyond anything she had ever known. It was as if the warmth of the cave melted away the control and the concentration that two days in the open had frozen into her and her whole body convulsed and twitched as she sat down, finally out of the driving snow.

If she had expected food, she was to be disappointed. There was none. There was no greeting for her, nor any kind word. Seven people were already in the cave – one man, four women and two small children of no more than six or seven years old. All sat staring lean-cheeked and moon-eyed at her. No one spoke for a long time while Tola lay out by the fire, her clothes steaming on her. Feeling was returning to her right hand but her left was numb, the skin blistered. All her limbs ached and then the ache became painful and she had to retreat to the back of the cave.

'That's it, girl, don't warm up too quick, you'll crack, so it's said,' said the stooped little man.

After a while the pain subsided and she began to feel cold again – but a tame cold this time, not the cold of the hills, that ice wind that cancels all personality, reduces you to just someone who, for that moment, is not dead.

There was no conversation in there, no wise woman for her to meet. Two of the women, at least, were foreigners – come over with the northern Vikings, maybe. There was an echo of other places about them, the smell of odd food, the tongue held in a strange way to curl out the odd, buttery sound of their language; a feeling of unbelonging. They had likely come over with Hardrada and been marooned when his ships went home. One had a black eye like a rotten apple. Slaves, probably. It was notoriously dangerous to beat Norse wives as they were adept at beating back.

Cedric from the top farm had married a northerner, Drifa, whose father had come with Canute. He beat her one day and she set about him with a spade while he was asleep. When he complained to her father that his wife would not cede to discipline, her father told him he wasn't beating her properly. 'What is properly?' Cedric had asked. Her brothers had dragged him outside the house and given him a good demonstration of what 'properly' meant.

The memory made her forget the present and laugh for an instant. Then she remembered – Cedric would likely be dead now, Drifa too, maybe even her father and all his beefy, bold sons. All those silly stories, all the misery, boredom, delight and love of their lives existing only in a friend's mind.

Ithamar and the stooped man were talking by the fire. She went to it and sat down. All the eyes in the cave followed her but no one said anything.

'Tomorrow we move,' said the stooped man. 'We'll head east with dawn and take the first shelter we can get, be it after an hour or, God forbid, near dusk. The going will be slow but careful and steady is better than quick into the arms of the invader.'

He glanced at Tola and she felt his irritation in prickles on her back. He did not like her listening to him – not because what he had to say was secret but because it implied she might have some opinion on it. She was mere goods to him. She ignored his disdain.

'Are men massing in the east?'

He didn't give her the courtesy of a reply.

'We must go east,' was all she got from Ithamar.

The men she was with could not hope to fight the Normans. There were six of them – young and healthy enough but badly armed, half starved. They had no more than clubs and farm tools for weapons, though the stooped man had a long knife. A single Norman horseman might account for the lot of them.

Tola thought it best not to make further enquiries before she was sure of what was happening. The attitudes of the men in the cave told her nothing. Some scarcely registered she was there. There was the familiar hot and restless sensation of lust coming from two of them but from the rest, very little. Tola wondered if Ithamar had told them why he had brought her here.

One of the men came towards her but the stooped man turned to him.

'Not her. She's our way out of this mess. Choose one of the others.'

The man snorted. Then he pointed at one of the women who was caring for the children.

'You,' he said.

She didn't argue but followed him to the back of the cave. Her mind was as cold as the wind on the mountain – she had cut herself off from everything that was happening. So that woman was a slave too, though she looked like a freewoman, by her dress.

'Don't look so appalled,' said the stooped man. 'She sold

68

herself and her children as slaves for us to save them. It's a fair bargain for the effort we've been through.'

Tola glanced at Ithamar but he avoided her eyes. She was under no illusions now. She was a captive.

10 Call of the Wolf

herself and her children as slaves for us to save them. It's a fair
bargain for the effort we've been through.
Tola glanced at Ithamar. [...]
under no illusions now. She was a captive.

Three horsemen returned to the village. They'd left one of the
houses unburned so as to draw the villagers back for shelter.
After three days they came back upon it in a wide circle, dropping in down the frozen stream that fell from the scar.

Freydis, the heat of Arabia long gone from her bones, saw
them coming. She was trapped in that country. When Harold
had shattered the Viking army at Stamford Bridge, Freydis had
tried to get back to the ships but the English king's army had
cut off her escape. She'd seen the smoke of the burning boats
in the distance and turned back inland, taking to the forest. It
was no difficulty to her to survive the autumn there. This was
an abundant land and the trees were full of berries and nuts,
birds and squirrels if she could catch them.

Of course, the Englishmen scoured the country looking for
the scattered invaders but she hid her sword, her spear and her
armour, and lay watching the farms as best she could. When she
could be sure she had found a family of northerners – it wasn't
difficult, many Danes and some others had stayed since the time
of Canute – she went to them and offered herself as a slave, saying she had been brought over as such with the Vikings. When
the farmer saw how she could dig, mend and cook, he took her
on and so she was saved, until the Normans came.

The farmer had stayed to defend his land but the women
ran to the woods. She'd had to leave them when a party of
twenty riders found them by the bridge at Weasel Gill. There
was no saving anyone and she had only just got away herself.
She couldn't give herself up to a farmer again – there was no
one to give herself to. So she had gone back and found her
sword and armour.

Winter alone wouldn't have driven her out – she had fire

and shelter – but she heard a call. At first she thought it was a wolf but its voice was in her mind, not her head. The rune that lived inside her seemed to shiver. That alone made Freydis want to know more. The rune was a burden to her now, its presence stronger and stronger. At the battle of Stamford Bridge she had felt swallowed by it, consumed. Her hand was faster, her aim surer than it had ever been, but the battle rune had not calmed itself when she had won her distance and fled.

Nights were full of strange visions – a spear flying against a storm-black sky, a field of the slain where she walked among the dead and dying with a bloody sword, killing some and leaving others. In the daytime she ached for vengeance on the English who had fallen upon her. She could not understand that. Men might fill up with resentments and anger, men could not stand to be beaten. She saw it as simply part of the business of war – someone had to win; someone had to lose. Any warrior who did not accept that and expected always to be the victor had to be a fool. But the rune, the blood-wanting rune, filled her with thoughts of shattering the enemy, using his head to adorn the prow of her ships, taking his gold and his lands for the pleasure of taking them, not the pleasure of having them.

The wolf's voice had quietened the rune. It was coming from the north. She went north, to this village.

The cold numbed her mind and clouded her thinking. Only when she had warmed herself for a day in the house did it occur to her why it might have been left.

There was even straw there, which she'd slept in, to make it more inviting in the cold. She hadn't lit a fire, she wasn't that stupid, but she saw straight away her mistake as she heard the blowing of an approaching horse. Her footsteps were in the snow outside. Had the wind blown them away? She couldn't be sure. Now she wanted the rune to express itself and she looked for it inside her mind. It shone, a silver spear, and she imagined herself grasping it.

She put her armour, her shield and her sword in the straw,

lay the spear against the wall by the door, and waited in the cold darkness. The horses drew up and she heard the Normans' voices. The rune hummed and sang like a spear striking wood. She sat in the cold darkness, flattening down her skirt like a wife waiting for her husband.

She heard the Normans talking outside. They were arguing with each other, or rather one was upbraiding another. She guessed they wouldn't come in by the door.

She was wrong. The door was booted through and at first it seemed that one of their tear-drop shields stood on its own in the doorway. The warrior crouched behind it, anticipating a spear or an arrow. Confronted by silence he peeked over the top like a child playing a game. He smiled when he saw her.

In two bounds he was inside the room, wheeling to see if anyone was behind the door. He saw the spear and laughed, threw it to the floor. Then he turned his attention to her, as the two others came in behind him. The spear rune hovered before her in the dark, pointing at his throat. The man spoke and one of the others curled up his face as if tasting rancid butter. The other held up his hand in a gesture of refusal. She saw what he was saying. 'Not for me. I have standards.'

The first man, younger than the rest, drew his dagger from his belt. She stayed looking at him, still as a woman listening to a fireside story. The rune sang and screamed, the spear burning bright in the darkness. He smirked and turned his head to glance at the others for approval. By the time he turned it back, half his jaw was missing as she brought the sword up from the straw and cut him in one movement.

The men behind him took a heartbeat to realise what was happening. They had no heartbeats to spare. She thrust the sword up under the next warrior's hauberk, sticking half of its length into his belly. The remaining man jumped backwards out of the house, trying to get the time to free his sword. His hands were cold, though, and he was surprised and scared. He fumbled for his blade but she had the spear, the weapon that embodied the rune. She charged but the man stepped back, stumbled and the spear missed. He scrambled to his feet and jumped on to his horse, digging in his heels so the animal leaped forward as if scalded. She threw the spear and missed, catching the animal instead in its rump. It bucked and kicked, terrified, throwing the rider down into the snow on his head. He went down hard and heavy, not even getting out a hand to break his fall.

She looked at her hand. The spear was still in it. She hadn't thrown it at all but sent the rune forward with her mind. She walked over to the man. He looked up at her from the snow. She jabbed him with the spear. His eyes were full of panic but he didn't move. It was obvious he had broken something, maybe his neck. It was very cold and near dark. There might be others behind him but she doubted it. She brought the horses inside the house through the animal door and stripped the bodies inside. The man outside moaned, his voice wet with blood. When night fell he became quiet.

Her own kit had suffered badly in her months in the open. It was good to get into the Norman's warm padded gambeson. Few of the invaders had bothered with full mail and were wearing the sort of coat made to act as armour all on its own – big enough to fit over her own underarmour, greased against the snow and very warm. She ate some of the provisions the Normans had with them – good bread, cheese, smoked ham, legs of chicken and chicken breast. The land was bountiful and they had taken what they wanted.

She ate, wrapped in the Normans' cloaks, and thought how easily she could have been these men's allies. There had been Normans at Novgorod, urgent, excited men who said that the English king was sick and the throne promised to their lord. They were heading back to Normandy with gifts for Duke William – rare spices, fine clothes and slaves, hoping that their generosity would be rewarded with gifts of lands in the new country.

They were curious people, the Normans, like her own – some even speaking Norse still – but very different in many ways. More Gallic, less flexible. They were convinced they were right, those people, and looked to teach the world, not to learn from it. Their tales were fascinating, and they listened respectfully to hers but always they told her what she should have done, how a Norman would have handled the situation. 'So simple,' they'd say. She admired their confidence, even if it did make her want to pitch them into the sea now and again.

So she could have gone to William's court and been with the victors in the south rather than the losers in the north when England was attacked. She might have even earned her keep and plunder with the men whose bodies now lay outside in the snow.

But no. She bit into the bread. Outside the wolf was calling. She'd follow it in the morning.

11 Breaking Free

The boy was a lousy cook, or if he wasn't, the Normans made him one.

He shivered and hogged the fire as he roasted the meat in the farmhouse and Giroie thought him too eager to be warm. The Normans, all twenty of them, were packed into the longhouse, each man a devil in the firelight.

'Get away from that fire, boy. You check the meat every little while, not all the time like that.'

He kicked the boy backwards. They'd tied his legs so he couldn't run and he fell heavily on his arse. Robert followed in with kick after kick, driving him away on his belly.

'You'll kill the boy,' said Loys. His hand was agony, swollen and already blackening to a bruise. He swallowed and tried to ignore it.

'You're right, I will,' said Giroie. 'That is, after all, why we're here.' His Norman was rough for a knight – one of those who'd won his rank at Hastings rather than inheriting it. In a generation, thought Loys, his children would speak like courtiers. In ten generations, what? Would there even be a court then?

'Well, try not to do it before we're served. And he has to mend the hole he made in my coat.'

'If you were half a man you'd make a hole in him for that.'

Loys smiled. Half a man. There were times when he hadn't even been that.

He touched the wolfstone.

'What is that you're always fiddling with?'

Loys said nothing. It was only the fact Loys had paid a good sum to be taken and offered a sum more if he was brought back that he was there at all.

'Looks unholy to me. The wolf is the sign of the northerners and some of those have no more knowledge of god than ...' He paused, presumably thinking of the right comparison. 'The devil.'

'I should have thought the devil would have a very good knowledge of God,' said Loys. He had never lost his scholar's habit of thinking that statements invited debate. Among warriors, generally they did not.

'Why did we bring this smart arse with us?' said one of the warriors. Loys hadn't bothered to learn his name.

'Just let the boy cook.' He held his hand.

'Maybe you should cook. You haven't earned your keep by killing.'

'I asked to accompany you, not to join you,' said Loys. 'What plunder have I taken?'

'What are you doing here, foreigner?'

Loys said nothing.

'Perhaps we should cut you lose.'

'Or just cut him.'

Maybe it was time. He wouldn't get the young woman back to London in one piece in this company. London was where he needed to be. The well manifested there, its waters nourishing the city, helping it grow. There he would go to the waters to help him understand what he needed to do with her.

'I'll go tomorrow,' said Loys. He wondered how he would survive, even if he found the woman. He was a Norman, or had been a century before, but that would not protect him when he came across other bands of warriors scouring the land. If he had something they wanted, and they would want a woman, they would take it and kill him to do so. If there were enough of them. If he let the wolf free inside him, he would be a danger to the woman himself.

'Not so easy. You owe me when we're back in London.'

'You'll be paid.'

'We have only your word.'

'My father was a northerner, of the Ice Lands, a Viking

true. When we give our word, we give it sincerely. You will be paid.'

'The vow of a northerner means nothing. How many times have the people of this country and ours paid them silver to leave, only to find them back next summer?'

Loys didn't bother pointing out that paying off one band of Vikings was hardly likely to carry much weight with any entirely separate group that turned up.

'What, then?' said Loys.

Giroie shrugged. 'Leave some token we might reclaim.'

'I have nothing save my sword, which I will not give up.'

'I don't want that bent bit of iron,' said Giroie. 'Perhaps you'd have more fight in you if you had a straight sword like a man.' He pondered for an instant.

'Give me that stone you wear about your neck. It is precious to you, I can see.'

Loys touched the stone again. It was his anchor to normality, to thought rather than instinct, to reason rather than rage.

'Ask for something else, Robert.'

'Don't Robert me. I'm sir to you. I demand the stone. Hand it over.'

Loys touched the pendant at his neck with his broken hand.

'I cannot undo it. Why don't you take it?'

Giroie understood the challenge.

'Filocé, take that stone off the foreigner.'

Filocé, the pale-faced Norman warrior who had won his scars at Hastings, came up behind Loys with a knife. He snicked away the cord and took the stone, holding it up to the firelight. The pebble was secured by a strange triple knot woven into a kind of cradle. He swung it over to Giroie, who caught it and inspected it.

'Pagan?'

Loys's face was impassive. The brawl of smells, colour and sound scrambled and thumped in his head as the wolf inside him opened an eye.

'Yes. I had you for an idolater the moment I saw you with

that cloth wrapped around your head like you were afraid your brains would fall out. Your brains haven't fallen out, have they?'

Loys still said nothing.

'Well, now we have something you want I'll let you go and take your little bugger boy with you. You can have it back when I get my pay. Make him serve the pork!' Giroie took a big swig from a wineskin and Loys gestured for the boy to serve the meat. It was burned but not so black that it was inedible. The warriors seemed satisfied with their victory in obtaining the stone and ceased their bullying of Loys. He nursed his bad hand and watched them drink. The time for horses was over. He would have to walk and the boy would have to walk with him. Who would have to die? Whoever kept watch. If his boots were decent then perhaps he would be the only one. If they weren't, then a warrior of near the boy's size would need to go too.

The men drank and ate what they had – which was plenty, because most of the winter stores were still intact. The people had been too hurried to spoil whatever food they couldn't take. They drank well, though Loys only took a little ale. Smoke and fire, red against black but in the way Loys preferred. The comforts of the hearth were dearest to him, though he had lived much of his life in the east where a night fire was not necessary for half the year.

He remembered Beatrice, when they had come to the palace at Constantinople, marvelling at the hot baths, the heated floor. What it had been to live as a Roman.

The warriors slept all in a pile, drunk for the most part. The boy wisely stuck to the animal pens, under the same roof, separated from the fighting men only by a low wall. They were empty of beasts now but not their shit or their stink.

Loys let himself doze. He would kill Giroie and the watchman. When the air was thick with snores and farts, he rose as if to piss. He was careful in opening the door and shut it quickly. The icy draught might wake the men as easily as a noise might and he didn't want to have to try to kill them all. He felt sure he could not take so many. The Normans were not the Pechenegs and knew that, if you are losing when you face your enemy directly, the situation will not improve if you turn your back. They lacked the insight to recognise what he was and the good fortune to be scared of it.

The man outside was stamping around the remains of the fire.

'Come to relieve me, foreigner?'

Loys was on him in half a breath, crushing his throat with his good hand. The scent of death filled his nostrils, the cinnamon-sweet kidney-and-onions succulent aroma of slaughter. He laid the man to the ground as gently as a mother would a child. His boots were the right size, he felt certain. The huddled horses fretted. Murder would call forth the wolf, for sure. He looked down at his victim, the expression wide-eyed as if he were surprised to be dead. He was recognisably human. Four, five more days and the corpses would begin to look like food. Loys could not be in this dead land without the stone.

He returned to the hut. Giroie was wedged in between two of his men. Stepping light as a deer, Loys approached him. He thought to kill him, to leave him dead among the sleepers in the morning, a lesson that they should not follow. No. Hold back from unnecessary killing. Preserve the human and deny the wolf. Loys reached inside the Norman's big coat and took out his stone. He would not put it on yet. The nimbleness he possessed without it was too valuable.

He roused the boy in the byre, putting his hand across his mouth to prevent him crying out. Then he cut the bonds and shoved the boots into his hands. The boy took them and put them on. He seemed to understand well that his time in the company of Normans was very limited.

They went out through the animal gate, pausing to strip the cloak from the corpse. The boy's eyes widened when he saw the body. Loys gave him the Norman's sword and the boy quickly pulled off the man's breeches, so much better than his own. Loys let him – no point in rescuing the kid if he was going to freeze to death.

No time to put them on. They made their way out into the flat dark. The clouds hid the moon and there was no light at all. Loys took the boy's hand, leading him out towards the woods. He smelled the leaf mould, the dens of squirrels, the warm bodies of the things that slept in hole and burrow. They trod carefully but made good progress.

In the morning, Giroie would come to search for them. The only answer to the humiliation he had suffered was death. Even if he discovered the killing with the change of watch, he couldn't hope to follow when he couldn't see.

Loys walked on, the boy's breath rasping in his ear. He had saved him, and slowed himself. Giroie would track them easily on the snowy fields but Loys doubted he would risk the woods. The English were hiding in there and they knew the paths. Perhaps he would find her there. He put his nose to the air. She was about somewhere in this country, he had her scent – not a scent just of the nose but of the mind. He would find her.

In the long distance a wolf howled out its thread of sound. He understood perfectly what it meant: 'This is my land, a land of the dead, where I am king.'

They heard the shouting from the farmhouse behind them. The boy almost whinnied in fright but Loys pulled him on.

'It will be all right,' said Loys, in Norse, which was as near to Old English as he knew. 'They won't harm you.'

'I'm frightened,' the boy replied in the same language. 'I should never have come on the boat.'

12 To York

They left the cave and went south – five men travelling with Tola, the women and a guard left behind with the children. Tola wondered how the families would eat so high up. She didn't think about it for long. They wouldn't. She put it from her mind after that. Death confronted her daily in those hills, face to face, no terror-summoned spectre but something that could be smelled and touched – the burned remains of a house or the bodies of those who had died in the open.

Her companions knew the way to York across the hills but the progress was slow. They couldn't risk getting caught without shelter so they would only walk from dawn until early afternoon.

On that first day, the wind died and stillness came over the valleys – a low mist clinging to the farms, purple in the morning sun. Smoke was still on the air and they could not risk going down. It was as if the whole valley before them was a great cauldron full of a milky broth. That was her hunger talking to her again. To the south a patch of the mist changed from purple to black. As they walked the morning it glowed red, a dragon's eye looking up at her. It was a fire, another farm.

Tola walked as well as any of the men, not showing the pain of her ribs. The dark shape she saw in her mind crawled after her, hurrying her on. She didn't like her travelling companions. The stooped man – who she now knew was called Ceoluulf – was easy to read. He hoped to gain from his association with her. On him she smelled the smoke of the ruinous fires in the valley. He moved, she thought, with a slinking, creeping gait and she imagined a fox approaching a hen house, a wolf creeping around the edge of a flock.

Except he was not a wolf. The wolf followed behind,

81

troubling her dreams, such as they were. It was impossible
to sleep properly, wedged into some crag on a hillside, where
she accepted the proximity of these rough men or she froze to
death. Hands were on her in the night and the only thing that
saved her was that an argument broke out about who should
have her first. Ceoluulf and Ithamar agreed that the answer
was no one. It caused too many arguments, she was too valuable a commodity.

'To whom am I sold?' she asked.

'Who said you were sold?' said Ithamar, invisible behind
his wall of fear.

'I feel it.'

'You are mistaken. You are going to meet great men and
help throw these Normans from our lands.'

'You do not care who your masters are. What does it matter
to you if you steal from a Norman or an Englishman? You're
still in the woods, freezing or baking, haunting the roads.'

'I am no bandit, lady,' said Ithamar.

She could see she had wounded his pride.

'Then what are you?'

'Just a man.'

'Bandits are men too,' said Ceoluulf. 'He's a magician, or
says he is.'

'I hear the gods of the wood,' said Ithamar.

'Men can't hold magic, so my mother said.'

'Not as a woman can. To see magic, to hear it, is not to hold
it.'

'Make it summer,' said Ceoluulf. 'If you're so clever.'

'If I did that the Normans might think it good to come up
to the hills,' said Ithamar. 'The cold keeps them locked in the
valleys.'

Ceoluulf shrank into his furs.

'When this is done, I shall travel south. They say it's warmer
there.'

'Couldn't be any colder,' said one of the men.

Tola thought of escape, but to what? These men had some

82

provisions with them, at least, and their bodies kept her warm in the night. The evening sky was a sword, the colour of dirty iron. As the sun fell it was as if the light froze, dropping cold on the hills. They lit fires where they could and pressed around them like misers around a hoard of treasure.

'What is York like?' asked Ithamar, one night when no one could sleep for the cold. They were in a tiny hill cave, just big enough for them to squeeze into, and the ground had been too hard to dig a pit fire, so the one they had gobbled all their wood too quickly.

'It's big,' said Ceoluulf. 'Bigger than anything you've seen in your life.'

'And what are its people like?' said Ithamar.

'Rich ones, those that I've met,' said Ceoluulf. 'They say the markets have all the world's wonders in them. A hippogriff of the east was sold there within living memory.'

'You've never been there,' said Tola.

Ceoluulf snorted. 'And why should I? There are men there who would cheerfully cut off my head and everyone would know me for a stranger. I meet its people when I rob them.'

The cloud cleared and a bright moon came up so they set off before dawn, hungry and cold but glad of the warmth that movement would bring.

As the yellow sun forged the sky into a cold blue blade, they crested a hill and looked out over a broad plain.

Ithamar's mouth dropped open and he said:

'Woden spoke:

"Vigrid is the plain where in fight shall meet
Surt of fire and the gods;
A hundred miles each way does it measure,
And so are its boundaries set".'

'The end of the world,' said Ceoluulf.

Tola stared. The whole vast plain was studded with fires.

In the valleys of her home the Normans had burned the farms but they had been isolated houses, set well apart. The plain in front of her was flecked with little villages and some not so little. All were on fire. All. In the far distance burned the biggest of them all – a vast plume of fire stretching up into the sky as if the land had given up on the sun to warm it and stretched up arms of fire to show it how it was done. York was burning.

The soldiers swarmed the plain, horses at the trot.

'I heard they had left it alone,' said Ceoluulf.

'They've just gone north first,' said Ithamar, 'and come round behind it.'

'Why? Their lords would be pleased by this land, it's so fertile,' said one of the men.

'When a farmer catches a fox on his lands he doesn't train it as a guard dog,' said Ithamar. 'He cuts off its head and mounts it on his gate for all to see.'

'This is a sermon on disobedience,' said one of the men.

'And the Normans are harsh priests. It is a sermon of fire.'

'Where, then?' said Ceoluulf.

'To meet our benefactor,' said Ithamar. 'It changes nothing.' He jabbed a finger towards a great forest of trees to the west of the town. 'Wheldrake Wood. That is where she will be waiting.'

Tola was almost deaf to what he said. 'Do you think the people had warning?' she asked. Screaming was in her head, panic and despair, she felt love sundered and smashed under pounding hooves, fire and destruction reigning as kings of the land and more. Down there on the plain something as old as death stirred. Her skin prickled as if pierced by thorns. She saw a shape like a battered cross floating above the woods, felt a desire like the downward pull of a mountainside drawing her towards it, saw fire flashing from it.

There were other shapes there too. She couldn't see them but she could sense them. They were calling to her in voices that chimed and breathed, that whispered and roared.

The shape inside her, the absence, stirred, slinking to the forefront of her thoughts. It was a low wolf crawling forwards from the night of her mind. It threw back its head and howled, so loud that the voices of the symbols by the woods were drowned. Its voice was all the shrieking notes of terror that emerged from the valley, moulded like clay, made one thing.

From behind her, way in the distance, she heard another voice, answering the one in her. This too was the call of a wolf but, instead of terror or agony, its voice brought nothing at all, no resonance or recollection. She could not read it. It was an end, a negation, a night that did not need a day to define it. Death? She thought so.

She tore her mind free of the valley's agonies and tried to send it towards the howling in the north to gain a better sense of it. She could not. She dare not. It was as if she stood on the ledge of a great precipice and any step would be her end.

She looked out over the burning plain, towards the woods. The symbol there spoke no threat to her but it frightened her too. She had never seen anything like it, not even in her dreams. People represented themselves in different ways in her mind: as a bird on the wing, a swampy field, or even a moon over the meadows. These images were expressions of their mood or their habitual dispositions. The symbol in the wood was attached to no person, was not a picture or a representation of something but a thing in itself. It was strange and frightening yet it was more appealing than facing whatever it was that was howling into her head from the north.

'What shall we do?' said Ceoluulf. 'We can't go down there.'

'Ask the girl,' said Ithamar. 'She is a seer. That's why they want her.'

'What then, girl, what? I don't believe in seers but any idea's better than none.'

When she spoke, Tola didn't really know what she said. It was the odd thing inside us, the winding, slinking shape that seemed to speak for her. 'Fear what follows us, not what is ahead.'

Ceoluulf crossed himself.

'Could we make it to the woods?' said Ithamar.

'I don't know. With luck, maybe. Not in the day. We'll need to wait for night.'

Tola crossed herself. 'There can be no waiting,' she said. 'We must press ahead.'

'Then we're dead,' said Ceoluulf. 'How many Normans do you think are down there?'

'We can make the woods,' said Tola. 'I will guide you.'

The men talked among themselves and were of the opinion that to go back was to die, of cold or starvation. To stay was to die.

'To go on is to die too,' said a bandit.

'Yes,' said Ceoluulf. He nodded towards the burning plain. 'But it might be that we die warm.'

13 The Opposite of Magic

'You're a northerner?' said Loys.

'Yes,' said the boy.

'How did you get here?'

'I came with Hardrada's army and when the English king threw us down I had nowhere to go. Our ships were burned and those that weren't had run for home.'

'So how did you finish up here?'

'By luck. I was captured by the people of these farms but many of them are of my country, or their fathers were. An old man spoke up for me, a warrior of my land who had come with Canute.'

Loys scented the air. He had a strange sense. The horizon towards the south seemed heavy. He would go there to seek the girl. The boy was a problem now. He wanted to travel as he'd travelled in the Dneiper Woods, the stone at his neck at night, in his pouch by day. The wolf inside him was not a domestic thing like a horse, to be let out or stabled as he chose. Always there was the chance that he would not be able to tie the stone back on, nor want to. He knew very well the smirking, self-satisfied feeling that came over him when the wolf stirred. It had taken a vision called by the sorceress Styliane to replace it last time. He would have to put it back on at the first hint of elation, to stop the spark before it became a fire to engulf his mind. But, as a human, the cold would dull his senses and put both him and the boy in danger.

The boy watched Loys as he decided on a path. 'Where will you go?'

'I have to find someone.'

'A loved one?'

'Something like that.'

'They'll be dead if they're around here. This is a place for hate, not love'

Loys shrugged. 'We're not dead,' he said.

'You're a Norman. They won't kill you.'

'They will. I expect Robert Giroie would like nothing better now.'

'He was the chief of the band you were with?'

'Yes.' Loys turned to his chosen path. 'We head south.'

The boy was terribly slow, even in his boots and cloak. He shuffled like an old man but he didn't complain about the cold and tried to remain in good humour. He sang a song as they went about warriors who walked ten days through a country of white bears to their ships and whose names were known ever after, and Loys could not be bothered to tell him to be quiet. If the Normans were close enough to hear them, they were close enough to see them among the winding valleys.

They took a wrong turn – a path heading south veering suddenly and seemingly permanently east so they had to turn back. Loys looked at the snowy hills. He could go over them but he could not take the boy – he would die up there. He tried to distract him from the cold by asking him about his home.

The boy's name was Gylfa and he was the son of a great pirating family who went Viking from spring to autumn every year. He'd gone with them.

'Though I confess I am not much of a fighter,' he said.

Loys thought that extraordinary. There were as many Viking cowards as in any other race of men but no northerner ever admitted to that fault. Gylfa must have been despised among his men, though Loys admired him for admitting it. So many men boasted of their bravery but were too cowardly to admit any trifling imperfection.

'So what are your talents?'

'I can smith,' said the boy. 'I think that saved me with the people here. They welcomed my skill with iron. To bend it if not to swing it.'

How much had he changed that he found this admission startling? He himself had been a monk, no fighter at all, and had valued learning far above skill at arms. Swordsmanship did not hold up the dome of Hagia Sophia in Constantinople, nor plan its aqueducts or build its bridges. The man he had been a century before spoke: 'I am no swordsman myself.'

'You killed the sentry very easily.'

Loys laughed. 'You learn a few tricks when you've been around as long as I have.'

'Some trick.'

'I am better with a pen.'

'I don't know what a pen is.'

Loys shrugged. He had abandoned his books after Beatrice died. That alone should have told him he had had enough of the world.

'I'm so cold with this wind at our backs,' said Gylfa.

'Walk in front of me,' said Loys. 'I will shelter you.'

They came to a wood on the first night and dug a hole with their knives, built a platform of branches within it and put a roof of branches over it.

'Tie this about my neck,' said Loys, his smashed hand still making it hard for him to knot the cord for the stone.

The boy tied the stone around Loys's throat. 'What is this?'

'A ward against bad luck.'

'Then take it back to the man who sold it to you, for I'd say it is faulty. Much as I enjoy your company.' They lit a fire using Loys's flint and tinder. They might be seen but better that than dead of the cold.

'So you are Norman,' said Gylfa.

'Yes. Though I spent a long time in the east.'

'Was there plunder?'

'I didn't go for plunder.'

'For trade, then. Though where is the merchant who hasn't paid in steel rather than gold when the odds favoured him?'

'I was a scholar.'

The boy looked nonplussed. 'I don't understand.'

'I was a man of learning. I read books.'

'And books brought you gold?'

Loys smiled. 'No. They brought me the company of great men, which was poison to me.'

'The favour of great men brings only joy,' said Gylfa.

Loys watched the flames. He had lived too long to argue. Once he had loved passionate debate but now he watched the sinking of the sun and the rising of the moon; saw the shooting green of spring and the falling gold of autumn as an animal sees them, without curiosity.

The fire was smoky but it was near dusk. Perhaps it would not be seen. Loys dozed for a while, frozen on the back, a little too hot on the front, but glad of the sleep after the day's efforts.

'What will you do?' said Gylfa.

'What do you mean?'

'Is there a world now? Is there a place for me?'

'I don't understand.'

'Will you go east again? Will you take me with you?'

'I am no sort of mentor, Gylfa. I am going on to find death. I saved you from an immediate danger. Perhaps we will go to somewhere you will be safe. I cannot promise that. I have my own destiny to follow, or rather to spin myself.'

'So why did you save me?'

'So I would not see the horror of your death.'

'And that was all? Not for your honour or your soul?'

'No.'

'Then why save me only to abandon me to death?'

'I do not wish to kill you. I do not wish to see you die. But die you will, so I prefer to get you to a place where you will do that out of my sight.'

Gylfa looked puzzled. 'Then bid me walk into the woods alone.'

'That would be to kill you. You may travel with me as far as I go and if you reach safety I'll wish you well.'

'Yet you say I will die?'

'You are a man. You must die. Now or later. Time is an ocean and you and I are specks upon it. What difference does it make if a speck sinks on the first wave or the third? It is still sunk.'

Gylfa pointed to Loys's strange curved sword. 'Then take out that and end your life,' he said. 'Today is no different to tomorrow, tomorrow to twenty years hence. If you believe what you say, sink now like a speck on the tide.'

Loys pushed his foot towards the fire, so close it might burn his boots.

'If it were that easy, I would.'

'How could it be easier? You cut your throat and in ten breaths you are dead.'

Loys kept quiet. He knew what he had seen at the World Well. Endless lives, endless rebirths. A tale played out down the centuries that had now ended but whose echoes were left sounding on through time – its players scrabbling in the chaos of existence, no meaning, no story, just the agony of glimpses of each other, of knowing connection and love only to see it swept away by death and the years.

'You're a hypocrite, then,' said Gylfa. 'You say you don't value your life but you do. Why are you so cowardly as to fear to see a man die?'

Gylfa's face drained as he clearly feared he had said too much. Loys wondered about his frankness. Call Varangian warriors hypocrites, even jokingly, and you were likely to encounter the honesty of an axe or sword.

'I'm sorry,' said Gylfa.

'You want my advice,' said Loys, 'I'd offer yourself to the Normans as a slave. Theirs is the future.'

'You are Norman,' said Gylfa.

'I am, or once was, a Norman. Now I am just an old man seeking death,' said Loys. 'I will have no part in the future of this country, no lands and no cattle. Go to the south if you can. Offer yourself there. It's warmer and the fields are bountiful. You can live out your days in peace.'

There was movement through the trees. A rider. No point in putting out the fire now, they would have been seen. Three, four, five riders. A party of Giroie's men – there was a big dappled horse Loys recognised.

Gylfa grabbed Loys's arm. 'What shall we do?'

'Take off this stone,' said Loys, tapping the pebble at his neck. He felt terror grip him but mastered it. He knew well it was a useless emotion, the vestige of a man he had been. He might die but he would live again. And even if he was to die forever, his beating heart, his sweat and his dry mouth would not save him from that fate.

'That will not save you!' Gylfa's eyes were wide with panic.

'Do as I say or we will die!' But the boy was gone, running away through the trees. The riders hallooed, wheeling their horses, each man a dragon in the steam of his horse's breath. Loys took out his knife, left-handed, and cut away the thong. The stone dropped to the ground and all his senses fired. His heart rate calmed and his mouth moistened and then became wet. He felt the shift in his perception from human to wolf, from prey to predator.

There was no point trying to use his sword with his hand so broken. The Normans had no lances, just swords, and he was thankful for that.

The horses came trotting in.

'We're to bring you back alive, foreigner.'

Loys bent and picked up the wolfstone, slipped it into the top of his boot, away from his skin.

'Still fiddling with your pagan icon?'

The horse and the man crackled with a deep aroma like the crisping of bacon. He smelled the sweat, the shit and piss of man and beast. Already the animals were nervous of him, a steel tang to their smell, lathering even in the cold.

Loys had his knife in his good hand and loosened his fingers on the handle. He would need to be quick.

'Kill him, Filocé, and we'll be back in a hot farmhouse within a couple of hours.'

'Giroie wants him brought back in one piece.'

'Why?'

'He wants to bring him before the king. I think he wants this man's lands after he dies.'

'I have no land,' said Loys.

'He has no land, Filocé. We should kill him.' The rider pointed his sword at Loys.

'He has land. No one who talks so fine and knows so much is landless. See his sword, see his fine clothes. He has land and a few days in the company of King William's inquisitors will reveal where it is.'

Behind him, Loys heard the boy's footsteps pounding through the trees.

'So will you come with us easily,' said the rider called Guillame, 'or shall we beat you and drag you?'

Loys saw no point in replying.

'Take him! Gentian, Gilles, with me.'

Filocé kicked his horse forward. The animal hesitated, its steps stuttering before he mastered it. Loys threw back his head and screamed to the heavens, all the misery and anger of his many years pouring out of him. The horse fretted, kicked and span. Filocé shouted at it to calm down and tried to dismount but Loys cried out again and the animal jumped backwards on its rear legs, tossing Filocé down into the snow. The horse bolted. The Norman got up as the other riders dismounted and tried to tie their animals to trees.

'A long way to the warm now, Filocé,' said Loys. 'Collect your horse and go home. I don't want to kill you. There's enough blood here.'

The Norman drew back his sword to strike. He was a big man, much taller than Loys. Loys tried to think of him as an opponent, not as so much sweating meat.

'You, who never fought. You with your smashed hand and your pagan charms. *You* don't want to kill *me*?'

He closed the ground between them. To Loys, free of the touch of the stone against his skin, the Norman seemed a

93

lumbering and slow thing. He could run, he thought, but then he'd be leaving the boy to these men or to the cold. Filocé shouted and charged and the hostility found its echo in Loys. The sword swung its lazy arc but Loys turned his shoulder aside and let it pass him. He drove his knife into Filocé's eye. Blood splattered over Loys's face as the Norman grabbed at his shoulders and they grappled like old friends greeting. In an instant Filocé was a dead weight and Loys let him fall to the floor.

Loys licked at his lips. No. Blood. No. Loys. No. The wolf was free inside him. The Normans came screaming in, hacking and slashing. Loys tore and ripped, cracked joints, split bones, peeled flesh. His good fingers worked their way beneath skin to lift it like the crust from a pie, his bad fingers hardly troubling him. Elation rose up in him like the sun filling the shade of a morning valley. One man tried to run. Loys howled through the trees after him, the human who would have let him go torn away by the wolf who could not. He heard a tight, ecstatic rhythm and knew it was the beating of his own wolf's heart. Iron and salt were on his tongue and in his nose. The fleeing man turned an ankle on a tree root. He limped deliciously on, every step an enticement to murder. Loys did not kill him quickly but held him to the ground, feeling his panic, delighting in his struggle and his death.

He sat, hot-minded among the human debris. The sudden stillness lulled him and he toured the corpses, sniffing at each one, tasting the blood. No, Loys. No. Verses from the Bible were in his mind, the Greek he had heard echoing through the great Church of Holy Wisdom at Constantinople.

'Heap on wood, kindle the fire, consume the flesh, and spice it well, and let the bones be burned. Then set it empty upon the coals thereof, that the brass of it may be hot, and may burn, and that the filthiness of it may be molten in it, that the scum of it may be consumed.'

'Who pluck off their skin from off them, and their flesh from off their bones; who also eat the flesh of my people, and flay their *skin from off them; and they break their bones, and chop them in pieces, as for the pot, and as flesh within the cauldron.'*

Loys giggled, snot dribbling down his nose. He put his finger to the dribble, licked it. Blood. He picked flesh from his teeth. The beating in his breast grew weaker, slower.

'Something wrong here, son.' It was his own voice, speaking out loud.

The snow was red. 'Is all snow red in this strange place?' The words fell into him like a fish hook into water. Human thoughts nibbled around them, finally snagging, dragging to the surface of his mind.

Don't do this, Loys. He fumbled in his boot, took out the pebble. Even the touch of it against his skin calmed him. He gazed about him, the snow blooming with blood. He felt sick at the sight, touched his mouth. No, Loys. He held the pebble tight. His right hand was still broken but it was already feeling better.

How long would it take him to transform, to become what he had been by the Dneiper? It need never happen with the stone against his skin. It would save him and he had done the most important thing: held it again.

The wolf's appetites devoured reason and while it commanded his thoughts, it seemed very odd to take up the stone, to turn his back on the odours of blood, the sizzling scent of panic, the cascading flavours of warm meat.

He tried to tie the thong back on but still couldn't manage it. His reason returned; he was tempted to put the wolfstone in his pocket until his hand healed. How long would that take? A few days. But he might be lost to the wolf by then. The flesh of men fed it and it thrived upon it, growing more present physically and mentally with every morsel.

He pressed the pebble into his palm. If the horses were still there in the morning the wolf might be quiet enough inside him for him to ride one. First he returned to the fire to check it was still going. Then he followed Gylfa's footprints through the trees.

The boy was easy to find, hiding on the bank of a frozen stream.

'You're alive!' he said.

'You need to tie this on me,' said Loys, holding up the stone.

The boy took it. 'You're covered in blood.'

'They were full of it,' said Loys.

The boy stammered out a laugh but Loys hadn't meant it as a joke. His mind felt heavy and leaden. Literal. The men had been full of blood and now they were mainly empty of it.

They walked back through the trees to the corpse field. Gylfa crossed himself.

'By Thor's great cock, you are a mighty man,' he said.

He ran to the bodies and began stripping them for what he could find. He took rings and shirts, fine belts and the best sword, four purses. He offered it piece by piece to Loys but Loys turned his eyes away and Gylfa went back to rifling the bodies as if he feared they would wake up and ask for their possessions back if he wasn't quick enough. He stood up, dressed in three cloaks, his fingers adorned with rings, two swords at his belt, four purses. He looked like a pirate and would last not a heartbeat if the Normans caught him like that.

'I have a pair of boots that fit!' said Gylfa. 'Fine boots, fit for a lord.' He extended a leg and flexed his toes.

From the south Loys heard something. A keening howl; a long tether of sound drawing him on. The boy had not heard it and just said he'd see if the Normans had any food on them.

They spent the night by the fire, wrapped in the clothes of the Normans. Gylfa tried not to stare at Loys but his eyes kept being drawn back to him.

'What is that stone, sir?'

'An anchor,' said Loys.

'For a tiny ship.'

'I'm cursed by the fates,' said Loys. 'This stone keeps that curse away.'

'Then it is powerful magic,' said Gylfa.

'It is the opposite of magic. It is its end.'

'But sometimes you choose to be cursed. You remove the stone.'

Loys poked the fire.

'Three women sit at the centre of the world, spinning out the fates of men. This is a pagan lie, or so I was led to believe. I have seen those women. The weft they weave is strong and subtle. You can try to break free of it but, even as you do, you will find you snare yourself more.'

'I don't understand you.'

Loys laughed. 'To take two steps forward, sometimes you must take a step back. That's all. I would throw off my curse, which means sometimes I must give in to it, just as a scholar who wishes to be a better debater must sometimes be bested to improve.'

'I do not know what a debater is,' said Gylfa.

Loys smiled. 'There aren't many in this land, son.'

They slept as best they could, not bothering to move the corpses or their fire. They ate well from the Normans' provisions – salted pork and dried apples.

Loys did not dream but he thought of that howl in his mind and what it meant. The girl he sought was near and he could find her. Until now he hadn't even considered what she might be like – a fleeing Englishwoman, a Norman princess. There was no point. Long years had taught him that speculation was usually a waste of effort and it was better to consider only the possibilities he could affect. The English people had suffered, no doubt. He hoped she was a Norman – it would be much easier for her to survive. He heard the voice of the rune inside her, so she was still alive. But for how long, with the Norman armies swarming the land? He quelled his thoughts and watched the fire while he tried to sleep.

The next day Gylfa caught the horses and they headed south, towards the heavy horizon and Loys's destiny.

14 Fog Spectres

They could not travel by day now but moved as wolves move, under the ice moon. Snow had fallen and frozen and the land was white, trees black against it like things wrought, not grown. Tola was glad to just keep moving. Columns of smoke lurked like demons in the moonlight – some from the burning villages, some from the houses and halls the Normans were using as bases. She could taste the fear here – acid and harsh, clamming her tongue to the roof of her mouth.

It was so cold and the distant fires mocked her – lit by industrious Normans toiling late into the sunset to destroy and burn. Shapes moved in the night – two terrified dogs running from the slaughter. The group clung to the hedgerows and slunk by walls and ditches. The sound of voices drifted clearly across the frozen air – Normans singing. Tola didn't know the words but she was sure the song did not praise God.

They pressed through a small copse. It was trackless and the long grass soaked Tola's skirt and leggings. The air here was brumous and she imagined that the whole land was on fire and the mist was its smoke.

One of the men spoke. 'Here. We should stop here. There's shelter enough and we might not be seen come tomorrow.'

'We go on,' said Ithamar. 'This is open country. We can't risk being seen.'

A noise sounded up in front of them and the whole band crouched, Tola included. Someone was coming. At first Tola thought it was some sort of creature native to York. It made a low whooping noise. Through the mist it appeared like a beast from a story, tall at the front, many legged at the back, a dark spider crawling through the forest. She felt its misery before she saw it clearly. It wasn't a spider but a woman, pressing on through the copse with her children hanging off her skirts behind her. She was sobbing and all the children were sobbing as they staggered forward, crippled by the cold. She was not dressed for it – her mantle was wrapped about a girl child of around eight. There were three children – wrapped in blankets. Their mother had none.

When she saw Tola's band she sank to her knees and cried out in despair. She thought they were Normans.

'Don't fear us, sister,' said Tola.

The woman put up her hands to beg them. All the words had been burned out of her, along with her home and her livelihood, Tola guessed. Tola went to her, taking off one of the big Norman cloaks to wrap around her.

'Tola, there is no time for this,' said Ithamar. 'We have to press on.'

'They're going to die if we don't help them.' Tola was already even colder without the cloak and could only imagine how the woman must be suffering. The woman was too numb even to be relieved. Tola saw images of despair when she looked at her – a well bubbling blood, not water; a table full of food that teemed with worms and flies; a wedding but the groom and bride dead on the floor, a union of corpses.

'They're going to die anyway,' said Ceoluulf.

The woman let out a shriek at his words.

'Tell her to shut up,' said Ceoluulf. 'Make her be quiet right now or she'll have half the Norman army down on our heads.

'Shush.' Tola took her in her arms but the woman continued to sob. Her children too were all wailing. The youngest had a split in his shoe that Tola thought would cost him his leg if he didn't get in front of a fire soon.

'We need to go,' said Ithamar. 'Take back your cloak, Tola, I can't have you die before I get you to our friends.'

'We have to do something for them. They're our people,' said Tola.

'They're of York,' said Ceoluulf. 'No kin of mine.'

The woman tried to stifle her crying but great bubbles of anguish forced their way through her throat.

Ceoluulf drew his knife. 'Three more breaths,' he said. 'If she can't be silent, I will make her silent.'

At the sight of the knife the woman let out a great howl. Ceoluulf sprang at her but Tola came between them.

'No.'

'She's going to get us killed.' The children jabbered and wept. 'Them too!' He pointed with his knife.

'Then you'll need to prepare for heaven and having her blood on your hands will do you no good at all with our maker.'

'I have enough already to send me to Hell.'

The breath of a horse. A word in a harsh foreign tongue.

'They're here!'

Ceoluulf grabbed Tola and bundled her down a bank. He held her flat on the frost-sharp grass. The woman and her children had not moved, the fear and the cold freezing them where they stood.

'There are not many.' Tola, her mind a wide and sensitive thing, thought there were only three horsemen at the most.

'Not now, maybe, but there will be if we fight them'.

She heard a cry.

'Hooo! La!' Fear swept over her, so sharp she thought she might vomit.

Hooves beat the ground; she could almost feel them, so close were they.

She heard one word, screamed by the woman.

'No!'

Then a thump. All the children howled. More thumping. Now silence.

Tola lay with her face to the cold earth.

The riders spoke to each other, the easy tones of men discussing a day's harvest. The hooves went away.

Ceoluulf shoved her and silently reproved her with his eyes. 'Next time,' he seemed to say, 'listen to me.'

They lay for a while until the thumping of their hearts

subsided and they felt cold again. Tola was the first to rise. She saw Ithamar further down the bank.

She had to go back up to the bodies because she needed the cloak. They'd been killed quickly, at least there was that. She looked at the woman's face. It was more peaceful now she was beyond the horrors of the night. Tola realised she was much younger than she had first thought. She might have been the children's sister, not their mother. She took her cloak, wet with blood.

Ithamar put his hand on her shoulder.

'At least you are going somewhere that you will learn to harness the magic in you and make these bastards pay for what they've done.'

'Am I?' said Tola.

He held her gaze and she felt his fear again. She saw it for what it was – not like the dead woman before her had felt at all. This was something he called into himself. It was a mask.

'You are heading to betray me,' she said.

'No,' said Ithamar.

'Yes,' she said.

She put the cloak about her. The blood would dry with the heat of her body.

'If you're so sure of that, why stay with us?' said Ceoluulf.

'Because there is the alternative,' said Tola, looking down at the dead woman on the ground. 'I cannot walk on alone. I will not sit here and die. So all I have is the company of treacherous men. You have a talent for staying alive, all of you. You were hunted by lords when King Harold reigned and no doubt Edward before him and you are still alive. With you I have the best chance.'

'Think how bad the world has grown when we're someone's best chance,' said one of the men.

'We should keep moving or we will freeze,' she said.

The men moved on through the woods, the fog thickening as they went.

'We must make camp soon,' said Ceoluulf. 'We could get

stuck in the open and when this fog lifts I don't need to tell you what could happen.'

'We need to find our benefactor,' said Ithamar.

'This is ridiculous,' said Ceoluulf. 'I couldn't find my cock in this brew if I didn't know where it was.'

'Are the woods enough cover?' said Ithamar.

'They're going to have to be.'

Tola looked out into the flat, grey fog. Icefalls, a lover plunging a dagger into his father's back for his refusal to let him wed, the wet smell of turf thrown up by the charge of horses, a light from afar guiding a traveller home. All of these things were out there, or rather their essence was, distilled in magical symbols that no fog could cloak, no night could hide.

She saw them in the dark, one made of fire, another of silver, still another that shone like a black horse's back, another that was just a candle. No, not just a candle. All candles. All light that stands against the dark.

They spun slowly around a woman, their light illuminating her face. She was old, not as old as they were but she controlled them and directed them. They were not her servants but rather aspects of herself, indivisible from her.

'You're looking for a sorceress,' said Tola.

Now Ithamar's fear did prick. No mask, this, a real clench of the stomach, knee-tightening lurch.

'Yes.'

Tola stepped into the mist and the men had no choice but to chase after her.

15 Two Witches

Styliane hated this cold country. All her life she had lived in the sun and, though Constantinople could be cold, the palaces were heated and she could be conveyed to social engagements in a palanquin, deep beneath furs. Here, she and her men needed to move stealthily. The runes were useful to her in this but she did not feel comfortable using them overmuch. At present, she had them under control. But if she allowed them to the forefront of her mind for too long they would take over, start calling for their sisters. At the point she allowed that, and the wish to become a god rose up in her, she would be lost as a person. Her brother, a century before, had lost control like that and the wolf had torn him, scattering his bright runes to the four winds. That was when they had entered her. She would not make the mistake he had made.

Dýri the Varangian stood close by her. Styliane had three of her guard with her and without such men she was sure she would be dead. They brought their tents, built the fires and kept low in the country. Her Varangians could pass for Normans and had cut their hair in the brutal, shaved style of the invaders. It had taken some persuasion to get them to do that. It was not manly to hide away from your enemies, to deceive them, they said.

It was much less manly to be cut down for nothing, having gained nothing, she said. She reminded them of one of the stories of the old god Thor, when the giants stole his hammer and demanded the hand of Freya if he was to have it back. Thor dressed as a woman and pretended to be Freya. When the giant presented the hammer, Thor picked it up and ensured the giants knew him to be manly enough, despite his wearing a bridal gown.

'You're not cold, Dýri ?' she said.

'It's half cold here,' said Dýri. 'A miserable, seeping chill but not a strong one. You compare this to Hordaland and it's like the Bosphorus in spring,' he said.

'My father wouldn't have bothered with his shirt in this,' said Agni.

God, how she missed civilisation and the company of intelligent people, rather than these boastful, showy warriors. She recalled all her homes, to try to make herself feel warmer. She remembered the flower garden at Baghdad, a tall beaker of sharbart in her hands. There she had thought ice a luxury – her drink chilled with it, brought all the way from the northern mountains. Here she hoped never to see another crystal of it again.

They were in a big, frosty wood and the Varangians had built a fire hidden in a depression, placing their tents around it. She had no choice but to sleep under the same canopy as the men, though she resented it. She was very aware that she would resent freezing to death more.

She was sure the girl was in the country. She could feel the nervousness of her own runes at her approach. They knew what she would bring in her wake. Would she be able to use her runes to get into York and find the well in the presence of that snarling, crawling rune? Probably, she thought. It was the wolf that followed that would bring the problem. No magic could stand before it. She would have to work quickly. An attack on the bearer of the wolf rune would summon the wolf. The girl needed to die before it had chance to reach her.

'This fog is not natural,' said Agni.

Styliane thought him an idiot. It was entirely natural. It was also very cold.

She allowed the Kenaz rune to light inside her, its light and warmth spreading through her body. Was the girl near? She could feel the wolf rune snuffling and rooting in the dark and something else too. Another rune was out there, she could sense it like someone standing on the shallow edge of a lake senses deep water beyond.

She let the rune burn brighter. The Varangians couldn't see it but they could feel it. Rannvér loosened his tunic, hot even in the icy fog.

'Will she find us?'

'She is finding us,' said Styliane. 'Ithamar has brought her near enough; she'll sniff out the way.'

'I don't like that sorcerer,' said Agni. 'It's not manly to use magic.'

Styliane said nothing. Agni's entire life seemed ruled by consideration of what was and was not manly. The ability to split a log with one blow from an axe, to best an enemy and outdrink a friend, was how these men valued each other. The most impressive man she'd ever known was her brother and he had been a eunuch; perfumed, hairless and long limbed. He'd been a lion among men. He would have been little use in that comfortless wood, she had to concede. The Varangians were peerless fighting men and if you wanted them for their prowess at arms you could hardly complain their dining manners would have disgraced a starving dog.

Ithamar, of course, was not a sorcerer. He was a man who had sought the gods and had been taught a few impressive tricks of the mind but his was a male magic, all discipline and repetition. Hers moved to the forces of the universe. The runes that guided the path of the moon and told the sun to rise in the morning were in her. She felt the tides stirring in her body, the winds tearing at her mind.

He'd been useful, though, sensitive enough to hear the girl's wolf rune howling, resourceful enough to get her through the country to where she needed to be. She'd seen him, one night in the desert, clear as if he had been standing in front of her, peering at the runes that spun and sparkled above her. Then she had spoken to him and sent him on his quest.

'What was that?' Styliane spoke involuntarily, looking

weaker and more worried than she would have liked before her men. She'd heard a sound, a guttural snort.

'I heard nothing,' said Dýri.

The white wall of mist was unyielding.

'No, there is something.' Big Agni drew his sword.

'You're there?' A girl's voice through the mist.

Styliane – who in her natural lifespan had served the dark Goddess Hecate; who now knew that all gods were the same god, of triple nature – paled. Hecate, virgin, mother, crone. Odin, all father, all hater, all wise. Christ, Father, Son, Spirit. Styliane had torn knowledge from the gods in ritual and suffering, most of all at the World Well where her brother had died and made her immortal.

She was still shocked by what she heard. The girl's voice was exactly as she had remembered it a century before. Styliane had watched her die.

'Yes.' Styliane walked towards the voice. She shivered with more than the cold. The rune she had lit inside herself illuminated and she saw the wolf rune writhing in the fog – long and sinuous, low to the ground. It turned its head towards her and its three meanings burst upon her. Storm, wolf trap and werewolf. She saw them now as she had never seen them before. Of all of them she had least understood the storm. The werewolf was self-evident, the rune drew a man who was a wolf. The trap was obvious too – the wolf was drawn on to die. But the storm? She had never penetrated its meaning. Now she did. Ragnarok. The end of the gods. Had that happened? She thought so. But the rune raged in front of her, rumbled with thunder, crackled with the smell of lightning rain.

The Varangians could not see the rune but they sensed its presence, exchanging anxious glances.

Rannvér now drew his sword. 'What is this?'

'What can you see?'

'Nothing. But it's like a goose has walked over my grave. Is this the hag?'

Styliane's attempts to explain the nature of her mission

had met with incomprehension from the Varangians and, in the end, she had told them they were going to apprehend a witch who was a threat to her and to the stability and prosperity of the Varangian Guard in their favoured position as the Byzantine emperor's bodyguard and, some said, controllers.

'I think perhaps it is.'

'Then I'll kill her here.' Dýri's voice was an urgent whisper. He was afraid. He would not have concealed hostile intent from any man but he feared what was out there in the fog.

'That won't be possible or practical,' said Styliane. 'We'll stick to my plan and I'll hear no more about it.'

'I am here.' Styliane heard the howl of the rune, which was the howl of the wind, the howl of a wolf and the howl of a tormented man all at the same time.

The girl emerged from the mist and it was as if she had stepped from Styliane's memories. She had been pregnant then, terrified. She was not even a person, thought Styliane. Just a role to be played in a story throughout history. Now that story was over, what for its players?

The woman terrified her. She knew what she was – a Norn, one of the women who sat spinning the fate of men at the centre of creation – her own people called them the Fates. Or rather, she was the dream of a Norn made flesh. To kill her was to kill destiny. Which was what Styliane intended to do.

The girl stepped further out of the fog. She was not tall, though she was taller than Styliane, and she was blond and ruddy with the cold.

She looked at the Varangians with their drawn swords. Fear was in her eyes – Styliane's guards were the biggest men of a big race and seemed as giants beside the ragged English bandits who took shape at Styliane's side. The two women stood looking at each other.

'You are not my people,' the girl said.

'No,' said Styliane in her soft Norse. 'But you understand me?'

'I understand. My father was a northerner.'

107

'Then be welcome. Share our fire.'

Styliane allowed the rune to fade inside her until it was just a candleglow in her mind. She saw the wolf rune writhing above.

'I'm afraid of you.'

'Yes. And I of you.'

'Am I right to be scared?'

'Perhaps. We may, however, work to our mutual advantage. Do you know what follows you?'

'It's like a wolf. It's there in my dreams.'

'Well, perhaps we can get rid of him.'

'I want to help my people.'

'You will. He is cursed. You have heard of Ragnarok? The end of the gods?'

'Yes.'

'He is Ragnarok. The final encounter is begun but not finished and it will try to play out here on earth, through him. In the east war trailed in his wake and now in the west it is the same. To free your land of slaughter, you must free it of him.'

'You said we'd be paid. You said we'd have passage south,' said Ceoluulf.

'I need you for a while longer,' said Styliane.

'For what? I've done what I was asked and now I want paying.'

'I require your service still. We're going in to York. You will travel as if my slaves but you may be required to protect me while I'm there.'

'That's suicide,' said Ceoluulf.

Ithamar was not so bold but the bland mask of fear he had maintained in his mind for their journey now came down. He emanated a much more human, various fear, a sharper one too. He was scared of Styliane, scared of the Norsemen, scared of Tola.

'I may need that from you,' said Styliane. 'But I promise a warrior's death and a favoured place in the afterlife.'

'Bollocks to that,' said Ceoluulf. 'Give me my money now!'

'Or what?' said Rannvér. He spoke in English. He wasn't the biggest of the Varangians but he was a head taller than any of the bandits and his arms were as thick as their thighs.

'You're a big man but to me that's just more to aim at,' said Ceoluulf.

Rannvér cut off his head. The movement was so quick that no one had time to react before Ceoluulf's body hit the ground, his head rolling away like a turnip from the back of a cart.

'Aim then,' said Rannvér to the corpse.

Tola did not flinch but Ceoluulf's fellows fell upon his body, stripping it as quick as they could.

'You owe us weregild for that,' said one. 'Compensation.'

'Easier to kill you all,' said Agni.

'What's the price for ridding the land of vermin?' said Dýri. 'You should pay us. I'd say that's your booty they're looting there, Rannvér.'

'Let them be,' said Styliane. 'We have more to think about. When shall we make the town, Agni?'

'How long will the fog last? I'd say dawn is a couple of hours. It might be good to get into the town now and hole up there until nightfall if the fog lifts. If it doesn't, we do as we please.'

'Then now.'

'We can't go in there,' said a bandit. 'The Normans have the whole land.'

'We look Norman enough,' said Dýri.

'It's too dangerous.'

'A man lives for danger.'

'A man lives for his belly.'

'Look at you and look at me,' said Dýri. 'Ask which philosopher eats better.'

'We should go,' said Agni. 'Or make ready to stay the day. We can cover our tents with brush and sit out the day.'

'Rannvér?' said Styliane.

'I say now. Last night the fog lasted until mid-morning. If it does the same tonight, we'll make the town easily.'

'Then prepare to go.'

'How will you know your way?' said Ithamar.

'I'll know my way,' said Styliane. 'And so, I dare say, will she. Are you able to go, my dear?'

Tola looked around her. 'We have come a long way without sleep.'

'Can you go a little further?'

'Yes.'

'Good. You are an example to the men.' She put her arms around Tola. She needed to say something to her, there was a pressure inside her, something that would not be contained. The girl would need to be killed. But that was not what she told her. 'I swear, by my Goddess Hecate, by the runes within me, by Odin and by Christ, that I will not harm you. You are under my protection now.'

The girl hugged her back and bile rose in Styliane's throat. She had been quite clear this girl needed to die. Why, then, make an inviolable oath to protect her? This was magic, beyond reason. Carry on with the plan. Take her to the water. There, all would be clear. She shivered, not with the cold. What price would be asked of her? Last time it had cost her Freydis, a guard she had loved, perhaps more than one should love a guard. This time? She put the thought from her mind.

The men stamped out their fire, flattened their tent and buried it in leaves. After a squabble, the Englishmen agreed to be disarmed for the sake of looking like slaves.

They set off into the fog, almost sightless across the fields. Styliane did not hesitate. She could feel the well drawing her in and she could hear the wolf behind her, its cry eerie and flat through the dead air.

She saw Tola cross herself.

'You want to answer,' she said.

'Yes.'

'Don't. He is destruction. Come. We will rid the land of this blight.'

16 Fate's Knot

Heading south, Loys left the stone in his purse and tucked it inside his coat. The air was full of iron and smoke. He was on the trail of the rune and he could feel it winding its way through his thoughts, its presence long and lithe, drawing him on. He wondered if the others the Fenris wolf had set its eye on before him had felt this way. His friend Azémar, so long ago, had carried the curse sleeping within him. In the dungeons of Constantinople it had come crawling forth to save him. Azémar hadn't had the stone to hold him to humanity. Had there been others, in lives before? Sometimes he thought he could hear them and at other times he thought he was mad.

The way was easier for the boy now he had a horse. He could almost pass for a Norman from a distance, until you realised he slumped on it as if coshed. No Norman rode like that, only the Norsemen – many of whom grew to manhood without ever seeing a horse. The horses would not go near Loys while he didn't wear the stone but he ran behind, which at least encouraged the animal to keep moving.

He followed her trail across the hills for a while. The path she had trodden was clear to him; he could smell her, an odour that sent him back a hundred years to a girl in a rented room in Constantinople. He remembered he'd once bought her a peach from a stall and thrown it up to her. He saw it now, rising like a little golden sun against the blue of the sky. She'd caught it. 'Thank you, serpent,' she'd said. It was a joke. The Greeks – or Romans, as they preferred to be known – called peaches Persian apples. She bit into it and smiled at him. He hadn't known it then but he'd been happy. It was the last time.

His hand was healing. Had he eaten when he'd killed the Normans? It seemed so. He didn't heal so quickly in that way without it. By the end of the third day they were in deep fog. His hand was entirely better. He considered killing and eating the boy, or rather, it was an idea that kept nagging him, like the thought of warm bread might nag a labouring man on a cold day. He found his hands flexing, found himself recalling the satisfying click of a neck being broken. He spoke to his appetite as he ran, telling it that it would not be sated.

They stopped by a sheltering cliff, a good overhang that would keep the weather off if it rained. The boy called out 'Here?' and Loys held up his hand.

It would be easy not to put on the stone. He wondered how the boy would look in his death throes. With the wolf rising inside him, he found nothing so fascinating as the way that men die. He thought to leave the stone off. He breathed and looked into the fog. It was as if God was inviting him to kill, saying 'I have sent you this fog as a sign that I am not looking.'

He put on the stone with quick determination, not allowing himself to even think about it, like someone jumping through ice to bathe in a pool.

His thoughts calmed as he watched Gylfa cutting up a bush for their fire. When he smelled the smoke, he approached the camp. He felt human and cold and the horse did not fret as he drew near. Still, when he first put the stone back around his neck he always felt as if he had left something behind, a little piece of him for the wolf to munch on.

'I've never seen anyone like you,' said Gylfa.

'I've never seen anyone like you,' said Loys. 'An honest Norseman, who admits to being scared like the rest of us.'

'I only said that for the pity it would bring.'

Loys said nothing. He knew what the Varangians who guarded the emperor in Constantinople would say to that. Better twenty deaths than an enemy's pity.

He'd thought them idiots when he'd first encountered them but now life seemed such a fleeting thing for mortals that to try to delay its ending by ten or twenty years seemed to be missing the point. The years were an invading army, sweeping all before them. Dying at one moment was very much like dying at another. Unless you didn't die. Unless you saw the invader take everything but leave you standing in the dead dust of love.

Gylfa irritated him. He sat clinking the coins he'd taken from the Normans as if fascinated by them. Loys forgave him. He had never known true poverty – his parents had earned a good living and he'd gone into the monastery as a boy. The kid had been raised on tales of plunder, no doubt, but never thought to see any.

'How did you come on the boat?'

'My father took me. He said it would be good for me.'

'You could have finished with a good farm in England.'

'Yes. I fought, you know. I had to. The English army came on us so quick.'

Their fire was a small one – the wood had been hard to come by. Loys stretched out his hands to it. Without the stone he rarely felt cold.

'May I ask,' said Gylfa. He was stumbling for words, clearly afraid of Loys.

'Ask what you want.'

'May I ask. Are you a devil? You are bound to answer me if I ask, so says my priest.'

'I am only bound to answer if I am a devil. And then you would need to confine and bind me with holy symbols and the name of God.'

'You know about such things.'

'I was a scholar.'

Glyfa scratched at the dirt with his foot. 'Are you a devil?'

'What makes you think I am?'

Gylfa crossed himself. 'You run all day without tiring. You kill many men yet you don't look like a warrior. Your hand, which when I met you was swelled up like a pig's bladder, is now whole and mended.'

Loys held up his hand to examine it. It still seemed miraculous to him that he could heal so quickly.

113

'I am a man. But the priests would say I am possessed by a devil.'

'What would you say?'

'I think it likely. But it is not as I imagined it when I read of possession in my studies. This devil can be faced down.'

'By prayer?'

Loys did not like to think about this. He had not considered the state of his immortal soul for years. He would rid himself of the demon the best way that he knew – by dying. That was not suicide. He had no intention of killing himself, because that was a sin. The girl would do that for him. But his very existence challenged everything taught by the holy church. He had tried for years to make it fit but it did not. In all obedience he could accept the teachings of Rome but his scholar's nature made him attach weight to what he saw with his own eyes, felt in his own heart.

The Bible contained no mention of the fiend that had set its eye on him.

'Prayer will not do. This devil needs to be faced on its own terms.' He tapped the stone.

'The priest says that is a graven image and the work of idolaters.'

'He has seen my stone?'

'Items like it. Trinkets, the horns of animals, the hammer of Thor.'

'Are you guided by the church, Gylfa?'

'I try to be.'

'So do I,' said Loys. 'I don't want to be this.'

'What?'

'What I am.'

'I would love to kill ten men, to run like a horse.'

'I killed four,' said Loys.

'But you have killed before?'

Loys threw some more twigs on to the fire.

'You will burn in hell for that and for treating with dark powers.'

'I don't treat with them. They treat with me.'

Loys felt guilty for telling this young man his secrets. He had hidden his true nature for so long simply to avoid the attention of men. An emperor who knew he had near him a man who had lived for a hundred and twenty years might wish to question that man, might regard him as dangerous, even imprison him. Loys was a formidable warrior but even he couldn't stand against ten men – not the disciplined Varangians of the emperor's guard anyway – and, even if he could, he didn't want the fuss. He had been open with Gylfa for one reason: he thought it wasn't going to matter because the young man was going to die.

Gylfa offered Loys some of the bread he had taken from the Normans. Loys held up his hand.

'You have it,' he said.

'You don't need food either?'

'I don't need it yet and neither do you. I do want it. That's different.'

'How different?'

'You can ignore what you want. You can't ignore what you need. That would seem to me to be an essential difference between the two words.'

'You talk strange,' said Gylfa.

Loys had forgotten, for a second, that he was talking to a northern farm boy, not a scholar of the Magnaura in Constantinople.

He did feel hungry but he thought the boy needed to eat more than he did. Hunger, like pain, passed.

Once he had thought that feeding his human appetite might quell that of the wolf. But it didn't work like that, he'd found. The wolf's hungers were deep fires and could not be fed by meagre fuel.

They lay down to sleep, pressed up against each other. Loys had travelled before and had had to share too-small beds with strangers but there was something about this forced proximity to another human that rankled him. He felt close to death, or

115

close to a chance of death. The boy was almost certainly going to die in such a hostile place. He would have liked a better companion than a farting, angle-some boy he had tried to save in a gesture of sentimental futility. He thought of Beatrice. He could hardly remember her face now. She was just blond hair and a few snatches of remembered conversation. She was gone, utterly gone, but his love for her remained; an ache that had outlived her.

He was gone too – the ambitious scholar, the hopeful husband, even the father to the child she had left him. He'd sent the girl away, hoping she would grow up free of the attention of the gods that had cursed him and her mother.

'Is it you?'

A woman's voice but none he had ever heard.

'It is you. I know you by this stone. It is you. Wake up and free me.'

'Hey!' Gylfa was on his feet, his sword drawn. Then he was sitting down, his sword somewhere else.

Loys jumped from sleep, his hand on the wolfstone. In front of him was an extraordinary figure, squat, bulky, wrapped in two large coats and giving the impression of being wider than it was tall. Its face was thin, though, a great squashed turnip of a nose poking out from a scarf. Its left hand seemed enormous, a huge black glove on it. Its right was a normal size and had only a stained yellow glove in addition to the sword.

It steamed at the mouth like a monster out of myth. If Loys ever met a troll, he thought, it would look like this lopsided barrel of a creature, though he saw he had no reason to draw his sword. The figure had surprised them, the wolfstone damping down Loys's senses. If he had wanted to kill them it would have been the easiest thing in the world. He?

'You are the wolf. Is it you who has been calling to me?'

Her voice was incongruous, melodious, feminine. No man spoke like that, not even the eunuchs of Constantinople.

'You're a woman,' said Gylfa.

'Are you him?' She ignored the boy.

116

'I can't be bested by a woman,' said Gylfa. He half crawled, half ran for his sword.

The woman seemed unconcerned. Loys noted the blue sheen on her blade. Damascan steel. A sword like that cost fortunes and would only be bought by a professional warrior. It was an investment, a bet that it could make you more money than the price of the farm it would take to pay for it.

'Leave her,' said Loys.

'She means to kill us.' Gylfa pointed his sword at the woman. He looked more like he was offering it for her to take. How did a Viking, raised to war, finish up with so little skill at arms?

'I'd say not. Who are you, lady?'

'Freydis of the Varangian Guard.'

'Is she a shield maiden?' said Gylfa. 'I've heard of them but I'd imagined them a sight better looking!'

'I could make you call me beautiful,' said Freydis.

'Not while I still have eyes.' Gylfa danced back and forth, pulled forward by the string of his manliness, pulled back by that of his cowardice.

'Well, tearing them out might be one way to go about it,' said Freydis, 'but, looking at you, I'd guess I'd only have to show you the sharp edge of my sword to have you declare me the light of all the north.'

'I won't kneel to a woman.'

'You will if I cut you off at the knees.'

Loys held up his hand. 'Gylfa. Put down your sword. We have enough enemies in this land without searching for more.'

The boy took a pace back. All he had needed was an excuse to dodge the fight and Loys had provided him with one.

'I was of Constantinople,' said Loys.

'I've heard of you.'

'From whom? You have been with her?'

He didn't need to say who he meant. No one else knew his secret, only Styliane.

'Yes. I am her servant.'

'Have you followed me? She can't want me dead.'

117

Gylfa wafted his sword about, as if trying to bat away a fly. 'She's not going to kill you, is she? I'd like to see her try.'

'She sent you here?'

'No.'

'You are not here by coincidence. There is a world for us to be in. Why do we share this spot?'

'I came here to get away from her. I only followed you since I heard you call.'

He looked around to the cold hills, floating like their own ghosts above the fog.

'I haven't spoken, lady.'

'I heard the voice of the wolf.'

'Not my voice. How did you hear it?'

'In my mind. I have a curse upon me. I think you can cure it. There is a rune in my heart and you frighten it away.'

'Now? Is the rune afraid now?'

'No.'

'And why do you want it to go? A rune is a great gift.'

'It brings a destiny. The runes want to be together. My lady has four. I have one. My rune wants her runes for company, she told me as much on the Galata bridge. If I am near her when I die then the rune will go to her and she will be nearer to resurrecting the god; nearer madness.'

'If you kill her then the runes will go to you. You could be a queen.'

'Or a madwoman. I do not want to kill Styliane.'

'Why not?'

'I love her. I served her by her side and now I serve her by keeping away. She has lived a long time and I would have been happy to grow old in her company. Now I must live, at all costs.'

Loys put his hand to the wolfstone. Freydis would not be there by accident. A shattered story was playing out, repeating, stammering, falling to nonsense. If she bore a rune she was part of it, sent by the will of a god now dead, Odin – the world sorcerer – so powerful that his desires lived on after his death. He thought he should kill her. But if he did, then where would her rune go? To Styliane, maybe, who would be one step nearer the divine. Could Odin take flesh on earth, even if he was dead in the realm of the gods? Loys didn't know.

'You are a famous killer, I think,' he said.

'Yes.'

'Then perhaps that's why you're here. I am trying to die.'

'You are the wolf, you cannot die, Styliane told me.'

'I think I can, in some senses. But if I do die then the story begins again, with me as an unknowing participant. I want to die properly. Will you help me?'

'I am a mercenary. What is my fee?'

'When I find who I am looking for, I will take her to the world well as it appears in London. There we will ask it for guidance. I will ask how you might be rid of your rune and the destiny it brings. Though I tell you clearly, I do not know if I will be answered. The well asks a high price for its knowledge and I have nothing to give, no lover to lose, no kin or friend.'

'Odin gave an eye at Mimir's well and he hung on the tree for nine days,' said Freydis.

'He was a god. Lesser beings are asked for more.'

'Would you give an eye?'

'Whatever is asked,' said Loys. 'All I ask is your protection.'

'How should I protect you?'

'Not me.'

'Then who?'

'There is a girl. I have tracked her here. I'll know her when I see her. She is my killer. You must protect her until the murder rune inside her can grow and prosper.'

'You are a mighty man and need no help from a woman. Protect her from who?' said Gylfa.

Loys said nothing.

'And you will ask at the well?' said Freydis.

'I swear it.'

'Then I swear too.'

'She's not coming with us, is she?' said Gylfa.

'She's coming with me,' said Loys. 'Whether she comes with *us* depends on whether you choose to follow. Now saddle your horse and keep it away from me.'

'You're afraid of horses?' said Freydis.

'No,' said Loys. 'They're afraid of me.'

They slept pressed against each other and awoke to a murky dawn. The cold was numbing, mind altering, clouding his thoughts with ice. Loys pressed his nose into the horse's flank, taking just a little warmth and comfort before the journey. When Gylfa and Freydis were ready, he took off the stone and walked behind his horse, Freydis well ahead. The animal had worked hard all the day before and he knew that, if they flogged it for another day, it might go lame, which would leave Gylfa having to walk. Besides, the boy was happier when the horse went slower.

The hills and the passes were dusted with frost, though the wind still did not blow, which was a mercy.

They rounded the shoulder of a hill and looked out as if over a sea – the fog obscuring all the land below therm.

There were human tracks in the grass. Loys sniffed at them. Four or five men, one woman, all moving in fear. He could taste it in all its heart-thumping, sweat-stained exhilaration. These people thought they were on the edge of death and Loys, his wolf mind chewing at the edges of his human thoughts, felt his mouth grow wet.

Loys heard the wolf rune cry out – its howl a shiver made sound.

Noises drifted up from the valley – voices raised. At that distance it was impossible to tell if they were crying out in exultation or anger. A sound like the fall of a great load of something. Loys recognised that – men charging into battle. Gylfa did too.

'What is that?'

Loys sniffed the air.

'Hard to say. War, in one of its various forms.'

'And we're going towards it?'

'I am,' said Loys. 'You must do as you please.'

'Master!' Gylfa fell to his knees in front of Loys. 'Let us go away from this land! Let us be great pirates somewhere. A man of your fighting prestige would find it easy to raise a crew and I know all the most profitable shores. Ireland still has its treasures, the east too. Think what we could take. Kings would envy our gold. This woman could join us if you so please.'

'We're going down there.'

'To death?'

'Yes,' said Loys. 'I have taken you as far as I can, Gylfa. Now it's up to you what you do. Come with me if you want. Or go on. The fog is your friend. You can see where the sun comes up and where it sets, so head south. The lands there are not under such a heavy burden of war and you may find employment.'

'I fear to go on alone!'

'Then stay by my side.'

Gylfa crossed himself. 'I will die down there.'

'And if you stay up here you will die. For most men death does not submit to choice in the question of its occurrence, only in that of its timing.'

'You talk too well for me, sir.'

'It is a sign of nobility,' said Freydis.

A howl echoed from the valley below, an ancient sound, full of loneliness, agony and exultation. Loys's muscles writhed on his bones in response to it. The rune called him, she was down there. He ran down the hillside into the fog and Gylfa scrambled to mount the horse.

Loys followed her scent on the damp grass. The trail was fresh and clear. She was near. His lover, his killer, and she was in danger. She could not die; she had to survive to help him thwart fate.

17 Discovered

They passed across the plain hardly breathing lest they disturb any plunderers still at their work. Villages appeared as ghosts of themselves, insubstantial, broken in. They were there for a second before the mist claimed them and made Tola wonder if she had seen them at all.

At first Tola thought the mounds were the markers for farming laines but they were too close set, too numerous. The frost gave an explanation. It had broken up the shallow earth all along a low-lying hollow and a grave had split like a hideous pie. The man inside it had been dead a little while. She glanced at him but looked away, having seen enough of destruction.

The bandits, however, fell upon him, searching for valuable clothes or for rings. There were none and they cursed him for being such a stingy, nasty corpse.

'That man is a Norman,' said Rannvér.

'His hair betrays him,' said Agni.

They went on as if over a frozen sea, so many were the undulations. Waves of dead. Tola was sure of one thing.

'They're all Normans,' she said.

'I'd say King Sveinn has got busy here,' said Agni.

'Who is that?' said Tola.

'Our ferryman. He brought us over from Denmark, or rather his men did. England's in too bad a state for any true Viking man to ignore. His army may have been bound here. I don't think even they knew where they were going when they landed. Perhaps there will be no Normans in York.'

'There will be Normans,' said Styliane. 'Some, at least.'

'How so, ma'am? There's a mighty field of dead here, fit to please old Odin himself,' said Agni. 'Can there be so many left?'

122

'There can. They buried them,' said Styliane. 'King Sveinn would just have put them all in one pit, or burned the lot of them. There will be Normans here.'

Tola stumbled on through the sightless fog. Another army in the land. More killers. The Varangians, with Styliane leading, moved at a breakneck pace, seemingly uninhibited by their virtual blindness. The lady worried Tola. She could not read her properly, or guess her intentions. Those magical symbols, that had burned so bright from afar, were not visible now. She still heard them moaning as if in an underbreath, chiming and sighing as the group strode towards the town. At least, she thought, it was towards the town.

For the first time she wondered what she was doing there. In the company of the bandits she had been simply fleeing, feeling any servitude or slavery must be better than falling to rape and murder. Now she was walking blind to a destiny as the servant of a woman she felt sure meant her no good. She went with her for the same reason she had gone with the bandits – there was simply nowhere else to go. It was a choice between people she suspected wished her ill and running into a land full of Normans who she was certain did.

How long was it since she had eaten? A very long time. She was dizzy and she was cold to the marrow.

She glanced at Ithamar. His shield of fear had dropped but now she could sense a deep and complex disquiet. Something like dawn greyed the clouds but she could see no further than the person walking in front of her. She could smell the fires, though, the noxious smoke of flesh and thatch tingeing the mist.

The Normans were nearby. Her mind had contracted with the cold of standing still, and the only thing that mattered was the numbness in her feet and hands, the shivering and the feeling she would die. The warmth of movement let her mind drift and she could see the invaders as if she were one of them, sitting by their fires, calming their horses, waiting for the fog to lift to commence the slaughter again.

123

The northerners would allow no rest – they said that to stop was to freeze. The smoke grew thicker, with that dry, bitter, funeral-pyre smell. Finally, a huge structure loomed above them. Tola drew in breath. She had never been so close to anything built so big in her life. The walls of York stretched out into invisibility in the mist.

Styliane led her men quickly up to the walls and huddled against them for fear of being seen. Tola could see the walls were a hotchpotch of stones, faced with crumbling earth. Some attempt had been made to shore them up with wooden logs. Her consciousness went running along their length, quick as a hare.

Agni leaned on his sword. 'Will there be guards on the gates?'

'There are two, near here,' said Tola.

She could feel them, almost *be* them. They were angry they'd been set such a ludicrous task as standing look-out in such a fog. Resentment tasted soft and tarry in her mouth. One was a well-born man and he hated doing sentry work – he would prefer to be out on his horse, raiding.

'Only two?' said Styliane.

'Yes, on the gate.' She sent her mind into the town. So much distress in there, so much agony – all the anguish of the villages but boiled down, concentrated in one small place. Not everyone felt unhappy. There were warriors in there, some exultant, some weary. One man felt tired and had clearly seen enough slaughter to last him a lifetime. Another was excited, looking forward to the fog lifting and the terror starting anew.

'Many more within,' said Tola.

'Which way is the gate?' said Styliane.

Tola pointed along the wall.

'Are the guards vigilant?'

Tola stood tapping her tongue on the roof of her mouth like someone trying to put a name to an odd flavour.

'They are cold and one wants to play dice,' said Tola. 'The other doesn't because he fears being cheated.'

'You can tell their thoughts?' said Rannvér the Viking.

'No. More their feelings.'

'So what am I feeling?'

It was easy to tell. Cynicism poured from him like the taste of bad wine.

'Can't you tell me? You are a more reliable person to ask than me, who only sees glimpses.'

He snorted.

'You doubt me?' said Tola.

Rannvér put his eyes to the floor. 'If the lady believes in you, it's not for me to call you a liar.'

'What to do?' said Agni. 'Do we go in as if these were slaves?'

'Is your Norman up to it?'

'No.'

'Then what?'

Agni looked up at the walls. They were intact.

'The Danes must have been let in,' said Ithamar. His voice was hardly more than a murmur. 'The city's full of Norsemen or their descendants. It couldn't have been too difficult to get the gates opened.'

'Either that or they just sailed up the river,' said Rannvér. 'Sounds a lot simpler to me, particularly as you've got your ships there for a quick retreat if things get a bit warm.'

'The Normans will have killed everyone inside. They won't be expecting trouble from within,' said Agni.

'How do you know?' said Rannvér.

'What would you do if someone betrayed you to your enemies?'

'Fair point.'

'Let me take them and be quick by the gate when I do. There are only two, you say?'

'Yes, two,' said Tola.

The sweat was freezing on her again now.

Agni tested the crumbling earth of the wall. It came away in his hand. He moved down to the wooden logs that had been used to shore the wall up. He managed to wedge his boot between a log and the wall proper. This was enough to lever him up to a level where the original stone was exposed, uneven and broken. It was easier to climb and up he went. In no time he was on the top of the wall and he lay flat, only his boots visible above them. The boots disappeared and Tola guessed he was climbing down.

'Too easy,' said Dýri.

'Not so easy with men pouring fire and stones down on you,' said Rannvér.

'Can you imagine climbing Constantinople's walls like that? Whenever anyone's tried to lay siege the legions have just had dinner and watched them until they get bored and go away.'

'No. But that is the Roman Empire. This is Rome gone rotten.'

Styliane held up her hand to silence the men.

'We'll die here, lady,' said Ithamar.

'I'm looking forward to it,' said Dýri. 'It'll warm me up.'

'I thought you said this was only middling cold,' said Rannvér.

'It's a dishonest, creeping cold,' said Dýri. 'You can fight the cold in Hordaland. Here it creeps up behind you and mugs you.'

'Like we're doing?' said Rannvér.

Styliane clicked her fingers and glared and they both were quiet.

They sidled down the wall towards the gate, Dýri in the lead, Rannvér behind. The smell of burning here was strong. Footsteps behind. Tola turned. One of the bandits had fled into the fog. Styliane again held up her hand. No one moved.

Too close to the gate to talk now. Laughter. The rattle of dice. Were they that close? Someone spoke a couple of rough words in what sounded to Tola like the Norman tongue. Dýri strode forward. There was a sound like a sack dropping from a cart and Rannvér motioned for them all to come on. Dýri and Agni pulled the bodies of the Normans to one side, away from the gate, and Ithamar and the two remaining bandits fell upon them, stripping them of whatever they could.

Styliane gestured to the fog behind them, to where the deserter had run.

'He'll be dead soon one way or another,' said Dýri. 'Chasing him's a waste of time and effort. Come on.'

They went through the gate. It was nowhere near as big as Tola had thought – just big enough for a man to walk through. She guessed the main gate must be somewhere else. The door that secured it had been torn away at its hinges.

They stepped through into Hell.

Every building she could see had been burned down. Tola could sense people in the town, warm and happy, so other buildings must be standing but everything around her was blackened and smoking, the remaining beams of the houses sticking up like the ribs of a slain dragon.

'Surt,' said Agni. 'Fire giants. I wouldn't be surprised if they were with them.'

'Just men with brands like any other,' said Dýri. 'Move.'

The smouldering town was much warmer than the country had been, though the fog was – if anything – thicker, mingling with the smoke.

'Where?' said Agni.

'Ahead,' said Styliane.

Tola walked on. The misery seeping from the houses was almost overwhelming, a chill beneath the heat. She saw things at her feet she did not wish to see. Bodies – many of them. The fog allowed such a limited view that it was all she could do to avoid stepping on them. So many connections had been broken here. Mothers, daughters, sons and husbands. All so much ash and smoke; the taste bitter in her mouth. At what looked like a crossroads the fog thinned to reveal more burned houses, bodies recognisable only by a black arm or leg. They reminded her of the women she had seen on the hill. The houses themselves were like plants that had withered, the remaining timbers reaching up like reeds that had rotted where they stood.

'If we become separated, dear, head for the well. Can you feel it here?'

'I can feel something,' said Tola. 'There's a great body of water.'

'That'll be the river,' said Rannvér.

'More than the river,' said Tola. 'All the water of the world is moving. It's bubbling up. It's like it wants to be free.'

'That is the well,' said Styliane. 'Find it if we get separated.'

'For what?'

'For your destiny.'

Norman soldiers sang somewhere close.

'Shouldn't my destiny find me?' said Tola. She kept her voice low. 'Isn't that what makes it a destiny?'

Styliane laughed under her breath 'You only look and sound like a country girl,' she said. 'Do your fellows remark that you can talk so?'

'My fellows are dead and remark nothing.'

Styliane stopped for a moment, judging the way.

'Do you wonder why you see the world as you do? Why you talk with me, a high lady, as easily as you can a thrall on your farm?'

'I wonder how I'm going to stay alive, or if it's worth trying,' said Tola.

'It's always worth trying,' said Ithamar.

'It's right for a woman to try to stay alive,' said Dýri. 'She needs to raise and nurture the next generation. A man should value his life more lightly. He will give it up to avenge an insult. He will give it up for gold. He will give it up for the joy of battle alone.'

Tola felt fear coming from Dýri as sharp as that she felt from Ithamar but nothing in the big Viking's face betrayed his feelings. He was trying to talk himself into courage. Ithamar, by contrast, skulked through the streets like a beaten dog. Styliane was scared too but her fear was not directed towards the men who sang invisibly somewhere away through the filthy air.

128

'Save the philosophy and concentrate on the task in hand,' said Agni.

'This way,' said Styliane.

They strode on – no point in creeping. To any nosy pisser or wandering drunk they looked simply like three Norman warriors escorting a great lady and her slaves. They'd draw more attention to themselves by trying to hide than by walking boldly.

The fog was definitely getting thinner – it was as if the smouldering buildings had burned it away. Ahead was a wooden bridge over a wide river and behind that Tola could see a castle taking shape up on a hill – wooden walls that had survived the fire, a wooden keep behind it. Downstream, the river had been dammed and its course altered. The Normans had made a moat. Had they sat behind that while the town burned?

The bridge was built in the solid Norse style – a functional structure of heavy logs with no rail or barrier to stop an errant cart or a panicked horse ending up in the water, two men's height below.

They stepped onto the bridge, Styliane falling in behind her guards. They were a quarter of the way across before they saw the Normans coming the other way. Ten of them, on foot. They were armed and armoured – the town had only just been subdued and it was clear they were taking no chances.

The Vikings didn't break stride but walked on purposefully. Tola felt the excitement coming from the warriors, the shaking, wet-mouthed fear of the bandits. Styliane alone was unconcerned. She glanced behind her, not ahead.

Halfway across and the Normans a quarter of the way on the other side. They would meet right above the water. As one the troop of warriors stepped aside as Styliane approached, the leading man – a big, raw-headed individual with a scarlet surcoat – bowing to her.

Styliane inclined her head and walked past. The Vikings met the Normans' stares boldly but the bandits – as was appropriate for thralls – avoided their gaze. They had gone ten steps back when a voice called after them. Tola didn't understand it. Styliane stopped her men and said something in reply. The Norman was pointing at one of the bandits. Tola felt her guts lurch as she realised – he was wearing the fine gloves of the man who had been killed on the gate. The Normans were telling the lady one of her slaves was a thief.

The man in the scarlet surcoat came and grabbed another of the bandits, shaking him. He rattled with the money he was carrying. The Normans seized the other bandits, Ithamar too. They found Ceoluulf's gold and two warriors bent to examine his boots. All too fine for a slave.

Tola went to press on but a warrior grabbed her, seizing her cloak and shouting. She felt his fury. Her cloak was good Norman workmanship, not suitable for thralls. He saw the blood dried onto it and his hand was on his sword in a breath.

Everything moved so quickly. Agni came forward smiling and laughing, shaking his head as if the Norman had made a simple mistake. The man returned his smile, willing to listen to an explanation of why a thrall girl was wearing two good Norman cloaks, one of which bore a substantial blood stain, excellent riding boots and such a good stiff coat. No one dressed their slaves so fine but she, by her ruddy face and coarse hands, was certainly that. Agni put his hand on the man's shoulder as if reassuring him. The man let go of Tola and Agni shoved him into the river, drawing his sword in the same instant. Time now creaked and groaned in the cold night. To Tola it seemed that everyone moved as if through water. Swords, all over the bridge. Agni charged, hacking at the Normans. They were taken by surprise and two hit the water quickly. A bandit rounded on his Norman but the man was too strong and quick. A squabble of limbs and the bandit went flailing to the water. Death was there, in his glory. Tola saw the women on the hill as if they were flesh, floating above the battle, gazing down, spears in hand, ready to strike. Panic was all around – hot waves of distress as might come from a

130

strung pig at the first prick of the knife. The bog-black faces of the women looked down at her. Were their spears poised for her? She ran.

Ithamar leaped towards Styliane, trying to grab at her purse but Dýri punched him hard in the face, a short, jolting attack, throwing the weight of his body behind the blow. His hand hardly moved but Ithamar went flat to the bridge. Tola sprinted for the bank, Rannvér coming past her to engage the Normans.

The Normans bellowed at the top of their voices, calling for aid from their fellows, no doubt. Styliane screamed at Dýri, too fast for Tola to understand. Dýri grabbed at Tola but she slipped by him. He was a big man but not fast and she plunged forward into the fog, ran up a hill. Here the houses were still intact and the road was narrow. She ducked down the side of a house as eight Norman warriors came plunging through the fog, swords drawn. Eight more were behind them.

She heard Styliane cry out. She saw that, across the road, a cart was leaned against the side of a house. She took the risk and ran for it, hiding underneath. From here she could just see the bridge through the fog. Styliane had gone, as had Dýri, but Agni and Rannvér were still on the bridge, corpses piled around them. Normans were pouring in now from both banks. They'd won the first battle with surprise on their side, but they couldn't win this. They were outnumbered twenty to one, surrounded on both sides.

Agni held up his sword and shouted out at the Normans.

'It is a man's death I will die today, and a noble one. It's a gift from the gods to die so. But I am not a selfish man, to keep such treasure to myself. Come, my friends, and share in it!'

His words were lost on the Normans, who shouted back in their own language. Tola wanted to run but she had no idea where to. She looked for the strange women she had seen floating above the battle. Were they there? The line in her mind between what she saw and what she imagined had always been a faint one and she couldn't tell whether it was the women or just their memory that seemed to congeal from the fog. The Normans were hesitant. She could only just make out the bank but she saw them arming with shields. A shout and they advanced from both sides. Agni and Rannvér were shadows in the mist, back to back. Such big men but so many enemies. The Normans closed, she saw shadows falling into the water, shadows falling from the sky; heard cries and screams. The mist covered the bridge and, when it moved away again, the two Vikings no longer stood.

Tola had been unsure what Styliane and the Vikings wanted to do with her but they had at least provided a direction. Now she felt utterly alone. She pulled the cloaks tighter. She could not stay beneath the cart forever. The Normans would search for her. She lay still for a few moments, just to collect her thoughts.

Flat across the water came the howl of the wolf, binding her to it with its long tether of sound. It chilled her, more than Styliane, more than Ithamar or any of the bandits. She would have to move. But where to? She tried to free herself from the grip of the wolf's howl. Close by she felt the mass of water, lapping through her thoughts, submerging them almost. There were bright things in those waters, the symbols she had seen in Styliane. They were submerged there yet also in Styliane, simultaneously existing in the water of the well and growing in the mulch of the lady's thoughts. That something could be in two places at once struck her as strange, fascinating almost. It absorbed her for a while. Odd ideas sparked in her. That shape was such a horsey, stampy shape. Here's another that was the mother of the world, yet one more that thrived on mould – a bright, living thing sprouting from the bodies of the dead.

There were corpses in the water. She could not see them clearly, only catch glimpses of their pale fishy flesh, bleached and bloated by long immersion.

Soldier's boots were on the road. She flattened herself. They were searching the houses. She stilled her breathing, tried to keep silent but she was fighting panic, the urge to run away. The Norman's harsh voices came closer. Only the fog protected her now but it wasn't enough. Boots in front of the cart. A hand rattled it.

A cry came from down by the river, footsteps sprinting away. There was a shout from very near her and the boots in front of her turned and disappeared. She heard more men running down the hill. More screaming, shouting and calling through the fog. The Normans had seen someone.

Again the howl, winding through her thoughts. Could anyone else hear that? She had no one to ask. She was alone but for the dark shapes which still seemed to hover in the fog.

18 A Beggar God

Tola had to do something before dawn. She couldn't stay for
the whole of the day freezing beneath that cart so near to the
water. The fog thinned and she could see glimpses of the town
under a smudged moon. The only intact houses were the ones
right about her. Everything else was charred and burned. In
the grey river the shattered hull of a longboat raised its dragon
prow above the water, casting its malignant eye out over the
mist. The Danes had been here, then. She sat watching for
a long time. There were corpses in the river, she was sure,
floating face down, only their white necks showing. The mist
moved over the moon again and it was very dark. She was
glad of it.

She could not be certain of remaining unseen now, so had to
stay where she was for at least a while. It was dreadfully cold
and very hard to keep still but she endured it. She tried to
distract herself by saying the names of all her kin. Alta, Ceade,
Evoric. All dead. It didn't work.

She let her mind float free of her body, seeking Styliane or
Dýri. They were the nearest she had to allies now. She could
not sense them and she guessed they must be dead. All around
her the Normans fussed and bothered.

Something hummed and groaned beneath the ground. She
felt as if she was sitting on the back of a great sleeping beast.
She put her hands to the earth. It felt very cold, but not the
sitting, sucking cold of the ground in the forest or in the hills.
This had the tug of current, moving away from her, down
towards the river. Could this be the well?

Why go there? Why go anywhere? She had been lied to,
she was sure, but why not believe the lie, even for a while?
It was better than the truth of the world now, a truth burned

into the land like a great black scab: that death was the ruler of all peoples and that all were equal before him, being nothing.

She would go to the well for the same reason she had come to York. She had nowhere else to go. Go south and she was a foreigner, a lone woman at the mercy of whoever might claim her. She had no idea what those lands were like. People from the farms said they were packed with charlatans who would part you from your money in a wink. And if she did go south, who would want her? Perhaps she should have responded to Ithamar's advances, become his wife and lived in the wilds.

No. She could not abide him, even if the alternative was death.

But where to go? Already she had moved further away from her home than she had ever been in her life. All future and purpose had ceased to exist, been burned into the ground with the crops, the houses, the cattle. She sought the well because she sought the well, just as she lived because she had not died.

The clouds thinned and the moon came back into view, gazing down with its white, rotted corpse face. All around her she heard the sound of men and horses but it was still very dark. There was no song or laughter, just hushed voices. They'd lost friends that day and no one was in the mood for jokes. She wished she could understand what they said so she might hear news of Styliane or even Ithamar. A door was opened and firelight flickered. It closed again and only the moon gave her any light to see by.

She put her hand to the stamped earth, feeling the movement of the waters. It led north. The ground sang with its flow.

The houses were only intact for thirty paces. After that, all was burned all the way to the solid stone block of a great church. This, she thought, must be the minster – famous throughout the world. It was enormous, bigger than any building she had ever seen, though it had not escaped the fire. Its arched windows were stained with soot, giving them the appearance of black eye sockets staring out of a stone skull,

135

and the sloping roof that faced her had caved in. The great church was a long way away – five hundred paces through the rubble of the city. She had to get there or freeze. At the very least it would provide some shelter.

She stooped forward through the houses, the ash dry in her nose. A scrabbling from her right. She stood very still. A dog stood looking at her, not twenty yards away. It was a mangy creature, though not thin. God knew there were enough corpses around for it to feed on. It came towards her, its head bowed low, its tail wagging. She glanced around her. No one in sight. She put out her hand and it nuzzled its head against it.

'There, boy, there.' She said it so quietly it was almost a thought.

Tola's gift of reading people did not extend to animals, though it was plain enough what this dog was looking for. Affection. Love. Someone to make order out of the chaos that had engulfed its life. She couldn't wait, it was so cold, her breath was freezing in the moonlight.

'Go on. Go on.'

She crept away from the dog but it kept following her, nudging her with its nose.

'Go away! Go away!' She shoved the dog away but it wouldn't go, thinking it a game and shoving back at her, its tail wagging. 'Hsst. Hsss! Go 'way!'

She shoved it again and now the dog barked, a great loud *woof* far louder than she would have thought it capable of producing.

'Go away!''

She ran but this was great sport to the dog, which ran after her, jumping up at her skirts and barking in excitement. It was a game she might have played with it on a summer day on her farm. She felt the Normans' curiosity spark before she saw them. The minster was still over two hundred paces away, the nearest house only a hundred.

They would be upon her in an instant. She had no choice.

One of the burned houses had a sunken floor. She dropped down into that and lay flat. The dog stood above her barking madly, pushing its two front paws into her side as if it would dig her up. Norman voices.

'Chen! Chen!'

They were calling the dog. She felt hostility like the sting of a nettle from one of the men, simple curiosity from the other.

'Chen! Chen!'

The dog turned from her and pricked up its ears.

'Chen! Chen!'

Something more was said in Norman. She had a winter feeling inside her – that of days spent locked in the house, aching to go out but forced to stay in by wind and rain. One of the men was deeply irritated by the dog's barking. The other had come out simply because he had been bored by the fireside and wanted to stretch his legs.

'Chen! Chen!'

She wanted to grab the dog, to make it stay, but she couldn't. It had to go to die if she was to live. She lay absolutely still, trying to quell the dog's interest. It lolloped over the bank of earth that had once been part of the house's foundations and went wagging up to the men.

The men made cooing noises, trying to attract it, but one man was seething, the other laughing. He was a bully and smirking as the dog snuffled unsuspecting to its fate. One said something to the other. She couldn't understand it but the emotion washed over her. 'Finish it,' he meant.

For an instant she thought she had stood up, begged them not to hurt it, appealed to their gentler nature. It seemed stupid to feel sorry for a dog when so many people had died, but she did. It had come looking for human comfort and was to receive only cruelty.

Another voice. Someone else had arrived. She heard a sigh, a long note like a grandmother might make when she saw a bonny child, though a man's voice. Then a long whistle. From the sounds of chuckling she guessed the dog had approached

137

someone and was presenting itself to be patted. More words were exchanged and she heard some very like 'no, no, no!"

A wave of resignation, resentment. Someone had been denied another kill. The cold of the ground was excruciating and she needed to move. One of the men took a long piss and she heard another calling and whistling to the dog. 'Coo, coo. Coo, coo.'

He was encouraging it to go with him. She felt like crying in thanks. She had thought all kindness burned out of the world. To see someone, even an enemy, show any delight in life, to welcome in the dog for the companionship it would bring, gave her hope that all the destruction would one day be at an end. One day the invaders must put away their swords, as the Danes had done before them, settle down, farm and restore the land. There would come a moment when peace returned to the dales and, even if she wasn't there to see it, the idea made her glad.

She waited for a long time, her hands and knees numbed by the cold earth. She tried to control her shivering but couldn't. It was intolerable now. She had to move or die of the cold.

Tola looked up above the bank of earth. No movement from the houses.

She crawled up, so cold she felt on the verge of passing out. Her vision was blurred and her hearing was subtly altered. It was as if her ears were blocked by water, a heavy feeling inside her head.

She wondered if she was dying, but not with any great anxiety, only curiosity. The minster loomed above her. She thought it might fall, it almost seemed to totter. It could have been a tree, she thought, a gigantic tree stretching up to the heavens.

No, this was God's house, and God needed a big house because God was so big.

God was not at home. He had given up on England and left it to the hordes of the devil.

A man walked towards her through the frosty night. She

hadn't the strength left to run. He was a strange figure, very tall and pale, red hair burned to patches on his scalp, great welts covering his face, blood everywhere. He wore a tattered cloak made of feathers, which he wrapped around him tightly. He was shivering deeply as he came on. This must be some poor Englishman, left for dead by the Normans, now coming to his senses among all this desolation.

'Hello, sir.'

It seemed natural to address him so calmly, even in the midst of the Norman camp.

'I'm so cold,' said the man.

'I am too. You have been used badly by these men of Normandy,' said Tola.

'I have been used worse by what follows.'

'And what does follow?'

'Follow who?'

'Follow . . .' Tola's mind felt fuzzy, half asleep, as if in that just-woken moment where the world is seen but not interpreted, where familiar things seem strange.

'I don't follow.'

'You don't follow?'

'No, lady, I am followed but only by my followers, of whom he is not one, though he follows. *A* follower, rather than *my* follower, if you follow. Let me explain. Though you do not follow me, you may yet follow me. Well, he's not the same. He doesn't follow me not because he doesn't follow me but because he follows me all too well. He had faith but now no longer follows. That follows.'

The minster loomed above her like a thunderhead.

'Who does he follow?'

'You. Do try to follow, though you are, strictly speaking, more followed than following. Listen to the following. He is following as night follows day, that is to say to eat it.'

'Who is he?'

'He is the wolf. The land is fallow because of that fellow, which follows because the fellow is followed by fallow, that is

139

to say death, who follows all humanity, save him who follows even death, that is to say he who pursues it. Death is the only thing he really follows. So what follows from that, you who he follows?'

The man's words made some kind of sense to her. He was a victim of the wolf she could hear howling in her mind.

'You are a god.'

'I am wounded and bitten, though no sinners were saved by me. I could not even save myself.' The red-haired man seemed very sad at this idea. 'What do you do when your anger is slaked, your revenge complete?'

'I would not know. My anger is frozen in ice. One day it will thaw and then pour hot over these Normans.'

'And when they are gone, what if hating has become a habit and all joy is gone from the world?'

'All joy has gone. I cannot replace it for myself. I can only make sure I destroy it for my enemies. The Normans planted a weed in me that will grow to choke the garden of their delight.'

'Oh, that wasn't the Normans who planted that, not by a long way.' He laughed at this, his bloody, torn hand coming up to his face. He pointed at her. 'Your inheritance is death.'

'Isn't that everyone's inheritance?'

'Not Wolfie. His father is immortal and his mother, well, to be frank I haven't heard from her in years. Spawning a monstrous brood tends to put quite a strain on relationships. I mean, a wolf! She said he had my eyes!'

Tola looked into the man's eyes and they were indeed those of a wolf, a burning yellow like polished amber.

'Why are you here, sir?'

'As always, lady, you cut to the nub of it, which is apt as you are the nub of it and this is next to the nub of it, it being one of those words that can mean many things, so does it.'

'Answer me.'

He smiled and crouched to his haunches, put his hands upon the ground as if he was searching for something on it, or beneath it.

> *'Three times nine girls, but one girl rode ahead,*
> *White skinned under her helmet.*
> *The horses were trembling, from their manes*
> *Dew fell into the deep valleys,*
> *Hail in the high woods.'*
> *'I do not understand you, Sir.'*
> *He smiled and said,*
> *'May the first bite you in the back,*
> *The second bite you in the breast,*
> *The third turn hate and envy upon you.'*

The words were glorious to her. She imagined herself high above the clouds, a spear of lightning in her hand, a horse of thunder beneath her.

'What am I?'

'A spinner of fate.'

'What is my fate?'

'You are one of the few to whom it is given to spin their own. That is what it is to be a god.'

'I am not a god.'

'Which brings me to the reason I'm here. I need someone to kill a wolf and I think you can do it.'

Tola didn't know what to make of this.

'Let me explain,' said the man. 'My time has gone. I would like to die. My former magnificence is dimmed and passed. But the time of the gods of the North has not finished. The wolf has not been killed. He needs to be killed. Things will not move on. The world will always be locked in strife.'

'The wolf?'

'The very same. He is destruction. Now I know there's always been rather a lot of that when Odin was hopping around the place but it had something of a creative aspect. One civilisation destroys another. I weep for the loss of a particular sort of beauty, whether of the face of a Scythian boy, or the curve of one of their vases, or of the Egyptians who flattered me and called me the Typhonic Beast but I did not see that this

141

allowed other things to flourish. Odin the mad, Odin the wise, Odin the king of magic and, yes, Father Death. But he had a sliding, slippery nature that made the death of one civilisation the manure that fertilised the achievements of another. I saw him as one thing but he was many. He couldn't be pinned down, which was one of the reasons he was always popping up as a woman. Your fellow, however. Oh dear ...'

'My fellow?'

'The following wolf we talked about precedingly. He has no dual nature. He is one thing only – a cavern, a space into which everything falls. He is an end to things. Look around you. He is here. He's been sleeping awhile but when he wakes, he howls, and the world howls with him.'

'The Normans did this.'

'And he came with them. I have glimpsed the future and there are many more of these destructions to come. He drags them in his wake. So we need him to die. And you are the one who can kill him.'

Tola wondered if she was dying, if this was a vision of the devil brought on by the cold.

'How?'

'You may have to hang on the tree for a while to find that out,' said the man. He gestured to the wall. In sparkling lines the image of a huge tree stretched up the walls of the minster, its roots reaching down beneath her feet. The ground was insubstantial, invisible, and the roots merged in a ball of light which she thought, strangely, might be the well she was look-ing for, then stretched away to become rivers. She felt them running away, some freezing, others with a close, sultry heat she had never experienced before, one that summoned strange cries inside her head and sparked visions of fabulous birds with feathers the colour of church jewels.

The tree sprang from the well, the well was the tree, all of a single shining substance. She looked up to see the silver leaves spreading out as stars.

'We are the light of this tree,' said the god.

142

'And he?' She meant the wolf.

'The darkness.'

'What must I do?'

'Kill,' said the man. 'Kill her, kill others. All of them to die.'

'All of who? You are the devil,' said Tola.

'Well, one man's god is another's devil,' said the man. 'Look at these Normans, marching under the cross. Whose work do they do? If it is a god's, ask how a devil's could be worse.'

'I think you are the devil. I will not listen to what you say.'

'I am trying to help you. You carry a heavy burden inside you, lady. Even now I can feel it writhing.'

He put his hand to her belly but she drew back. The man bowed his head. When he looked up, he was weeping.

'You recoil from my touch. No mortal woman has ever done that. There was a time when the offer of my kiss would have been an irresistible lure to you. My powers have waned. My light was only borrowed, it all sprang from him. Oh Father, oh deceiver, you even tricked me in your death. I did not know it would make me beg for my own.'

She was convinced this was a fever, brought on by the cold. Still, she had to run away.

She went up the steps to the minster, turning round to glance behind her before she turned back to open the door.

'All is broken,' said the man. 'It is for you to fix it. You must kill him, for I tell you true, he will kill you.'

The wolf's howl called cold across the burned city.

She shoved at the door of the minster.

'You will be here again if you don't act,' said the man. 'You will stand in rubble, weeping the loss of everything you love again and again, endlessly pursued, bringing misery and destruction behind you. The story must end!'

'Get behind me, Satan!'

The man pulled the cloak about him and hobbled off through the ruins.

The minster was vast but almost lightless, its windows high and small, just daubs of moonlight on the blank face of the

143

wall, the hole in the roof dropping a veil of shifting silver.

Careful, she moved on. The building seemed to intensify the darkness, to boil it down to a solid and glutinous thing. She could not see and felt for the wall. There it was.

Now a little light seeped in from the windows. A flat-faced angel looked down at her from an arch, its feet ensnared in vines. The stones of the great church's floor seemed to murmur, as if water flowed beneath them.

She was cold, so she drew the cloaks tight about her.

On and on she walked, past the dark mouths of arches that lined the walls. The great altar was quite bare. A body lay there, but she didn't stop to look at the horrible thing. A priest? A man? A woman? None of those things now. The current under the stones led her to beneath the hole in the roof. Ten paces further on was a broad flight of steps descending into deeper darkness. The waters were coming from there. Could she go down into the dark?

A noise behind her. Someone was coming into the church. She hurried as quietly as she could to the steps and went down out of the light, lying flat to the stones, just beyond the lip of the first step. Whoever had come in had no light either but they didn't need it – they stepped confidently forward. A spark, a glint; like sunlight on water. Tola peered over the step.

It was Styliane, a rune shining from her like a beacon – the shape of an arrow head. Tola didn't know if she could really see the rune floating there in the darkness or if she imagined it. It seemed very real, a torch shining out, but other things too – it was the fire of the hearth, of the smith's creation, something to shape and mould. Styliane was using it, Tola could sense, to encourage herself, to beat out the iron of her thoughts as if on an anvil. Dýri was behind Styliane. He moved more hesitantly. Tola could feel his worry bleeding from him.

The rune seemed very bright. Around the walls the flat faces of angels, saints and beasts looked down, all their eyes on her.

Styliane walked on, past the great altar. From deep behind

Tola a noise sounded, like the rush of great waters. The light appeared at the top of the stairs.

'Lady,' said Tola, standing.

'Take her,' said Styliane to Dýri and the big Viking ran down to grab Tola.

19 Breaking the Seal

Styliane had seen him, of course – the sly one, Loki, skulking by the steps of the church. So battered and cut now. When she'd last gone to the well he had been magnificent – a pale giant, his hair red as fire, whose gaze brought fear and excitement all in one; a heartstopping creature. He had come to her, of course, at the well and tried to reason with her, stood shaking and bleeding in the desert night.

Reason, though, was not his strength. In his pomp, he had begun where reason ended. He was abandon, he was wildness, he was a future thrown away for the pleasure of destruction alone. To see him stammer, to hear him talk of how the story needed to finish, how she should find a way to kill the wolf was almost pathetic. She had told him so. And Odin himself, master of magic, had not killed Fenrir. How could she do it? He had wept then and spoken of the story breaking, of how it needed to end for good or be mended. There was a girl who bore a dark rune. She could kill the wolf, the story could end and all the old god's mad magic would leave the world.

And if that girl died?

'The story goes on, broken,' said Loki. 'The rune flies into the world to be reborn.'

That would suit Styliane very well. A broken story had kept her alive and young for over a century.

'But the girl will not die,' he had said.

'Why not?'

'As you are a fragment of a god, she is the expression of a Norn. To kill her is to kill fate. That cannot be done easily.'

'Fates are shaped in the water of these wells,' said Styliane. Was it an insight, was it something the god had put into her mind? 'I will find her and take her to the magic waters. They reveal all secrets and will offer me the secret of her death.'

'You have been twice,' said Loki. 'Three is Odin's number.'

'Odin is dead.'

'He gave his life to the Norns. What will you give?'

'Best not ponder that,' said Styliane. 'I am wedded to these magics. I can have no other course.'

She was almost sad to see the god so beaten. Once Loki had flown among the stars, burned the heavens like a comet. Now he ran from the church steps like a beggar who had got enough for a loaf.

The Normans were asleep. She had summoned the runes to hide from them and regretted it had been necessary. She could feel them like a whirlpool, tugging others in. There was at least one rune nearby, maybe more, aching to join its sisters. No to that too. The Norse gods were not her gods and, though she would use them, she would not serve them unless it suited her.

The sly one knew better than to approach her. Once her runes would not have been enough to cow him. Now he feared her and fled her. He was a servant of fate, a servant of the story of the Norns that said on the last day of the old gods the wolf would slay Odin and then die. Well, she was an enemy of fate. She would be no one's sacrifice. If she had been more certain of the outcome she would have used the runes to kill him. Gods, though, could split, as Odin had split, sending pieces of their mind into mortals. Alive and whole, Loki could not harm her. She would not risk killing him. Too much uncertainty.

Dýri behind her shivered deeply. He had lost two good friends but showed no sign of grief. She knew how these Varangians thought. His friends had died a good death, surrounded by enemies, killing many. It would make a good story, should he survive to tell it, and they would be famous – a prize greater than gold to their people. He was quiet, though. It was not grief he felt but, she thought, a slight shame that he hadn't shared their fate.

'You'll get the chance to prove yourself, Dýri,' she said.

'Sooner than we might like if we stand in the open like this,' he replied. 'The Normans piss like any man and will be out and about to see us if we're not careful.'

'Inside then. Follow the girl.'

They went up the steps, Dýri first, his sword drawn. She doubted there would be any warriors in there and she had no intention of letting them see her if there were but Dýri would be needed to help with the ritual and, if it made him feel better to draw his sword, so be it.

Inside, the church did not seem big compared to the magnificent cathedrals of Constantinople. It was, however, dark. The presence of Loki showed her the time for discretion was over. The die would be cast here. She allowed the Kenaz rune to come forward in her mind and the church was bathed in a fiery light.

Dýri murmured under his breath 'Volva.' It was his people's word for 'sorceress'. The gold had been well plundered but the altars remained in their arches and the faces of saints peered down at her. It was called a 'great church' by the people of England. It seemed a poor, boxy, ill-finished thing to her – five of them would fit inside the Church of Holy Wisdom at Constantinople. However, the world well manifested here, so the stones were not silent. They almost breathed as she passed, humming with the spawning power of the well. Men built things to honour it even if they knew nothing of it – great cities sprang up around the well's manifestations, civilisations expressed themselves in art and violence. The wolf was coming, though. The devourer.

The rune bred insight and she sensed the girl was in there, sensed her sensing her. The rune inside her seethed and spat. The little Saxon was so dangerous; the thing she carried inside her offered her huge protection. Styliane felt the Kenaz rune gutter as the growl of the wolf rune rumbled.

Killing her would not be easy; banishing the rune to the realm of the gods would be even harder. The ordeal would be very great. Styliane touched her arms. She bore the scars

148

of many rituals there. The lesson of her own god, Hecate, was that there was no creation without pain. The goddess presided over childbirth and magic, death and darkness. All those things were linked in fundamental ways, a knot of agony. Men could not hold magic because their natures were not attuned to the eternal rhythms suffering and begetting. When a man made, he did so with the smith's hammer or the saw and sword, beating, cutting and killing to achieve his ends. These were not the ways of magic. It came from inside, like a child, and with pain.

The well was like a vortex here, a whirlpool to the river eddies of her runes. The girl stood on the steps, her breath a plume. There was no point tricking her now, this was the time for speed. She told Dýri to seize her and he did, picking her up in one arm like a father might a child.

The girl was too scared and cold to resist. The steps went down to a crypt. Six stone sarcophagi were in there, their knot patterns writhing like snakes in the runelight. The well was below the floor. There were no more stairs down. Dýri put the girl into a corner. She was beaten, Styliane could see, and just curled in on herself, pressing into the wall.

Styliane felt the sucking of the well. Its centre was beneath the flagstones set between the two biggest sarcophagi. She pointed to it and Dýri set his pick into a crack, to lever up a stone. It did not come easily.

'I could smash it,' he said. 'But ...'

Styliane held up her hand to silence him. He didn't need to tell her the effect the noise of excavation might have on a still, cold night full of sleeping warriors. She summoned up a rune, one that stamped and snorted like a bull, that shone with umber light and stank like an animal stall. She sent it to him, not to enter him but to shine upon him, to empower him.

Dýri staggered as the rune worked its influence upon him. He recovered himself, glanced at Styliane and snorted, then inserted the pick beneath the stones again, this time shoving it much harder. It sank in and he levered up a stone easily.

'By Thor's cock, lady, I wish you'd done that for my friends when we faced the Normans at the bridge.'

'There is a cost to this magic,' said Styliane. 'Remove the stone.'

He levered the stone aside. There was flat earth underneath it, dark and pungent.

'Dig,' said Styliane. 'Quietly.'

Dýri worked the pick in, not swinging it but rather scraping with it. He went down a forearm's length, then an arm, loosening the soil with the pick and then scooping it away in handfuls. The girl in the corner didn't move but the rune inside her seethed like a cornered wolf. He dug. How long had it taken? About as long as she'd thought. It was not yet midnight and there was no reason to expect the Normans would come into the church, even at dawn. They'd had what there was to be taken. She listened for the wolf outside but heard nothing. Dýri was now leaning into the hole, scraping away.

'I can't go any further in without taking out another stone, ma'am. There's no room to work.'

'How long will that take?'

'To get down to this level, the same again if you don't want me swinging the pick.'

'It's near.' The girl spoke.

'What?'

'I can hear the water. Can't you?'

Styliane crouched by the hole, though it was beneath her dignity to do so. Yes, it was almost as if the current of the river pulled at her hand. Its cold flow was very near.

'Hit the soil,' she said to Dýri. 'Strike it with the butt of your pick.'

Dýri reversed the pick and drove it into the hole.

A rattle of falling soil. He stepped back and Styliane leaned in. By the light of the rune fire she saw the soil had fallen through. There was a cavern below and in it glinted a stream of what looked like fire.

150

20 The Oathbreaker's Cavern

The Viking tied off his length of rope around one of the pillars that supported the roof. Tola thought she should run but the rune Styliane had lit in herself was warm and its light comforting. She could no longer feel what Styliane planned — when she sent her mind towards the lady all she saw was the bright rune, casting its beams up into the sky as if the stone of the cathedral was no more than a veil.

Dýri was not hostile. He had an almost fatherly aspect to him. She felt he was afraid on her behalf, wanting to protect her, but she felt too his efforts to dismiss those tender thoughts.

The waters pulled and sucked beneath the floor. She would not leave, even if she was to die in that place. The wastes of the dales were too wide, the rest of the country too unknown for her to carry on alone. This was where she was meant to be. It was important, she could feel it.

Dýri approached her.

'There's no need to grab me,' she said. 'Where am I to go? What better destiny is out there than the one you have for me in here? I cannot defy my fate so I will walk to it without the need for you to drag me.'

'Good girl,' said Dýri. 'A warrior's answer, even if you are a woman.'

She approached the hole and looked down. There was a trickle of water down there, going across the floor of a sloping cave.

'Can you climb down the rope?' said Styliane.

'Yes.'

Tola tried to take hold of the rope but her hands were still too cold to grip it properly. Instead she wound it around her forearm, then around her body. She lowered herself down, a

151

stifled cry of pain on her lips as the rope cut her arm.

Styliane came down after her, followed by the big Viking.

They were in a low passage – just about big enough to crawl down. The water ran in a channel through the centre. She saw the tunnel was not natural – too square, carved. On the wall a winding serpent was etched into the grainy rock.

'Down,' said Styliane.

Tola could no longer see the rune. It was Styliane who emitted light. Was she the rune herself? An expression in flesh of an eternal magic?

She crawled through the tunnel, the others behind her. It was colder here. She couldn't feel her hands. The Viking moaned as he came on. He was a big man and, where the women could crawl, he had to slither on his belly.

The water on the floor of the tunnel flowed down but it had a weight to it that seemed disproportionate to the size of the stream. Tola seemed drawn by it as she clambered down the passage. The way became narrow, the ceiling low. She went on, wriggling on her belly.

'I can go no further,' said Dýri.

'Wait at the top, then. Kill any who try to come down. Kill her if she emerges without me.

'Yes, lady.'

Dýri backed away.

Tola thought of the words of the bloody devil. She should kill this woman. But she was not sure she could even go on, let alone commit murder. Styliane was her enemy, she sensed that, but the devil's instruction – and her own nature – made her draw back from attacking her. Ithamar had said there would be something for her in York and she had sensed he was telling the truth – or rather *a* truth, even if he believed it to be a lie. Here, beneath the stones of the minster, was something very important to her.

Styliane squeezed through after her, her fine dress now filthy in the mud. The passage extended into a darkness not even the rune light penetrated.

152

'There is something down there,' said Tola. 'I can feel it pulling.'

'It pushes too,' said Styliane. 'As this river flows in, there are others that flow out.'

'What is it?'

'It is the heart of the world.'

'In Yorkshire?' The idea struck Tola as almost funny.

'Wherever it chooses to be. In many places. I have found it in the desert and at the centre of the world in Constantinople. I will find it here. In what aspect, I don't know.'

They climbed down further, the passage becoming steep.

'What is an aspect?'

'There are many wells. Some of wisdom, some of magical power, some unknown to me. All are contained in the well of fate in Constantinople.'

'What is here?'

The howl of the wolf seemed to squeeze the tunnel in on them.

'I don't know.' Styliane glanced behind her. 'I am not sure.'

'You are afraid.'

'Only a fool wouldn't be. Now down.'

The passage dropped into blackness, the water splashing down. It was nearly vertical – a shaft more than a tunnel. The stone was damp and crumbly.

Styliane hesitated. Tola did not. She jammed her back into the shaft, pushing into the wall to stop herself from falling. Then she began to wriggle down. Her fear had gone, though the water beneath her sighed and moaned and the stream made the tunnel slippy and her back wet. The effort kept her warm, though she could feel her damp clothes clinging to her back.

The shaft turned again after a little way and, while she still had to dig her legs in to the walls to stop herself from tumbling, the descent was not as steep. The gritty stone was in her mouth, nose and eyes. She wanted to wipe it away but feared that if she let go her grip she would fall. Above her,

Styliane came down in a shower of dirt, crying out as her foot slipped momentarily.

The rune light guttered but it did not fail. Now, at the shaft's bottom, Tola could see the reflected gold of water and feel the pull of the well very strongly. The sensation was more than physical. It was as if her mind was being drawn there. Her thoughts would not hold but seemed to leak from her as she looked down into the bright waters.

'This is very strange,' said Styliane, her voice full of fear.

The waters below seemed to breathe like a great animal, glittering like a dragon's back. They were whispering to Tola, though in no language she knew. They were bubbling with heat. Yes, they were hot.

Down more and still more. Tola had been to this place before, or one very like it, she was sure. The tunnel opened onto a rocky ledge in a large cavern. All over the walls carved snakes slithered in the wavering light. On the ceiling of the cavern was carved the body of a great serpent, its teeth sinking into the roots of a tree. The cavern was flooded with water that steamed and bubbled.

"Hvergelmir!' said Styliane. 'This is the source of all the cold rivers. It is a harbinger of treachery. Where are my runes? What is happening to my runes?'

Tola drank in the heat of the well. Why was it hot if it was a source of cold rivers?

She saw that the body of the snake on the ceiling had runes carved on it.

Styliane saw them too and read:

'Now may every
oath thee bite
That sworn thou hast,
By the water
bright of Leipt,
And the ice-cold
stone of Uth.'

'What is it?' said Tola. The words were resonant to her. She saw brother against brother, waves rolling on a wide ocean, blood on the sand of a beach.

'A Valkyrie's curse.'

'This is a place where oaths are broken,' said Tola. 'You swore not to harm me.'

'Yes,' said Styliane. She slipped her scarf around Tola's neck and pulled tight. Tola saw white lights flare at the edges of her vision, felt her head bursting with pressure and then she saw no more.

21 A Voice in the Dark

'What is the stone at his neck?'

Freydis walked besides Gylfa while Loys strode ahead. She shivered. The rune was with her again, undaunted by Loys's presence. And yet, when he took away that stone from his neck, she felt the symbol trembling within her.

Hers was a violent, flying, stabbing rune but before Loys it was unsure, fazed – though not quite cowed. It was the symbol of the god Tyr, king of war. He had dared to put his hand into the wolf's mouth as assurance that it would not be tricked and tied forever. But the wolf was so tricked and tied and Tyr lost his hand, though not his courage. The rune danced forward and back, as Gylfa had danced when she had confronted him for the first time. She had seen that dance many times before – warriors in a battle, lined up against their opponents, goading them to advance – afraid to strike the first blow, afraid to be the first to run. She had fought in Italy against the Normans and had noted that, if you attacked as a line of men were coming forward, they would usually oppose you. Attack when they were dancing back and there was a good chance they'd flee. It was as if their movement was a current. Push against it and be opposed. Push with it and be carried.

'It is a protection against magic.'

'Then why does he remove it and retie it?'

'His own magic.' Gylfa smiled.

Freydis did not warm to this boy. He had spent a while sulking that she was coming along but suddenly changed his tune and become friendly. She saw him for what he was – a user, though not a very accomplished one. His smile had come too quickly, he was too eager to please. Men like that didn't last long in the company of warriors.

'You are from the north?' he said.

'As you can tell.'

'What part?'

'Hordaland.'

'They are fierce men there. And ladies.'

'Not fierce enough. They could not defend me so I took up arms.'

'You were married!'

Gylfa apparently found this funny. With a mouth like that the boy was lucky to have lived. He'd have swum home on any longship she'd been on.

'I was better looking in the days when I sat at the milking stool instead of swinging a sword. Ugliness is the fate of old warriors. You're good looking enough, I notice.'

'I wouldn't be interested in tumbling you,' said the boy. 'You are a hardy woman and not made for softness, I think.'

'Who brought it up?' said Freydis. 'If I were to choose a man he would be of tougher stock than you.'

'Give yourself to our leader,' said Gylfa, nodding ahead to Loys. 'You would have mighty sons by him.'

'I've had my sons,' said Freydis.

'Were they strong men?'

'Until they died.'

'If you have grown sons you cannot have long to live. And yet you are strong, I grant you.'

'None of us has long to live,' said Freydis. 'Look around you. Do you expect to get out of this?'

'I hope to.'

'Hope is for cowards,' said Freydis. 'The warrior seeks only a noble death. How can you go into a battle thinking of life, of old age, a fire and a mug of ale? Think instead of great deeds, strong enemies, a fight worthy of the skalds' songs.'

'You are not seeking death,' said Gylfa. 'Why come to the chief asking for help? Why not throw yourself into the first battle you see?'

157

'I've thrown myself into enough battles,' said Freydis. 'And I have something to live for beyond glory.'

'What?'

'Love,' said Freydis. 'It can make cowards of us all.'

'So you have a man?'

'I love the lady I serve.'

'It is to be expected,' said Gylfa. 'You have acted like a man too long and now think like one.'

Freydis laughed. 'As if I could be so stupid.'

They passed an ash-black village, just three houses, all personality burned from them. Freydis recalled her own long-house – how it had bowed at one end; how the green moss grew on the landward side of the roof, though the seaward side was bare but for snowdrops that grew there in the spring; how her husband had built the door low, which kept out the draughts but made it hard to get the cows in during bad weather. He was away a lot and had never quite remembered to duck enough on his way in. If the house had burned it would look no different to these.

Loys made them keep walking well into the night. It was very dark but he found his way easily. The boy moaned that it was too cold. Loys told him, rightly, that it would be colder if they stopped moving. The boy said he was hungry. Freydis saw no point in that. They were all hungry, and they would stay hungry. May as well say that he was breathing, though in this place that seemed itself unusual enough to be worthy of comment.

'What's that?' Gylfa pointed ahead, his voice low.

A blur of yellow light was visible through the hazy night air like a daub of paint on a grey wall.

Loys sniffed. 'Men,' he said. 'The town, I think. Death keeps his larder here.'

Freydis thought that an odd thing to say but, then again, Loys was a famous warrior. It was right he should speak poetically.

Freydis peered into the mist. 'It's a watchfire,' she said. 'It's lighting up the city wall behind it.'

'Do we need to go in there?' said Freydis.

'Yes,' said Loys.

'How?'

'We'll ask. I'm Norman enough still. Say nothing. I will play the high man so they'll address their questions to me. You ...' he addressed Gylfa, 'keep your cloak close about you. Do not let them see what you have plundered.'

They pushed forward through the mist. Freydis thought of the fire. It would be good to stop by that for a while, to thaw her bones. She saw Loys tie back on the stone. Immediately her rune lit up, humming. She felt directed, aimed like an arrow. The rune wanted to go inside the town. It was as if she was being tugged that way, so much that it was difficult to think of anything else but going through the gate. She heard a strange music in her head – chiming and rustling like the wind in trees, the breath and stamp of a horse, the crackle of a fire, too close to be the watchfire. The sensations combined within her, sparking the memory of light on water, brown eyes regarding her, the touch of a soft hand, kind words. Styliane.

No, not here. She had fled that destiny, understanding how the lady's safety depended on staying away from her. Styliane was a creature of the sun, the warm light of the ocean, of olive groves and fountains. She would not be found in this desolate place. The magic was playing tricks on her, Freydis was sure.

Loys shouted something in Norman. Freydis knew enough of the language from fighting in Italy – if 'Hello', 'Look out' and 'my people will ransom me', were enough.

A reply, the voice flat in the soupy air. Loys spoke again. Another reply and Loys gestured them forward. Freydis buried her face in her scarf. She knew she could pass for a man easily enough but she had killed Normans when they had chased her to the woods and superstition made her think some of these fellows may have been with them.

There were four men at the gate, wrapped in so many coats and scarves that they too could have been women beneath, or children, or perhaps even just piles of clothes stood up in place of guards.

Loys spoke to them for a while. She heard a name. 'Robert Giroie.'

The men nodded and pointed up through the town, gesturing directions. Loys patted one on the arm in thanks. They were through and into the desolation of York, a sweep of black leading down to a grey river under an ash moon.

It was as if the air of the town had been burned, the hanging mist bitter with the taste of cinders. Out of earshot, Loys spoke, low, to Gylfa.

'There has been a raid by bandits on the town. Most of them are dead but the Normans are looking for survivors. We need to declare ourselves quickly to any who challenge us. The men who captured you are here. I said I was part of Giroie's troop and they said he had arrived yesterday.'

The boy looked around him, as if he thought someone would leap at him from the night.

'What shall we do?' he said.

'What we are here to do.'

'Which way?' said Freydis.

'On.'

They descended to a bridge over a river, the logs slick with moisture, slippery underfoot. They went carefully, the body of a great church looming above them like rocks from a sea mist. The night was clearer here, the mist low and the round moon sharper. The rune in Freydis pulled forwards. She felt like a thrown spear, impelled to go on. There was movement from her right. Four men were descending from the intact houses on the hillside. They were warriors – one carried a long spear.

'Keep going,' whispered Loys.

'Where?'

'The church.'

'We should run,' said Gylfa.

'No. At the walk,' said Loys.

'It could be Giroie,' said Gylfa. 'What if he recognises us?'

Freydis could see panic rising in the boy. She took his arm and walked towards the church – its stout tower rising as if made of shadow rather than stone. That was where she needed to be, where the spear rune wanted to fly.

The men spoke a word and Loys said something in reply. The men passed by behind them, over the bridge.

'What did they say?' said the boy.

'In here?' said Freydis.

Loys removed the stone from his neck and, though the rune shrieked and keened like an angry wind, now it did not go but clung to its determination to lead her through the door.

'In here,' said Loys.

They opened the door of the church. Freydis felt as if her guts were being pulled from her. The rune so much wanted to be free of Loys and go down into the darkness of the church that it was all she could do to keep herself from running. Again Loys sniffed at the air of the church.

'She's here,' he said.

'Who?'

'My enemy. My friend is here too. And one more.' He gestured for quiet. Then he moved into the church, carefully and quietly.

She followed him, Gylfa behind. It was very dark, the moonlight dim through a hole in the roof.

Down steps to a crypt. A sudden movement, or the idea of a movement.

Loys exhaled heavily and then was gone. A terrible noise sounded below, a snarling, screaming sound like that of a deer caught by dogs. A man's voice cried out loudly in Norse. 'No!'

Freydis came to the edge of the steps. She could see nothing down there. It was flat dark. Still the rune wanted her to go on. It was as if she sat on a tipping ship in a storm. She heard things calling in the dark, saw bright lights that floated without illuminating what was below. There was a stirring wind, hot like fire through trees. She had to go down. The rune impelled her.

She felt her way down. It was wet underfoot and she slipped slightly. Her foot caught something on the floor. She bent to feel what it was. A man's head but it was light or, rather, there was no resistance to moving it. It had been severed. She was used to such horrors but still it gave her a start. She padded forward on the floor, feeling a hole.

'Loys.'

No reply.

'Freydis, don't leave me. I'm on my own up here.'

'Shut up, Gylfa.'

'Freydis!'

'Do you want the whole town down on us? Be quiet!'

More lights, more noise. Then, in front of her in the darkness, she saw a shape – like an arrowhead, a triangle missing one side, all in flame. Her own rune, the spear, shook and quivered, longing to join its sister.

A rune. She had never seen it in Styliane but it made her think of the lady, of her clarity, her decisiveness, her passion.

'Styliane?'

She said the word and the rune shot forward, spinning around her with her own rune in a wild dance. She saw the fires of illumination burning, as if banks and banks of candles stretched out before her into the darkness. She saw a wide land beneath her and it was as if she herself was the sun; she felt the hearth fires of the earth stretching out into the ice-black night, she was suddenly warm and the truth became shiningly clear. Styliane was down there. These echoes of her were her runes reaching out. The lady was dying.

The rune cast its light over the crypt. There was a hole in front of her where the flagstones had been moved away. The headless body of a big man lay battered and torn beside it. Inside, down there, other runes were calling, bringing with them the memory of Styliane. She saw her lady reclining on her divan in the great palace at Constantinople, walking in the garden of Baghdad, she heard her breathing next to her in their tent in the deserts of the south. Styliane. Down there.

She lowered herself into the hole and into the little space below.

'They're leaving me. Oh, Goddess, help me!' Did Freydis hear her, or did the rune inside her scream out the lady's distress?

Freydis put her hand to the wall, as if the solid earth beneath her feet was no more than the wood of a storm-tossed ship. She felt as though the floor might crack open and she might fall, down and down into unknown darknesses, to chambers that had never seen light, to depths where she would lie broken, beyond hope of redemption.

It was her voice, Styliane's.

'My love,' said Freydis and scrambled down into the dark.

22   The Price of Lore

Styliane heard the wolf calling all the way down the passage and she knew her time was short. The girl must be parted from the wolf rune as quickly as possible. It was a delicate matter. If she died too soon, the rune could slink off to someone else, or re-enter the world to menace her in twenty or thirty years, by coming again to offer the wolf death.

She loosened the knot at the girl's neck – only two knots. The third, the one that would stop it from ever being loosened, save with a knife, would cement it as a holy symbol, honouring the tripartite nature of God. It was Odin's knot, the Valknut, but it was a crossroads too, sacred to her own lady Hecate – a juncture between life and death. It was even a symbol of Christ – three in one.

The girl started to breathe again. She had broken the oath – that was part of the magic, she was sure. The girl had provided the answer herself. This was a snake's chamber, a backbiter's temple, a deceptive and treacherous place. The water was hot but it flowed cold – or not so much flowed as writhed and coiled. Nothing was as it seemed. She had wondered why she had made such a solemn oath to Tola. It had seemed such a right thing to do. She hadn't seen that it would be the source of her magic. Something so profound, so deeply held as the value of an oath could not be violated. And yet she had violated it. The guilt, the shame of that were both an offering to the well and something to smash away her ordinary self, to access things deeper underneath. Already she felt a little madder and a little more in control of the runes than she had before. She could take on this girl, remove the rune, and live safe again.

What could she offer the well? Her guilt and her shame. Her peace of mind. The girl's life was nothing to her but the vow felt sacred. She shivered as she realised what that meant. She had emulated the gods. Odin himself was called the treacherous backbiter. Was his magic bound to him by chains of guilt? The howl came cold down the passageway. No time to think about that.

She put her arms underneath Tola's armpits and pulled them both into the water. It was so warm – like a bath in the great palace of Constantinople – and for an instant she forgot herself. She had been cold so long. What a temptation just to sink into the waters and be warm until death took her. No. That was the well. She had come to the right place. The well of Uthr beneath Constantinople was a place of all possibilities. Now she could feel the cold flow leaving the pool at her feet, dragging her down. The water was not deep – on tiptoe she could keep her mouth above it. She held Tola's head up so she could breathe. And then silence. They were two women in an underground spring. She had thought the well like an animal. Now it held its breath.

She heard a short cry from the top of the passage. Then that howl; all the terror of the burning land made sound. Oh God, she had left Dýri in the dark. The dark was nothing to the wolf. She needed to call on the runes properly, not just to summon them as shadows to light her way or heat her. She needed to do something she had never done before, to allow the runes to flower properly in her mind. She had always known they could run wild, cling like ivy around her thoughts, consume her. The wolf nearly upon her, it was worth the risk. She let go of her thoughts and called them forth.

Kenaz, the beacon rune, blazed, shining into her, lighting all those parts of her she had hidden, an arrowhead, sparking stories and pictures in its wake. She saw herself as a little girl, taken by her brother from the slums of Constantinople to the city itself, saw her servant initiating her in the mysteries of the goddess Hecate that her dead mother had held dear, felt her brother's love that he had cultivated for its own sake but also so that he might betray it when his mind needed the shock to his sanity to access his deeper magics. She saw how the runes had entered her, growing within her at the well to which he had carried her and where he had died.

She saw the rune Algiz, spreading its antler arms wide. It would be her shield but she saw it spinning and turning, whispering threats. Odin, the dark god, was present in her in part. Odin would be whole again. She would be consumed. No. She reached forward as if to grab the rune, to turn it back to its defensive posture, to shape her own destiny.

Now the horse rune stamped and sweated, its chestnut sheen filling her mind. It would carry her away, change her. No. It meant a partnership. Was it telling her to drown Tola now? She pulled the girl up by her long scarf. Should she tie the knot that would kill her, cement the betrayal that would offer insight? Again the howl and now, from within Styliane, she heard the rune answering in kind, a lonely voice calling to its kin, the wolf.

The final rune whispered its name. Othala. A vision of a chest of gold. It meant reward, inheritance, the receipt of dues. This had always been the furthest rune from her mind, the one whose use she could never fathom.

Duty. It wanted her to leave the girl who carried the howling rune, to honour her promise. Yes, that was the price the well sought for insight. Defy the rune, go to war with the magic inside her, and live forever in a state of inner turmoil. But live forever. She pulled Tola backwards and looped the final knot.

'I'm sorry,' she said. 'It's you or me.'

She forced Tola down into the water. The girl's eyes opened wide, staring up at Styliane and then Styliane saw it – the girl's rune, the low wolf slinking shape crawling across her face, the shadow of the wolf that stretched out to meet the real thing. It was a trap, but for who?

For the wolf. For anyone. She saw the rune writhe and turn, stretch up towards her.

'No!' said Styliane, but the rune had twined its way through the eye of the Othala rune, winding around it like a cat winds

166

around a post but ensnaring it, pulling it in. The receipt of dues. Time to pay, Styliane.

'No!' Styliane spoke again but the wolf rune had seized the Othala rune and would not let it go.

Styliane coughed, choked. Tola's hands, she realised, were around her throat.

Something else was in the water too. She saw a face close by her, its nose a squashed bit of clay.

'Freydis!'

'Lady, I am here to save you,' said the warrior.

23 The Wolf Rune

Tola felt the rune inside her coil out to grab at the bright symbols all around. The constriction at her neck was terrible. She scrunched up her eyes, afraid they might pop out if she did not, but still she saw the shapes floating in the darkness, whispering their names. Fire, Protection, Horse and Gift. The shadow rune inside her snapped and guzzled at the one that shone like the gold of a dragon's lair in a story, ripping it from its orbit and throwing it aside.

Then she was in front of a mighty white tree that stretched to the stars and she saw the runes hanging like shining fruit upon its branches. She reached up and snapped off the burning rune, the one that was shaped like the head of an arrow. It fluttered like a bird in her hands and she let it go. Then she snapped off the horse rune, feeling its great beating heart as she took it down. It wanted to be free to gallop. She let it go. Finally she took off the shield rune and saw it wasn't a shield but a stag that snorted, tossed its head and looked at her with liquid eyes. Then it was gone, turning into the darkness as if into a forest.

She wanted to be sick but she couldn't. Something was at her throat. She felt a heavy blow against the side of her head and fell back. Warmth swept over her and she knew she was in water. It was very important to her to remove the pressure at her neck but she had something in her hands. Her head pounded and water filled her mouth and nose, it was important to hold on to the thing in her hands for just a few moments longer. It was a living thing.

Her head broke the water, or she thought it did. No light now, nor any air, but a scream filled up the chamber. It was coming from the thing in her hands. She burst to breathe out as much as to breathe in. She let go of the thing in her hands and fell back into the water. She didn't know up from down, water from air. Inside her she felt the shadow rune howl, calling out, trembling and shaking. Another voice answered it, a keening that turned her bones to powder.

The well swirled around her, a whirlpool of images and sounds. She saw a barren island, a grey sky, green turf. There was something below the turf. Treasure? The rune she had taken from Styliane glinted and shone. Not treasure, an inheritance.

In her vision she dug with her nails, tearing away the grass and soil, scraping down and down. She didn't know what she was digging for but she felt it was the most important thing on earth to find what was buried there. Mounds of earth behind her. Still she dug until a knuckle of wood became visible. She kept on digging, scraping down around the wood, exposing more and more until she saw it for what it was – the figurehead of a ship, a carved raven, inscribed with runes. She counted them out. Twenty-four. The sky had turned black, the sun on the horizon lighting it up like iron in a forge. The runes caught the red light, shimmering as if inscribed in gold.

Someone was buried there. Her grandfather had talked of kings who went to the afterlife in burning boats, or who were buried in them – sometimes along with their servants to aid them on their journey to the lands of the gods.

She stepped back from the grave, horrified. The soil on her hands was wet with blood.

'Where am I?'

'In the boiling, bubbling, blubbing spring from which all cold things flow.'

'I am on an island.'

'You are on a grave.'

She looked down and she saw what she had taken for the prow of a ship was the head of a great black raven. It crowed and strained, as if trying to lift itself from the soil, but it couldn't. Blood dripped from the bird's beak.

Tola wanted to help the animal and ran forward to try to dig it out but the great bird pecked at her, cawing, its eyes full of anguish. It would not allow itself to be freed but its terrible voice would not be quiet. She would do anything to silence it. She picked up handfuls of earth and flung them back into the hollow she had dug, then she kicked and pushed the piled earth back on top of the bird, willing it to be mute. She felt the ground tremble.

'Where is this?'

'This is the graveyard of the gods, where their old bones lie.'

Whose voice was it? A woman's. The voice of the well?

She kept pushing the earth back on to the screaming bird.

'Let me free,' she said. 'Let me free.'

In an instant she was the bird, looking up in agony as great clods of earth came down upon its head. She felt a blow and the light went out as if carried by a giant who had stumbled and dropped it, a flicker and then nothing.

Hands were on her and she fought them by instinct. She saw a light, the flash of a knife. Then the pressure at her neck relented, grit and gravel scraped against her knees. Someone was dragging her up and out. She tried to kick and fight but all she could hear was the rasp of her own breath, harsh as a blacksmith's blast bag.

'Who is this? Who is this?'

'The runes will not go to the murderer. They fly to the lover.'

The question would not come to her lips, though the rune inside her shook and sobbed. She felt its loneliness, its desire deep as thirst.

A confusion of limbs thrashing in the water. Someone had her, tugging her up the tunnel with incredible speed and force. Her back tore against the soil, her hands ripped on the walls.

Her clothes were pulled off her. She resisted on reflex. Her mind would not yet come back to the horrors of the everyday world with its mundane killings and rapes – she was still consumed by the shivering, beseeching rune inside her that whined and implored like a dog at a gate.

She was pulled up to sitting, a tunic put over her head and her arms lifted roughly – like a mother helping a reluctant child to dress. Hose were pulled over her legs, a big fur coat put around her.

'You're all right,' she heard a voice say in Norse. 'You're all right.'

'Who is this?' Another voice, younger. A man too.

'Someone who can help me. Now we need to get her away.'

She was lifted to her feet, plunged through the nightblack and moonsilver of the ruined church. From outside, noises, footsteps, but bringing with them the resonance of calamities – of dear Aeva, dead in childbirth, her baby too, the echo of her husband's cries; the time when the ox in the top field had backed Bryni against a wall and broke his leg. They'd heard his cries as far as the next valley, it was said. The leg had turned bad and left his wife a widow.

Tola snapped to consciousness.

'We are discovered,' she said.

She was shoved on again, to the side of the church, into one of the side chapels. It was utterly dark in there but the man who held her moved unerringly, driving her on.

'Will they find us?' It was the younger man's voice.

'Shhhh!'

She heard the church doors open and a prowling, thorough presence enter the church.

It was the man she had sensed on the dale, the one with the tricks for flushing out the villagers.

She heard a barked order in the Norman language. She didn't need to understand the words to know what the man had called for.

The image of a burning torch appeared in her mind. He had sent for light.

24 A Wolf Cage

The man guarding the entrance to the tunnel died quickly, mundanely, his neck snapped back then torn, the delicate flesh peeling beneath Loys's fingers, the vertebrae severing as easily as the cooked bones of a fish.

Before that moment and after it, under the power of the wolfstone, Loys would think of the horror of it all. The blood, yes, the salt beef smell of it, the chicken leg crunch of the spine, the little breath the man gave as he died – as if trying to say something profound or moving, not accepting fate had denied him the time even for that. All those horrors, yes, he would think of and the littler, quieter horror that niggled at the corners of his sleep like a draught at the fireside: the horror of knowing he no longer found such things horrific.

Before that moment, and after, he would think of the words of Saint Paul in his Epistle to Timothy: 'Even though I was once a blasphemer and a violent man, I was shown mercy because I acted in ignorance and unbelief.' And he would wonder if grace could be extended to the man who had gone the other way, who had slipped from knowledge and faith to the level of a brute.

At the moment he tore Dýri's mortal soul from its flesh, he did not think at all and there was no horror. A man opposed him. A man fell. By the time Loys jumped into the passage beneath the crypt, Dýri was just the taste of blood on his lips – a nectar that set his body tingling and burned away the human fog that sat on his senses.

He could see nothing but that was unimportant. Water was ahead, he could smell it, people too. Behind him he heard Freydis and Gylfa arguing.

The passage was low – he could feel it touching his head

even though he crouched. Even if he hadn't have touched it, he would have known it was low. It smelled low, the air had a squeezed, musty tang to it. She was down there, he heard the rune mewling and calling for him, hooking him on.

He was forced to crawl. The soil was damp and pungent. This was bone-rich earth, rotting treasures all around. He had a strong urge to dig at the wall but he did not follow it.

He knew that he needed to put the wolf stone back on like a six-cup-drunk knows he needs to stop drinking. He felt no urge to do so. For an instant he sat, puzzled, forgetting his purpose, wondering why he was not in the crypt guzzling the wet feast he had prepared.

Things were shirking from him in the darkness ahead, as if fear was a bow wave that preceded him. The runes. He could not tear them, he could not kill them. Why did they fear him? That human thought was a lodestar to him, leading him from the darkness of his wolf mind.

'The point is not to want to do it; the point is to do it.' The voice in his head was not his own. Whose? His tutor at Rouen? The man had a name, had been important to him, though he could recall neither his name nor his importance now.

Something ahead of him was in distress. His lips were wet with drool, his body tense with a greedy excitement that rose like an echo of the thrashing panic before him in the dark. The howling, creeping, calling rune he knew in his dreams was there, but something else too. Their scent told him all he needed to know. Two women, stinking of sweat and fear, fear so lovely that his teeth itched. You don't have to want to do it, you just have to do it. *Want* is the fire and the hearth. *Do* is the cold night full of painful duty.

His fingers made shapes at his neck, a weight fell on his chest. He had tied the stone about him and it was as if he had stepped through a door, out of the light into darkness. He could see nothing now, nor smell it. The air was not tight nor the earth full of sweet decay. Anxiety gripped him – but not fear, for the long years had eroded any terror of death he

173

might ever have had. He needed to find his killer, to protect her.

He blundered down the passageway, his head hitting the ceiling, his elbows catching the walls.

'I'm sorry. I'm sorry.' A woman's voice called. The voice spoke in Greek. 'I must. I ...'

The sentence was not finished. A great cry with a close echo sounded. Splashing and slapping, a scream and a shout. He scrambled on, the floor dropped away and he fell heavily into the water. He plunged blindly towards the noise, the screams and the splashing, the keening and sobbing – or where he thought it was. The cavern was small and the voices loud and echoing. He stretched out his hands but found nothing but a wall.

'They're going. Where are they? They're going.'

Styliane, her voice right beside him. Someone hit him, he grabbed at an arm, then a torso. Frantic hands clawed at him and he shoved and pushed to defend himself. He needed to find the girl, his killer. He was certain she was here but with the wolfstone at his neck he couldn't tell where. But to face Styliane with the wolf free in the forest of his mind was to risk killing her, freeing her runes, moving the god closer to resurrection and he could not do that. If Odin came again then the story might restart, telling its tale of misery and death for aeons to come.

He must even be careful how he struggled against her. If she lost consciousness here or fell then she might die.

'Lady. I'm here. I will free you from this hateful woman. Where are you?'

Styliane screamed and fell from his grasp. He leapt after her, grabbing into the blackness. Someone else was there, bigger than the tiny Styliane. He had her and then he lost her. She was gone. There was nothing for it. He took off the stone.

It was light and all around him were runes, shimmering in the air like the moon on water. The pool was no longer water but a cascade of stars. The runes shrieked and shook as the wolf woke in him, flying away. The stone on the thong in his hand was a hole, a sphere of darkness.

The girl lit up in the starlight, all shiny wet. The liquids on her skin interested him greatly – water of stone, water of salt, water of iron that was called blood and lovely to lap at. She could not see him but she had something at her neck.

His mind was sand, but the sand of mould like a blacksmith uses, she the metal burning within. They were expressions of each other; non-existent, useless alone. He had been in such waters before with another woman who he wished was alive in his place.

He took out his knife and cut the cord at her neck, her weight collapsing into his arms, her breath a wet rattle. A hundred years before he remembered a woman in the water. The shoulders were different, bigger this time, the arms not slender like a princess's – these thick from years of toil, piglet-lifting, cow-shoving, pail-swinging arms; shoulders to lift a yoke to the ox. Still her, though. The girl who had died to save him, reborn as the fates had cursed her.

He did not remember her at the table, saw only glimpses of her in their bed. He remembered her there, though, at the world well beneath Constantinople, at the well, the flower of knowledge that seeded the world.

'Don't die. Beatrice. Don't die!'

'See my blood in the water. It is a ribbon of light that has pulled you back from the realm of the gods,' she said.

The memory of her voice was such a ribbon to him now, pulling the man from the jaws of the mind-wolf. I am Loys, of Normandy, formerly the Quaestor of the Chamberlain of the Byzantine empire; formerly husband to Beatrice, Lady of Normandy; scholar and father, a man of pen and parchment.

He pulled her to the ledge. The girl was silent. Another presence shoving by him. The woman – not blind, but not seeing him, only looking to the water. His wolf mind had a sense not known to humans – the ability to detect attention. He knew without thinking if someone had seen him or if they had not. Freydis, splashing into the water, had a gaze focused like sun through glass. He followed the scent of the Varangian's blood above back down the tunnel.

'Sir, help me, I think they are coming for us. There are voices here.'

It was Gylfa, his voice a harsh whisper. His fear sizzled and snapped like bacon frying. Loys wanted to eat it up, to feel the secreted oils of terror, greasy on his teeth.

'I'm going to lift this woman. Pull her up,' he said.

'We will die, sir. We should run.'

A thought snapped through his mind. *You should run. It would be good to hear your heart pumping, the uncertain stutter of fleeing feet on the icy cobbles, to catch you and watch your entrails steaming in the cold, starred night.*

'Gylfa. This is death's kingdom. You dwell in his hall. Trying to avoid your fate will only speed it along. Pull up the woman.'

Loys lifted the girl above his head. She was light and he was wolf-strong. Gylfa reached down and pulled her up by her tunic as Loys pushed. Loys climbed the rope.

The light was very dim but now he saw his breath was freezing, hazing the air. The girl would die if he didn't get her dry. She was sucking in breaths in great sobs. No point asking her to be quiet, her gasps and retches were the sounds of her fighting death. He stripped the Viking. No time for this. No time, Gylfa was saying.

'Hide behind a tomb. If they come down here, strike at their backs.'

'What if there are many?'

'Then there are many and your death is a glorious one. I will tell the tale.'

'Will you live?'

He didn't answer. The Varangian's clothes were ludicrously too big for the girl but they were dry. She tried to fight him momentarily, mistaking his purpose, but he soothed her, spoke to her in Norman and in Norse. 'I am your friend. Vinr. Vinr.'

Voices and footsteps far away, near the door, he guessed.

His mouth flooded with saliva and animosity shook his flesh on the bones. No. He couldn't fight a whole camp of them and what if the girl died? He picked up his curved sword, tied it back on. A shout from the darkness in Norman.

'Who's there?'

The girl coughed and heaved.

'Shut up!' Gylfa grasped her big wool coat.

'Who's there?'

'Can't a man get his end away without starting an inquisition?' Loys shouted up in Norman.

'You've got a woman in there? Give us a go when you're finished. Robert just killed our last one and this weather's frozen my cock solid.'

'This one's mine. Find your own.'

'Now don't be selfish, son.'

The girl mastered herself, was silent. Her eyes were full of fear. Loys supported her under the arm and lifted her to the deep shadows on the side of the crypt. Gylfa came scuttling behind.

There were three of the Normans, their steps heavy, clinking with mail as if someone were manhandling sacks of coin along the cathedral aisle.

'Where are you?'

Gylfa's breath seemed very loud to Loys, the boy's efforts to suppress it rendering it a stuttering sob. Kill him. No, too noisy. Offer him to the Normans, throw him out there, the role of the weakest is to die for the pack. No.

'What's your name? Come on, son, this isn't funny, there have been all sorts of night trolls skulking about tonight.'

Loys could just about see them. The light from the hole in the roof only touched their heads, so that they floated through the mirk as if disembodied.

'We're not going until we've found you. That woman could have important information about those rebel bastards who were here earlier on.'

'And it's our responsibility to fuck it out of her.'

177

A tight cackle. One of the men, at least, found that funny. 'Get a brand lit.'

Fumbling and a curse. Flint on steel, the sparks monstrously big in the deep dark. Then the kindling glow and the fluttering light licked at the shadows.

'I see who you are.' She spoke Norse with a heavy accent and her voice was close at his ear. He put his hand to her mouth to silence her and he wondered what it would be like to snap her neck like a hock of lamb.

She took his hand away. 'Over here,' she said loudly.

The torch swiped lines across the blackness, the men shouted. 'Where are you?'

'Bitch!' said Gylfa and from the wave of hate that came from him, Loys knew the boy would have killed her if she had not been under his protection.

The girl stood. 'Here!' Her voice was hoarse.

They had her now and advanced, nearly invisible behind the blinding light of the torch.

'What's going on here, chief, sharing her with your servants?'

'She looks remarkably unfucked to me.'

The girl spoke again in her native tongue, spitting out the words as if they were gall in her mouth.

A soldier stepped forward, shoved her. She hit him, smack, right on the nose. He raised his hand and Loys could not say what happened then. Afterwards, Gylfa would tell him the Normans had died quickly.

Loys knew nothing until he found himself on top of the headless corpse of one of the soldiers, his hands red with meat, his voice shouting jumbles of sentences, chewed up sounds, wolf-torn words.

'I kill and meat this everyone purpose of death this! Teeth kill come the more men, here come and die us. Wolf I, eye of wolf! Stone, stone. Turn the wolf to stone!'

His mind was slow with blood but his thoughts had a terrible momentum, like a great door swinging shut over the light. Blood was in his mouth and he wanted more. He bit and tore, stopping to examine the way a last strand of a sinew clung to the bone, long white and taut.

'Oh, Lord, save my soul!' Not meat, not a sizzling liquor to savour but human blood, human flesh and bone. Gylfa had placed the stone about his neck, crept up and tied it on.

Gylfa?

The boy crossed himself, uttering oaths to Christ, to Thor, to the elves of the land and the saints of the church.

'Thank you.' The red mess beneath him had nearly claimed him. He'd had enough human flesh to fire the appetites of the wolf. The desire to replace the stone might have left him. Still he felt as though he clung to the edge of a crumbling cliff, only the stone holding him. He could not remove it again, not for a while. It might take a week, maybe a month, for the wolf to be quiet enough inside him for him to risk that.

A torch guttered on the floor. Voices outside, many voices.

'Where's the girl?' said Loys.

'She's gone.'

Loys got to his feet. The church door banged open. It seemed as if some fire spirit stood in the doorway, so numerous were the torches.

'The rebels are about, lads,' said Loys. 'Look what they've done. Let's find them before they flee!'

'My God, look at him. You're covered in blood, man.'

'They were here. My servant and I beat them away. Ten of them.' That was weak. His mind was disordered and seemed to slosh in his head like a cloth in a pail of water. That was weak, Loys, it would not do. It did not do.

'I saw no ten men.'

'Hang on,' said a voice. 'I know you. It's the coward of the North. Loys, with your airs and graces. The lord wants your bollocks on a plate. What have you done here?'

Loys touched the stone. He could not take it off but he could not get away if he did not.

'Take him. Take them both!'

The Normans advanced and Loys knew he was lost.

25 The Corpse Shore

Moon-bright and star-light, a dark hill against a dark sky. Styliane walked on a sparkling black beach by a sparkling black sea.

'Where am I?'

All along the limit of the tide she saw slick shapes lapped by the little waves. At first she took them for seals, but they were not seals. She knew what they were. What? She could not say, but she knew. It would come to her when her thoughts settled.

'I am far from the sun,' she said. An old chill gripped the beach and there was ice at her feet. For a moment she feared the Northern bears she'd heard the Varangians talk about. One of the guards in the Great Palace at Constantinople wore a white fur about him, the head of the bear sitting on top of his own. It was enormous and the man said it had cost him two friends and his arm to get it.

The sand crunched beneath her feet. She walked up the beach. No. This couldn't be. The land of the dead?

Would the goddess be here to meet her? Hecate. She listened for dogs, the goddess's companions. There were none.

The beach rose for a little while before giving way to glass-black grass with big, sharp blades rising above the ankle. Beyond the grass, trees. Not the lonely cedars of the east nor the tanglewood of England. These stood straight as temple pillars, black lines in the dim distance. She had not known there could be so many shades of darkness. Behind the trees rose a mountain and she could not see its top. Though the night was clear it was far away.

'I was somewhere else.' Her voice was flat in the still air. The ocean sucked at the beach but there was no other sound – not the night chirp of insects nor the call of owls.

'She drowned me.' It was almost as if she expected someone to answer, to come forward and say 'No. You are not dead. This is a garden beneath the earth kept by monks according to ancient magical wisdom. There is nothing to fear here. See, the stair is clear behind you. Go back to the light if you wish.' No one said that.

Styliane saw what she took for a small hill between her and the trees. Having no other aim, she walked towards it, wondering if she could make a survey of the land from on top of it and work out her options. The grass was wet and the dew on it caught the moonlight, shining back to the sky as if it were a field of stars.

The hill was not a hill. It was a hall, white as bone. She approached and saw that it seemed covered in tiny bristles. Coming even closer, she saw it was woven from the spines of snakes, their bleached skulls left with their jaws wide, as if they might live again and snap at any intruder.

For the first time she was afraid. She looked for her runes. They were not there.

She had been before to the realm of the gods but this was not what she remembered. She thought of the wolf, groaning on the black rock where the gods had tied him. Was he here? Had he laid waste to the land like this? If this was death she had been right to fight it. The hall filled her with dread but, if this was the land of the dead, could she die again?

She looked for a door but could see none. She walked around the hall and walked around it again. On the third time she came around, a woman was sitting on a low stool by a doorway, another similar stool next to her. Now the smoke vent breathed smoke and there was light within the hut. The woman had a small knife in her hands and she used it to cut turnips into a dish. But, though the turnips fell and the woman's hands were quick, no slices could be seen in the bowl. Styliane saw that one hand was young and pale but the other was eaten by rot, but she could not say which hand seemed the living and which the dead. The woman's face was beautiful and decayed too, so that in one instant it seemed Styliane was looking into the face of a young woman, in the next at a corpse that had lain a long time.

'Lady Hecate.'

The lady said nothing, just gestured to the stool beside her. Her face shifted in the flat light. This had to be Hecate, Selene, lady of the moon, virgin, mother, crone.

'I have killed the black lamb for you. I have walked on bare hillsides beneath the cold moon. At the meeting of the ways I sacrificed to you and called your blessed name,' said Styliane.

The lady cut another turnip, the fleshy slices falling into the bowl and disappearing.

'Gods have many names,' she said.

'What is yours?'

The lady shrugged and cast her hand out wide to the land, as if to say, 'This'.

'That is not the question you came to the well to ask.'

The lady's voice was dry as city dust.

'You are death.'

The woman laughed. 'Not he. Sit.'

'Where is this place?'

'Nastrond. The corpse shore. Those dead by water find their way here.'

'So I am dead.'

The woman shrugged. 'You are a magician. Though you have lost your magic, I think.'

'Is it here? Are the runes here?'

'No. But I can show you where they were.'

'How will that help me?'

'I am not a helper, lady.'

The woman got up and walked and Styliane followed her. The moon waned in the sky, dropping to the horizon before rising again, filling to a bloated face and thinning to the blade of a boning knife. Men were in the woods, dead men, lying half buried by root and earth. Their flesh showed the stain and rot of death but their eyes followed her as she walked.

It was never day and they had walked a long way before they came to marshy ground. The women waded on through it, ankle-deep, thigh-deep and eventually the water reached Styliane's middle. The water was dark and full of loam, and the straight dark trees rose above her from where the ground was high enough to hold them.

'This is the well.'

'It is a well.'

'What is it?'

'Each well is every other well, or an expression of it. This one feeds the rivers of the land of the dead.'

'And what is here?'

'The god that died and would live again.'

'If he lives, I die.'

'You no longer bear the runes. You will die anyway. I will welcome you to these lands.'

'What does he want?'

'Look into the waters.'

She looked down. A dark shape was in the water. It was a man, his body tanned black by the bog, his hair white, stretching out from him like the roots of some light-starved plant. Even dead, an expression of unimaginable ferocity gripped his face.

'What does he want?' The question seemed more important than anything in the world.

'He wants me to let him go'

'He is dead?'

'Yes, or he would scarcely be here.'

'So how can he be freed if he is dead?'

'Gods die and are reborn. His magic is working, even still. Perhaps it is why you are here.'

'He wants my life for his?'

'A life. Death for life. There is no other coin in this place. You must give something you hate to lose. That is what sacrifice means.'

Styliane reached down into the dark water, her fingers searching for the corpse. She felt the leathery skin, the sinewy

183

arm. He was cold and his body was hard as bog oak. She pulled at him and pulled again. The body came up to the surface. She had thought revelation would come in a rush as the runes had come, shrieking and chiming, sending her mind plunging towards madness. It did not. She was a woman in a cold wood, in water, holding the leathered body of an old man with one eye, and she knew the truth as surely as something she had always known. Perhaps it wasn't even a revelation. To have her runes back the god would have to live again on earth, to be killed by the wolf again. Then, as the god's soul shattered under the teeth of the wolf, the runes would fly. Some away, some to her, as they had before. The god had something for her. His dead eye, she saw, had a stone in it, the colour of blood, the size of an eye. She plucked it out and held it up to the moonlight. It sparkled ruby red. Within it curled thorns and a sensation of prickles shot up her arm, through her mind. A gift from the god. A rune. Not inside her, not to be used as easily as she might speak a word but a rune, nevertheless, trapped in a gem.

'I will call you from the waters,' she said to the God.

She needed to do what she had fought against for years. To call the rune bearers and to have them die. Twenty-four must be brought to the god, taken to Hel to revive him, brought back to the realm of the living for the wolf to kill. She could not hold all those runes or she would die herself. She had let them go from her, floating away like desert dirt in a cooling spring.

But the girl had slipped through her fingers and might still go on to kill the wolf. If that happened, disaster. If Odin was reborn he would not be torn and his runes scattered. What then? Whatever it was, the world would hold no place for her.

She let the god slip back into the water, felt a thump at her neck. The dark wood blurred and faded. It was dark and it was cold and the goddess's voice rang in her mind.

'You must give something you hate to lose.'

She heard a voice, 'My love!' and she was pulled from the water.

26 Human Frailty

Loys had to let the Normans take him. The blood-glutted wolf had been fettered inside him but he could feel it stirring in its bonds. It was a smirking, simmering presence, biding its time to chew on the bones of his humanity.

'There's no need to seize me. I am not afraid of Giroie and will face him willingly.'

His words were useless, five men were on him, six, grabbing his arms and legs, lifting him bodily off the floor. He lost sight of Gylfa, felt his sword lifted from his side, his boots snatched from his feet. Three heavy blows were driven into his eye and the pain shot down to his guts. They were stripping him, robbing him at the first excuse.

He was not afraid to lose his fine shirt, his cloak, his trousers, even his hose – but he was afraid to lose the stone. The weight of blood in his mind would drag him down, undo him. They didn't want the stone, of course. Who would want a pebble when there were fine gloves to be had, a golden ring, a purse full of gold?

In a thicket of torches, they ran him out of the church like plunder. The night was full of memories. Hagia Sophia, the great church of Constantinople, its gold burnished by torchlight, so many with their faces to the flagstones like Saracens at prayer but dead to the last man. He saw a broad, flat island, a church under flame. He had never been there but it appeared to him as clear as the memory of his last meal.

They carried him out into the freezing air. A torch jabbed into him and he cried out with the pain. It jabbed in again and once more.

'Leave him, Richard. Giroie will want him in a fit state to speak.'

185

Heading up towards the unburned houses, they grew tired of carrying him and dropped him to the ground, kicking him on. All the breath went from him as a boot smashed into his back. He staggered, was shoved forward. The cold burned his feet and the sweat of the fight froze on his skin. On and on, through frozen alleys, up to a hall.

They stopped, holding him tight against running away.

'Hey, Giroie, come and see what we have for you!'

The door of the hall swung open, an oblong of firelight framing Giroie's big shape.

'If it's an Englishman, kill him.'

'It's the foreigner, we found him in the church.'

Giroie came out of the hall, stepping up to Loys, his head jutting forward like a dog who has caught a scent.

'A traitor. You cost me a prisoner, foreigner, how are you going to pay for him? You don't look as though you've prospered since leaving us.'

The cold was making it difficult for Loys to think. He could not let these men kill him, to be reborn, perhaps not knowing what awaited him, growing to adulthood and then seeing time stop for him, watching parents, brothers, lovers rot and die, feeling the animal snarling behind his eyes, the wolf padding through his dreams, dragging in his jaws the destiny of death.

'We should have done this a long time ago,' said Giroie. 'It doesn't do to bring a foreigner with us. It's bad luck and, as we've seen, we can't trust them. You killed Gervaise, didn't you?'

Loys said nothing. Even if he had wanted to speak he would have found it impossible. The cold had gripped his jaw, rattling his teeth and numbing his tongue.

'You're too cowardly to admit it. That skulking little boy you were in love with surely didn't.'

'He was with him, sir, but the little bastard gave us the slip in the dark. We've got men looking for him now.'

Giroie snorted, the steam at his lips, the firelight at his back, like a dragon before his hoard.

186

'He won't last the night without this one to keep him warm.'

Giroie leaned in to Loys's face, taking the wolfstone in his fingers as he did. Loys looked down at it. To him it didn't seem a stone at all but a tight sphere of darkness anchored at his neck.

Giroie lifted it from Loys's chest. All the night scents burst over Loys, the burned pig bones in the fire in the hall, the pork on Giroie's breath, the campaign dirt of the soldiers' clothes, horse sweat and human sweat, chalky soil and ashes, farmyard and riding tack. The wolf stirred inside him and the men holding his arms sprawled to the ground as Loys snarled, his teeth snapping for Giroie's face.

The knight jumped back and let the stone fall. The fog of human senses came down on Loys again. All the wind went from him as a Norman threw him down. The cold earth stung his knees, his belly.

'Look at him,' said Giroie. 'The man's a savage. He'd slaughter us all if he could. There's one penalty for murder,' said Giroie. 'Get him down to the river.'

Loys felt his legs go and didn't at first realise he had been hit. The pain in his back only registered as he sprawled to the floor and rolled to see a soldier above him, raising the butt of a spear to strike him again. He curled up to shield himself and felt another blow sharp in his ribs.

'That's enough,' said Giroie. 'Defiance doesn't warrant an easy end. Get him down to the water.'

They sank a stake in sight of the bridge across the river and hung him from it. The mist had thinned and a pink sun smudged the steel sky but it was a cold sun and it brought no warmth. The day was windless and the river was grey and flat. Loys could not feel his arms, tied above his head, nor his feet. On the stake, so close to the ice of the river, he was reduced only to his breath. He marked each one, in with pain, out with pain, until his consciousness was just a pendulum swinging between two agonies.

He forgot who he was or why he was there, his mind bound

with cold. He thought he heard Jesus talking to him, telling him that his suffering was equal to the suffering of the martyrs, that many saints had enjoyed an easier death but that he was not a martyr nor a saint, but one of the damned, to whom the torments of the flesh were but a prelude to the torments of the soul. 'As you abandoned me, I abandon you,' said Jesus. Christ said this to him, Christ who was the pink of the dawn light, Christ who knew what it was to hang on such a tree and suffer. Loys tried to cry out that he had not abandoned Jesus, that he still walked the road of righteousness but that one other walked beside them – a grim companion he could not shake.

The thought took form as a god. Odin came to him, also hanging, and spoke of runes and destinies and old pacts struck that could not be denied. He told him that the suffering was a gate through which you could walk as if into a perfumed garden. The river ran to the well and the well from the river.

The wolfstone lay on his chest and he was tied in such a way that he couldn't move it if he'd wanted to. It was a slab to seal his tomb. The wolf inside him watched with cold eyes. It was waiting for him.

'Take off the stone,' it seemed to say. 'I shall not harm or eat you.' He could not take off the stone, even if he wanted to. To remove it was just to choose another kind of death, an oblivion. The wolf would hunt the girl and kill her as it had done in lives past. No. Then what?

In an instant of clarity he saw his error. He was thinking as if he still had choice. The ropes on his hands and feet had taken all choice.

The cold of the day now burned him. He heard jeering and felt a thump in his face. Some soldiers were throwing snow-balls at him. It was dark and even colder. He was an icicle hanging in a cave, water made rock by cold.

He saw Giroie's face sometimes. He had Loys's sword, the curved sword, the Moonsword. It was poisoned with the dreams of witches. That could kill the wolf. Perhaps he could strike a pact with Giroie? No. The girl needed to end it for him or it would just all begin again. Where was she? The Norman offered the edge of the blade to Loys's torso, as if offering to kill him. Then he took it away.

'I'm going to eat,' he said and his words were gongs, struck in a vast cavern.

Perhaps he was wrong. Perhaps the vision he'd seen in the well so many years ago was wrong. The rebirth would not happen. He would die and be as unthinking as a stone for eternity or he would pass into heaven. Or perhaps he was dead and this was Hell, just a continuation of his earthly sufferings.

It was night and the ice moon looked down on him, big and full-faced.

'You got nothing.' That was a voice nearby.

'You got nothing.' It spoke in Norse. 'Is this a thing of power? Can I have this, my dead man? It brought you no luck but it is the symbol of my god so I take it as a sign.'

He couldn't see the man or even know if he was real.

The wolfstone was lifted from his chest.

Pain everywhere, from his toes to his fingers, his hands not quite numb enough to ignore the terrible constrictions at his wrist. The weak human who could not face his pain had fallen away, the strong wolf had risen. He cried out in his agony and bucked and twisted against his bonds but he couldn't shift them. Then the man was gone.

27 The Runes Unite

'It's all right, it's all right, you're where you belong. You're with me now. You're with me.'

Freydis held Styliane close, cradling the lady's slender frame against her. Five runes spun about her. She was wary of them and she sensed they were wary of her. If only Styliane could awake and use them. The lady had described them to her, told her each of their various powers. One was burning, a fiery arrowhead. The lady needed warming.

'Wake up and call your magic to you, lady. Look there's one here that is blazing. I feel its heat. Take it to yourself, gain comfort by its fire.'

Styliane was insensible. Freydis saw she had cruel bruises at her neck.

'What have they done to you? I should have stayed with you to cut down your enemies as they came close.'

Freydis thought the wellspring of her tears had run dry years before with the slaughter of her kinfolk and her adoption by their slayers. She was a practical woman. But she wept now.

She looked up at the runes, shining in the darkness. The walls of the tunnel were nothing to them. They seemed to float within the rock, even take their character from it. Here was one marking out its shape like a seam of gold, so like the real thing that she would have run back for a chisel in easier times. The one that burned like fire, the arrowhead rune, made the walls a dark glass.

The horse rune was only a smell, but a smell that marked its shape in her mind. The torch rune lit the passage. She had never seen Styliane's magic symbols before, though the lady had spoken of them.

190

'Why don't you go to her?' she said. 'Why don't you wake her?'

She reached for the fire rune, physically reached for it in the dark. It came into her hand, or rather the idea of it came into her hand. It sat there burning, like the odd curved sword of the wolf man, bright and warm. 'I wish you would warm her,' she said. 'She is your mistress. Make her live.'

The fire rune spread its light and Freydis felt the warmth fill her. The physical sensation was very welcome but it brought with it ideas too, the fire of the hearth, of the camp, the fire that wards away the bear and the wolf, the fire that bakes and boils.

She sat for a while, cradling Styliane's head. She wanted to move, to get the lady out of that grim place, but the warmth robbed her of all real will to do so. It was the warmth of the bed on a frosty morning, of a lover's glow.

Styliane stirred.

'Lady.'

'Freydis.'

Styliane hugged her like a child hugs its mother in a storm.

'Lady, I have tried to stay away but I was drawn here.'

'Why, Freydis? I have missed you. I thought you had run away and the .. Ād had enslaved you.'

'I would never run from you, Lady of the crossroads, Lady of blessings and abundance.'

Freydis recited some of the words of Styliane's prayer to Hecate, her goddess, the one the Christians called Mary mother and Mary Magdalene and Mary Virgin, the one the northerners split into three and called the fates.

'But you did, Bellona of the Battles.'

All women are aspects of the goddess, Styliane had said and Freydis, though unusual, was no different. Bellona was the goddess in war.

'There was a mistake. At the desert well. There was a mistake.'

'What?'

'The rune entered me.'

Styliane crossed herself and then made the triple touch, shoulder, shoulder, head of Hecate.

'And you ran so you could not harm me.'

'Yes. I must get you to safety and leave you now.'

Styliane looked around her.

'They have gone.'

'What, lady?'

'The runes. My magic. My immortality. I cannot see them.'

'Don't be foolish, lady, they are here. They warm us and keep us safe. Can you not see them?'

'I see nothing.'

'Then how do you see me, with no rune light to guide you?'

'They are in the well, then. The well has taken them, or captured them. We must cut them free. If you have a rune inside you, use it to call the others.'

'I have no need to call the others. They are already here. See, here's the hoof rune and the lamp and the hearth rune and here is one like a seam of gold. They are wondrous things. Do you dwell every day in their company?'

Styliane grasped at Freydis's arm.

'I can see the light. I can feel the warmth. But I cannot see them.'

A noise from above, a curse. Weeping.

Someone dropped heavily into the tunnel.

'Oh, God and gods help me.'

Freydis had her knife free. The space was too small for a sword.

She crawled down the tunnel towards the noise.

'Don't kill me!'

It was the lump of a boy the wolf man had kept with him. Immediately, with a warrior's sense, she knew something was wrong.

'What?'

'The woman is lost, he is taken and the Normans are searching for me.'

192

'Keep your voice down. Nothing will be helped by your wailing.'

'I'm sorry, I'm sorry.'

She turned back to Styliane. 'Lady, dim your magic lights.'

'I can't. They are not with me.'

'Can you use them to affect harm to these men?'

'Some. Perhaps. But they're not here.'

'Dim the light, you bitch, or you'll have the whole Bastard's army down on us.'

Freydis took the boy by the tunic and spoke softly.

'Insult the lady like that again and I shall present her with your tongue,' she said.

A voice shouted above, a question by the tone of it.

She heard 'Non', which must be 'no', and a stumble, a cry. More cursing. A man had tripped in the dark. They had no light.

Then more words.

'They can see the light!' said Styliane. 'He's asked "what is this?"'

'I wish it would be dark,' thought Freydis.

The light went out as if by command.

The boy's breath was too loud, stifled sobs. She'd have killed him with the knife or by strangling there and then if she'd been sure it would make no noise. She couldn't be sure, so he lived.

They heard the men shuffling around above them. It would be only a matter of time before they got a torch and discovered the hole in the floor.

'You help me up,' whispered Freydis to the boy.

'How? We shall be undone. We shall be killed. Master Loys is the best fighter I ever saw and they took him easy.'

'I shall not be taken easy,' said Freydis. 'Get me up there.'

The boy knelt on all fours and she stood on his back, her knife in her hand. The light of a torch flickered. She kept her head below the lip of the hole. The light became brighter. More words. She guessed they'd seen the hole in the floor.

193

Two men came near. One did not see her but the other let out a cry of surprise as he looked down into the hole. She drove the knife hard into his lower leg and left it there.

The man screamed and cried out again, gripping at the knife. A bad warrior. He ought to have attended to the enemy before attending to himself. Pain was a luxury he could not afford.

Out of the hole, she grabbed her sword and ran, the torch was on the floor, the shadows gobbling at its light.

Four men. Now three as she hacked into the side of the head of the man with the injured leg. If she survived this fight it would be her right to boast of it, her duty, to set an example to other warriors. Then she might say, 'He wore no helm but the helm of blood,' or say, 'Littleclaw liked to feed so well, he could not be pulled from his feast'. She could dress it up how she liked: the sword caught in the bone of the man's skull and was dragged to the floor with him as he fell.

Three opponents left.

The torch guttered and went out. Confusion and fumbling. The torch rune lit inside her and, to her, it was like day. Three of them slashing at darkness, their mouths distorted by fear. One, more calm than the others, slashed with his sword while he felt for the steps to the crypt with his foot. She had no time. The noise might have alerted the rest of the camp. She retrieved her sword. Littleclaw was a good weapon – forged in Damascus by magical smiths. No need to kick it straight.

No. No need for more killing. Or rather, a need not to kill. A wounded enemy was more of a drain than a dead one. The calmer man found the steps, reaching backwards with his foot to confirm where he was. She brought the sword down hard over the back of his leg, cutting in deep. He cried out and fell, cursing.

The other Normans fell to panic and one caught the other a glancing blow with his sword, the blade biting into his arm. The man immediately retaliated, cutting a violent arc with his sword that took his fellow at the throat. The man fell, holding his neck and calling out, oaths or curses she couldn't tell.

He might be mortally injured, he might be scratched. Freydis knew that wounds to the neck filled men with fear. Hit a man in the arm or the chest, cut him deeply, and he might fight harder. Catch the neck, part the skin and draw blood and his fingers would seek the wound. Only heroes, those in the songs of the Skalds, smiled to take such wounds and threw themselves harder into the scrap.

She took her knife from the leg of the now dead man at the hole. Then she stabbed the only standing warrior hard in the buttocks. He screamed and she kicked his legs from under him.

'Quick,' she said down into the hole. 'We need to go.'

Styliane climbed up on Gylfa's shoulders and she lifted her out, light as a bird. The lady shook and shivered, the shock of her ordeal engulfing her. Gylfa was a harder pull but she got him up well enough. She wondered why she bothered. He was slow and he couldn't fight.

Perhaps for that reason. He would be easily caught, which would give her and the Lady Styliane more of a chance to slip away.

'I can't see,' said Gylfa.

Freydis had no time to wonder why that was but she welcomed the fact. She stripped off one of the Norman's cloaks for Styliane, then one for herself. The lady had fainted away but she was still breathing. The runes kept them warm for the moment but she wouldn't be able to rely on that.

She picked up Styliane and carried her up the steps, leaving Gylfa crying and howling in the dark, asking where she was and weeping that he would die.

28 Lights

Gylfa lay on the floor of the crypt, the cries of wounded men all around him. He called out for Loys and for Freydis and then he cursed them both for abandoning him.

The woman in particular, if one could call her a woman, he hated. Until she showed up he'd had a good thing going with Loys. The man had saved him from persecution, might have taken him south, during which time the good warrior might have revealed his secrets to him.

He crawled around the floor, the flagstones hard and cold on his palms and on his knees but he couldn't find the stairs to the crypt and was afraid he'd bump into one of the screaming Normans. They could still defend themselves, he was sure.

He had gone to the ships too soon and all because of the taunts of his brothers. They had grown up tall and strong, easy with spear and axe. He had grown up tall, but that was where the similarity ended. He was given to fat, though he only ate what they did. He was as much a danger to himself as to an opponent with a spear, and the name they had for him had tormented him. Little girl. So he had begged to prove his worth.

'I am as tall as any man, Father,' he'd said. 'Let me do a man's job by coming raiding with you.'

His father had let him, not for any tender feeling for his son. Gylfa knew why. His father was ashamed of him and thought that, if his son could not make a famous warrior, he could at least make an honourable corpse. They had sailed with Hardrada.

He remembered the ships on the ocean. Hundreds of them sailed from the flat waters of the Sognefjord, like swans, his father had said, flocking to a feast. They reminded him more of rats: dark, low to the water, full of sinister purpose. He should not have come. He should not have come.

'So mighty,' his father had said, gesturing to the fleet.

'So fragile,' he had felt like saying, though he only nodded.

'You're doing right, Gylfa,' his father said. 'You'll feast at King Hardrada's bench or at Christ's in heaven before the winter comes.'

'Will I feast with the king?'

'You do mighty deeds and maybe. Though likely not. You'll at least feast with your brothers and be able to look them in the eye as you drink.'

'Will I look Christ in the eye?'

'Fight well and you will. This god blesses those who fight in his name.'

'Some of the men call on Odin.'

'Odin is a treacherous god. Christ stands behind you. Call on Christ to strengthen your arm. Odin asks too much in return.'

'You pray to Odin.'

His father smiled. 'I pray to both. Too long a merchant. I want the gods competing for my soul.'

They travelled as much by oar as by sail – the wind was forever too high or too low. Shetland, Orkney, Scotland, picking up troops all the way. He'd thought then that no one could stand against so many men.

They'd made landfall easy. The country was a funny one, no mountains but rolling hills that bore all the menace of mountains, though little of their splendour; squat things hunched like beaten dogs on the horizon. It was cold too. Not the biting cold of Hordaland, the deep-locked snows and ices, but just a nagging dishonest chill that never quite left, even at the fireside. Why had they come so late? His father said other plunderers were in the south of the country and that, unless they got there quick, there would be nothing left to conquer.

'We'll all be lords!' Hardrada had screamed when he'd

197

addressed the army. He was a magnificent man, a head taller than any of his fellows, arms that looked strong enough to pick up the sea in a bucket.

They'd had an easy victory at Fulford and took York without a fight but it had bred slackness among the men. At Stamford Bridge – he now knew its name – the English king had found them far from their ships and armour. He had come down on them like the tide upon a sand bar. They had not expected him; the scouts had said he was far away. Yet Harold had moved quickly.

He had lost his father that day. He'd hadn't seen him killed and, for all he knew, he had made the ships. Gylfa only wanted to return to his lands, to hug his mother again, sit by the fire and tell stories of war. He'd had enough of participating in it. These men, that woman, they'd all called him coward, or implied as much. But he was not a coward. A coward would still be on his farm, shoving some resentful cow out to pasture, tilling the stony soil. He almost laughed. His ambition now was to be a coward, to live a coward's life.

He crawled forward. He felt something, a little disturbance in the ground. The start of the steps? The warrior beside him cried out. A voice answered in the same language. They were coming. There would be torches and he would be discovered and blamed for the carnage here. He edged forward, the ground gave way and he fell.

He had blundered into the hole in the floor and fallen into the sightless black tunnel. All the breath left him, his straight arm was driven up hard and he gasped in pain. There were shouts above him. He felt his shoulder. It was very painful and he thought he might have dislocated it. Where to go, where to go? He tried to stand but his head was spinning from the fall.

A torch came into the black space above him like a terrible comet presaging doom.

He couldn't see the faces of the warriors behind the brightness of the torch but he heard one of them spit at him. The torch moved away and its light was softer. He saw a glowing rectangle of light above him where the slab had been removed.

He wondered what the scraping was at first. It was dull, loud, near. A Norman face peered down at him, smiling. He didn't understand the word the man spoke but it issued through a smile and he knew that smile was not friendly.

The scrape. A brief squabble, as among workmen who disagree how best to bang in a nail, and then the scrape again. At the left hand edge of the rectangle of light, darkness encroached, darkness with a regular, hard edge.

'No!'

They were putting the slab back across. He tried to stand but too late. The slab thudded into place and it was dark. On his feet, he shoved at the rock with his good arm but it was at the very limit of his reach, he could do no more than put fingertips on it. And what if he did push it aside? It was only the Normans waiting for him.

His heart thumped like a fish on a deck.

'No! No! No!'

He heard no reply. He kicked at the walls, tore at them but it was no good. He just brought earth down on himself, clogging his nostrils and gritting his mouth. He had to think; think like a brave man.

What thoughts did the brave have that cowards did not in such situations? Gylfa thought of his mother on the farm. He thought of his dog and of his sister; the hunger of July, the bounty of September; all the mild torments and pleasures of a man who had not tried too much.

What would a brave man have thought? Not much different. Or perhaps he would have envisaged them less powerfully. Gylfa could almost see his mother there on the hillside; he could hear the shush of the summer sea; he could feel his sister's hand in his, the bones more delicate and precious than anything he had known or could imagine in this world or the next. The brave man would be less imaginative and less hopeful. He would think, 'I have had a good life. I have held my son's hand and known that I will be remembered and that my kin go on. I have piled the plunder I got from the sea at the door of my house and seen the respect and the envy of my neighbours, narrow-eyed on their faces. I have done enough and I do not hope to do more.'

Gylfa lay for a long time. He did not hope for a swift death. He was not afraid of pain but of extinction.

He touched something embedded in the wall and realised it was a skull, its teeth still in its head.

'Here I lie. Bones among bones,' he thought.

He was cold, though not as cold as he had been on the hills, and he was thirsty. There had been water down here, he was sure. That gave him hope. He would wait a while here and then he would scrape the mud from the walls, use the soil and bricks that had fallen in when the excavation was made, to make a pile. He could stand on that and then push away the slab.

It was a large one and beyond his power to move on its own but maybe he could dig around it, do ... What? Something. No, nothing. Black despair came down on him like grave dust. He would never get out, never be free and he would die a coward's death and pass to Hell or to the dead lands where the sick and feeble go, where women go, cut off from Odin's mead bench and the eternal life of a great warrior.

Stupid thoughts. What if Hell was like this? What if Hell was not dying but living forever in this blind tomb? Gylfa cried for a while before he mastered himself.

Brave men did things, his father had told him. When others dithered, they acted. But anyone would be brave in such a place. There was only the desire to get out of it and that begged action. He began to make his pile, shovelling bricks and mud with his cold hands, swallowing down the pain of his shoulder. Even as he removed the bricks of the wall, he feared he would bring the ceiling down. He piled as many as he could find without losing his way in the blackness and then packed them with mud. Leaning carefully on the wall, he stood. He could not afford to push now, only to test if he could hear anything. He reached the slab. He would not test its weight. To do so was to risk it moving and drawing the attention of the Normans. He listened. How futile. If he heard anything he would not lift the slab. If he heard nothing, he still would not lift the slab. He sat back down again.

After a while he began to get very thirsty. He was used to being hungry, so much so that a few days without food were no discomfort to him. Thirst, though, could not be denied. If he could drink, it would be a little victory against the circumstances. There was a well down there. He knew it was stupid to move but he didn't see how he could fail to find his way back to the pile of earth and the slab in such a tight tunnel, retracing his way.

He crawled down the tunnel, counting his elbow steps. His shoulder was painful but not dislocated or smashed, he guessed, or he wouldn't have been able to move. Five, six, seven. He got to thirty before he heard water.

He swallowed, his dry throat commanding him forward, all his common sense saying go back. The tunnel dropped here, it was definitely on a slope. What if it fell to nothing? He stretched forward his arm, patting at the earth, wary as a cat trying a lily pad.

The ground was solid. He crawled forward, trembling. 'Odin, you are lord of the dead and I am among the dead, preserve me. Christ, you rose from a tomb. Show me how you achieved that feat, oh great magician. Help me here. Please help me. Jesus Odin, Odin Jesus. Saint Thor and Saint Michael, angels and elves, help me here!'

A few body lengths on, he felt moisture on the floor. He put his hand to the wall to test it there. Yes, wet. He slithered on. The earth of the floor gave way to slick rock. He could hear the water trickling now. Forward again. The rock dipped sharply. He stopped, stretched out his good arm again to test the way. The water was louder – a waterfall? Now a further drop and, just on his fingertips, water.

He leaned forward to scoop it up but he was not quite near

enough to do more than wet his fingers. He licked at them but that only provoked his thirst. He wriggled forward, got a good scoopful of water, raised it to his lips, slipped and plunged headlong into the pool.

Gylfa did not know if his head had struck something. He saw a white light, breathed in water, spluttered and hacked it out. He was underwater, no sense of up or down, no air to cough into.

He thrashed and kicked, the cold a bear squeezing his chest. Something thumped against his hand. He had gone down when he had thought to go up, he breathed in, only water. He was dying, he was sure, and he did not want to die. Raging for air, he turned, kicked again and struck the bottom once more. No. Up! One thrust of the legs and he thought he broke the surface. He couldn't tell. His face was numb with cold, he couldn't see or feel that he had left the water. He coughed, breathed in, coughed. He was in the air, he thought, he must be in the air. He breathed in, rasping, wheezing. Yes, he was alive. No sight, no other sense, no idea of where he came in or how he might leave, he said the word that brave men and cowards alike find easiest on their death beds.

'Mother!'

Above him, a tiny glow, no more than a distant candle in the darkness.

'Help! Help!' Oh, the horrid cold.

No one replied. He moved towards the light. A peculiar thought struck him. This was the oldest instinct, to move out of the darkness into the light. As he got nearer to it, the glow got bigger, more diffuse. He made out a faint archway, a depth that said this was another tunnel. He swam forward towards it, gaining the side of the pool. Yes, a light. And somewhere, in the tunnel's distance, someone was singing.

29   Unknown Enemies

Tola stepped out of the church into the misty night. It was very dark but a moon looked down at her, its face blurred as if seen through ice. She had escaped but now she had no idea where to go. For a few moments she couldn't even place where she was in the town. Everything was unfamiliar. She seemed to be at the bottom of a hill whereas she had been sure she'd come up one. It was then she realised she'd exited through a different door to the one she'd come in through. The houses here were more or less intact, though some had been burned.

Away in the darkness she heard shouts and more shouts answering them. The slaughter in the cathedral was drawing warriors. She crouched and ran a little way, then stepped over a burned wall and lay down, trying to marshal her thoughts. All around was confusion, anger, fear. She had escaped the terrible warrior with his presence like the deep water of meres, like the darkness of the forest and the tomb, but now she didn't know where to go or what to do.

She tried not to think of what she had seen at the well. Styliane. *Oh Jesus save me*. Had she killed her? She didn't know.

A press of warriors came towards the great church. She watched them, peeking above the ruined wall. Already she was cold – her hair wet and freezing against her face. She couldn't stay there all night but where else to go? Perhaps back to the church. It was huge and full of dark nooks to hide in. It wouldn't be warm but it would have to be warmer than these frozen ashes.

The wolf rune stirred inside her, crawling and slinking. It wanted to go back, to meet with that man, that non-thing. Even unpleasant people came with resonances she could understand. Ina the traveller had come to the farms with his goods and a stink of fox. He had the sly eye of a fox and when she remembered him she envisaged him prowling, fox-footed, around the farms, looking for what he could loot. She had no idea if Ina ever had stolen anything and she doubted that he had. He'd have been mad to. One man – only occasionally did he travel with a woman or some children – alone in the farms would be the first to take the blame should anything valuable go missing. In fact, were anyone planning to steal something, the appearance of a pedlar was as good a time to do it as any because people naturally distrusted outsiders.

She hadn't liked Ina but she had understood him. Other people she disliked brought resonances of burned hair, mithering weather, sticky and warm, even the feelings of an annoying puppy, forever tugging on her skirts.

The warrior brought almost nothing. Just a weight, like a rock, like the sea.

She could not go to him. Alone for almost the first time since the burning of her farm, all the horrible sensations of memory came back to her. Pleasant memories were the hardest to bear: a sunny day with Hals at the start of July, too soon to go hungry, too early for the toil of harvest; a butterfly landing on her breast like a bright blue brooch, a piece of the sky fallen just for her – those memories were the memories of the mind. The memory of the burning was a memory of the body and it was as if her bones and flesh could only hold so much. She shook as she recalled the cry of alarm from the bottom farms, the panic of the flight north – running beyond endurance over hard, cold fields up to the hills, not because the hills offered safety but because there was nowhere else to go. She relived the sensations of the scramble up the fell, climbing slopes she would have thought too steep or too perilous not a day before. Hiding behind the wall now it was as if her body wanted to keep running, re-enacting the movements that had so far kept her safe. Tola knew that tactic was no longer open to her. The dales would kill her if she couldn't find better protection than these oversized warriors' clothes. She would need more cloaks, someone who knew how to live in the open, other bodies to lie next to for warmth in the night.

She waited. There was a lot of shouting and cursing from the church, which went on for a long time. The doors came open and she clamped shut her jaw to stop herself crying out. A naked man was carried out, held aloft by seven or eight warriors, all hurling insults at the man above them. She couldn't understand a word that they said but she knew they were promising him death. Other warriors streamed behind, bearing torches, and the sight of the fire triggered a deep shiver, the idea of warmth deepening the cold.

The shouting moved down to the water and she wondered if it would be safe to go into the church. It had to be. 'Safe' wasn't a word that meant very much any more. To be safe from one thing was to be in danger from another. Flee the sword, face the cold. Flee the cold, face the sword. She had the odd thought that she wouldn't mind being stabbed if only she was stabbed warm.

That was the sort of grim joke her mother was fond of. Tola hadn't seen her die.

She ran back down the hill to the minster, dropping quickly into the shadow of its tower. The poor door was in front of her and she opened it very gingerly and stepped through, then through the leather curtain that separated the vestibule from the main building. The weak moonlight picked out a scene of slaughter. Four men lay dead, killed in the most hideous way. Their bodies had been reduced to carcasses, torn meat. She couldn't think about that. Two of them still bore cloaks. She scuttled forward, grabbed one and returned. It was soaked with blood on the bottom but it was largely dry. She put it about her and drew it close.

Men were in there, she could immediately tell – the hard-headed, obdurate note that made her think of castles and palisades. How many? She let her mind wander the church. Four? Five? Someone else was there, not like them. This person was ardent, full of passion, fear and defiance. The presence was like that of a warrior but it was female. She didn't understand how that could be. The symbols from the well were still there too, chiming and sighing. Tola crossed herself. They terrified her, even more than the women up on the hill.

The thoughts and dispositions of the people in the church floated in the darkness. She put herself into the mind of a warrior to see what he would want. Her mother had said Tola could read minds but that wasn't true. She could imagine someone fully from the invisible scent they left as they walked, the way that the air seemed subtly altered by them having been there, to bear still a light that suggested the colour of their eyes or the sheen of their skin. She drifted towards the Norman warrior, imagined him – a tall man, uncomfortable in boots he'd stolen for their quality, telling himself the pinch would go once they were broken in. He wanted to go back to the fire. If any rebels had been there, they had gone. Tola cried out, a pain at her throat. The man had been struck, and hard, across the throat. Panic welled up in her, dread. She withdrew from his mind. Were her countrymen still here? She could contact them. Maybe that offered a way out. There was no feeling of them in that place.

Screaming and shouting from behind the altar, down towards the crypt where the well had been. If the soldiers outside heard they'd be back very quickly. The darkness seethed with panic. The warrior's presence faded. There was only the woman left. Freydis heard the sea sigh of the runes, saw the light of a moon on water ascending the stairs. The wolf rune inside her tensed and trembled. The figure who carried Styliane could have been mistaken by others for a man. Not by Tola. The warrior was a woman, despite her mail and her sword. Tola withdrew behind the curtain.

Should she offer herself to this woman? No, she was an ally of Styliane's, Tola sensed it. That woman had tried to kill her. Yet the wolf rune still keened for its sisters in the church.

'What are you?'

A woman's voice, through the curtain. She saw a burning rune like an arrowhead, or rather envisaged it, floating by the poor door, lighting her up, questioning her.

'Someone trying to live.'

'Then stay away from me.'

The runes moved on as if dragged away, like dogs from their food; the woman's footsteps were heavy – flat and dead through the thickness of the curtain. Far away the church men were crying out in agony. When she heard the footsteps returning, she thought that death must have come for her but she lacked the strength to run.

The curtain moved back and a weather-beaten, flat-nosed woman stood opposite her, Styliane on her shoulder, her breath rasping.

'You led me here,' she said.

'I don't know.'

Someone away in the night was calling out the same word over and over again, a tone of agony. She sensed it was an invocation to God. But God had not intervened when his house was burned and his treasures looted, why would he come to help a man in pain?

'You did. I think the magic is afraid of you. You have magic in you too. You carry the wolf rune.'

'I have never given it a name.'

'I heard it howling in the hills.'

'It has been calling to something. I thought it was her.' She nodded to Styliane.

'Maybe too. Maybe it called us both,' said Freydis. 'For that I thank you because it saved the lady's life. For that, though a wolf snarls behind your eyes, I offer you my protection.'

Tola glanced at the good sword Freydis wore at her side. Sword! She wouldn't have to worry about that. Freydis could crush the life from her with her hands. If Styliane awoke then she would be done for.

'I cannot accept it.'

Tola felt and heard the runes around her now, rather than

saw them. They burned, snorted, jingled and fluttered. Her own rune prowled around them, like a fox around a hen house, and they began to sing – a high, piping, off-key music like wind in the mouth of a shell. It was a call, she felt it, they were sounding like the shepherd sounds his horn in the hill, like the warrior in battle or even the pedlar in the dales. It was a drawing, pulling, imploring sound, 'I am here,' it said. 'You should be too.'

Two men cried out together. 'Seca! Seca!', or something like it. They were begging for help, their need was so sharp she felt it in her guts.

'You will not come with us?'

'The magic inside me tells me to make my own way.' This was a lie but she could not tell her Styliane was her enemy. Tola felt like crying and, when she spoke next, it was as a child to her mother. 'What shall I do?'

'Die, I think, if you will not come with me. It is not such a big thing. Or perhaps not. You have survived so far,' said Freydis.

'Who is that warrior who pulled me from the well?'

'You were in the water?'

'Yes.'

'He is an enemy.'

'Whose enemy?'

'Everyone's.'

'Like the devil?'

'I think so.'

'How do you know?'

'I travelled with him a little way.'

'He is not your enemy, then.'

'I thought he might offer me a way forward. He only brought me back to where I started.'

'But he didn't kill you?'

'No. I found him ...' She searched for the word. 'Kind.'

'Can the devil be kind?'

'God can be cruel, so why not?' said Freydis.

She put her hand to Styliane's throat, checking her pulse.

'What happened in the waters?'

Tola wanted to say that Styliane had tried to kill her but she was afraid of what the warrior woman would do if she told her that. So she said nothing, though she could feel her lower lip wobble and knew she was close to throwing herself into this woman's arms and telling her everything. Despite the runes, despite this woman warrior's loyalty to Styliane – a thing she felt emanate from her like the love of a child – the warrior was the first person since the burning of her farm who seemed straightforward and honest.

'It is a magic well,' said the woman. 'Odd things happen there. No wonder you cannot speak of them. I am Freydis.'

'I am Tola.'

'You cannot stay in this church, Tola, and you will not come with me. What will you do?'

'Stay here a while. Perhaps the Normans will move on.'

'You will be safe here for a short time. It's the poor door. None of these warriors will come through it or leave through it even to save their lives. Thank God for the vanity of men. You are a magical creature?'

'My father's people called me Volva.'

'A sorceress?'

'Not willingly.'

'Nor I. Where will you go?' said Freydis.

'I will try to live in this land until it's warmer. Then I'll go home. They can't keep burning forever.'

'Perhaps it's the end of the world.'

'I think it is. But I'll try to survive just in case it isn't.'

Freydis smiled.

'Spoken like a warrior, not a witch. Goodbye, Tola. I am frightened of you.'

'Goodbye, Freydis. And I of you.'

Freydis tried the poor door and peered through. Seeing nothing, she went into the dark night, Styliane across her shoulder. When the door was closed again, Tola sat in the darkness, the cloaks pulled tight about her. She heard warriors streaming through the church and she pulled herself tight to the door arch, her back to it, hoping that anyone who looked in would miss her. She needn't have bothered. The screams of the men in the church pulled everyone past the door. After a while, when a washed-out light crept under the poor door, she heard the men leave. She let her mind wander the church. They were gone.

For the first time, she slept, her thoughts drifting from the cold of the floor to the cold of the well and then back out again.

She sensed the Normans at their fires, she sensed the skulking Ithamar, moving about by the river like a rat, and she sensed agony. It hit her so sharp that she cried out, jolting herself from sleep. The man who had come for her in the water, the void-minded enemy who Freydis had called kind, was alive in her mind. She had not been able to find him, not wanted to. But now it was as if he arose from a sleep and stood before her, like Christ on the cross, tortured and forsaken. The wolf rune in her stirred and called and there was an answer, an animal miasma drifting through her thoughts, a howl-stink, a demented scream like the sound of a snared fox.

The emotion was like a fire to the frost of her thoughts. He was fear, a nightmare come to life. But she would go to him and she would help him. The wolf rune howled and she cracked the door of the church to see when it would be night and she could move.

30 Merkstave

Gylfa crawled down the tunnel. It was not like the other tunnel, lined in sharp bricks, but instead it was like a wormhole dug through rock. As he moved on he saw other tunnels coming off it and he was reminded of the meat in the bad Last of Goat stew they'd eaten on the farm – all little pipes and knots. Better than no meat, though, as this was better than no way forward, no light.

The song sounded in the passageway. It was in his own language.

'Two without fate on the land they found,
Ask and Embla, empty of might.

He recognised it as the poem about the formation of the earth. The first men, Ask and Embla, were powerless before the gods breathed life into them and, with it, destiny. To live was to have a destiny. His father had told him that – no dodging it, no hiding. Strap on your sword, grip your shield and get ready for whatever yours might be. The voice was cracked, full of agony, singing as a man who had broken his leg might sing to distract himself from the pain.

He crawled on.

'What is this place?' he muttered.

The singing stopped.

'Who's there?'

'I am.'

'Where are you?'

'Here.'

'Ah, a liar. You are welcome at my table. Crawl forth so I might see you.' The words came out in gasps.

Gylfa crawled on. The passage opened into a cave hung with icicles, great teeth of rock jutting up from the floor. On a plinth by a trickle of water that fell from the wall sat a torn corpse. It was tall, two or three heads higher than any man Gylfa had ever seen; a shock of bright red hair on its head, its body pale and ruined. Half of the torso had been torn away, most of the right arm too. The corpse wore a cloak of hawk's feathers but apart from that it was naked. He had seen worse in war but he could not rightly remember quite when.

'Sit and eat,' said the corpse. It must be a corpse, thought Gyfla. No man could survive such wounds. 'I have plentiful food.'

'Now who is the liar?'

'You sir, you. You said you were here when I see plainly that you are there.' The corpse smiled and blood burst in a gout from his lips. It did not seem to trouble him any greater.

'You say you have a fine table when I see nothing,' said Gylfa.

'I said I had plenty to eat. Nothing's plenty for dead men.'

'I am dead and you are the devil.'

'Oh, that again,' said the corpse. 'I always get that.'

'Always?'

'Lately. Since Christ climbed up his tree and became the king of pain. A good idea, really. So much pain, such a large kingdom, so many subjects in it, eager to bow the knee.' The corpse inclined its head, not its knee, in a little bow.

'So am I dead?'

The corpse cracked a wide grin. 'Well I don't think you're very well. Not very well in the well. Well, well, well. All's well that ends well but all's not well that ends in a well. We'll see what wells in the well. Well or ill, well met, ill met, well we've met in a well, what do you see?' He fell to coughing, leaning hard over the table.

'You make no sense, sir.'

'I was ever in tune with the times. You are a coward, I think.'

The boy felt himself colour. 'I have tried to be brave.'

'They all try that. All men are cowards, especially the true heroes. They run into the enemy's spears, they fight the wolf and the bear but they do so because they fear what men will think of them. Have you ever met anyone as dull as a hero? Have you ever met a hero?'

'I was with one. A strong man. He killed many men.'

'Was it a man you saw? Or a beast wearing a man's pelt?'

'A berserker, I think. He fought like a bear.'

'What you saw was not a man. It was a wolf creeping in a man's flesh. What was he doing?'

'He said he was seeking death.'

'A coward, true. I am seeking death too.'

'Are you a coward?'

'I thought I was but I have disappointed myself with my bravery. I have lost an enemy and don't know what to do. I would have him back.'

'Who?'

'The king of battles, the Lord of Slaughter, Odin, Woden, he who loves the sight of blood, death himself, he who hung ... Am I boring you?'

'You are puzzling me. Death has not gone. Death is everywhere.'

'Had his people not abandoned him ... Had he lived then would old Harold have caught you napping by the bridge? There is a rightness to slaughter, I see that now. Tribute paid to fate, warriors to fill the halls of the dead god and ride at his side. That makes the gods happy and the land bountiful. But this? The women cut down, their children too, the land ravaged. This is not his work but that of the Christ god, who hates all nature, who would call the cycles of life sinful and shameful, who obliterates all passion but that for him in his suffering. And let's face it, he got a better death than his followers are granting the men of this land.'

Gylfa felt dizzy. He could taste iron in his mouth and he had the sense that behind the light of the cave lurked blackness.

He was in a bubble of light that could pop at any moment and return him to the freezing dark of the well.

'What do you want from me?'

'Spoken like a northern man, always ready to slice to the nub of it,' said the corpse. 'This well contains the old symbols, the runes, the fragments of the god. You need to take them on. Then you need to find the others. Some of them left here and some will be called to find you. They will be buried.'

'Where buried?'

'In human flesh. You will need to dig them out. Take the girl and kill her. She is the key. She carries a powerful rune and, if she can kill your friend the hero at the appointed place, then the god will be dead forever. If you are there when the wolf waters the soil with her blood, however, the god might rise in you. I have told her a story. It will lead her to where she needs to be.'

'I don't understand you.'

'Kill the girl. You'll be divine. No more "woman" taunts there. No one will question your manliness. Or godliness. Or whatever-you-say-you-are-ness. It'll be up to you.'

'Is not magic womanly and beneath the warrior?'

'Or godly and above him.'

'And the alternative?'

'You might survive. You might die. But you will live on without fame. You will likely die of the cold or at the spears of your enemies. I'm aware I'm not painting a very attractive picture here.'

'I will take the runes.'

'Good.'

'Where are they?'

'Here.'

The corpse stretched a long finger to the wall and Gylfa saw it was not a wall at all but, as he had thought, the skin of a great bubble.

'No!' he shouted, but it was too late.

The long sharp finger breached the skin of the wall and

the black waters smashed in upon him. Sowilo, the day rune, turned in his mind. He felt energy coursing through him, felt his cock stiffen to the point of pain, felt full of a hot energy; he saw a vision, two men he knew to be brothers, striking at each other, a mother slain by a son's hand. Fehu lit up inside him and he was back on his farm in the north, tending the cattle but the cattle were sick. He felt dull-headed, stupid and afraid. Finally Dagaz lit with its pink dawn light but he knew it was the light of journey's end, the light the hero faces, returned home, failed.

'What gifts are these?'

'Gifts and burdens. You will carry them to where they need to go.'

'They are a poison in me.'

'To ascend godhead, to conquer them, you cannot be a man.'

'What must I be?'

'That revelation comes at greater price.'

Gylfa kicked and swam towards the light of the dawn. The air burst on him and he sucked it in, in desperate gulps.

> 'Where is he?
> Where is he?
> The god of the hanged and the battle dead.
> Over the sea,
> Over the sea,
> Lies the king of murder, the earth his bed.'

He had no idea what that meant but, for an instant before his hand struck the rim of the well and he realised he was in darkness, he thought he saw three women looking down at him, and in their hands were skeins of sinew and skin, a warp for life, a weft for death.

He pulled himself out of the water and the day rune lit inside him, lighting the passageway as clearly as if it were noon but its light was hard upon him, like sunlight to the hungover drunk.

He saw what he needed to do, to get out of this water, to go to the girl, find her, make her work upon him, help him control these singing symbols sprouting inside him. Then he would decide who to kill. She was a sorceress, Styliane too. He needed to find them. He had to get out. All he had to do was lift the slab.

31 The River

Tola was sure she could not wait too long to cut Loys down. She was numb with the cold herself, so she was sure he could not survive for long nearly naked. She saw the magician Ithamar sneaking to the stake to cut the stone from Loys's neck. A big risk for a small trinket. If he could move in the half light, so could she.

No. She dare not. Ithamar had got away with his daring, meaning he might have used up all the luck to be had. The stupidity of that thought was not lost on her but still she felt it fundamentally right. The Normans did occasionally venture out to piss or to change the guard on the gates. There was a limit to the number of sneakers and creepers they could miss.

She had plenty of time to find something to free him with and, after a little searching, settled on the deformed blade of a knife she dug from the cold ground. It was no bigger than her finger but still, despite the fire, held an edge. It would do. And if it did not? The cold froze all thoughts of failure from her. It had to work. They had to get warm somehow.

Night sucked the light from the land and she became colder, which she had not thought possible. Tola had to go now. She made her way down through the blackened stumps of houses, her legs entirely without feeling at first, then exploding into pain as the blood and the heat came back into them.

She had no idea how she would move Loys but she was sure she could carry him if needed. How far was another question. The dirty moon was on the river, giving just enough light to see by. She sensed he was alive but, when her mind explored his further than that, she recoiled. Whatever was prowling in his heart did not welcome her thoughts mingling with its

217

own. He chilled her. In place of the void she had felt within him was something nearly as terrifying – an animal, stinking, snarling, presence. The only solace she took was that it didn't seem hungry. Its animosity just sat and simmered, there was no need impelling it, nor any sense that she was a particular threat.

It was only when she reached the stake that she realised he had been tied higher than she could reach. Was it worth trying to release him?

She touched his leg but could not really feel if it was cold or warm. Her fingers were like stone and told her nothing. She tried to climb the stake but her frozen hands could not be made to grip the wood.

Up on the hill, two men were talking. There was no humour in their exchange, just a sullen grief, an anger about the men they had lost. In the cold, still air, the sound of their pissing was like a waterfall.

She searched the burned quay. There was a good sized stone that the fire had dislodged from a house. She rolled it down towards the stake, her hands agony against its cold. It was heavy, though the slope towards the river helped her and it rolled easily enough. Too easily. She lost control of its movement and it tumbled forward to thump against the stake. Loys stirred. The pissing stopped. She stood counting her breaths. She got beyond her numbers before the men up the hill started talking again.

She stood on the stone, holding on with one hand to the stake while the other gripped the blade of the knife as best as she could. His hands were tied above his head at the very limit of where she could reach and she stood on the wobbling stone sure she must fall or cut the man on the stake. He moaned and shifted.

'Don't cry out, I'm cutting you down.' She would not say 'rescuing you' because she knew how particular even the farming men of the dale could be about accepting help in physical matters from a woman. How much more so a warrior?

218

The rope frayed and stretched.

Normans stamped and hallooed. They must be changing the night watch.

She hacked still at the bonds.

He murmured again. What was he saying?

He leaned forward off the stake. All that was holding him was a thin sinew of rope.

She sawed at it. He found his voice.

'Not yet,' he said. 'Do not cut me down. Not yet. It is not safe for you.'

The rope frayed and snapped and he dropped to the ground, not slumping, as she had expected but onto all fours, an animal crouch. His ordeal had not harmed him.

'Run from me,' he said. 'I am not yet my own master.'

He sniffed at the air, craning his neck around, trying to catch a scent. He paused and stared out over the bridge.

'Survive,' he said. 'Live. I will come back to you.'

'I'm afraid. You must help me.'

He led her down to the water, where a little rowboat lay like a cranefly killed by the cold.

He lifted her into it and she could see that, despite the freezing weather, he was sweating heavily.

'Lie flat,' he said. 'And when you are away from here and get the chance, make a fire. Don't fear it. I will find you. Please. Go. My mind is full of rage.'

He held her hand. The dark, coiling, sinuous wolf that wound its way around her thoughts, called him on, wanted him.

'I need you,' she said.

'And I you.'

'Please.' She squeezed his hand, her fingers so numb that it felt like stone.

'I am an enemy of destiny, an enemy of death,' he said.

'Then keep me from destiny and death.'

He put his arms around her. 'I've missed you for so long,' he said. 'I ...'

She didn't know what to think of this but she felt a terrible attraction to this man, well beyond lust or infatuation. He was necessary to her. Fulfilling. She felt guilty when she thought of Hals. She loved Hals. This was something different – the attraction of the moon to the night. Unanswerable. He felt it too, she didn't need to be a seer to realise that.

'Lie flat,' he said.

She lay back as he said, looking up into the thin mist and the ice-locked moon.

He put the oars inside and shoved the boat out into the water. How could anyone bear to wade out like that? How could a man spend so long hanging naked in the cold and emerge unharmed?

He stepped into the boat and lay beside her, his warmth against her so welcome.

The river bore them on and she pulled the cloak about her as tight as she could. The old kings had gone off like this, so it was said, but in blazing ships not frozen ones.

32 Giroie at the Well

They found Gylfa in the church, kneeling as if in prayer.

'How did we miss him?'

'Never mind. Kill him before the boss gets back. None alive.'

'He might lead us to the others. I tell you there are more Englishmen than we've found around here, it's giving me the creeps.'

'Can you speak to them?'

'Nope.'

'Kill him then.'

Gylfa did not turn to see them, did not wonder how he understood them. He sensed them as little burning flames behind him, delicate, almost precious, like a candle in a draughty house. Gylfa thought he was perhaps in two places, odd as the idea seemed. One was the church, its solid buttresses stretching up to the broken roof. He was also at the root of a great silver tree, the runes settling in its branches like silver leaves. One rune was like ivy, clinging to it, its white stem climbing up into the stars from his eyes and ears, its roots in his head, curling around his brain, protecting it, making it something new. Another grew from his belly button, anchoring him to the floor with silver, shining roots that sang when he looked at them. He understood the men perfectly in a way he had never understood anyone. Their words were plain to him, but also their souls.

One of the men was a willing adventurer, driven on by the prospect of plunder in new lands, his mind humming like the grass in the wind at the prospect of confrontation. The other was a more stolid presence, a man who had come from hard, flinty soil that blunted his harrow, yielded few crops. He was numbed by slaughter, his mind labouring as if into a headwind, enduring, waiting, until the winter and the mundane work of killing, the confrontation, was gone and he could get what he had come for – red soil, golden crops, a full belly and some strong sons. He was subordinate to the adventurer, tired of him, but still following out of long habit.

A heavy boot landed in the middle of the boy's back, driving him forwards.

Gylfa's hands went onto the flagstones. He felt the rumble of the rivers that fed the magic well beneath them.

'Kill him.' Gylfa said.

'What?' The subordinate man spoke.

'He speaks Norman,' said the adventurer. 'Kill who, you pig? Don't give me orders. Don't . . .'

Gylfa allowed the silver tendrils of the root rune to grow from his mouth, engulfing the lower man's legs, snaking up his body, pushing tubers into his throat and his eyes. Red soil, thick red soil, clodded the Norman's mind, a clinging goo of resentment. He smashed his sword down across the back of the adventurer's head. Gylfa saw light splurge to the ceiling, pool about the floor. The warrior was leaking light that was blood and blood that was light.

Gylfa stood. He was warm, full of energy. And then something horrible. The feeling reversed, it was as if he had a great stone on his chest, he convulsed in a shiver, fell down.

'This is witchcraft!' shouted the remaining Norman. 'What have you done to me? I did not do that. I did not kill him.' The bloody sword in his hand told a different story.

Gylfa retched, tried to stand, but his head felt fit to burst. More noise from the back of the church. 'What's happening? What's going on?'

Oh, lord, he recognised that voice. Giroie, the Norman he'd escaped.

'Lord!'

'What? Christ, get light, I can't see anything in here. Why is it the English can see to kill us but not us them?'

'Lord. I have one of them. He's a sorcerer. Careful, he is rich in magic.'

222

A torch was thrust into Gylfa's face. The tree still stretched above him but the runes on its branches seemed rotten fruit now, unpleasant to look at, never mind to touch.

'This isn't a sorcerer, it's a shitting farm boy!'

How could Gylfa understand the Normans, he wondered. The runes. It had to be the runes.

'I swear, sir, he made this sword leap out of my hand and strike down Geoffrey!'

'Great lord,' said Gylfa but the buzzing in his head undid any further thought.

Giroie drew his knife.

'No,' said Gylfa. 'No.'

The day rune lay before him, floating in the air, its closed X almost palpable. 'Do not, sir, do not.' He tried to think. He didn't want to incriminate Loys. The warrior had helped him and, besides, if he found out Gylfa had betrayed him then Gylfa's days might be few. Who?

'Loys, the foreigner, he was seeking a witch. She is the source of all his magic. She has gifts to give. She could make you mighty.'

'I am mighty, I am the Conqueror's right hand. I am ...'

The day rune lit, its harsh light aching in the eye. Gylfa retched again. The pain in his head was fierce but he allowed the rune to shine through him.

'He has a stone. A magic stone. She gave it to him. He used it to escape from you. No ordinary man could deceive a great lord like you.'

The rune shone on Giroie, its light playing on his face like sun on water.

'What is this light?' said Giroie.

'It was planted in me in there.' He pointed back to the crypt. 'Under the earth. They were all delving down there, all of them, delving for magic.' If only Gylfa could make the runes kill again but he found even the light hard to bear now.

Giroie crossed himself. 'Show me.'

'Lord, I am weak.'

'No bother, I am strong.'

Giroie picked up Gylfa by the scruff of the neck, bundling him down the steps. The other Norman followed, a torch in his hand, flickering against the rune light.

'Should I send for the others, sir?'

'Why?'

They approached the crypt and saw the scene of slaughter.

'This is what the magic did, this is it!' said Gylfa.

'Christ's nuts!' said the Norman.

Giroie looked around him. 'There weren't enough English to do this. This would have taken a mighty force.'

'Magic,' said Gylfa. 'I told you. There was one, a woman. She went into that hole as nothing and when she came out, this. This slaughter.'

'It's safe for me in there?' said Giroie.

'Yes. I came in and out.'

Giroie pointed at Gylfa but he spoke to his soldier. 'If I don't come out of there,' he said. 'Kill him.'

'Yes, lord.'

Giroie lowered himself into the hole, taking down the torch. Only the rune light shone now, cold and shifting.

The Norman did not sheathe his sword. Gylfa was too weak to stand. He wanted the day rune to dim its light but it would not. They sat for a long while, Gylfa's eyes on the sword he was certain would kill him.

Shouting and lights from within the church.

'Lord, lord, the foreigner has gone! He has cut himself down and fled! Lord!'

Six soldiers ran down the steps towards the rune light.

'Where is Lord Giroie?'

'In there!' said the Norman.

A great cry came from down the tunnel. Without hesitation two warriors climbed into the hole.

'He had better live, sorcerer, or ...'

The Norman's voice was hoarse with fear.

'What is this bright thing?' It was Giroie's voice.

A scraping and thrashing from below. A soldier's head appeared at the hole.

'Help me,' he said. 'Help me! He's raving!'

The soldiers reached down and Giroie came coughing from the darkness. He was soaking wet.

'What?' said a soldier.

'Fill in that hole,' said Giroie. 'Move over the slab!'

He grabbed Gylfa. 'What is it in there?'

'Magic,' said Gylfa.

'How do I get it?'

'I don't know. The witch is the key. She knows everything. Find her.'

'The foreigner was searching for her?'

'Yes.'

'Then he will know how to find her. Get me to the waterfront.'

'The foreigner is gone, sir. Downriver, I think. A boat is missing.'

Giroie coughed again. 'Do you know where he's gone, boy?'

'Downriver, sir. That's where the witch said she was going!' said Gylfa.

Giroie stood haltingly. A soldier went to help him but he waved him away. 'Get me dry clothes and let's get after him! I want that magic stone and I want that witch.'

In the dark air of the church Gylfa caught a glimpse of something else – a rune like a glittering icicle. Giroie had taken the magic. He gazed up at the symbol twinkling in the dark. No one else seemed to see it, no one but Giroie, who turned his eyes from it.

'That is a curse,' said Gylfa.

'I know,' said Giroie. 'Let us find the witch.'

33 Pursued

She lay beside him in the boat as it slipped through the mist of the grey river. Loys was naked, though not yet cold and he feared what that meant. His mouth was wet and he had a strong urge to chew. Her smell was sharp in his nostrils, fear and dread sizzling on her skin like spices in a pot of pork.

He itched to kill her, but the smell that goaded the wolf inside him brought other, kinder memories too. He was a prince by an expanse of bright water, this woman at his side who he would never give up; he was a wildman trudging through another snowy country, leading a reindeer sled on which the same woman sat in deep furs; he was a man in a green wood, shaking crippled limbs into life, amazed and appalled at the transformation that had come over him. That was when the god had lived, when the story was still being told. Now the god's story was shattered and its players enacted its fragments. He had thought her like Beatrice, his lover, so long dead. But she was not Beatrice, just someone who stood where Beatrice once stood as one May Queen stands where generations of others have been.

The story was gone, or made no sense any more, like a fireside tale of heroes that lacked any foe, any monster, or a tale of monsters without heroes to face them. He imagined how you would tell such a story. 'Listen, and I will relate, a tale of a man and woman who lived forever under the eye of a wolf. They were called to kill the old god Odin when he took flesh on earth, to die with him, so he might offer a sacrifice to the Norns who spin men's fate at the well of worlds, pay the price of pain and live eternally in the realm of the gods. The bargain was not met. The god died. They lived and now the reason for their sacrifice is gone. Only the sacrifice remains, repeated in many lives and forever.'

This woman beside him, shivering in the boat, was not Beatrice, his wife, reborn; he was not the prince by the water or the wolfman with the sled or the cripple in the forest reborn. But she stood in the place of his wife in the god's broken story, as he stood in the place of the figures he glimpsed in his memories as the wolf awoke in him. She looked so like her that she could be her but her accent was strange, her face ruddy from a life of toil, her hands rough and her limbs thicker.

He wanted to tell her again he'd missed her for so long, to hold her and comfort her, but he knew he would only be comforting himself. The woman didn't know him, was afraid of him. He could not even risk being kind to her. She had to have the steel to kill him when they reached the appointed place. Nothing could intrude on that.

The rune within her writhed and simpered, representing itself as a shadow on her face, a shadow on the water, a shape in the mist that turned out to be a tree branch when the boat floated closer.

The current took them and he risked sitting up. The fog was thicker here, the banks just shadows, and at points they could have been in the middle of a lake or a still ocean, only the washed-out light of the moon to see by. Even he, with his wolf-keen senses, could see very little, though here and there fires ambered the mist and he didn't know if they were fires of life or of death. The girl was freezing on the boat, she was pale and her lips were blue.

She would be red inside; her flesh would split like a pomegranate yielding its colliding flavours of perfume and iron.

Chase away that thought. He needed to find the stone before they went on. He was on the edge of control now. If they were confronted and he was forced to kill, that control might slip. Without the stone, they would never get away, he would never be able to guide her first to find the necessary place and then to kill him. And if she died he was lost. She had survived in the bitter cold so far but the boat was freezing.

He needed to find shelter for her and then search for his stone. He could scent the thief on the damp air, the pelt he had worn about him seeping in rot, still with the fear of the animal's death upon it. It had been trapped, not hunted, and its secretions told a story of long agony.

He was north but so were others. Loys smelled leather and horses, iron and sweat. Something more. A noise like the fall of water in an ice cave. Runes? They would run from him, he knew. He had to protect Tola.

He took her hand. It was cold as a river rock. She wasn't even shivering any more.

'Lady.'

She stirred, sleepy. He shook her. 'Lady!' But she would not be roused.

It was clear to Loys that if he didn't get her to a fire soon she would die. Smoke was on the air, but smoke had been on the air for as long as he could remember in this country. The boat slid along on the gentle current, or he thought it did. The mist was so thick that it was difficult to tell if they were moving at all. Only a suddenly looming branch or turn of the bank confirmed they weren't floating motionless.

A noise behind him. Oars in the water, heavy breaths, the scent of torches and a breath moving to a different rhythm. A dog. The Normans must have discovered he had gone and were pursuing them. They were at a distance, maybe a mile, but he would not be able to outrow a party of men.

To remain in the boat was to be caught – to kill and to risk his mind sinking into the blood mire. That would place the girl in danger. But a dog might find them in the mist. The Norns spin what they spin and here, on this river, they spun death. It was impossible to avoid it; destiny was a knot that could not be untied. He steered the boat in to the bank and tied it to a stump. The girl was frozen and he hugged her, trying to revive her. It was no good. Fire soon or death. The dog's sawing breath was nearer, the beat of the oars on water too.

He slipped into the river, the water taking his breath momentarily. He swallowed down his shiver, allowing the wolf to rise up in him, its hostility and vigour coursing through his mind, the warmth of its anger loosening the freezing grip of the water on his chest, allowing him to wade forward. He made his way out along the branch of a fallen tree, twenty paces away from where he had moored the boat. The water came up to his chest but he squatted down until only his head was above the surface and he peered out through the branches.

Their voices were clear on the still air now.

'We'll find nothing in this mist, lord.'

'We'll find nothing if we don't look.'

'If there are Englishmen here we could fall into a trap.'

'The English are beaten. We are ten warriors, what are you afraid of?' He coughed. There was a rasp in his breath. Giroie was not well. Did he have the rune?

The hound barked; short, hollow, gulping bays. Loys's mind was vacant. It was cold. There was noise. The world was reducing to bare facts. Mist, river, prey. An echo of himself sounded in his mind. No blood. There must be no blood. Ten men. He had thought there would be more. Giroie among them.

'He's got a scent!'

'Of a corpse in the water.'

'Be quiet!'

The Normans stopped speaking but the hound kept on barking

'Look!'

'There's our boat!'

'Approach it on the bank. We're dead in the water if they've got archers.'

'He hasn't got archers, he hasn't even got any clothes. Row towards it.'

Giroie stood up on the prow of the boat, peering forward like a man trying to spear a fish. Loys saw now that there were runes but, even as he watched them dance, they fled from him.

229

'What's happening. Gylfa, what's happening?'said Giroie.

'I don't know!'

'Is the magic lifting? I can't feel it any more.'

'I don't know. Lord, I don't know.'

'Was this a trick?'

The prow of the rowing boat came past the branch, five paces away. Loys swam under the water, the cold tightening his scalp onto his skull. Three strokes and he was at the boat, seizing the side. He had meant to tip it away from him but his feet slipped on the river bed and the boat did not capsize, though it rocked violently and Giroie and another man were thrown clear into the water. He threw his arms over the side of the boat and bore down. Panic and the rush of the soldiers to arms did the rest. The boat tipped towards him, four warriors splashing in around him, crying out to Mary and St Etienne. He had his arms around one's neck and, in a quick twist, he had broken it. In the confusion and the darkness the soldiers drew their weapons. He dragged another man down. His friend came to his aid, hacking into the water with his sword but striking only Norman flesh. Blood was all around Loys, the smell, the taste, as sweet as another sip of wine to the three-cup drunk. He stood, driving the heel of his fist into the swordsman's temple. Not to tear, not to rip, not to sink his claws into his own humanity.

'Foreigner!' Giroie called out from the other side of the boat.

'He's here, lord, here!' Another warrior was backing away, the water around his waist, his sword in front of him shaking like a branch in the wind. His fear hit Loys like a waft from a baker's oven.

'I can't see you, Philip!'

'Here, here.'

Loys struck, dashing the sword aside, going for the throat. The warrior drew his knife but Loys snapped his arm, the knife snagging the warrior's thigh, which burst to the surface with a deep meaty enticement of blood. It was as if he stood on the edge of a great precipice, ready to cast himself down. No

Loys, no. His fingers itched at the man's neck, his lips drew back from his teeth and a snarl rattled in his throat. What of her? He could protect her from the Normans but not from himself. He threw his man back into the water. The warrior turned on to his hands and knees, hacking like a sick dog.

The smell of the blood called forward the wolf, slinking and hungry in his mind. Kill, eat and kill. Kill again.

'Philip, are you there?' Giroie spoke.

The panic was ripe and slaversome. Words split and disintegrated in Loys's mind. Instinct told him his eyes saw what Grioie's did not. It was flat dark for a man. Not for a wolf.

The girl cried out on the bank, her voice bringing him back to himself.

'Leave me, Giroie. I give you your life if you flee now,'said Loys.

'There are ten of us and one of you!'

'Not so many now, and that tells me you cannot see me. Know that I am the possessor of a great magic.'

'It didn't save you when we tied you by the river. Andrew, Robert, Pierre!'

No reply, just the gasps of the man Loys had strangled.

Loys peered through the darkness and mist. There was Giroie. The water was only up to his thighs and he cast around him, looking for enemies.

It could end here. The pursuit need go no further. Rage bubbled up inside Loys like a boiling spring. The girl cried out again. If he killed, could he stop killing? Could he snap a neck, tear a throat and not lick the jewels of blood from his fingers? More precious than gold, blood was transformative. Even the smell of it seemed to feed his muscles, opening new voids of hunger inside him.

'I'll kill you, foreigner!'shouted Giroie.

Loys was on him, driving him backwards into the water, holding him down. Kill and rejoice, kill, hunt. No difference. What is killing if not hunting, what is hunting if not eating? The thoughts would not separate. To hunt was to kill was to eat. Giroie clawed at Loys's face as he tried to drown him, cried out as Loys bit him, severing a finger. The blood burst in Loys's mouth, a warm frenzy trickling into his throat, exulting him, lifting him up, making the night crackle with sounds, heartbeats, breath, the shivering of limbs, the music and percussion of murder.

The woman cried out for a third time. Loys spat out the finger. Death, not to be its servant, but to make it serve. Loys threw Giroie down, turned back to the bank.

'I can't see him! I can't see him!' The one remaining warrior was shouting out.

Loys made the bank.

'Follow me and die!' he said.

He went to find the woman, spitting the savour of blood from his mouth.

34 Mortal

'What are these things, mistress?'

'These are the runes. They are the magic of the gods. They make the gods.'

'Then use them to get us away from here. Let us go to a place which is warm. I have one inside me. It is tangled with the ones you showed me at the Galata bridge.'

'I have no runes. They are gone.'

'Lady, they are here. Can you not see them? Here is one that breathes like a horse and another that sighs like a mountain wind.'

'They are gone.'

Freydis looked down the hill. There was a commotion by the river. She couldn't see much through the gloom but men were calling out, splashing; launching a boat, by the sound of it.

'There may be a distraction, we can get away. Use your magic to hide us.'

'I have no magic.'

'If only we had a horse. They might mistake us in this night and we might get away.'

At the word 'horse', the rune that shone bronze like the back of a bay mare stamped and blew. Answering it, from up near the intact houses, a chorus of neighing and whinnying. Voices raised to quiet them.

'There are others. In the church,' said Freydis. 'Other runes are in the church.'

'You have taken my magic at the well, or it has been given to you,' said Styliane. 'We must go. The runes will want to unite. Then you or whoever bears them will be nearer to being a god. The cycle will start again.'

'What cycle?'

'Birth and death, forever. I do not want to die, Freydis, I fear it.'

'You will not.'

'We must find the girl Tola. If she kills Loys then we are all lost. The god exists in opposition to the wolf. While the wolf lives then the god is needed and might be reborn. If he dies, the runes are gone from the earth. You die. I die.'

Freydis looked up at the shining symbols in wonder.

'But without these you die anyway?'

'Yes.'

'Then what shall we do?'

'It is right you die for me, as my servant,' said Styliane. 'But we must walk a perilous path. When the god dies on earth, the runes will scatter. It happened before and it could happen again. Then, at the right place, I might receive my magic back.'

'The god is already dead.'

'So he must be reborn. In you and with whoever has the runes in that church. You must come together and the wolf must tear you.'

'I am ready to face a thousand wolves for you.'

'Good. But first, we must kill the girl. If we can do that, then the wolf is safe.'

'And then?'

'The story will unfold as I have striven to prevent it unfolding all these years.'

'But if the god gives his sacrifice to fate, will not the cycle begin again?'

'I will reclaim my magic. From there I can plan.'

'I fear these symbols.'

'You are right to. They are keys to knowledge and to madness. The god Odin boiled his brains when he took them from the well.'

'Then let us find her. How?'

'Think where fear is. Think where you do not want to go.'

Freydis thought. The night was alive to her. Even in the

frost she felt creatures, burrowed beneath the earth, their slow breath, their still bodies, waiting for spring. She felt the seeds of the fields, the bulbs of the flowers sleeping, and she felt fear. On the horizon something did not sleep but stirred and swirled like a river whirlpool. Some strange nothing, a negation, a darkness folded in darkness lay beyond the horizon.

'You feel him.'

'As I did before. It was my instinct to follow him.'

'No instinct. The runes have a will. It is hard to know it from your own.'

Shouts from the church. A crash. She wondered that the men of the halls did not come to investigate but it was cold and a fight in a camp was no unusual thing.

'How will we travel?'

As if in reply, a horse whickered away by the city gate.

'I will get us a horse,' said Freydis, 'I will kill the guards and be gone.'

'The runes you have are not runes of death.'

'I have the spear rune but I will not touch it, nor call it to my mind. I don't have your strength, lady, and I feel the runes pulling me to madness. For you, I need to be clearheaded. I will kill them as I've always killed, then we will take their horse and be gone.

The men on the boat splashed out into the night. Freydis wondered what could be urgent enough to make them set off in this blackness. She kept the runes quiet inside her now, taking Styliane by the hand and creeping down towards the water.

Behind her something stirred and rustled like the wind in the trees. The runes she had sensed in the church. She felt the ones in her keening for them. No time to think of those now. She steeled herself and made the water, tracing it along in the direction she guessed the bridge would be. She was right.

Over the slick logs and out towards the gate.

She gestured for Styliane to stay, then crept forwards. The horse was fretting at the gate and the man was trying to calm it. She took out her knife. No way to hurry this, better a slow, silent approach than quicker and raise the alarm. She made the wall and rested. A few breaths and she sidled along towards the gate. The fire at the gate was enticing but she could not stop to enjoy its warmth. Three men there. How quick could she be? Very quick.

She was close enough to hear the men breathing. The spear rune quivered in her mind, begging to be used. Let it. She saw it as a white shaft against the black sky. One man died immediately, his head half severed as her sword stuck, though she lost it as he fell down. She did the other with her knife, driving it up under his chin into the root of his tongue, leaving him to drown silently in his own blood. The third ran and shouted. It was too much of a luxury to chase him.

'Lady!'

Styliane came running.

Freydis freed the horse, tightened its saddle and nearly threw Styliane up onto the big war saddle before jumping up herself. There was no real room in the saddle, so she stood up in the stirrups, spurring the horse away into the night. She heard the man hallooing back into the town behind her but she heard no answer. The town was silent.

She didn't know which way she rode – just away; the night was clear to her by the rune light but she wished it wasn't, she wished she could damp down the magic that was lighting inside her, filling her with elation. Or was it just her love for Styliane? When they were clear of the town, she would lead the lady on the horse and she would walk. She saw herself strolling with the lady through a green landscape, spring warm about her and she did not know if that was a glimpse of the future, born of magic, or just a wish for what might be.

35 Insight

Tola was being carried when the cold released its grip on her mind. He had her across his shoulder, striding forward as if she was no heavier than a cloak.

The night was darker here, the clouds had buried the moon and she saw very little. They were crossing a marsh, she could smell that, wet grass, frost. Behind her was distress, humiliation and fear. Hearts beat quickly, the bodies were warm but cooling beneath wet clothes. She imagined him, the leader, his pride shattered, desperate for revenge, angry at his own impotence.

She felt nothing from the man who carried her. He was a void still, a falling away into darkness, and when she tried to assume his thoughts, she feared to step into that darkness. He moved so quickly, almost running, and she knew, if she had not known before, that she had stepped into a story where fantastical things were everyday and all the certainties of life were gone.

Her body convulsed in a big shiver and he gripped her more tightly. The heat of his body brought her out of her numbness and she realised how uncomfortable she was, his shoulder pushing into her belly, her legs cramping.

'I must stop.'

He kept going, jogging and bashing her.

'I must stop!'

'There's blood in the water. There's a river of blood.'

'They will not find us in this night. Stop and let me get my breath.'

'I have killed,' said Loys. 'I have heard the Valkyries' song as they choose the slain from the living.'

'Set me down!'

237

He stopped and dropped her to the ground. Her legs would not support her and she stumbled but he caught her. He trembled as he held her and he could not look at her.

'What?'

'I am slipping away. I cannot defend you. I killed them.'

'Who?'

'The ones in the boat. They came for me. I cannot defend you.'

'And yet you have.'

'From enemies without, yes. But I have an enemy in here.' He thumped his chest. 'He is waking and he is hungry. If he eats, his hunger grows.'

'You have not killed me yet,' she said.

'But death surrounds us here. Soon we will have to defend ourselves again and that will call him out. The teeth. In the darkness. In here.' Again he thumped his chest. 'I must leave you where it is safe.' Loys gently let her go to stand without support.

'Don't leave me. It's safe nowhere.'

'I need to seek the man who took my stone. I can smell him on the air. He is near enough. Two days and I will find him, reclaim myself.'

Something moved in the darkness. Loys turned and crouched. He didn't draw his knife, as a warrior might have, but rocked forward onto his hands, like a wild animal ready to pounce.

Heavy sawing breath in the dark, a splashing and plodding.

'Hold, hold! I can't see where I'm going!' She did not know the voice.

'Run from me,' said Loys. 'I cannot answer for what I do if I kill again.'

'I can't run. I can't move!'

'Run! I am a monster. Run!'

She tried to get away but her legs would not carry her. All the strength had gone.

Three short, gulping barks, a low answering growl from Loys.

At first she thought he was another creature from a story, many-legged, short and squat, but then she saw, in the gloom, that it was a man, almost dragged by a dog.

'Lord Loys, is that you?' he said.

'Gylfa!' said Loys. His body shook and Tola guessed he was trying to master himself.

Closer, she could see the man was soaking wet, shivering deeply.

'They forced me,' said Gylfa. 'They forced me to lead them to you. I was glad to do it. I know your fame, lord, I knew you would free me.'

Tola could think of only one thing.

'Do you have a flint? Steel?'

'Yes, but my tinder is soaked!'

'Never mind.'

'A fire will reveal us!' said Gylfa.

'But the cold will kill us. We need fear nothing in this fog. You took your plunder, I see.'

At Gylfa's side was the strange curved sword.

'I brought it for him. I knew we would find the lord again. He has cured me. I have things inside me but he frightened them away.'

'What things?'

'Runes,' said Gylfa. 'They fell into me at the well but I do not like them.'

'You are a man, you can't bear runes,' said Loys.

'Well.' Gylfa smiled. 'Perhaps you have reminded them of that and they have gone away. I am glad of it, they pain me.'

'Draw them,' said Loys. 'Here in the mud.'

So Gylfa drew. The Algiz, tree roots reaching down into the ground; Fehu, the two short staves propping up the long one; and Dagaz, two triangles kissing at their point.

'Merkstave,' said Loys.

'What does that mean?'

'They're upside down. The day rune is the only one you have used?'

'Yes.'

'It is the only one that cannot be reversed, though it can oppose the other runes. Do not open your mind to the others. You have been cursed and you carry the curse inside you.'

'But they are gone.'

'With me here, yes. When I leave they will return.'

'I would not be cursed!' said Gylfa.

Loys smiled. 'Me neither. Though you may be part of my curse.'

'Don't cut me free, lord. I am a man better owned than owning, better told than telling.'

'I have never seen the runes reversed before,' said Loys.

'That sounds like a bad thing!' Gylfa grinned, though he wrung his hands.

'I don't know,' said Loys. 'Most people who carry them the right way round die. It may be a sign of good fortune.'

'You said it was a curse.'

'For you, not me.'

'You were leading them to us,' said Tola.

'No, I swear, they forced me to follow.'

'Why?'

'I don't know. I don't speak their language.'

'Why did they let you keep the sword?' said Tola.

'I took it from the boat. I need to defend myself. Without you, lord, I need to defend myself.'

He untied the sword and passed it to Loys.

'It's good you brought it,' he said. 'This is the needful weapon.'

'For what?'

Loys did not reply, just sat down on the floor. She wondered that he did not shiver or complain of the cold, or seem ashamed of his nakedness. She distrusted Gylfa but his fear of Loys was palpable. He would do nothing to her while she was under his protection.

Tola took her knife to a birch and stripped it of its oily bark, feathering it to take the flame. She collected twigs and, because the grass was damp and useless, cut a piece from the stuffing of the Norman tunic she wore.

They chose a thicket of trees for their camp and hoped that would be cover enough. The fire didn't come easy but it came, a strange, gaudy thing in that grey land, something that played and danced in the stillness.

'How long before the rest follow?' said Tola. She had not known how cold she was until the fire began to warm her.

'Giroie and another survived,' said Gylfa. 'But they have been chastened. They were shouting "Fen Monster". Sir, they couldn't believe they fought an ordinary man. I'm sure they will not dare to face you alone.'

Loys sat naked in the firelight, the light of the flames shifting on his pale skin. Tola crossed herself. His eyes had changed. The irises were big and deeply coloured – difficult to see what in the firelight, maybe green, maybe amber. He had a watchful expression and sometimes inclined his head as if hearing something. She could hear nothing beyond the crackle of the fire. The dog was wary of him now, though it came to the fire on the opposite side to Loys, not sleeping or resting, but nervous, its fur steaming, stinking. It was restless, its legs half creeping forwards, half back, pulled on by the warmth of the fire, wary of the man who sat beside it.

'I need to find the stone,' said Loys.

'Can you not sniff it on the air?' said Gylfa. He had taken off his cloak and was holding it up to the fire to dry it.

'No. It is invisible to me, as is the man who took it. He must have put it on.'

His breath was heavy and his mouth was wet with drool.

'So where does that leave us?' said Gylfa.

'Dead,' said Loys, 'if we are attacked again. I have a wolf in me and his hungers grow with feeding.'

'So what do we do? We will not survive without you.'

'I survived without him before,' said Tola.

Tola, now the cold began to leave her bones, could concentrate on this little man. He had a huge fear in him but not like

Ithamar. This was not a wall of fear, put up to block thought, it was fear that sparkled like sun on the morning fields, a shifting, sharp thing. This man was afraid of so much that it almost over-rode any other emotion in him. She felt an animosity towards her but only that which many cowardly men felt with death all around them; a despair at the evil of the world but no desire to oppose it, only surrender to it; a willingness to become its instrument even as it destroyed them. It wasn't rape she saw in his mind. Something else. She couldn't quite understand it. It was a feeling half between wanting to protect her and wanting to harm her. She'd had that before from the young men of the dale, as she felt their minds hover between desire and fear of rejection. So that? Maybe? The man was very young and perhaps unused to the company of women. She saw him as a river thistle, clinging to hard places; a burr, an irritation that snagged you as you passed, something to be picked out and discarded. It did not bother her. There were no friends left and she had been in the company of hostile men ever since the Normans had burned her home.

'We go north in the morning,' said Loys.

'Why? The land is in flames and the Normans are all around,' said Tola.

'It is where you were. Where I was looking for you.'

'And where you search, that is where I must be?'

'Yes. It's the way of it. We need to go back and to consult, to find the appointed place.'

'What appointed place?'

'Where we will both be free. You of me and me of everything.'

'How will you find this place? By magic?'

'I am the end of magic, a hole into which it sinks. I can't do any magic. Women and gods do magic. I am neither.'

Tola leaned in to the fire. 'You think I can?'

'You know you can. Why are you alive among this slaughter, in this cold? You survive because the god's story, or the fragment of it you are enacting, says you survive, because he

242

has put his magic in you like a seed.'

'Then I don't need you.' She didn't believe those words. She needed Loys because he offered a purpose, a place to go, an idea that the running and hiding might end.

'This story does not end well, lady, for any of us.'

'What should I do?'

'I don't know.'

Tola watched the fire. As a child it had seemed to her that an invisible river flowed through her valley beside the real one. It swept over her, trying to carry her away. Sometimes she dreamed that it was not a river but a sparkling yarn of gold and silver, soft to the hand. She followed it through the dale, out and away over strange lands. She knew now that it was the thread of her destiny that had led back to the well at York.

She nodded into the heat of the fire, searching for it again. All men are spun. All men. She saw the yarn that stretched over Gylfa, a net of red jewels; she saw her own stretching away from York, like spun ice, twisted with tiny diamonds. All men are spun. All men. There was no net for Loys, no thread either, just a sense of unseen depths, like a cave that plunges into fathomless darkness.

She took up the thread in her hands. The hill. The women, with their skins of beaten leather, their hair of spun gold.

'I know where to go,' she said.

36 Abomination

She led them back the way they had came, over the hills. There was warmth at the White Horse cave at least.

'This way we have shelter,' she said, 'to break our journey.'

The cold had lost some of its grip on the land and only the high hills were touched with white but the wind was bitter. While they moved she was all right but rest sent her muscles writhing on her bones. She built the fire as Ithamar had shown her, in the lee of a great rock, the small hole feeding the bigger one, and Gylfa marvelled at it. Had it not been for him, they would have frozen. He had the knife, he had the tinder.

There was nothing to cook. Movement kept the hunger at bay but, in front of the fire, the memories of the hearth at home sharp in her mind, it came back, burning in her guts as if she'd swallowed the embers of the fire. She felt irritable and restless and could sense that Gylfa felt the same. Loys, as ever, was dark to her.

'There's something following you,' she said to Gylfa as they crested a stony ridge.

'There's something following us all,' said Gylfa.

'Yes. But magic things.'

She saw them in the night, catching the edge of her vision only to fall away when she turned to see them properly. Bright flashes came with whispers of birdsong, movement that suggested tumbling water.

'It's to be expected,' said Loys.

'Why?'

'We are together. The story has moved on.'

'You said the story was broken.'

'I believe it has been and it may be told differently this time.

But still its parts seek each other. That is what you're seeing in the darkness. Something that is trying to be.'

'You are something that is trying not to be,' she said.

'You have a great magic in you.'

She said nothing, too numb to think about what that meant.

The hill lay out before her like a collapsed animal, dead of cold. The dog followed behind, at a distance, skulking forward at night to lie by their fire, always wary of Loys, its eyes never leaving him. In the daylight she saw he had changed again. His blue eyes were now shot with amber, the muscles on his neck stood out like the roots of a hill. The boy Gylfa offered him his cloak but Loys refused it. The priests said the first man was naked and knew no shame. Perhaps Loys was the last man, returning to the way he had been in Eden.

He constantly craned his head and sniffed at the air.

Tola had to ask him directly. 'Is this the end of the world?'

'I think the world is ending,' said Loys. 'But it may not yet be the moment of the end.'

'Will it pass, the danger to us? Your danger?' she said.

'I don't know. If we meet an enemy you must run and keep running. I will face them. After that, hide from me.'

'You will harm me?'

'I will try not to. But I cannot swear it.'

Fog came down again on the high hills and Tola moved as if blind. Loys led them, his hand in hers, Gylfa taking her cloak.

'I can't see anything,' said the boy.

'Then neither can our enemies,' said Loys.

Sight gone, she found herself counting her breaths. One, two, three, four, one, two, three, four. She timed them with her footsteps, a step a breath. In the greyness it was the only thing that convinced her she was alive. She saw an arm's length in front of her, no more. The going was slow, even with Loys leading. Something brushed her leg. The dog. It was coming nearer. She felt Loys shiver.

'You're cold?' she said.

'At last,' he said.

'You can't stay naked in this.'

'No. Let's find your cave. I can smell it. There's a fire.'

'How do you know it's the cave fire?'

'It's not a free breathing fire. It's enclosed,' said Loys.

'Not much further, then?'

'A day.'

'You can smell a fire a day away?'

'For now. I can smell the drop at our side too. Don't go any more that way, the air deepens so there will be a fall.'

Gylfa shot back as though the fall might leap on him and bite him.

The hills were heartbreaking – she had no idea how long they went on for. Always as a child when she had climbed the long rise to her Gran's she had glanced at the summit and then not allowed herself to look up again for a while, surprising herself with how much nearer she was. She couldn't do that here so there was no way of knowing when the effort would subside. When it did, the cold came on again, and she longed for the warmth of another climb.

'Are you hungry?' said Gylfa.

'Of course.'

'We need food soon or we will starve. I haven't eaten properly in weeks.'

'We're all in the same mess,' said Tola. 'Talking about it makes it worse.'

'Are you hungry, lord?' said Gylfa.

Loys said nothing.

The fog did not lift, a grey day became a black night and they built what fire they could from the sparse bushes. It was not much but it kept the cold at bay for most of the night and after it faded, they all slept huddled together in the way of travellers, the dog made confident enough to lie beside them, its fear of Loys overcome by the promise of warmth.

She dreamed that she was in another place, lying with her arms around Loys, a very strange place near blue water, the sun strong in the sky. The warmth made her happy but she shivered herself awake with the dawn, to find Loys shaking too. The hunger had receded now, though her throat was raw from the wind.

'You need clothing,' she said.

'No. Not yet. Pain is man's burden. I will be a man, not an animal.'

They walked on for a long time, though she couldn't say if it was morning or afternoon when Loys sank to his knees.

'It's gone,' he said. 'The wolf is gone, for now. It's asleep.'

'We're out of danger?'

'I can't lead any more. My senses are muted.'

'Then what?'

'We have to wait for the fog to lift.'

'We could die here,' said Gylfa.

'I think so,' said Loys. 'Perhaps the story is broken beyond repair. Perhaps this is as much as there is.'

'Then you've led us here for no reason.'

The hound stabbed out its short bay, its black body sliding into the fog like an eel into water.

After a while they heard it barking and something else – a distant word.

'Steady!'

'People?' said Gylfa. 'What language?'

'English,' said Tola. 'Our people.'

'I am Norse, he is Norman and you are English. We can be certain of finding friends and enemies in anyone we meet.'

'Come on,' said Loys. His jaw chattered as he spoke.

They trod carefully up the hill. After thirty or forty paces, they smelled the fire, a tinge on the fog. Still the dog barked. Tola felt its excitement in its voice. Someone else was there too – a man, pleased to see the creature. She felt the man's long pain and the relief to see the dog. It was more than the end to loneliness, to him the presence of the dog was the kindling of hope. Then came fear.

They heard him stamping down the fire, the sound carrying on the sodden air. Loys held up his hand and gestured to Gylfa.

'Me? You are the great warrior.'

'Go,' said Loys. 'If it's trouble, come running. I can't risk a fight. It will wake the wolf. You go. Go!'

Gylfa nodded and stepped forward into the fog like a man unsure if his next step would send him hurtling from the mountain.

Loys shivered deeply and Tola went to him, wrapped her cloak around him and hugged him.

'Can you die?' she said.

'I think so.'

She felt his body trembling.

'Help! Help!'

An angry voice screamed out in English. 'You'll keep away. Keep away or die!'

'If I draw blood ...' said Loys.

'I will try.'

'Friend. We are friends!' she shouted.

'No friends of mine!'

'We mean no harm, we're looking only for shelter.'

'There's none here!'

'He's a liar, there's a great cave!' came Gylfa's voice. 'Come on!'

The hound barked and she heard a skittering of stones. Gylfa was going into the cave.

She felt his excitement, the man in the cave's fear. More than fear. Shame too.

She scrambled up through the fog, guided by the barking of the hound, Loys beside her.

A waft of hot air came from the cave, like a rancid breath, a dirty, fetid air but sweetened by the smell of a heather fire.

A loud sobbing came from inside.

'What is this?' Gylfa's voice.

'Do not judge me,' said the man. 'We were facing starvation.'

Tola scrambled down the scree slope and into the cave. Its mouth breathed with warmth, hot and fetid as a dog's.

248

Loys came down too. A fire was within. And carnage.

Gylfa was already by the fire, kneeling to warm himself, his head bowed to avoid the sight of the bodies.

There were three of them – one larger, two smaller. The smaller figures had their faces turned to the floor. The larger figure had been stripped for meat. It had the flesh cut away at its arm. The pot on the floor bore a hand, the flesh boiled and picked at.

'We were left here too long,' said the man. She recognised him from her first visit to the cave. He was no thinner. 'They said they'd come back. There's no food in the land. There was no choice.'

'All of them?' said Gylfa.

'Could you eat a mother in front of her children? Or children in front of their mother? I killed them in their sleep, they never knew.' He gestured to the bodies. Even in death, he had turned the children's eyes away.

'Tender feelings,' said Gylfa.

'So you'll be wanting none of the meat?'

Tola shook her head.

'We should bury them,' she said. 'It's the Christian way'.

'I don't think I could stomach it,' said Gylfa.

'Of course you could. You can eat a pig, a horse, a dog or a rat. Why not a man?'

'I am hungry,' said Gylfa.

'I would rather starve,' said Tola.

'Good. More for me. There's a deal of meat left on even them that have died of hunger,' said the man.

'Loys. Speak to them!' said Tola.

There was no reply. Loys was gone.

Tola walked outside the cave. The light was dying and Loys was crouching on the grass, his head in his hand.

'There are clothes for you inside,' she said.

'I am cold.'

'Then come in. There is a fire. I will take the bodies outside if you can't face it.'

'It's good to be cold,' he said. 'The wolf is never cold.'

The moon lit the low fog and she looked down the long granite scar of the hillside, disappearing into murk. The heather tufted from the snow, like ash. It was as if all the world was burning and this was the only place left.

'Why did you come here?'

'Looking for you,' said Loys.

'To die?'

'Yes.'

'You would have thought it would be easy here. Everything I have is gone. Everyone is dead. Will you come back inside the cave? I will move the bodies.'

'I cannot face them.'

'They are a horror to you, after all you have seen in the dales?'

'I am a horror to me.'

'You are the only thing I am not afraid of,' she said. 'Though my body trembles when I see you, though my legs want to run, I am not afraid inside.' She was surprised at herself for the question that came to her. 'What do you hope for?'

He looked puzzled. 'Hope seems a strange word for it. I don't know. I aim for death. Do I hope for it? I don't know. And you?'

'Not this,' she said. 'Anything but this. I could have fallen into Hell. I wonder if I was killed with Hals on that hill and it is part of my torment not to know it is torment, to think I can escape, to hope for better things. We cannot go back to what was. What will I do when I have helped you fulfil your purpose?'

'I don't know.'

She studied his face, the wolf's eyes, the skin smooth and young, his naked body pale against the snow.

'Not without the stone. The smell torments me, even here. I must remain on the hill until you move on.'

'Let me fetch you clothes.'

'I need the cold.'

'And the clothes. They will offer little protection but if you look like a man, you might begin to think as a man.'

She slid down the slope to the cave. Gylfa smiled at her through the firelight, his mouth greasy.

She only took what clothes remained – a big pair of hose, a shirt and a tunic. She tore the woman's dress to make a cloak. The corpses did not bother her. How quickly, she thought, we can bear things, how quickly a dead child looks no more horrifying than a slaughtered pig.

She brought the clothes back out to Loys.

'Put them on.'

'They smell of meat.'

'We all smell of meat. You too, very likely.'

He climbed into the hose, then the shirt and the tunic. Finally she gave him a blanket. He looked like any other refugee from the Normans, dressed in scavenged or torn things, things made to serve the wrong purpose. She was the same in her huge cloak, her man's breeches. It was as if a flood had swept through their lives, jumbling and overturning everything and, when it had receded, the detritus had clung to the living like weed to rocks.

A horse breathed down in the valley. Then many others, as if it was a speaker and the other horses were murmuring their agreement with his words. A dog barked as if in disagreement, throwing great scoops of sound through the dead air.

'We need to move,' said Tola. 'They'll find the cave if they have dogs.

'They'll find us anyway if they've got a dog. Fetch me my sword,' said Loys. 'I'll try to use that. The rest of you, run!'

37 Run to Earth

Who do you pray to? To the gods you have seen and who you know hate you? To the god you have never seen who says he loves you? Loys did not pray, nor even cross himself. It was hard to be a god, or a devil, and to have no one to call to for help beyond himself.

Tola and Gylfa scrambled up the hillside, away from the main track, the man they had found in the cave huffing behind them.

The world around him seemed to sizzle with the scent of excitement, men, dog, horses, as the hound gave voice and bayed towards them.

He heard the girl's voice. 'Come on!' and sensed its panic. Her breath was loud to him, like an answer to the hound's questing sniffs. The dog said, 'Where are you?' She said, 'Here', with every breath.

He weighed the sword in his hand. The dog would have to die, it made tracking them too easy. The animal broke from the mist at about twenty paces and Loys was disappointed to see that it wasn't some fierce fighter but a flop-eared thing, low to the ground, its face expectant as if he was going to give it a morsel of meat.

He edged towards it, not raising the sword, only cooing to it. Grey and green spun before his eyes, the smell of blood was in his nose and his ears rang. He was on the wet ground, his senses clearing enough to know he had been struck by a charging horse. The smell of its sweat and the wet leather of a strap or saddle clung to him, gave a flavour to his pain.

Four more riders came bursting from the mist, hooves trailing spumes of bitter soil, the dark smell of the animal bodies filling his mind.

'Up there! Up there!'

The Normans were pointing to where Tola and her companions were making a run for it.

'Where?'

Tola shouted out. 'My ankle!'

Loys stood, the ground like the deck of a storm-tossed ship to him. A horseman rounded on him, levelled his lance. Loys's head was not clear, his nose was full of blood. The deathbeat of the hooves commanded his legs to run, the point of the lance bobbed like a distant seal's head on a field of grey. He stepped under it and swung his sword hard. Another thump and he flew backwards – the horse had struck him again, his body humming like a door struck by a ram.

The horse wheeled and spun. It was as if the rider was turning tricks in a square for the amusement of a crowd, nearly falling off, throwing his legs high to cast them back and fall slumped onto the saddle. The horse screamed and collapsed. He had put an ugly wound into its head.

Loys thought he had broken his collarbone – the pain was awful sharp there – but he had no time to think of it. Age did not wither him, he could take ten times the shock of an ordinary man, but he suspected he was far from unkillable.

Another charge might put him down so hard he could not get up. What then? Rebirth, finding himself anew, misery and death forever. The sword was gone, knocked from his hand.

Tola had gone up the hill, so he needed to lead the men down where their horses could not go. He scrambled down the scree to the mouth of the cave. More riders now, nine or ten of them. He ran inside, ducking under the low ceiling until it opened out into the higher cavern.

'Halloos' and 'hoys!' Some speech in bad English.

'Where?'

'Up!'

He recognised the tone of voice. It was the man who had taken the stone.

A spear poked through the cave opening.

'This is a rebel dwelling!' said a Norman. 'It's warm in there!'

'Whoever goes through will be risking a royal clout on the head,' said another voice.

'So how are we going to get him out? The boss won't be happy now we've had sight of him if we don't come back with him.'

'Five at a time,' said the first voice. 'He can't do for us all, and if we go in spear-first we can drive him back. I don't think he's armed anyway.'

'As good as any plan.'

Loys did not want to risk killing now. Already the wolf seemed bright-eyed inside him and the only blood he'd smelled was his own. He couldn't stay in the cave either.

The dead here, stripped like so many pig carcasses, were too much of an incitement.

He sniffed. Water and the smell of the deep earth below the aroma of human butchery. There might be a hiding place there at least, where he with his sensitive ears and nose could find his way more easily than the Normans, staggering on in darkness or by the uncertain light of a torch.

He went past the small fire and down into the shadows at the back of the cave. He sensed an exit, a colder area among the fire-warmed stone.

'Here we go then!'

Clattering from the entrance as the Normans rolled into the cave with screams and curses.

Then: 'My God, these people are savages, look what's happened here!'

'Where is he?'

'In there. He certainly didn't come out.'

'God, I'm going to retch. That's a thumb joint in that bowl.'

'I'd rather starve! Do you think he's been up to this? Let's find him!'

Loys crawled into the deeper darkness. No sword now, only the animal weapons to defend him. He hoped he wouldn't need them.

254

Through the rock of the cave ceiling, through the soil and grass that covered them, he heard the call. The long rune was howling. Tola was in danger. If she died all his plans, and her chance of peace, were gone.

He needed to get to her but he couldn't risk the wolf emerging. His instinct told him to go down into the dark, so he did, slithering on his belly into the sightless blackness. One of the Normans brought a burning ember from the fire nearby but the light was not enough to see by.

'Can we find him?'

'No. Wait until he comes out.'

'That could be forever.'

'Now there's an idea.'

Loys heard them rolling the rock into the mouth of the cave. It took a lot of them to get it there by the sound of it. Should he attack? No. He'd have enough strength left from his partial transformation to shift it when they were gone. He hoped.

38 A Prisoner

The excitement of the riders was all about her, buzzing like a swarm of wasps. The Normans had to go the long way around the hill as their horses wouldn't climb the steep rocky section above the cave.

'What shall we do?' said Gylfa.

'We're going to have to fight them,' said the bandit. They had not asked his name and he had not offered it.

'With what?'

'You have a sword. I have a knife. He has a knife,' said Tola.

'They're mounted horsemen, veterans of battle, we can't face them!'

'We have to. If you don't want to use the sword, give it to me!'

'Here!'

Gylfa passed her his sword. It felt too heavy, too unwieldy in her hand. Her people had been poor and the only time she had seen a sword before was worn by a Norman.

'I'm going to offer myself as a slave,' he said.

'A lot of good that did my countrymen,' said Tola.

'Give me the sword,' said the man from the cave.

She passed it to him.

'Now let's see if they catch me!' he said. 'The enemy never looks where he's been.'

He bounded down the hill, on the edge of falling all the way.

At the bottom he rolled onto the valley floor, turned and gave them a wave of 'goodbye'. He looked over his shoulder. He'd heard something. Hooves. The warhorse hit him hard, the rider not even bothering to use his lance, the man completely surprised as the Norman emerged from the mist.

The sword flew from his hand. To Tola he seemed to strike the ground in little slices of movement. First the horse struck, then his head snapped back, his left arm not registering the attack and appearing to continue to wave and he slammed into the earth. As the rider turned to face her through the mist, it seemed that all the little slices of the bandit's death were pressed together and he had died in an instant in a jumble of limbs, human and horse.

She screamed, against herself, and the rider pointed at her with the spear and ran his horse around the path. Men were dropping down the slope from above her now. Gylfa curled up into a ball; she waved her knife but a Norman warrior was on her, smashing her in the belly with the butt of his spear, sending her sprawling down the hillside.

She lost her knife, she lost her bearings. She stood, finally knowing up from down. A white light exploded above her eye. She'd been punched and she fell to her knees. The Normans were barking at her in their strange language. One of them hit her again but she was beyond pain. A warrior had her by the hair, dragged her up the slope.

She tried to kick at him but all the strength had gone from her legs, and she only stumbled, screaming as she was dragged to her feet by her hair.

There were three horsemen, all dismounted, at the top – another two who had pursued her down the slope.

One drew his sword but the other one cupped his balls. 'Too cold,' another seemed to say. None of them were serious about raping her just then, she felt the ice in their joints, their soaking feet, the chafing of the coats at their necks. No, they wouldn't rape her right then. They'd wait until they had a fire and some food so their cocks weren't shrunk to nothing by the cold.

They tied her hands and then lashed the rope to a horse. A Norman came up close to her, his nose almost touching hers.

'Our. Friend. Dead. You.' He drew his finger across his throat. 'Souffrir, souffrir.'

Another horse came clopping up, ridden by a very young warrior. Behind it, led by a rope binding his hands, was someone she recognised. Ithamar! His wolf pelt was gone but she would know him anywhere.

One of the Normans said something to him in slow English. 'Woman? Right woman?'

'Yes,' he said. 'She's a sorceress. You will be able to make her bring you many blessings. You will ...'

He didn't finish his sentence. The Norman put his spear through Ithamar's chest. The hedge sorcerer looked down at it as if it was a strange butterfly that had landed there and he couldn't make out its sort.

'Sorry,' he said to Tola. He slumped down onto the cold ground. As she was dragged away she saw the wolfstone at his neck.

39   A Wolf's Larder

The rock would not budge. Unfed, the wolf inside Loys had all but closed its eyes. His senses were duller, the smell of the cave rank to him, not enticing or intriguing, though his eyes were still keen and his ears sharp. He had no desire to sniff around for the bodies, to push them with his nose, to turn them to expose the uneaten meat of the belly, the hock of the shoulder.

The little fire had died now and he was glad of it. His eyes ran from the remaining smoke but he knew that if he waited it would go. He lay on the cave floor for a long time until the smell of the dead fire numbed his senses. Eventually it became easier to breathe.

He felt his way across the floor, the only illumination from the nimbus of light around the rock that sealed him in.

Was there another way out? Perhaps but, the wolf sleeping inside him, he would have no chance of finding it in the darkness.

The faint sounds of battle came from outside and he renewed his assault on the rock. It would not budge. He sank down and turned his back against the rock, feeling its coolness against his skin.

In the realm of the gods he had freed a wolf from its bondage and the wolf had attacked the gods. Was this their way of repaying him? No. He breathed in the thick air. Odin was dead. But could death die? Or were the Fates willing him to be the wolf, no matter how he struggled?

He remembered the three women, the Norns, who spin the fate of all men, sitting spinning by the waters of the world well. He had thought he could break free of them but it would not be easy. When he had met the bright god Loki by the

259

waters the god had called himself an enemy of death but he had only been playing a part in a story spoken years before by the women of the well. Loys was not an enemy of death. He was an enemy of destiny but here he was ensnared in its weft of flesh and bone, of torn bodies and dead eyes. To free the man, he must free the wolf.

He heard the keening of the wolf rune above him, a long cry of distress. They had caught her and, if they killed her, destiny had won the battle, a battle whose only aim was continuing the war, to trap him in a story without end, without meaning.

He sniffed at the torn corpses. They were not repulsive to him but neither did they draw the slaver from his mouth, the beast from inside him. The rune called again, a lonely note of distress.

He approached the slaughter trove. He could make out little more than the hunched shapes of the bodies in that darkness.

'You must eat!' His mother's voice. 'You need to be strong for your labours!'

'Eat!' his fellow monks had urged him. 'Think of the poor who would gladly have your bowl. Think of me, who would gladly have it if you don't want it. Eat'.

He remembered other times, other lives. He was a monk in a wood, tortured, bound by infirmity, forced to swallow the blood-slick liver of a friend. He was a man in a dungeon, beyond starving. He sensed his previous lives dimly, or the lives that had mingled with his under the eye of the wolf. He knew he had never done what he was about to do by choice, only coercion.

He picked up a hand. It was small and delicate. The loss of a child, a terrible and regular occurrence in the cycle of human misery. There was no horror for him in the cold of the arm, the skin beneath his teeth, the blood, fragrant as any bloom, in his nose, in his mouth. It was just food. And that was the horror. All those memories, all that joy, reduced to this, the tug of the skin against his teeth, the slip of his teeth against bone as they pared the flesh away. Horror was the years, lived and unlived, the fleeting connections, the loving and losing. None of that in meat.

He fed and the wolf's eyes opened inside him. Immediately the cavern was lighter, his senses sharp and clear, his rational mind, with its questions and decisions, a little duller. There was meat, there were enemies. First the meat, then the enemies.

He had hoped to eat a little, to allow the wolf to rise in him enough to suit his human purposes. The wolfish appetite had been pricked, the blood stink in its nostrils. It did not nibble like a lady at dinner, it gorged and tore until it was glutted.

As he ate, he spoke to himself. 'I am Loys, a monk of Normandy. I broke my vows and ran away to the east with the duke's daughter and there God punished me for loving. I travelled to forbidden places and released the wolf that killed the gods. I am a man. I am Loys and I am a man, beloved of Beatrice, who gave her life to save me, who I would follow into death.'

Gristle, blood, bone. A cold feeling swept over him, like entering a frosty morning from a muggy house, beautiful and clean. He said some other words but they were just leaves falling in the forest, losing all definition as they covered the ground. 'What am I? I am Loys. What was I? I was Loys. I was Azemar, friend of Loys, forced to help his would-be assassins, the wolf's eye was on me and I didn't know it until the dungeons of Constantinople awakened my appetites. I am a wolf against the moon. I am a brother, two brothers. I am several, many. I am born to tear the gods but there are no gods to tear.'

He swallowed, the taste metal, lovely. He laughed. Familiar things became unfamiliar. The dark was nothing to his eyes now and he spent a long time looking at a cooking pot, unable to determine whether you ate from it, pissed in it or wore it as a hat. It contained things. Meat. He contained things. Meat. He giggled and licked a dribble of blood snot from his lips.

There had been a point to all this eating but he couldn't remember what it was. He had to save the woman. He couldn't remember why but it felt important. He certainly mustn't eat her. He should get out, he remembered that. But why? This place was warm, there was food. It was only when thirst gripped his throat that it seemed more desirable to leave than to stay. He would go, but for a little while, and to find water. Then he would return to his cave, the warmth and the meat-hoard.

The rim of the boulder blocking the entrance had lit and dimmed three times when he thought to move.

His nose was enough to tell him where the boulder was, the cold, wet air behind it. He put his hands to the rock and shoved. The boulder rocked slightly.

He shoved again and the top of the rock moved back to show a glimpse of the star-full sky. On his third push it turned to the side and he slipped through. The fog had gone and he was in a shining country of bright stars, a bloated moon, the grass sparkling in the wet light.

The smell of corpses was all about him, calling to him. He needed water but first he saw the body of someone he recognised. He did not know how he recognised him or where from but his smell, his proportions, were familiar. Loys sucked moisture from the wet grass.

He knelt to the body and tore at the skin of its face with his nails. His fingers were changing. They were longer, thicker, and the nails were thick and black. 'This country's good,' he said out loud and surprised himself with his voice. It was deep and rough, the words coming out as if through a grindstone.

He ate again, lay lapping at the grass and ate more. He was strong and swift but he had no urge to go anywhere. Why would he when the land was so bountiful?

He sprang up the bank above the cave. More bodies lay there, one a man who smelled of wolf. About his neck was a stone. Now he really did recognise that. What was it for? Not for eating. Then for what? He couldn't recall. It didn't matter. He pulled the body down the hill and shoved it into the cave along with the one he'd begun eating.

What a winter he would have here, the meat rotting into glory, the cave entrance sealed against wind and frost!

He sniffed the wind. There were others around, hostile men, he smelled their nerves and their aggression on the breeze. Would they find his den? He needed to scout them, to keep an eye on them and even kill them if necessary. This was his territory now and he would not have interlopers.

Another howl split the night of his mind and he saw a rune, writhing and turning as if in the air in front of him. The sound ensnared him, enchanted him. He had to go to it. He set off at a lope across the high fell, towards the sound of the rune, the smell of warriors and of horses.

40 At Rest

Freydis held Styliane in her arms. The fire crackled and spat in front of her, tucked into the little lea of the hill. Its colours were intense, glossy, more like the gems of the great church Hagia Sofia than ordinary flames. The runes were opening ways of seeing to her. She had wanted to use them to bring warmth to Styliane but the lady would not allow it.

It was days now since they had slipped out of York on a stolen horse using the noisy exit of Gylfa with the Normans as cover. They had run north. Styliane, when she had recovered from her faint, said they had an appointment with fate. They would look to keep it when free of immediate danger. That time appeared to have come.

'The more you use them, the more you grow used to them, the more they grow in you. You haven't my training, you haven't made my sacrifices to be able to control them. If you wish to relinquish them to me then you must not think of them. Send them to the dark of your mind.'

Freydis poked the fire. It was as big as she dare make it. The fog had come down, which gave them cover, but she knew the weather could change in an instant here, the wind spring up and leave them exposed to whatever eyes were abroad in that country.

'You took something from the well. Even when you were half dead you gripped it in your hand.'

Styliane reached inside her cloak and produced a stone, as big as an eye, the colour of old blood but with a deep sparkle to it.

'What is it?'

'A rune.'

'Then use it to warm us.'

'It is not that sort of rune.'

'What, then?'

'It is a tangle all of itself and a tangling thing. The god gave it to me.'

Freydis had seen so many wonders this almost struck her as normal. 'Well, we cannot fail with gods on our side,' she said. The horse breathed. It, at least, had eaten. Water was no problem, they had too much of it – dripping from every rock, soaking the grass, trickling beneath the ice of frozen streams.

'How shall we know where to go if I don't use the runes?'

'Think where fear is,' said Styliane. 'We'll go there.'

'It seems more difficult to go north. The hills seem steeper this way than any other, my feet heavier.'

'Are you afraid of the north?'

'I'm afraid of failing in my duty to you.'

'You will not fail, Freydis.'

'Must I die for you to return your runes?'

'I don't know. I lost the runes and I am still alive. Though now I will die. So yes, one way or another, soon or in many years, you must die. Without the runes you will age.'

'If I die with a sword in my hand I'll go to the halls of Freya to feast and battle eternally for that great lady.'

'You will be her best servant.'

'She will not be the best mistress. I have her here beside me.'

'You give me comfort,' said Styliane. 'As fierce as any man but not wanting to be small like a man. Do the runes let you see how the warriors try to reduce themselves, narrow themselves, so they are a simple thing – a man that carries an axe is fearless and well-loved by his kin? The scholars and priests of Constantinople are no better.'

'Women are freer,' said Freydis. 'Our lives may be bound by convention and rule but with each other we are free to be many things. A man tries to be few, to show himself a simple thing of honesty, wit and violence, though there are men who are gentle or thoughtful, who temper strength with humility.'

'Though few,' said Styliane. 'The world does not reward such as they.'

'Is the Norman like that? Loys?'

'No. He is one thing trying to be many. Or trying to be nothing. He was undone by love and he lies like a warrior stricken in battle, his guts spilled, waiting for friend or foe to come and finish him. But no one will finish him. He must do that himself. And we must stop him. He must live because, if he dies, dies properly, then the story is over.'

'What story?'

'The one that is telling you, telling me.'

'I don't understand you, lady.'

'You are a warrior, Freydis, you don't have to understand, only to do.'

'I am glad of that.'

They lay in each other's warmth until morning. The fog was lighter but not light. Spectres of hills loomed in front of them, bushes appearing like ghosts to sink again into the engulfing mist.

'I feel dread here,' said Freydis. 'I don't want to go on.' The horse stood and stamped and Freydis, walking beside it, stroked its nose.

'Then it's the way,' said Styliane. 'The scholar is the point around which everything must happen. If we find him, destiny will play out.'

'And what if your destiny is to die?'

'The story is shattered. Its ending can be rewritten. I am sure.'

'My people believe that our destinies are unchangeable.'

'And it suits a warrior to believe that – it gives courage. If it is your day to die, it's your day to die. How can you be scared of what you cannot change? But destinies can be changed. We faced the gods at the world well in Constantinople. I gave a brother. The wolf gave a wife. Our destinies changed.'

'How do you know?'

Styliane smiled.

'I don't. But I can't imagine a girl born in a slum outside the walls of the world city was destined to become an immortal.'

'Is what you believe and what you don't believe all there is to the world, lady?'

'I have travelled difficult roads to be where I am. I have seen death himself at the well. I have seen the women who spin the fates of all men, of you and me. I don't know the truth, Freydis. Sorcerers imagine they can gain true knowledge gazing into their fires, chanting their rituals. Perhaps there isn't a truth. There are just stories, told by the gods, and those of us who dare may take over the tale ourselves.'

'You are a brave woman.'

'I am a coward but I fight what I am afraid of.'

Freydis heard that voice in the hills, the long, cold stream of sound, the howl of the wolf. She shivered.

'What?' said Styliane.

'You didn't hear the wolf?'

'No.'

'Then it's him. Follow.'

Freydis kept the runes deep within her, so her feet froze and her cloak felt heavy.

In a dry valley she heard the damp footfall of many horses.

'Normans?'

'It must be. Be still.'

They waited, their own horse's breath sounding like a bellows, so loud it seemed. The horses passed by in the fog, their steps muted in the heavy air.

'We are hunted?'

'Everything is hunted here,' said Styliane. 'It's just a matter of whether we are their main quarry or simply sparrows who get trapped in the game-bird nets.'

Freydis began to feel very afraid, far worse than she had when she had found Loys the first time. This was the child's fear of the dark mere, of the depths of the woods that are black and cool even in the heat of summer, of the noise in the night when she knew her father was away raiding but the stories of creeping monsters and foul fen hags he had told her still whispered in her mind.

She thought nothing of it. Fear was a fact for a warrior, like rain and lice. It didn't stop the war, only made it uncomfortable.

When the fog was very thick they sat but as soon as they could see a few steps ahead they walked on. The horse breathed heavily, though Styliane was the lightest passenger it could hope for. It was hard to stop – nowhere dry to sit until the fire was built with curses and impatience, the collection of wood difficult, the taking of the flame harder.

They found tracks after a day or so – a great body of horses, dogs with them. They followed them a while until they reached a valley that split both ways. The horses went north, the main valley east.

'Can you find the wolf?' said Styliane.

'He is north. We're going the right way.'

'How can you tell?'

'The fear deepens with every step.'

'Good. Then step on.'

41 A Promise Of Magic

The rope on the horse jerked Tola along. The fog had lifted and the Normans' progress had become quicker.

Only her ankle slowed them. At first they tried beating her to make her move quicker but, when that proved of no use, they had to put her on a horse. It was almost worse than walking, the jolting, bumping trot, her hands tied, trying to keep herself on the high saddle.

The men had not yet bothered her, though they talked often of raping her. She didn't need to speak Norman to know what they were talking about. Their eyes lingered on her, they made gestures with their tongues and grabbed at their crotches. But this was only a ritual, to convince themselves that everything was normal, that the old certainties of domination – of the sword and of the cock – still held. They were afraid and would not touch her. She sensed an old fear in them, of the pooling dark of the woods, of moors and wild places, of things glimpsed between dreaming and waking.

They thought she was a witch, just as Styliane had thought she was, and Loys. The mad thought came that it was all for her – the burning, the murders, the destruction of everything she had valued. Perhaps God was doing it to spite her for not finding a way to damp down the magic inside her; the sensitivity that, with a moment's concentration, could feel the fear of a child in the next valley, the useless love of its father called to defend it against such numbers.

Cursed of God. She didn't understand the words of the Norman jabbing his finger at her but she understood the sentiment as clearly as if she had been raised in his alien land over the sea.

They took her down through the dales, the way she had

come. Her shoes were falling to bits, her feet swollen with cold and wet, the rope was scraping the skin of her hands raw, the sweat clammed her clothes to her skin.

The day was clear and bright, a good work day her mother would have called it – chilly but sunny, cooling to the labouring woman, cold to the idle.

The Normans were a band of five and afraid. There was movement in the hills, lines of men seen at a distance, watching them for a while before disappearing into the landscape. Her people, mustering resistance.

Maybe one of the lords of the north had finally come down to face the invader. Morcar? Was he dead? She'd heard it said.

She felt other forces, the giddying, ecstatic hum of the runes. Where? Somewhere up on the hill, watching her.

At camp at night she thought she saw the runes dancing in the heather fire, or sliding through the darkness. Styliane? She would not go back to be sacrificed.

She tried to alert the Normans. They doubted her, though, and one slapped her. They thought she was trying to get them caught.

The fog returned the next day, though it was less heavy. The Normans set off early but by mid-morning were arguing with each other. They had taken the wrong path, it seemed, and tried to retrace their steps. In the distance there were noises, chiming, a sound like a breath but not a breath, something that made her think of the sea she had never seen – a wide, grey thing, flat like a pond but many times bigger.

A big Norman pulled her off her horse and held up a knife. He was saying something but she didn't know what. 'Stop' maybe. He wanted her to stop.

'These things aren't from me,' she said.

From a long way away she heard a coil of sound unravelling – a howl in the hills. The Normans heard it too. This was not the sound she had heard in her mind but something real. The horses shivered. A slight man came to his bigger friend's side, put his hand onto his dagger arm.

'Leave it,' he seemed to say.

They shoved her back up onto her horse and went on. Another argument broke out. Two men pointed back down the valley, three of them up. The fog was thickening now.

Something went running past them, a dark body briefly visible, then lost to the fog. A soldier hacked after it with his sword but hit only the vapours of the air.

The howl came again, from behind. The Normans crossed themselves and took to their horses. Tola too crossed herself and a soldier shook his head in disbelief at her piety.

They spurred on, up a steep slope.

The mist shifted and swirled about them. She could see shapes in it now, shadows and things more substantial than shadows. Something loomed from the fog in the distance, upright, like a man. A Norman dismounted and fitted an arrow to his bow. It took him three shots to hit it. The arrow clattered against it.

'A stone,' said Tola.

'Eh?'

The bowman advanced through the fog, his bow drawn. Then he laughed and shouted back to the others. They advanced and she saw that it was the remains of a gate.

Another shape in the mist. A voice and the Normans gave shouts and waved. Horses appeared through the murk. More Normans – many more, twenty, thirty, more behind.

They rode forward to greet them with cries of exultation.

A great rich Norman rode up to her. He wore a broad, victor's smile and when he spoke he spoke slowly.

'This is hill,' he said. 'I have magic in here.' He beat his breast. 'At the water. Ice entered me. You make it work.'

She sensed his discomfort, the shiver within him he tried to hide from his men.

'We must go to Blackbed Scar,' she said.

42   A Leader of Men

Gylfa had run, the great boots slapping on his shins as he did. Behind him the sounds of a fight. They'd grabbed the girl, he thought, and were screaming at her, probably for the deaths Loys had caused. Their brothers.

Out of the presence of the wolf the runes returned, but he feared to look at them. He stumbled and fell. The fog was tight about him and he couldn't be sure that, if he ran too hard, he might not fall from a cliff or blunder into some sinking bog.

He lay still for a long time, his ears straining for sounds of movement, movement towards him in particular. That hound was still baying but he heard the hooves of the horses receding. They'd given up on him but he was not yet sure enough to stand.

He respected the god's warning against using the runes but, like a messenger charged with delivering an interesting parcel, couldn't help prodding and feeling at them with his mind. They sickened him. In the well they had chimed and rustled. Here they brayed, frustrated, like a horse left too long in its stable; grated like a swollen gate on rough stone, breathed fever-bed breaths. Their restlessness made his flesh crawl and he longed to be anywhere but that hillside.

He vomited, whether from the foul flesh he'd eaten, the magic inside him, from fear or relief, he didn't know. What now? Which way safety? He waited a day, the aching light of the dawn rune keeping him warm, keeping him ill. After two days he heard something at the entrance of the cave, a great crash like the fall of rock and he saw Loys scampering away. He thought to call after him but there was something in the way the lord now moved, low, very quickly but with an uneven lope, that chilled Gylfa. He was afraid of everyone, everything, and he cursed his fear. But plenty of brave men had died. He was still alive.

He risked getting up onto his knees. He could see no one around. Mist clung to the hill but down in the valley he saw no riders. He made his way down to the slope above the cave.

Night was falling and he doubted the Normans or Loys would return. The wind was rising, and with it a little hail, countless little spears blowing in from the North. He felt cold and, if he thought of the day rune to warm himself, nausea rose up within him.

He dropped down to the mouth of the cave. A big rock had been rolled away at the entrance. That puzzled him and he sat a long time thinking about it. Eventually, he went within. In the dim light he could see bodies, new bodies. A chance for loot, perhaps? He'd need what he could to bargain his way out of this desolation – to go where, he couldn't think.

He moved in. Here was the body of a man. He wore nothing but the wolf pelt still tied around him but, at his chest, the stone! How odd. He examined the man carefully. He was not Loys, for sure. Gylfa untied the thong that held the stone and lifted it up. A wolf's head, crudely etched. He tied it around his neck, pressed it to his skin as he had seen Loys do. Immediately the runes were quiet inside him, the dissonant, sick-making whirl of their orbit over.

So that was the secret of the stone. It damped down magic. Would it damp the curse that had been set inside him? It seemed so.

He felt much better but now he also felt cold. He took the wolf pelt and tied it around his head. He would stay in the cave – there was even a flint and steel with enough dry heather to make a decent fire.

The bodies bothered him. To put them outside was to invite attention but to stay with them was to go mad. The fatty taste of the cooked limbs was still on his lips, its smell like a floating headache in the cave. They had to go.

He dragged them outside and hid them as best he could. He

273

couldn't look at the children or the mother. The other dead didn't bother him so much.

He sat weeping for a while in the cave. By taking on the runes, by eating the flesh, he felt he had crossed a threshold but now he wanted to go back through it, to be what he had been before the madness at the well and the abomination in that cave. He had heard that men got used to slaughter and butchery but he knew he would not. He was a gentle man at heart, who wanted to be left with his goats and his sheep. By Odin's arsehole, he could hardly even bear to kill *them*.

The night was as cosy as any he'd had so far — there were blankets, a little lousy, and there was warmth from a fire and the pelt of the wolf. He laughed to think of himself so rich, in his stolen finery. He could go back now, to Norway, claim great deeds, be loved. The curved sword was on the floor of the cave. He took it out and studied the blade. He had never seen anything so fine nor handled anything so sharp. He ran his finger gently across the blade and he knew it would only take the slightest sideways movement to cut him.

'The needful weapon.' Hmmm. What did that mean?

The thought of the god at the well was like a weight in his head; his right eye felt heavy and sore, like he had slept too long in a draught. The God had tricked him, but what had he expected from Loki, the lie smith? He couldn't believe the god really meant him harm. He would be dead if he did. He dozed and was drowning in the well, waking to grip at the floor of the cave, as if he might float away if he did not.

Often he imagined he heard voices outside and pressed himself down into the shadows at the cave's rear. He let the fire die, choosing to be cold rather than discovered.

The morning dawned with a wet mizzle, fine rain like a shimmering net at the cave's mouth. He went out to see what might be there. Nothing. No one. So what now? He would need to eat but he could not go back to the bodies. He had sickened himself.

He knew he was taking a risk in the cave but life had become

274

one long enormous risk. It was a case of deciding where to take the risk, in a cave or the hills. He came to the conclusion that the only thing in his control was the temperature, so he stayed in the cave.

Nightmares bothered him, but less than his dreams. Gylfa had never thought of the future with anything but dread before. His happiest time had been as a young child, before his uselessness with spear and shield had become apparent, before the embarrassment of races with his cousins, before the whale had landed and he had been sick at its butchery. Life was a hill, he had concluded, and he was slipping ever down it, his only hope to hold on to the latest position of misery before sliding to the worse one below.

Now, though, the runes – however sick they made him, however frightening they were – offered him the chance to climb back up a little. He had met the gods, met a great hero who could best ten men on his own. They were adventures worthy of a saga. He should do something, he was sure. Heroes did things, killed dragons, confronted their enemies, rescued their friends.

Here, though, there was no clear course of action. Everything was an enemy. He wondered if the heroes of the sagas ever found themselves in such a position, becalmed in dangerous waters, no idea how to proceed.

'Carry the runes,' he'd been told. Where to? And why? To become a god. Gylfa imagined himself, one-eyed like Odin, sitting at a fire in the company of warriors spinning tales of his battle prowess. Yes, in such company he would be a god.

His third day in the cave, he heard voices outside. One word in English.

'Butchers.'

He lay still. A sudden rush and five men came rolling in through the cave's low entrance, axes and knives drawn.

Another word in English.

'Nothing.' Then: 'Hey!'

They had seen him so there was nothing to do but stand.

Five men – English, two freemen and their slaves by their clothes, though the difference between master and servant had been eroded by filth, weather and wear.

'You are the wolf sorcerer?'

Gylfa trembled. He could not make himself speak. It was as if a glamour was upon him and movement or reply was impossible. It was fear and he did not know how to fight it.

One of the men sank to his knees.

'We've been sent to find you. Lord Morcar is waiting. Do you have the sorceress? Will she help us?'

Gylfa unpeeled his tongue from the roof of his mouth.

'The Normans have her. We were surprised here.'

'You are not a man of Yorkshire.'

'I speak to the Danish gods of our fathers and they through me,' said Gylfa.

'You could not defend her?'

'They had horses and ran. You see the slaughter they caused and how I repaid them.'

All the men now dropped to one knee.

'You are a mighty man, strong and full of knowledge. Can we find the Normans? We have a great force mustering in the north under Morcar. We could yet take them if we reach them before York. They can't have gone far in the weather.'

'How did you get here?'

'To make our meeting with you, we would have travelled across Hell itself. This is Cedric, he is a man of this vale and has been finding his way around in this weather since he was a boy. He is also a rare tracker. Let us find them and confront them.'

'There were many of them.'

'There are many of us. We have a host of almost a hundred men outside. This is our country, our weather. They'll not leave these hills. It's good to be beside you, Ithamar, battle bold!' Cedric strode forward to embrace Gylfa.

Destiny. Yes, destiny. 'Have you a horse for me?' said Gylfa. 'I am no great rider'.

'We have a horse. Just hold on and he will follow the others.

With our swords and your magic, we'll send these invaders back south whence they crawled.'

43 Love and Death

'Where is he now?' Styliane, on the horse, shivered under her layers of clothes.

'Ahead.'

'What is that? Are they soldiers, can you see?'

They were on a good-sized hill above the mist and the day was blue and beautiful, the sparse snow speckling the green of the hills like cold flowers. The sun was sharp and strong and, with no wind, the effort of climbing and descending made Freydis hot.

'They are stones, lady. They have them in this country, I have seen them before.'

'What are they for?'

'No one knows. The English say they are magic. Are you cold?'

'Very.'

Freydis offered the lady her cloak. She took it without a word of thanks and Freydis was glad of it. The lady was recovering her former strength. It was natural for a high lady to put her own comfort before that of a servant, natural and right. Around them the tops of hills jutted from the mist like islands in a milky sea.

Freydis could feel the wolf on the hillside. They climbed but the wolf so weighted the world that the slope felt as if it was going down.

Freydis lead the horse on. They said very little, not just for the fear of being overheard. Freydis felt there was no more to say, that this moment, warm in a cold country, serving the lady she loved alone, all to herself, was the fulfilment of her dreams.

'Are you afraid, Freydis?'

Freydis shrugged and pursed her lips. She wanted to say that she was afraid for the lady, not so much physically, though there was clearly a threat to her in such ruination as was around them, but more that she would not be in her proper place as one of life's rulers. Styliane was born to command, born to master the runes. Without them she couldn't follow that calling. Styliane sought to command everything, even death. As was natural, as was right.

Freydis was called brave by many men but she knew that particular strength came from a shortcoming, not a virtue. She lacked imagination. Cowards might envisage a thousand ways to die. She kept her eyes and ears open and did not think of what might and might not happen. You could never truly prepare for battle, only accept it was coming and hope to see the enemy before they saw you. The armies of Constantinople spent a long time training 'what ifs'. It did them no good, because the enemy always did something you didn't expect, fighting harder or less than you had thought, being greater or smaller in number, better or worse deployed.

'I am not afraid. Were you afraid when you had this magic inside you?'

'Only of the magic.'

She still felt the runes but it was as if the wolf was a powerful wind, the runes merely ribbons she had attached to her hair, blowing away from where it came. She didn't mind; it made them easier to keep quiet.

For days they had followed the high hills, shadowing horsemen below them in the valley. She could not see them but she could hear them, the conversations of the men, the blowing of the horses. At night she sometimes smelled their fires. They had to be Norman – no Englishman would be so brazen. She held Styliane close, loving her, protecting her. Could she die for her? Ever since she had known her, she would have said 'yes' in a heartbeat. But, reunited by fate, it was the parting, not the dying, she would fear.

'I wonder how we are bound to these men,' said Styliane.

'I don't understand what you mean.'

'The story is moving somewhere.'

'You think we are nearing the end of the tale?'

'I don't know. When I had the runes I understood. You might understand now. It is in fragments. We may be going on to the end or we may be returning to the beginning. Perhaps the Norns are shuffling the pieces of the story until it fits their scheme.'

'Might I not write my own part?'

'That is what I have to believe. It's what I have believed since I started this. The grip of fate is broken. This is a new age. Perhaps it is as the Christians say, each man's salvation lies in his own hands.'

A woman's voice cried out from the mist below. 'I'm here!'

Soldiers shouted and cursed at her.

'That is Tola,' said Styliane. 'She senses us.'

'Does she not know we are her enemy?'

'If I have two enemies it doesn't mean they must be friends,' said Styliane. 'She seeks to set one against the other and see if she can profit by seeing them destroy each other for her.'

'I can't fight that many men.'

'You just need to kill the girl.'

'What will that do?'

'Deny the wolf the death he seeks.'

Freydis held her hand. 'If I die . . .'

'Don't say such a thing, my love.' The lady had never said those words before. 'My love.'

Freydis wiped a tear from Styliane's cheek. 'I'll go tonight,' she said.

44 The Scar

'Here?' The big Norman was alongside her, pointing with the stump of his finger. If he felt the pain, he did not show it. She sensed his men's love for him, their fear too. He seemed a giant to her, thanks to his size, but his presence was greater still. She imagined the scraggy raven that beat its way over the snow saw only him, that the creatures sleeping in their burrows woke as he passed, that the wind rose for him and the snow fell. She sensed too the magic within him, the rune he carried like a spear of ice in his side.

He was the future made flesh, violent, huge, foreboding, bleeding.

'This is the hill,' she said. 'This is where magic is done. I killed three of your men here.'

'Not my men,' said Giroie.

'You were in this part of the country.'

'I'd say so. Same to me.'

By that, she thought he meant that he couldn't tell one place where he'd burned and murdered from another. 'I'd say it must be easy enough to know where you've been,' said Tola but he didn't understand.

The Normans argued among themselves. There were so many of them to feed and they'd been out for much longer than they'd expected so they had only light provisions. There was nothing to scavenge, not a grain, not a hen, not a dog. They'd burned it all weeks before, stripped the land bare.

The men were annoyed at being taken out for so long without food, though icy streams and snow gave them enough water. A delegation of three came to Giroie but he struck one of them and insisted, 'On, on.'

When the men had gone away he grinned at her. 'Did too good a job here,' he said. 'Where? Up?'

'Up.'

'Cold up there,' said Giroie. 'But we see wide.'

The column made its way up the side of the hill, breaking free of the mist on the top.

Giroie had been wrong, they could not see the land. It was as if they sat already in heaven, she thought, the cloud below, the pale blue sky above, the moon's ancient face staring down at them. God had given it a face to remind men that He was always watching, her mother had said.

The riders settled down to make a fire. She didn't want to sit at it, it felt wrong to share the comfort of these men and she knew it would be dangerous. It might be difficult for Giroie to keep her safe from his men.

A wolf howled far off. She intuitively knew what it was saying: This land is mine. Keep away. She wondered if even it had found anything to eat.

The night was freezing and mist gave way to icy rain. There was nothing to stop her running, other than the certainty of a freezing death. The men sheltered under their shields but she was left out in the open, shivering, trying to edge nearer to the struggling fire.

All creation seemed split into red and black, the fire a cradle of light in a deep darkness.

At the edge of the camp she thought she saw something move but it was too late. A sharp pain in her arm, she cried out and the camp was chaos, men running and shouting everywhere. An arrow had caught her a glancing blow.

'What?' A Norman grasped her but a second arrow struck him on the boot and he gave a wail like a fox caught in a trap. He fell.

Giroie went thrashing into the darkness with his sword, other men following him, cursing and raging.

Tola lay still, flat to the floor. Her whole arm was gong numb; it felt as if the bone was an arrow, humming in a struck post.

A scream from the dark. 'Get him!'

A sound like someone hitting a tree with an axe. Raw panic, a jangle of panic that sparked sensations within her – the smell of something that should not be burning – hair, perhaps – the lurch in the stomach felt in the moment you heard a friend had died.

More thumping and shouting and Giroie burst from the dark, dragging a body into the firelight. Or not a body. The person was suddenly on his feet and kicking Giroie as hard as he could.

Light and hail, stamping and snorting. Runes! Bursting from the night, shrieking in wide orbits around the stones.

'Witch!' said Giroie and punched his captive hard in the face. The figure's head snapped back and it hit the ground, all breath coming out with the sound of great bellows. The runes vanished like the sun behind a cloud.

'More bastards? Any more?' screamed Giroie at her in his awful English. As if in answer, a horn sounded down in the valley.

'Not ours! Trapped us, witch?' said Giroie.

'English,' said a soldier.

'And bold enough to make themselves known.' He was still talking to her, his face twisted like a walnut in fury.

'This arrow ...' Tola tried to speak but she was faint.

'I saw those things in the darkness,' said Giroie. 'What are they?'

'Runes,' said Tola. She felt bile come into her mouth. The shock of being hit by the arrow had worn off and now her arm felt as though she was being shot again every time she moved.

'Like our fathers had,' said Giroie. 'These stories. As a child. Told.'

'They are of the devil, I think,' said Tola.

The big Norman grinned. 'No. My father old ways kept. All old country keeps them. What must be done? Possess.' Then he spoke in Norse:

283

'Know that I hung on a windy tree
nine long nights,
wounded with a spear, dedicated to Odin,
myself to myself,
on that tree of which no man knows
from where its roots run.

No bread did they give me nor a drink from a horn,
downwards I peered;
I took up the runes, screaming I took them,
then I fell back from there.'

He prodded Tola and she thought she might faint.

'How shall I have them?'

She sensed his greed, like an undertow, endlessly pulling.

'I don't know.'

'How shall I have them?' he said it again, in Norse.

Freydis, bound, held by two men, opened her eyes. 'The god is in the water,' she said. 'Go to the water.'

45   A Spell

Styliane waited until Freydis had gone. Her sacrifice to the dark god. She wept for a long time. Death for Freydis, but more than death. An eternity in the cold waters of Hel, in place of the god in the mire. Odin must be reborn and die at the wolf's teeth. Styliane would embrace the fate she had fought to avoid.

She fingered the knot she had tied in the cord of her robe in the waters of the well, put her finger inside the loop it made. She took the black blood gem she had found at the well's bottom, the gem she had taken from the god's eye, and held it in the crook of her ring finger.

The horse stamped and blew, its ears twitching. Other horses on the wind, perhaps. A distant horn sounded. Yes. Or if not that, something was unsettling it.

She thought of her days as a sorceress of the goddess Hecate, who had revealed herself to be Odin, who had revealed himself to be Christ and every other god that split into three, sacrificing himself for wisdom. Three rune bearers, three ways to die, a knot of three.

She pulled the knot tight on her finger and gasped as it tightened. She pulled it again, struggling to keep her finger on the stone. She looked at the knife for a long time before she summoned the courage. Without the bitter drink that had opened her mind to the realm of the gods in Constantinople, without asphyxiation or drowning, there was only faith to help her – a memory of magic.

She tried to summon a trance, remembering the knife she had used to cut herself when she had paid the blood price to have the truth of the wolf revealed to her.

Hel wanted blood. How much blood? That of a hundred men? It should do.

They were coming. The runes were trying to unite. Well they would, but she needed to guarantee the presence of the wolf when they did. Styliane gave one last tug on the cord, pain shooting from her hand all the way down her arm to her teeth.

She could hardly grip the bloodstone, so she put her hand on the ground, allowing it to nestle in her palm, against the finger of her seal ring. It was a tangling, tricky rune within it that would trap and trick.

She wanted to say the old words of her spell to Hecate, goddess of the meeting of ways, of death and the journey to death, but she couldn't be sure the goddess was even still alive. Was Odin an aspect of her? Was Christ an aspect of her? Or was she an aspect of them? So instead she said the words to the story:

'I slew death at the World Well under the world city. Now I must raise him to kill him again. I pay the old price of agony. I pay what Odin paid at Mimir, what Christ paid on the cross, what the priestesses of Hecate pay freezing in their midnight streams. Hecate. Hecate. She who helped Demeter bring her daughter Persephone from the underworld, who lights the dark of death's night, whose friend is the dog and who guards at the gateway. Open the gateway to the lands of death. Open them.'

The sound of horses drew nearer. Up on the hill the Normans were shouting, the urgent voices of men preparing for battle.

'A weft of skulls am I weaving. The warp is sinew and bone, stretched on a loom of pain.'

She cut deeply into her ring finger, the dark stone shining in an island of blood. She coughed and sighed with the pain. It had been a long time since she had worked such magic.

'All the rune bearers to die,' she heard herself say. 'This is death's land, he is coming, he has prepared the way with fire and blood and this will be his domain.' She waggled the knife to prise open the knuckle, retching as she did so. The stone drank in the blood. It was dawn and it caught the blue light and made it red. She cut again and the finger was severed, the knot falling loose, the stone cupped in her bloody palm.

No. The light of the stone took on a shape, a sharp, angular D. She recognised it immediately. It was the Thorn rune. Its light shone from the stone into her, prickling her skin, a delicious caress, half-pain half-pleasure. She felt the tendrils curling around her heart, the thorns tightening her chest and cutting off her breath.

'I do not want this.' Forget that mortal weakness. Forget the girl who was born in a slum outside Constantinople. Remember the priestess, the sorceress, the fearless fragment of a god.

The rune's other meanings flashed through her mind. She felt a step-mother's spite for an unfavoured child; a jealousy as between sisters, one pretty, the other with a rich husband who let his eyes wander. A word in Norse rang out in her mind. Slatrvif. Slaughter wife. The rune sang out other names too. Evil doer. Witch and plague upon good people.

A raven fell like a black leaf from the tree and picked up her finger.

'I have paid the price,' she said. 'The spell is done.'

The bird flew up and away, its baggy, black flight taking it up towards the hill. For the first time Styliane became aware of the pain in her hand. She held her cloak to the wound to staunch the flow of blood.

She watched the bird's sagging flight as it headed into the mist. She had given something because it felt right, cast a spell but a spell without an aim. Sometimes the reason for the magic was hidden from the caster. She knew that, had seen it happen with her brother in Constantinople.

She remembered Arrudiya, the slave who had taught her the rites and magic of Hecate.

'Magic is not written, it is not a recipe but a puzzle.'

She had done what was important – one sacrifice to ensure another.

She held her bloody hand and wondered if she had given enough and, if she had, what she had given it for.

From the distance she saw perhaps one hundred riders

coming in under the stormcloud sun from the east, bearing
weapons, bearing death, bearing blood.

46 Choosers of the Slain

Eight dead girls watched her from the edge of the moor. Freydis swallowed as the runes blinked back into her vision, swimming like the frogspawn that floats in the pond of the eye when you look up to a blue sky.

She feared to use the runes here. She felt the fascination they drew from the peat-stained women who stood in a circle on top of the hill. Each woman carried a cruel, fireblack spear and seemed hardly substantial. Fog spectres. Rain shadows.

The runelight poured from Freydis unbidden and she saw Tola with new eyes. A sinuous, stretching wolf, long and lithe, seemed to curl about her like a snake. Was it a wolf? Or was it a sign, something rendered by a scratch in the light? This was important, this was real, more real than the men who wrestled her to the damp grass, sat on her hands, bound and dragged her.

The skies seemed wider now, lightning purple, dark clouds blooming like blood in water. The hollow light was the light of dusk but unshifting, undying. Here on this hill the sun was always setting, never set.

A boot in her guts. A man shouted at her. She guessed he was asking if she was alone or had companions with her. It was what she would have done. Her body felt like a coat of wood. She was inside it, aware of the blows but indifferent to them.

Styliane was still down in the valley, hidden in a scraggy copse. She needed to succeed here for her. Yet the presence of the women of the moor set her thoughts jangling. The runes wanted her attention, wanted to present themselves before these women but she felt them tugging on her sanity. She saw herself at the head of an army of spectres, a rotten-skinned horde that had dug itself from tomb and grave to follow her. She could have that if she spoke to the runes.

She made a lunge towards Tola but the men held her back. She hardly saw them, they were like something from a dream, forces that held her back, only impressing more strongly her will to go forward. Punches and kicks crunched into her and the runes lit more brightly. She had a strange idea – that the runes were a wine and she the grapes. They were trying to beat them from her.

'All ravens here, ready for the feast.'

'All ravens here.'

The air was heavy with the sound of beating wings. Shadows flickered across her sight, but only two ravens fluttered down behind the biggest Norman.

The dead sisters intoned:

> *'How is it, ye ravens – whence are ye come now*
> *with beaks all gory, at break of morning?*
> *Carrion-reek ye carry, and your claws are bloody.'*

One of the ravens had something shiny in its claws. She dreaded it, whatever it was, glinting evil in the storm-blue sun.

"No!' shouted Freydis but the women continued to chant. The bird fluttered past, its beak red, its claws red. It dropped something to the ground in front of her. It was a finger and on it was Styliane's seal ring.

'Choosers of the dead.'

'Choosers of the slain.'

'We never-welcome women.'

'We shunned spear sisters.'

'I choose the slain, in Odin's name.'

'I choose the slain in Odin's name.'

'The god is in the water.'

'King Death is in the water.'

'He has what you want.'

'I want only the lady!'shouted Freydis.

'He has what you want.'

'Go to the water.'

'Take the runes to the water.'

'Give me back Styliane!'

'She will stand beside us.'

'No!'

'Some must stand beside us.'

'I will! I will do it!'

'Death is in the water.'

'Go to the water where the god lies.'

'Take me to the water where the god lies!'said Freydis.

'Where is the magic? You before,' said Giroie in his broken English.

'Along the scar,' said Tola.

'No. This is a trick,' said Giroie. 'You escape or kill us.'

Freydis summoned the Kenaz rune, let its light burst above Giroie's head.

'I bear the magic, I bear the runes,' she said. 'My lady is gone and I would join her in death. The runes are yours. I am a servant, a low woman. I should never have had them. They should go to you, a lord.'

Giroie nodded. 'Very well,' he said. 'Follow the English-woman. Let's get this done.'

47   The Gate of Death

Tola, who could hear the heart songs, to whom people appeared sparking memories and visions according to their dispositions, felt Giroie's anxiety as they heard the English horsemen approaching down the valley.

The Normans were rattled, scared. They thought there were too many to fight. Tola guessed they were outnumbered two to one. Giroie reassured his men. They had the high ground, they the bows.

Had they been seen? They must have been, burning a fire in such a high place with no regard for who saw it. Giroie and his men thought themselves the lords of the land. Well, now the English were striking back.

She saw the rune light up above Giroie, heard Freydis promise him her magic.

The soldiers cut Freydis free and she stood.

'You are a servant of Styliane? Did you come to kill me?' said Tola.

'Yes,' said Freydis.

Tola started backwards. The warrior smiled grimly.

'The time for that is gone. Here. I'm sorry about the arrow, let me help you.'

'No time!' said Giroie in Norse. 'I want the magic. I must have it working. It is a bane to me.'

'I will live,' said Tola.

'Then show me the god's grave.' Tola led Freydis down the long scar towards the mire.

Below them the horn sounded again.

Freydis held a ring to her lips and kissed it.

'A fine ring for a servant,' said Giroie.

'Too fine by far for you.'

The big Norman grunted.

With the rain and the snow what had been a mire was now a small lake, the marsh grass submerged under dirty water.

'You know how to do this?'

Freydis said nothing, just put the rope that had bound her about her own neck and tied the sticky, tricky triple knot that Styliane had shown her in the desert.

'Strangle me,' she said, 'and push me in. Then the spear. A triple death for a triple god, that will let the runes fly out.'

'You think this will work, sorceress?'

'Magic is pain,' said Tola. 'When I saw the sisters here, I had to suffer.'

'You cannot see them now?' said Freydis.

'Only stones,' said Tola. 'Though I hear them speaking.'

'What are they saying?'

'I can't tell.'

'Get on with it.' Giroie shoved Freydis in the back.

'Hey!' A Norman loosed an arrow down the hill. Tola felt the panic in the men.

A spear flew up towards them but fell short.

'Tighten the knot and then stab me,' said Freydis.

Giroie picked up the spear as Freydis knelt at the water's edge.

'This is the gate of death,' said Freydis. 'And I go through it now, offering myself for the lady.'

Giroie yanked the rope tight and kicked Freydis into the water. He thrust the spear down into her. The runes circled the moors, eight in an orbit, moaning and keening.

'They are for me!' said Giroie.

A burst of light like a second dawn and the English warriors charged the hill on foot, the Normans loosing arrows as fast as they could, then dropping their bows to the ground to draw their swords.

Giroie looked around him in wonder, lifting up his hands like a child trying to catch snowflakes. A flurry of hail burst on them, so much that Tola could hardly see. She curled up on the wet grass, sheltering beneath her cloak, nursing her wound.

Figures loomed from the downpour. An Englishman split a Norman's skull with an axe, spraying her with blood. A Norman hacked into the killer's throat with his sword, more blood bursting over her. Men fought in the mire, one holding another down to drown him.

The hail drove into the faces of the English but the Normans faced a light as bright as the sun.

'These symbols are mine!'

'No! Mine!'

It was the boy, Gylfa, the wolf head tied about him.

She rolled to avoid a stray horse trampling her. She couldn't let Freydis die now, she was all Tola had to protect her. She grabbed for the woman's body, freeing her knife from her belt.

A severed arm hit the water beside her but she cut the rope at Freydis's neck, pulled the warrior from the water. Freydis gasped and hacked, shoved at Tola, trying to force herself back into the water.

The fight went on in the mire, men hacking and cutting. She saw the grim sisters flying on their horses of shadow, moving among the men, casting down spears. Freydis punched Tola, sending her reeling backwards.

A runestorm swirled around her, the symbols howling and shrieking. The waters were bubbling with blood, bubbling with hail. A man smacked into the mire beside her, his veins blue against his white skin, his hands flailing, blood leaking from his skin and she knew he was dead of no natural cause.

The dead sisters screamed out oaths to Odin, he who died and would be reborn.

The runes howled and keened. She saw Gylfa running back and forth along the edge of the mire, no more than a shadow in the hail.

A cry. 'It's me!' in English.

The tumult ceased, the hail died.

'Well,' said Giroie. 'Now I see what needs to be done. All these runes have come to me.'

He held out his hand and every warrior remaining fell into the mire.

'The gate to death is open,' he said. He was never to speak again in this world. The wolf ripped off his head.

48   A Sacrifice

The Valkyries were gone. Only the stones stood on the moor. Freydis sat on the bank, shivering deeply. Tola stood facing the monster in the corpse mire, frozen to the bone.

It was a wolf, an upright, fleshy wolf, the fur in patches across its great head, its hands human but long and cruel-taloned. In one it held a head, staring at it as if to interrogate it.

Tola saw that the waters about her feet seemed to mirror the sky, black clouds burning with the sun. At her feet, the headless corpse of Giroie. Something moved at the side of her eye. At first she thought it was the wolfman, but no. It was someone like him, but without his assurance. Gylfa.

'Is that him?' he said. 'Is that Master Loys?' He held the wolfstone in front of him, as if to ward off the great wolf.

'Loys?' The creature turned its slow gaze towards her.

'Loys?' She spoke again.

Freydis emerged from the mire, which shifted and stirred with red light. She was heavily wounded in the side.

'This is the gate,' she said. 'This is where I will find my lady.'

'Fear me!' said the creature. 'I am a wolf.'

'A wolf does not say it is a wolf,' said Tola. 'It sees itself, the meat that will become itself and the earth that cannot become itself. Man is made of earth, so the priests teach. You cannot become a wolf. Here, clasp the stone to your skin.' She gestured to the stone Gylfa held in his hand.

'I will not. I glory in this slaughter. All men are meat, all men in me. I hear them whispering, Lei werreurs de Normadie son mor. Sur le table de Dieu.' He drew back his lips.

Freydis was alongside Gylfa. She took the stone from her and put it in her own left hand.

'Dread wolf,' she said. 'Be human again. I go to Hel, to bargain for my lady's life. I have nursed children and know they will take medicine in a sweetmeat.'

She leapt at the creature but it was too fast, too strong. It lifted her from the ground by the throat and drove its jaws towards her but Freydis threw out her hand, the one with the stone inside it, and punched it into the wolf's teeth. The creature opened its mouth and sank in its fangs, tearing and ragging at the arm, throwing Freydis from side to side. The warrior screamed and beat at the wolf with her free hand but in a twist and a shake of the head the ravaged limb was torn off and the wolf threw Freydis back into the mire.

It gulped and guzzled at the arm, throwing back its head to crunch and snap it down.

From on high the runes, like gulls, dropped screaming into the water after her, splashing down. The wolf dived in, snapping and tearing at them like a dog chasing a fly. It picked up the corpse of a Norman soldier and held it in its hand like a man holds a chicken joint, ready to crack.

The wolf hesitated, looking at the corpse as if it didn't quite understand what it was. It let the body fall from its hands, down into the water, and then it sat down itself. Tola watched the wolf for a while. It seemed entranced, distant. Gylfa stood mute, afraid to even to move.

The sun was up now and the water was stone grey beneath its light, all trace of the boiling red gone.

She thought to walk away, but where to? This place, with its whispering stones, with its memories of dead lovers, friends and enemies was where her journey into this madness had begun. Was it a gate between worlds? She sensed it was something more – it was where a fragment of a tale of death told by a mad god still hummed in the stones and on the hillside. She was part of that story and, if she left here, she would need to find the next part of the tale, to restore order and sanity, if not peace. Otherwise, all roads led back here. The hill was a vortex in a stream, always pulling her back.

She walked to the wolf. It watched her approach.

'You have the sharp rune inside you. You can cut the weft of fate. You know.'

'What am I looking for?'

'Death. The place that you will die.'

'I have tried to live.'

'You will cut your own destiny. I, who could tear you and guzzle you in a breath on this hillside, promise you, you are not to die. I, who rescued you and defended you, promise you, you are not to die.'

'And if you are no longer your own master?'

'I have the stone inside me. If it comes out, I will find it and wear it.'

'I need to be warm,' she said.

Tola came soaking and shivering from the mire. She made a fire from the clothes of fallen men, from the hafts of spears and axes. She watched its flames, warmer now in her steaming clothes.

The wolf sat down beside her. Gylpha joined them.

'How long have I known you?'

'The lives of twenty men,' said the wolf. 'And you will be here or a place like it again for the lives of two hundred more if we do not complete the story as it should be completed.'

'How is that?'

'When we reach the place, you will know.'

He reached out his arm to her but she shied away.

'I mean only to offer you comfort,' he said.

Tola lay against the wolf's side, his arm around her. Gylfa went off to rekindle a fire. He would not leave. Even he felt the pull of destiny.

'I have come back to you,' she said.

'Yes.'

'You will be a man again.'

'If I keep the stone.'

'Then let us go from this place to find some refuge where we can live out our days.'

'My days are numberless. There is no refuge, only respite. Be rid of me, Tola.'

'What were my names?'

'You were Beatrice and you were Aelis and you were Adisla, or they took your part in the story.'

She was sleepy, lulled by his animal warmth.

Over the hills she heard the wind carry a song of a woman who was loved by two men, one who killed the other and then died himself to please the god.

In the morning she awoke.

'Death is in the east,' she said. 'Across the sea. The god's bones hum in the deep earth and the song has found a singer.'

49 The Land of the Dead

Freydis fell through the dark water, through the tangle of moss and the roots of marsh violet, of fenberry and asphodel, past bubbles of shining light, in a wake of her own blood.

She fell through the sparkling white roots of a greater tree, roots big enough to bear icy rivers, and she fell through those rivers to a black shore under a silver moon by a black sea.

Giroie lay wheezing on the glittering sand.

She stood. Her hand was gone but it was not bleeding and she felt no pain. Her body writhed with runes, images of spears and swords flickering across her pale skin. She watched Giroie, a great wound at his neck, the runes seething on his face, making images of storms, of feasts, piled treasure, bright sunrises.

She felt for her sword. It was still there. Giroie got to his feet unsteadily. He was terribly hurt, a huge wound torn through the armour at his side in addition to the one at his neck.

'Alive again! Each one of us a Jesus!' said Giroie. 'But by Christ, what is this place?'

Freydis drew her sword. 'I'm going to kill you,' she said.

'Look at your sword!'

The blade shone, taking the light of the moon and fortifying it to an almost unbearable brilliance.

Freydis strode towards him but he put up his hands.

'Look around you. We were on a frozen hill in Yorkshire five heartbeats ago. Now we're here, where the air is warm, in a place we've never seen. It's as the waters promised. This is a magic land. This is where we might become gods.'

'Where are we?'

'The land of the gods,' said Giroie. 'Look at us! See how the runes shimmer and shine. They are part of us! We are made of magic like the old god at the well!' He coughed, held his side and sat down on the sands. He held out his hands, looking at the writhing runes.

'This magic does not sit well with me.'

'Magic is not for men,' said Freydis, 'everyone knows that.'

Giroie shook his head, mystified. 'This is a cursed treasure. Where is the future? What do we do? Is it this forever? I would go back to life.'

He ran to the ocean, splashing in up to his thighs but stopped as if he'd hit a wall and gave a great shout. Freydis ran to the water's edge. She saw it was full of corpses, white, fish-eyed, seaweed-haired, more like creatures of the ocean than the land. Giroie composed himself, like the warrior he was, and backed out of the black sea.

'No way that way,' he said. 'We came by water, could we not leave the same way?'

'Where is Freya?' said Freydis. 'She should be here to greet me. Styliane could only have died in battle, she must be here too. I want to find her.'

'She has fulfilled the bargain,' said a voice. 'Runes are here in the land of the dead. The god may revive'

Someone was watching them from the edge of the beach. He was a tall man, bearded and bloody, his eyes dead, his mouth slack with death but he stood, a great wound at his neck.

Giroie drew. 'A spirit!' he said.

The figure turned away and walked out into the grass, which sparkled like shards of black glass.

Freydis followed it.

'Is this wise?' said Giroie.

'I'm not wise enough to know,' said Freydis. 'It seems to mean us no harm, and we can't remain on this beach forever.'

They walked past a low hut where a three-legged stool sat on the ground outside. The hut was made of white snake bones and a noxious smoke poured from its smoke vent. The companions followed on, wordless.

Freydis was gripped by a great unease.

'Is this the land of Freya?' she asked the man.

'This is Hel,' said the man.

'My reward should have been Freya's hall, Sessrúmnir. I died fighting. My lady died fighting! A bird brought me her finger!'

'Valhalla is quiet, its warriors sleeping. The ways to the lands of the blessed are broken down.'

So was this it? Eternity in this strange land of wide night, silence and foreboding?

'Are you a man of this place?' she asked.

'He's an Englishman,' said Giroie. 'Look at him, he looks like a thousand other peasants I've butchered.'

The man extended his finger towards Giroie. The Norman crossed himself.

'How do we know he's not leading us into danger?' said Giroie.

Freydis snorted. 'I think the time to be worried about danger is over,' she said. 'Look at this place. Remember the stories our forefathers told. We are dead, and this is the land of the dead.'

'I expected a heavenly reward,' said Giroie. 'I have donated mightily to the church.'

'And I expected the halls of Freya,' said Freydis. 'So it seems we are both disappointed. You, dead man. Can you lead us to my lady? Styliane, Lady of Constantinople. Is she here?'

Silence.

They walked away from the shore, following the man through dark glades and moonlit clearings. All around them were fires and Freydis became aware they were walking through a great camp. As they forded a river, she saw men huddled around a fire. Freydis approached them and saw they all bore signs of battle. One had two arrows protruding from his chest, another half his scalp missing.

'A good wound, warrior,' said the man with the arrows to Freydis. 'Was it a dragon that took your arm? You see I was killed by a fine marksman. Two to stop me. One in the heart was not enough to stop old Ragnar.'

302

'A wolf killed me,' said Freydis. 'But no ordinary animal. This was a fen dweller, a giant and a fiend.'

'A great death!' said Ragnar. 'Sit by our fire and share your tales.'

'I am Norman. You are pirates and Vikings,' said Giroie.

'And we, like you, are dead. Our wars have been fought. Here there is only waiting.'

'For what?' said Freydis.

'For the goddess to release the god in the mire. For Odin to be reborn in Valhalla and all us dead scrappers go to our reward. The gates of Valhalla are closed and the god is not there to welcome the dead.'

'That is a shame,' said Freydis. 'What of Freya's halls?'

'The Valkyries do not carry people there any more. Those they choose come here. Our camp is mighty but our reward is scant. Where is my mead? Where my meat? Where the giants I should battle and the songs I should sing of it?'

'And how will the goddess release the god in the mire?'

'When runes are brought back to him. When another takes his place.'

'Who?'

'A goddess.'

'We have none of those.'

'I'd say we do,' said the dead man. 'I can see you, if you cannot see yourself, lady.'

'I am here to find my mistress and bring her back.'

'You are here because you are a god.'

Freydis smiled. 'Not I.'

'We see gods here, lady. You are a god, or a dream of a god.'

'Which god? How a god? She got torn in two pretty easy for a goddess!' said Giroie.

'The gods' dreams take flesh,' said the dead man. 'When the goddess Freya dreams of death she dreams of you.'

'You are wise in lore for a warrior.'

'I have been a long time here and heard many tales from many men. I have seen the dead dreams of gods collecting on

303

the shore, as I now see you, the mortal dream of an immortal.'

'All very well,' said Giroie. 'But is there a way out of here?'

'If the goddess lets you go,' said the man.

'And where might the goddess be?'

'Go to the god in the mire. She won't be far away. Your friend can lead you. And be brave, both of you. An army of men are waiting for Valhalla's gates to open again.'

Freydis shook her head. 'I care only for my lady. I have come for her.' She held out the finger. 'Do you see a woman here, one to whom this belongs?'

'Ask the goddess,' said the man. 'Go to the mire.'

Freydis glanced at the silent dead man. He turned and walked through the dark trees. She and Giroie followed and, as they did, Freydis offered a prayer that she was not a god. But a prayer to whom? To Freya? To herself?

'It seems you have a great destiny,' said Giroie.

'I don't want a great destiny,' said Freydis. 'I only want Styliane.'

50 An Army for Styliane

Styliane walked out onto the corpse hill, through the cold dusk. The wolf was gone, the girl with him. All around was the litter of battle – dead men, dead horses, broken spears, the gore-stained earth.

She took her knife, her little key to pain and to magic. Long before a rune had entered her she'd worked her spells and her body bore the scars to show it. A length of rough hemp rope was coiled at the saddle of a fallen horse. She took it.

'The story must be told again,' she said to herself and cut a good length of rope – a man's height. She spent a long time looking at the rope, teasing the strands with her fingers. A wind stirred, sharp with the promise of rawness to come.

It would take an army to overwhelm the wolf. Even then, she bore no hope he himself could be killed, at least not in his animal form. The girl should have been vulnerable. The runes had shown that. Freydis had at least taken the runes to the god. Now Styliane had to follow her, to show in pain and denial that she was worthy to strike a bargain with the goddess who ruled the lands of the dead.

She made the knot, three loops. Three the number of Odin, with his three circles of eight runes; three for the Norns; three for Hecate, triple faced; three for Christ, father, son, spirit.

For an instant, she saw herself as she used to be – a girl of the court under her brother's patronage, running through the sunlight in the olive groves of Constantinople. That girl would have shuddered to think of what came next. The rope. The water. The journey through death's gate and, with luck, with hope, with faith, the return.

A century before, she had learned the art of falling in on

her mind, falling away from the body and the human senses to glimpse the gods. She put the rope around her neck, waded into the mire, the cold like a dragon sinking its teeth into her thighs, sending spasms through her body. She mumbled to herself and it seemed to her that she could hear a song on the breeze, a song that told of lovers who died so a god could live. But the song would not finish, the last verse was unsung.

The words swept over her, through her, and her bones hummed like reeds in a breeze. Her skin was the skin of a drum, her heartbeat the rhythm it kept.

She pulled tight the rope and fell forward into the water. She was immediately human, choking in the filthy mire, desperate for air and light, frozen, panicking – a terrified woman, not a sorceress. She clawed at the rope but the knot was tied so that it only slipped one way. She cast her hands about her, feeling the cold limbs of dead men, their cold hair like weeds, their cold hands the claws of grave monsters dragging her down.

She let them, tumbling through blackness and light, through wide fields of the battle-dead where ravens cried in ecstasy, where blood rivers flowed through islands of corpses.

She was a warrior struck by a spear, a woman dragged to a ship then executed on the sand because there was no more room for cargo, a child among ashes.

'You've returned.'

The half-faced lady was on her stool, a bowl at her feet, the hut of snake spines sea- and wind-white behind her.

'I said I would not be long.'

'You're dying. The way back is closing behind you.'

'You can keep it open a while.'

'This is the land of the dead, lady. You have visited twice. There is no return journey a third time.'

'I do not ask for one.'

'Then what do you ask?'

'I have sent you a gift. Runes to raise the god and allow him to pay his price to the Norns again. He will return to his halls. Hel will be at peace.'

Styliane looked at her hands. Bubbles clung to them and she could feel the mud of the mire's bottom, though she could not see it.

'I thank you for it.'

'But the promise to the Norns cannot be fulfilled if the wolf dies first.'

'This too may be what the Norns want. They are more powerful than any god. Perhaps the time of the old gods is truly gone.'

'Then the lands of the dead are never peaceful. Hel is a place of war.'

'What do you want?'

'No living army could fight the girl. Eight valkyries attend her. Grant me an army of the dead. Let me lead them back to the world of men down the paths I have travelled. Let the warriors fight so their king might make his sacrifice and live again.'

Hel took up her bowl and dipped in her fingers. 'They are in my charge.'

'Release them. The god will wake soon. You do not want the wolf here, lady. He will not lie in any mire. These will be his lands, not yours.'

Hel flicked the water from the bowl into Styliane's face.

'I bless you,' she said. 'The girl is death's servant and his enemy. She should be here where I can watch her.'

The distant trees stirred and moved and, all along their line, helmets glinted, spears shone in the cold moonlight.

'Go!' said Hel.

The bubbles on Styliane's hands streamed upwards, the great host of men ran towards her. The moon was huge in the sky, the stars all rushing, smearing across blackness. Styliane had the knife at the rope at her neck, the freezing waters of the mire all around her. She cut through the rope but the cold gripped her. She staggered and splashed towards solid ground, falling and stumbling on again. She sat on the bank, convulsing with cold, retching from the pain at her neck.

The stars slowed and defined themselves, condensing to diamonds. The moon stopped dancing in the sky. She touched the bloodstone, held it to her, cradled its warmth.

At the rim of the mire the dead men stood, the blood on their faces black in the moonlight, their armour dripping mire water. There were a hundred of them, Normans and English, a united army of corpses.

Styliane crossed herself, said a prayer to Hecate. She could scarcely believe what she had achieved and fought down the glow of pride within her. Nothing had been achieved yet.

'Find Tola,' she said. 'Find the lady with the wolf and bring me her head.'

She gestured to a big Englishman who bore a wound at his neck. He instantly understood her and helped her on to her fretting horse.

'Calm,' she said to the animal. 'They are with us.' She pointed east and the host ran down the hillside, as many and as quick as rats from a fire.

51   A Battle of Nightmares

Loys vomited the stone on the third day towards the sea. From the coast they would find one of the great rivers of the world – the Esk or the Humber or one of the nameless rivers that must exist above or below those two – and from there a port. A port would have a ship and a ship would take them to the island.

'How will we sail it?' said Gylfa.

'You hold the runes?'

'But they don't sit well in me, they're all backwards and jumbled.'

'Because you are a man,' said Loys, his great tongue rough on his teeth, which seemed to him like so many swords. 'They will suffice. You will be able to use them.'

'Why?'

'They want to be free of you. They will take you to a place where that escape is possible. You came to the mire. You will go to the island.'

'Will I die?' said Gylfa.

'It does not matter in the schemes of the gods.' The wolf held the stone in its talons, studying it.

'It very well matters in the schemes of the me!' said Gylfa.

'I would have been glad to have been beneath the notice of the Norns. A twist of the fate yarn, a knot and a cut, then done. Be thankful for death,' said Loys.

'Well, being dead, I'm not going to be able to be thankful for anything, am I?' said Gylfa.

'Die well. Hope for eternal life in the halls of the All-father.'

'You have been such jolly company,' said Gylfa. 'I'm sure the company of dead men will seem festive by comparison.'

They camped against the lea of a hill, Tola and Gylfa huddled against the wolf's side for warmth.

'Dare we risk a fire?' said Tola.

'We can risk anything,' said Gylfa. 'We've got death on paws with us. I'd like to see the Normans face this.'

'Then I would need to drop the stone,' said Loys. 'My fury is weak when I have it. Human thoughts beset me.'

'What thoughts?'

'I think of my enemies at home in their fields or at their fires. I think of the people who wait for them to return.'

'And when you don't have the stone?'

Loys bowed his head. 'Then I glimpse myself as a shadow among trees. I am an echo of a voice, swamped by the noise of great waters. I am a leaf blown on a breeze and that breeze's name is hunger.'

'Best keep the stone, then,' said Gylfa, edging slightly away from the wolf.

Tola took Loys's great clawed hand in hers. 'With that stone, you could be human forever.'

The wolf fixed her with its huge green eyes. 'Human and forever are different things. What lives forever is not human. The inner man dies though the outer goes on. I loved you on a hillside full of flowers – or someone within me, something that entered me at the well did. I loved you when I took you to the caves beneath the earth, planting you like a seed that sprouted death. I loved you in a house in the forest and most of all by the docks of Constantinople, the sun on the water and, like this, your hand in mine. But you die and are lost and I remain, wanting you. I cannot do that forever.'

'I was promised to Hals,' said Tola. 'You couldn't have had me, even if I had been willing.'

'This is the curse of eternal life,' said Loys. 'I am the same man. You are born again, or the story tells you again, but you are told differently. Once you were promised to me, once I was promised to God, once we were married. Now ...' He took his hand from hers. 'Sundered,' he said.

They spoke no more after that.

At night they built fires where they could find valleys or

depressions deep enough to hide them, kept walking if they could not.

Loys slept fitfully, clinging to the stone as a man caught in a roaring flood clings to a branch. He was so much the wolf now, his teeth big in his head, his hands big and strong, claws like knives. The scent of the blood was less enticing, that was good, his rage on hold, but there was a dangerous resentment in him – why should he hold this stone? Why, when he was a god on earth, should he dampen his appetites, choose dull senses over sharp ones, weakness over strength?

Because. Because. Echoes of what had been and would never be again sounded in the vault of his mind. The Lady Beatrice, all those lives ago, holding his hand in the little cell. The child he had abandoned for its own safety, brought to its mother's court, given to its aunties. He was afraid for it, afraid of himself and what he might do to it; afraid of the gods. He could not raise it under their eyes. But still he had fallen into the mire of human attachment, with all its rot and decay, the faces of friends and lovers looming at him like the drowned from the black water of memory.

Even if he could be only and forever a wolf, he would not have wanted to live. That sort of extinction was unthinkable while he had even a chewed tendon of humanity securing his mind to that of the wolf. His ancestors had named the creature well: 'Slaughter-beast'. Loys, though he had killed many, was not a willing killer, nor would he be. One last murder. Himself.

He did want to put down the stone, just to hear the voices of his wolf brothers in the hills, to smell the fires on the wind and let the human smoke coat his tongue.

He was not falling out of his wolf form quickly enough. They would be at the coast and his body would still be this monstrous size, a terror to all men. He had no idea how long it would take. It was as if he was dozing on a boat on a summer river, awaking every now and then pleased to find he was still drifting, vowing to stay awake but quickly nodding off again. He was a passenger in the ship of the wolf, shouting directions

311

to a helmsman above the roar of a storm.

He wanted to kill the girl very badly and he wanted to stop, be a man, ask her to come with him to the sun of the east and spend his days with her on a farm on a mountain.

'No. No. Neither course. Let her go. Free her of the curse of you.'

The first of the dead found them by the riverbank on the second day. Loys would not have heard them coming if Gylfa had not woken him. The stone was dulling his senses, quietening the wolf piece by piece.

'Get up. There are things out there.'

The young man had been unable to sleep, terrified. Loys the man might have called the boy's leaping and jumping at every sound cowardice once. Now, having lived with the wolf inside him for so long, he saw it simply as he saw the caution of a bird – sensible, life preserving. Gylfa even hopped like a bird, his sword cutting at invisible enemies.

'There!' Tola's voice was a raw rasp of fear.

Loys was not even two steps on the journey to being a man again and his wolf senses pricked as he looked for the enemy. He smelled their rot, sweet as fermenting wine. He swallowed the stone again, gulping it down easy as the pip of an orange.

A shadow moved through the night and he touched it. He had caught a spear. The violence was a spark to the tinder of his rage. He had moved, there was a head in his hands and the head was not attached to a body any more. Three sword cuts, curious slow things, and he tore a warrior apart like a man breaking bread. A spear struck him from behind and then his mouth was full of meat, a mist of piss, shit and cold blood filling his nostrils. He smashed the last dead man on the top of his head, pulping the bones from his skull to his shoulders.

'We need to go!' shouted Gylfa. 'Odin's nuts, let's go! Look, the flesh is still moving!'

Blind blood slugs crawled on the ground, pieces of slick muscle dragging fragments of bone.

'I would stay a while,' said Loys.

He picked up a hand, felt it spasm in his teeth before he crunched it to nothing and swallowed.

'What were those things?' The girl spoke.

'Horrible,' said Gylfa. He hacked at a crawling torso, spilling its bowels like steaming worms into the cold air.

Loys lay down on his front, gnawing at a bone.

'Are you all right, Loys?' She spoke to him as if he were waking from a dream. He could hear her words, understand them even, but they were no more important than the rustle of the trees.

'Enemies?' said Loys. The two in front of him smelled less appetising than the dead flesh. Should he kill them and let them rot? Maybe they would walk again and he could tear them to pieces, have the fun of feeling their meat squirm in his mouth.

'Loys. It's me. Tola.'

She had a purpose but he couldn't remember what it was. Food?

He had her off the ground, lifting her from the waist in his massive talons.

'Loys!'

In Constantinople she – or someone like her – had called him like that before. He recalled sun, water, the smell of the fish cooking on the docks.

He put her down.

'Doesn't the stone help you?' The man spoke.

'Murder is sweet to me now, though the stone may cool my tempers in time. Run ahead to the sea. When you are there, call the rune from within you, Tola. I will come. I will wait for these dead things here.'

'We will die without you,' said Gylfa.

'You will die with me. Go. Now.'

Gylfa took Tola's hand.

'Come on,' he said. 'Keep these things from us, wolf.'

But Loys was lost to his feeding.

52   The Sea

The sea was not as she had imagined it. It lay silver, flat and wide under a grey sun. Her grandfather had said it roared but he was wrong. It whispered, as it lapped against the sand, as if trying to lull the land to sleep. But it was cold, colder even than the winter hills and she felt it almost sucking the heat from her. No chance of a fire here. A village lay at the mouth of the river and it was crawling with life – five longships on a dirty beach near a settlement by the broad mouth of the river, men conducting repairs on two of them. Smaller fishing boats lay beside them. This must have been where a good force of Normans had sailed up from the south.

Smoke rose from the low houses and men moved among them. The sounds of a smithy rang out up the hillside and, out at the limit of vision, a little boat cast nets into the haze.

'We could never sail one of those,' said Gylfa.

'There are the smaller boats,' she said.

'The sea is a serpent that coils its way around the world,' said Gylfa. 'When that serpent stirs it can swallow a boat like that in a blink.' He looked very pale and was sweating, despite the chill.

'Serpents or dead men,' said Tola. 'We choose our way to die.'

'If we hurry up,' said Gylfa. 'If we are slack, we will have no choice.'

'We should take a boat and cling to the coast if we can; find a part of the country where these killers do not rule.'

'I cannot carry what I have inside me for much longer,' said Gylfa. 'The wolf frightened the runes away but they are back now and they are a plague to me.'

'Loys says you are an omen of bad luck.'

'I'm still alive,' said Gylfa. 'Unlike most people in these parts.'

'Are these the final days?' she asked.

Gylfa scratched at his chin. 'The church says that on the final day, the graves will spill open and the dead walk again. I have seen this.'

'Monsters walk among us.'

'Thank God or we'd both be dead,' said Gylfa.

They waited until night, clinging together for warmth. Gylfa was hot as a loaf from the oven, burning up with a fever but she didn't fear to catch it. She knew what was inside him, gnawing away. She felt the wolf rune inside her stir. Was it calling to its sisters inside Gylfa?

Perhaps she was the cause of his pain.

The village was quiet and the moon a blade as they descended the hill. Tola had gone beyond fear. Having feared the risen dead, feared the cold, feared the wolf, feared Gylfa and Styliane she had become numb to it. There was no more room left inside her for fear of the men in the village.

Gylfa was in a bad way, limping as if his foot was broken. 'It's like my guts are on fire,' he said.

'Get to the boat. The big water must cool them,' said Tola.

They skirted the village, going too slow rather than risk too quick, always watching for signs of movement. Grey smoke from the vents of the houses was all that they saw. A fishing boat lay behind two big longships. It was grounded on its belly but the longships had been brought further up the beach to rest on logs. One ship had planks missing from its side, clearly under repair. They crawled along the scrub as far as they could but saw quickly that there was no way out to the beach that didn't expose them.

'What?' said Gylfa.

'You're the warrior.'

'You're the wise woman.'

Tola let her mind widen. There were no men awake, it seemed the Normans hadn't even set a guard. A dog stirred in the darkness whining to be let out.

It caught hers, whining and pleading. A Norman woke up. She felt his irritation. A curse. Someone else, cursing the curser. The dog still pleaded to be let out, thumping on the door of the longhouse. More cursing. More men were awake.

'We need to go,' said Tola.

'Where?'

She didn't have time to reply. The door opened and the dog came bounding over the sand towards them. Gylfa drew the Moonsword but it was no good. Killing it would only arouse more suspicion.

It leapt up at her, wagging its tail, barking out a big greeting. A man emerged from the longhouse, his hose around his knees, ready to piss. Then he saw them and gave a shout.

'Run!' said Tola.

'Where?'

'Up the slope!'

'There's no cover that way!'

'The boats then!'

There was no plan now, no careful weighing of likely outcomes. The boat was a desperate hope but it was at least some sort of hope.

'I can't run.' Gylfa was bent double, like a man who had taken a kick in the guts. She grabbed him by the collar and bundled him on towards the boat.

'Can you sail it?'

'You need to row it off the sand, there's not enough wind.'

'Can you row it?'

'I can hardly walk. You'll have to do it.'

'I don't know how!'

'This seems a good time to learn.'

They stumbled across the dirty sand. The dog chased them, gambolling and baying, wanting to play.

Warriors came out of the longhouse, carrying swords and spears, a couple with shields. She felt a wave of curiosity, annoyance from the men, the routine animosity of the conqueror. No anger just a weary resignation to the duty of unexpected slaughter.

There was no urgency about the way they moved. They seemed more amused than anything else at the sight of a woman and a sick boy crabbing their way across the beach.

Three came towards them, swords drawn, their manner casual. Gylfa untied the mooring rope from a stake.

'You'll have to push it off the beach!' he said.

'How?'

'Just shove it!'

She put her hands against the boat and heaved. It would not move.

A question in the Norman language behind her, the voice light and mocking. She guessed they were asking her if she wanted a hand.

'Get out! I can't push it with you in there!'

'Oh Jesus and Odin preserve us!' Gylfa climbed again to the rail and dropped over.

The dog left them. The men kept walking across the beach. Tola shoved at the boat. It moved, but barely.

'You'll have to help!'

'Oh God! This magic is a terrible burden to me!'

'Stop complaining and push!'

Gylfa half collapsed against the boat and it slid forward a painful pace. How many more steps to the water? Five?

'Push harder.'

The Normans had caught them. They didn't attack but stood in mock puzzlement. One had his hand on his hip, another held his head craned sideways as if trying to work out what they were doing. They spoke in Norman but Tola and Gylfa shoved again, the boat going forward another pace.

The dog barked excitedly away in the night. Then its tone changed and it cried out, a crazy squeal. The Normans looked up the beach. The dog stopped barking. A chink of mail.

Now the Normans were worried. They shouted up the beach for their friends. Six men went running over to the little cliff of the beach, jumping or climbing up onto it as their age allowed.

A soldier grabbed her by the shoulder, drew his sword. Another held onto the boat. Gylfa, his back to the prow, sank to the sand. Another Norman appeared at the top of the dunes. He had something in his hand. Tola took a moment to realise it was the dog but its head was gone.

The Norman with the dog gave a big shrug and then collapsed. At his back, the goose quill of an arrow stood up like a night flower. The Norman who had hold of Tola pointed up the beach with his sword and cried out.

'Guenipe!' a soldier shouted at her. The two standing Normans leapt towards her but she ran around the boat to avoid them, like a child playing a game.

More shouting from up on the dunes. 'Goubelin! Goubelin!' She felt the Norman's confusion wash over her. It didn't stop them moving. One went one way around the boat to get her while the other stood still. She couldn't avoid them any more and backed into the sea, knife drawn.

'Goubelin! Goubelin!'

Ten or so men ran out of the village to its perimeter. They'd found their armour and formed a wall of shields, six men staggering back from the dunes to join them.

The dead poured out of the night, many, many of them, howling and leaping, crashing into the wall. The soldier nearest to Tola crossed himself, slack jawed at what he was seeing. Tola tugged at the boat, fear lending her strength. The boat moved another pace. Two more and it would be in the water.

'Shove, Gylfa, shove!'

The young man moaned but she felt the boat move. She could not see him but he was pushing. The battle noise clattered down the beach, screams, howls, anger.

One more pull and the boat went light. It was floating. She pulled it three steps more. Gylfa was on his knees in the shallow water, spent. She grabbed him and dragged him to standing, almost throwing him into the boat.

Dead men threw themselves at the shield wall, screaming and skittering. She saw one take a sword through the eye but he kept stabbing with his broken spear.

One of the two Normans near her ran up the beach to face the enemy but the other stayed, looking at her, looking at his friends, stepping forward, stepping back.

The boat floated a little way out to sea but stopped again.

'A sandbank,' said Gylfa. 'It's beached.'

'What?'

'Shove. Again. Shove.'

Tola leapt out into the freezing water. It only came up to her ankles. She shoved but the boat would not budge.

The dead on the top of the beach broke the shield wall. The Normans were in disarray, each fighting three or four dead men. Cries and wails, a sound like a market shambles, chopping meat. The warrior who had run up the beach now tried to run back but three bounding dead men were on him, hacking him down.

The remaining Norman ran for the boat. Tola had left her knife on board and she stepped backwards.

The man ignored her, shoved the boat himself. It floated free. She splashed over the rail but the water suddenly deepened. The Norman warrior behind her was up to his waist. He chased the boat, grabbing at the side.

The dead were closing on the water. With an almighty effort she helped the warrior inside.

'Oars!' she said. He may not have understood her but he needed no instruction. He set the oars as a dead man splashed towards them through the surf, his axe high, his mail torn. He grabbed for the boat but lost his footing on the sudden drop. The Norman put his back into rowing and the boat moved free of the beach.

He shouted at her. 'Qu, qu,' or something like it. She understood and just shrugged.

'Don't know.' She looked back to the land, under the hazy moon.

On the edge of the little cliff, a woman watched her from a horse. It was Styliane.

She pointed to the longships and the dead men poured towards them.

The cold and exhaustion, kept at bay by terror, hit Tola in a blast. Inside, she felt the wolf rune calling, a long howl echoing through her mind.

'Come on, Loys,' she said. 'Where are you?'

53   To the Island

Loys lay still. The wolf raged inside him, despite the stone he had swallowed, and to move was to lose focus, lose humanity, to be just a monster stalking the night.

He slept for a long time and when he awoke on his bed of blood and bones under a cold moon an ember of disgust flickered inside him. He stood, squatted and shat, searching through the mess for the stone.

He held it again. The dismembered bodies around him moved no more. He coughed and spat, the taste of salt and iron in his mouth.

He had something to do. Someone to protect. Someone to harm. He cradled the stone in his hand like a candle in a breeze, a human light to keep the beasts away.

After a day he came back to himself, smelled the rot on the wind. The dead were moving. There were a lot of them; the gamey smell hung all over the trees. The wolf knew they had passed maybe two days before. The man knew that meant his promise to Tola had meant nothing.

A faint fog was still in the air and he moved towards the coast under a spiderweb moon.

There was no one and nothing around. He was unafraid of men when he travelled alone, so he dropped down among the little farms, not to kill but to see. See what? If life went on, if he was the last living thing on earth? That, he knew, was his awful destiny. Immortal, invulnerable as the wolf, to sit howling on the desolation of everything. What becomes of the killer, when there is nothing more to kill?

The farms were burned, all but one, and that was a corpse-hoard. Five Norman soldiers and three women lay dead by a house. Loys guessed they had preserved it for the shelter of troops moving inland. Someone had tied a blue ribbon on the thatch above the door. An emblem of life, lying limp in the land of the dead. He believed he could wander into Hel from here. His ancestors had believed Hel was a realm you could walk to if you went far enough beyond the mountains. This place with its burned settlements, bitter with the taste of ash, sweet with the tang of the fat of men and animals, could be Hel's hinterlands.

He touched the ribbon, thought of his daughters in Constantinople, thought of the child he had taken back to Normandy to be raised out of sight of the gods. Sun, blond hair, a sweet voice. That was all that was left of them, everything else washed away, people no more.

There had been a fight and the warriors had died bravely, it seemed. An arm lay twitching still on the wet ground. They'd asked the dead men to pay a price for their passage.

Loys felt the slaver drip from his jaws. More meat. He studied his hand in the hazy moonlight. The claws were black, each as long as a man's finger, the palm muscular and leathery. Not a wolf's paw but not a man's hand either.

He bent over the succulent body of a man. 'There is only one desire and that desire is death,' he said. 'All lesser wants must bow to it.'

He lay next to the corpse for a little while, drawing in its deep aroma, cuddling it like he was a child with a doll. He tried his jaws against the skull. Yes, he could crack it like a fox cracks an egg.

Enough.

A beast can't wish itself dead. Only a man can do that.

He ran, out to the coast, through the dead lands where burned hands reached up from the charred shells of houses like black briars, where a whole flock of sheep had been shut in a house and the house torched. Their bones lay black, piled on top of one another in a tangled heap like the carcass of a giant insect.

He tracked the dead down the river, the salt of the sea

already sharpening the air, bringing memories of cured meat, of a man and a woman on a boat going east, robbed and nearly penniless, of Constantinople, a meal, a sense of hope as he'd looked up at the giant edifice of the Magnaura university.

At the water's edge he sat down and looked out on the corpse shore. Bodies of men lay all around, hacked and dismembered. A severed head blinked up at him from the sand, a look of uncertainty in its eyes, as if it couldn't decide whether to die again.

A horse munched disconsolately at the salty grass of the dunes. He recognised it from somewhere, he couldn't tell where. Yesterday? Last year? Another life?

Two longships lay in the bay. The tar smell of the hulls sparked a memory – a blue morning, a cold breeze. He was a boy, shoving the longship out of the great hall where it had been kept for the winter. The memory was not his. There was someone else inside him, someone the wolf had eaten and yet not consumed, someone who lived in the back of his dreams.

He padded back to the river, took a big drink. She'd gone from here, he was certain, he could smell where she had lain on the dunes. He threw back his head and howled, sending a blade of sound out over the water. The thin moon looked down from its bed of gauze, but the water was silent.

Then, as the day dawned grey, he heard the rune calling across the water, an echo of his own wolf voice. 'I am here, where are you?' it said.

He put the stone beneath his tongue and set out into the water, swimming in the direction of the sound.

54 Rune War

They heard the longships behind them through the mist.

The Norman bent his back to the oars, pulling out beyond sight of the land. Tola felt his fear, bitter as the taste of an unripe apple.

She could not kill him but he could kill her. Gylfa lay holding his belly in the bottom of the boat. As soon as the mist swallowed the land, the Norman stopped rowing and put his fingers to his lips in a sign she should be quiet.

Across the water, she sensed the island calling. There was a rune there, a little whirlpool in the fabric of creation, pulling her in, wanting her. It was very far away.

She was terribly cold now, though there was scarcely a wind. The oars of the longships were loud on the water.

'They will find us,' she murmured.

'How do you know?' said Gylfa.

'They found us before. They are drawn to us.'

'Drawn to you. I never saw them before I met you.'

'And perhaps you. You have the runes inside you.'

The Norman made a gesture with his hands. 'Quiet!'

The beat of the longships' oars drew nearer. She heard the throaty calls of the dead men, telling each other where they were.

'You need to use your runes,' said Tola. 'You have magic inside you.'

'I cannot. The runes are curdling in my guts. I can see them but I cannot bear to look at them.'

'Do, or I will cut them out!' said Tola.

'Don't do that!' said Gylfa. He retched but had nothing to throw up.

'Mal,' said the Norman. 'Hot.'

Gylfa was indeed roasting, the heat of his fever almost comforting in the boat. The longship oars grew fainter and then stronger. A ruby light swept the water.

'It's a rune,' said Gylfa. 'I can feel the others calling to it.'

'Use one of yours,' said Tola.

'Which one?'

'I don't know. They are stronger than you. Let them choose.'

She heard Styliane calling, her voice flat in the fog.

'Talk to me, Tola, I know where you are.' The dead men jabbered and rattled their shields as if in agreement. 'I won't pretend that I mean you no harm but you will live again if you die. If the wolf gets what he wants, it's over forever. Come to me. Die quickly.'

Gylfa gave a great groan and the Norman reached for his knife.

'No!' said Tola, but too loudly. Styliane called to the longship crew, the red light of the blood rune flashing through the water. Tola felt Styliane's elation like a lurch in the stomach, even though she could not see her.

Tola tried to pray but could not. She felt the wolf rune stirring inside her, answering the rune that cast the red light.

'There. There you are!'

The blood light shone strongly on Tola. Then, from the mist, the prow of a longship knifing through the flat haze, dead men jabbering at the oars. The Wolf's hook rune howled out its note of terror.

'I am dying!' groaned Gylfa. 'I am ...'

The rune was big now, floating in front of the longship. Tola felt it as a sensation of prickling skin. Thorns, which made blood. Tola saw Christ on the cross, his blood dripping in beads from his head. Each bead trapping a rune? Was that a sacrifice too? Had Odin walked the earth as a man in Galilee?

Runes could call runes. She knew the runes could fall in love with each other. She had seen them dancing in their orbits at the well.

'Call to it!' she said to Gylfa.

'I cannot!'

'Call to it.'

She sat him up and the blood light of the rune caught him in the face.

'Merkstave,' he said. 'All reversed. All wrong.'

The dead men rattled their shields. Styliane held up the bloodstone, the rune floating above it, half seen, half imagined. The Norman was a skilled rower, the boat nimble and he ran around the bows of the longship, to its stern, putting distance between them and Styliane. But the lady ran to the back of her boat through the corpse warriors and shone the light on them again.

Thurisaz, the thorn rune. It seemed to speak a poem to her.

'Thurisaz causes anguish to women, misfortune makes few men cheerful.'

The blood light shone on Gylfa.

'All reversed,' he said. 'All wrong.'

Gylfa's body opened, it seemed, spilling images of men in chains, of lightning shattering a great tree, of a blind man staggering through an empty landscape. Styliane dropped the stone and she was soaked in the blood light.

Another poem washed over Tola in a voice like the rustle of fire in the gorse.

'The thorn is exceedingly sharp, an evil thing for any to touch, uncommonly severe on all who sit among them.'

Styliane screamed, falling, clutching at her neck. 'Thorns! Thorns!' she shouted. The dead men howled and yammered, jumping into the sea in their armour.

A wind sprang up and Tola saw it was no normal breeze. It was filled with dark shapes like leaves but all the same, tumbling stick shapes whispering and calling to her.

'Get the sail up! Get the sail up!' Tola shouted at the Norman, pulling at the sail on the deck.

He needed no translation and set to work. Soon the sail filled and the little boat lurched forward, powered by the magical wind.

326

Tola crossed herself. There were two more longships somewhere around and they could sail as well as she could.

'This is the wind of destiny,' she said. 'This is the breath of a god.'

Styliane's voice shouted across the water, her voice full of anguish.

'You cannot fight the Norns! You cannot fight destiny! I will kill you but I promise to be swift!'

Tola glanced at the Moonsword by Gylfa's side. She took it from him.

'Perhaps,' she said, to the air. 'And perhaps I will tell the tale differently.'

55 The God's Grave

Tola found the island by instinct. A heavy sun in the east; heavy clouds. It seemed as if the sea was tilted and the little boat ran on like a cart down a hill. The Norman was fearful of her. She saw now he was very young, maybe not yet sixteen, and he could not meet her eye, though he periodically clung to a little crucifix he wore at his neck.

When the fog cleared they saw the longships, bobbing on the horizon like caterpillars crawling on a dirty green leaf.

The rune wind kept them ahead, though they heard the strain of the dead at the oars across the water. Three ships. They could not fight. All Tola could hope was that Loys would come to rescue her.

They travelled for days, the rain sustaining but chilling them. There was no question of taking down the sail to stretch it across the boat as a shelter while the dead relentlessly pursued them.

The boat bogged down with water and they bailed as best they could, she with her hands, the Norman with his helm. Gylfa just lay, mumbling, rune-tormented, his face pale, his clothes wet with rain and sweat.

'I cannot keep it going night and day,' he said.

'Hold fast,' said Tola. 'It is but a little way now.'

'They are plants,' said Gylfa. 'I am the earth and they feed on me.'

Again the Norman crossed himself. No one had eaten in three days now. The nights were vast and full of stars, the dawns bright and blinding. At midday the sun scorched them, unless the black clouds bubbled in the sky, when it rained and they shivered.

They lost sight of the longships and she was glad of that,

though they sometimes still heard the beat of the oars carried across the water.

It was at dusk that they sighted the island, grey and flat, rising no more than three man heights above the waves, its limestone cliffs crumbling. To the south of the island a grove of trees rose and, at its centre, a single bare ash stood, its dark branches made shadows by the sun. Something was near the base of the tree. She couldn't make out its shape. A house? No. A ship? Perhaps.

The beat of the oars was distant but Tola was under no illusions: the dead would come. But here was safety, or a sensation of it, like when her mother had come to her in the night to tell her there were no mire beasts lurking in the corner of the room, when she had snuggled herself beneath the blankets between her parents and slept, warm in the winter night. That feeling of safety had been an illusion. In her life there had been no safety, just a suspension of the day of awful danger.

Tola gestured to the Norman to take the boat in but he shook his head, drove his fist into his hand and made a crunching noise. 'Bad place,' he said. 'Rochet.' He picked up a tiny stone from the bottom of the boat. He made a gesture of circling and she understood he wanted to find a safe place to land.

Gylfa's eyes were glassy and his breathing shallow. What now if he died? The rune wind would die too, as well as any protection the runes might offer from the hordes of dead men.

The Norman steered the boat around the island, looking for a place to land. At the south, just down from the trees, was a rough beach of stones and pebbles. The Norman steered the boat into it and it grounded with a lurch.

She felt the terror coming from the boy. He spoke. 'What now?' he seemed to say.

She didn't know, only that this place felt right, where she would make her stand. How, she didn't know.

'Him,' said Tola, gesturing to Gylfa. 'Carry him.'

The Norman struggled to get Gylfa out of the boat but, when she helped too, they got him on to the beach. Between them they could carry him only as far as the grove. It was some sort of cover.

Big spots of cold rain fell from the black sky. *God, let's have a storm. Let Jesus sink these demons of hell that pursue me*. She wanted to go up the island, to examine the shape she had seen from the sea, but night was falling fast, clouds had eaten the moon and it was very dark. It was safer to stay in the grove.

Jesus did not sink the dead men. In the black of the night she saw a red light floating. How far or near she could not tell, but she knew it was Styliane.

She felt sick with fear. Could dead men see in the dark? She sat frozen in the glade. The Norman was terrified and he hugged her like a child hugs its mother.

The woman's voice sounded across the water, backed by the beat of the oars on the water like some terrifying song.

'Tola! We are here. Your rune calls to us.'

Tola crossed herself. The oars' beat quickened and she saw the light shine over the low cliffs. They were looking for a place to land.

'Wait! Hold your oars.'

Silence. And then a sweet voice drifting down from above the grove, up towards the single ash. A woman, singing. In the darkness there was a flash. Someone, there on the island, had lit a fire.

56   The Fire Ship

Tola ran towards the fire, the young Norman behind her. Down on the shore the blood rune shone and she ran between two converging points of light.

It was so dark and she stumbled as she ran, falling and rising again.

The young Norman cried out and fell but she wouldn't wait for him. He had despoiled her land and, though circumstance had drawn them together, she was his sworn enemy.

At the top of the ridge she saw the fire. Beside it, a bright torch in her hand, stood a woman, terribly thin, half her face burned away, clothed in rags. Tola sensed a rune inside her, a deep, dark thing that crackled with madness, with poetry and with death. Beside the woman, she now saw what was beside the ash. A longship, eaten and bleached by the weather, its sail ragged, its mast warped. She gripped the Moonsword. Its presence made her feel no better. She could not fight or kill, she was a farm girl, not a warrior.

'Dead men,' said Tola. 'Dead men!' She didn't know what she expected this starved castaway to do about it.

'This island is full of them,' said the woman. She spoke in Norse but with an accent Tola had never heard.

'You understand me.'

'Odin is the lord of words and his rune is within me.'

'Use your rune to defend us.'

'I cannot.'

'Why not?'

'I don't wish to.'

'Then we will die.'

The woman said nothing. The fire played on her face and

it seemed to Tola that she was a spirit, perhaps even a vision born of madness.

'I have spent a long time singing to bring you here,' said the woman.

'You are a witch?'

'No more than you. You are the greatest of witches, for you spin fate.'

A great scream came from down the slope. The dead men had found the young Norman. There was no time now.

The woman took her hand.

'Go to the god. You can lead him from the land of the dead. This is your task. Your rune unites the others and unties them again. You are the storyteller and must go to where your rune can be heard.'

'How?'

'Go to the land of the dead. Bring the god here and he will release your land from its yoke of pain.'

'Must I die to go there?'

'How did the old kings travel there? On ships of fire.'

Tola looked at the boat. Ancient shields rotted on its rail, the mast was bleached by sun and salt, the whole deck piled with wood.

'Free Odin, let him come to the land of men to die, to pay the price to fate and be born again in eternal time,' said the woman.

The first of the dead men appeared over the ridge – a Norman, his face white and puffy from his time in the mire, his drowned-man's eyes upon her, terrible in the firelight.

Another ran up beside him. An Englishman, a great axe in his hand, his head half missing. She could not face them. Better death by fire than to be taken by these horrors.

'Hals is in the land of the dead,' said Tola. 'I will go to him.' She ran to the ship, jumping in beside the piled deadwood inside it.

The woman put her brand to the wood. It caught quickly. A dead Norman made the rail of the ship but the fire was taking hold. He tried to leap aboard but Tola struck at him with a branch and he fell backwards.

Tola spluttered and fell too, hot ash and flame burning at her face and hands.

'Help me!' she cried.

Her mouth was flame, her words were flame. The ship burst around her, dead men clawing at its rails, burning and falling back.

'Hals,' said Tola. 'Hals, I am coming to you.'

She had expected to die. But the ship groaned, lurched and turned, slipping forward, pushed by a billowing sail of flame.

The ash tree glowed white and the ship plunged down, as if falling through the earth. The clouds rolled away and above her the stars wheeled, the moon blurred, quick as a fish in the water. The ship turned and jolted, falling through black voids, the only light the fire of its own combustion.

Wreathes of flame blazed about her body but she did not burn. Tola went to the tiller and steered as she had seen the Norman do on the little boat. In front of her was a dark headland, a black river between mountains. She turned the boat that way.

The ship lit the dark water beneath the prow and it floated on as if on a wake of fire.

'Am I dying?' said Tola. No one answered.

A headland appeared, a pale light picking out the bulk of a hill. All along the shore, fires were burning, figures moving.

An army of dead men lined the shores, some exultant and cheering, others with heads bowed. The river opened into a broad reach. By the banks the dead were firing their ships.

The black shore was near, warriors with their torches thronging to meet her. So she had run from one army of dead men to another. The ship did not respond to her tiller now but fell towards the beach.

The boat beached and the warriors parted. Tola did not know the way to go but she had no real choice. The throng offered her but one road through them. She walked for a long time, through dark woods and fields. Dead men ran ahead of her with torches, lighting the way, strange women riding the fog of the air. They were the ladies of the vale, who she had summoned to save her up on Black Scar Tor.

'We are the maidens of death
The halters of heartbeats
The stoppers of breath.'

'Get away from me!'

But still the faces loomed at her, as if from the fog of a dream.

In the wood, by the mire, they stopped. Freydis and Giroie stood waiting. The dead men assembled around them, their torches blazing. Above them the strange women danced and swooped. And there, by the black trunk of a rotted tree, was Hals.

She could not speak to him, had no words, but he reached out his hand. She took it and kissed it. So cold.

She found her voice. 'I will not leave here without you,' she said.

'Who are these who travel with you?' said Freydis.

'Dark ladies. They wish me harm,' said Tola.

'You look like one of them to me, girl.'

Tola looked down at herself. Her clothes were black and tattered. She felt for her neck. At it was a noose. No, not a noose. A weft of yarn cast around her shoulders. Her fingers itched. She had a great urge to tease it, to find a spindle and spin it. All she had in her hand was the Moonsword. A spindle of sorts, to weave a weft of blood.

'I am not one of them.'

'So why are you here?'

'I ran from the dead men.'

'You picked a bad place to run, then. Here there's nothing else,' said Giroie.

'I am not dead,' said Tola.

'I wouldn't be so sure,' said Freydis. 'I cannot find my lady Styliane. Have you seen her?'

'She is still in the realm of men,' said Tola.

'Then I too have come to the wrong place,' said Freydis.

Beside her was a woman. Tola had not noticed her before, though how she didn't know. Her worm-eaten face was stark in the moonlight. Tola recognised her from her father's stories. Hel, goddess of the underworld.

'Am I dead?' she asked the goddess.

'You are in the lands of the dead.'

'Can I leave?'

'Few ever have.'

'The men who followed me did. The dead warriors.'

'They hover between this world and the realm of men.'

'And us?' said Giroie.

Hel ignored him. Instead she spoke to Freydis. 'I see what you are. A dream of a fierce goddess. You are Freya, first among the gods of women. Such as you will serve well to take the All-Father's place in the mire.'

Freydis wept. 'I am a simple woman. I have tried to follow my love Styliane but I have fled from her.'

'She offered you to me to take the god's place in the water,' said Hel. 'That is your destiny. Ask the lady of fate.' She pointed to Tola.

'Styliane wouldn't do that,' said Freydis. 'She would not betray my love.' Tola saw something she had never thought to see. Tears streamed down Freydis's face.

'No. She seeks eternal life,' said Hel. 'She loves you dearly and so gives you up. That is the nature of sacrifice.'

'You are dishonoured by her betrayal,' said Giroie. 'Take the god's place in the water.'

'If she does not want me, then any torment is bearable,' said Freydis.

'This is your task. To release the god,' said Hel to Freydis. 'The Norn brought you here. She ...' She jabbed a finger at Tola. 'Is the mistress of destinies.'

'And if the God rises?' said Giroie.

Hel pointed to the Moonsword.

'That weapon kills gods,' she said. 'It was forged to do so.

The gods die many deaths. That can finish them eternally. Kill this goddess. Kill this aspect of Freya and let the waters have her divinity, as they now have old Odin's.'

'And my Hals?'

'He is dead and cannot be reborn.'

'Why not?'

'I will not let him go and you, lady, for all your might, have nothing to give. Now send the goddess to the mire, let Odin live, or go and keep the world in torment.'

Tola weighed the Moonsword in her hand.

'Do as she says,' said Freydis. 'I am ready to die.'

The weapon felt light and shone under the starlight like a curved moonbeam.

Then she struck, not at Freydis but at Hel, sinking the sword deep into her neck. The lady howled and twisted, her head lolling, and she collapsed into the mire, the Valkyries sweeping down upon her like crows from a black sky, tearing at her as she fell into the water.

'What have you done?' said Giroie. 'What have you done?'

Tola struck him too, cutting off his head with a single blow and the rune burst out of him, splashing into the waters of the mire, which bubbled with blood, seething as if a mighty host of fish snapped for bait inside it.

The god stood from the mire, his peat-stained skin sparkling, his long, sinewy limbs levering himself from the water.

Spectre women rose from the water, flying up on wings of shadow to surround him. The god looked weak, standing on bog-blackened legs like a newborn foal.

'Fourteen runes with the god in the water. One from the dead man! Nine more runes to gather!' shrieked the Valkyries.

The god put out his hand towards Freydis and Tola saw bright shapes stream through the air towards him. Freydis coughed and fell. The god had simply sucked the runes into him.

'Twenty runes in the dark god's orbit, four more and the debt will be paid!' a dead man shouted.

'Odin is near to life! Hel is struck down. We sail to sacrifice the god on earth so he may please the Norns and live again in Valhalla!' screamed a tall Viking with a huge wound in his chest.

Tola pulled Freydis from the wet ground but the black shapes were all around her. Valkyries, sweeping her up.

They grabbed at Tola, and at Freydis, flying them back over the dark fields and through the dark woods to the beach where the ship still burned. The God flew with them, borne by his Valkyries, his skin leather, the noose at his neck streaming like a banner, his great spear shining but limp in his hand. They carried him as if he were a warrior, newly dead on the field of glory.

Tola jumped into the ship, the flames catching all over her body. There was an intense sensation of heat, a brief agony, and then the pain disappeared, as quick as it had come. A dead man took the tiller and the boat slid into the black water, a thousand other ships igniting behind it, the warriors calling Odin's name.

The black water was cool and deep, the flames reflecting within it, turning the mass of boats into a constellation of blazing stars. The river's mouth disgorged into a black sea and Tola felt the rocking of the boat, tasted salt on the breeze. The boat steadied and the sea was no more. She was floating with a thousand other ships in a night of sharp stars.

The ship turned and rose, the others following it. Below them light shone in the three colours of the rainbow, gold, red and blue. The ship fell into the beam and now the stars rushed like comets, fans of light stretching out over it.

Still falling, falling into blackness. Then a lurch, a jolt, a noise of creaking timbers and it sank towards the island, towards grey seas, a grey sky.

57 A Blow Against Fate

Styliane made the top of the ridge and stood beside the burning ship, its heat almost welcome after the cold of the journey.

'You have killed her?' she said to the ragged woman she found there. The story was unhealed, the god could not be born! Styliane's mouth felt dry. Had she achieved what she had set out to do? Was this the right place, where the girl's sacrifice would please the Norns?

'I have sent her on a journey.'

'Who are you?'

'Odin's servant.'

Styliane looked hard at Célene.

'I have seen you before, I think. You are weathered and you are old but it's your mother's eyes that you use to look at me. It's a gaze I have remembered for a century. You are the child of blood.'

'I am the child of blood. I sang my long song and called you here.'

'Do you mean to kill me?'

'This is not a place of death.'

'It is the grave of a god, I think.'

'The grave breeds life. All things contain their opposites. Listen to the flames. They speak with the voice of the rain.'

It really did seem that the sound of the flames was the sound of a great rain in the hills.

The ship creaked and groaned, its mast collapsing in a cascade of sparks. Styliane caught her breath as she saw figures taking shape in the fire – two women, one slender, the other squat. Around the squat one runes sang and spat, crackled like meat cooking on a pan, whistled like a log in the hearth.

'And now what?'

338

'The god is coming. His army of dead men is sailing on ships of fire. The girl who bears the wolf rune is with them.'

'Will I die?'

'I saw you in my dreams. You lived so long because the story shattered and the end was never told. Now the story is whole again. Odin will die forever, the wolf will be killed, the Norns' will obeyed, the runes will go from the earth.'

'No. The wolf will live! I will live!'

Now lights appeared in the sky, floating flames, descending to the island. The figures in the longboat pyre moved. She saw the god, his huge form in the fire, black against the flame, twisted like a hazel tree. Inside, she saw the runes sparkling.

Styliane tried to count them but could not.

'The god is on his way,' said Célene. 'But where is the wolf? Your time is gone, lady, your story told.'

Rage, so strong she could taste it, iron in her mouth, sprang up in Styliane. 'Kill her!'

Five dead warriors with axes and swords came towards Célene. The ragged lady smiled to see them.

'Twenty,' she said as an axe struck her in the back.

'No!' shouted Styliane, realising too late what her anger had made her do. A dead man struck again and Célene lay dead on the floor, her rune shrieking through the night to join its sisters in the flames. The god must not come until the wolf was there to kill him.

Tola stood before Styliane, her back to the great fire, a charred spear in her hand.

'You have done this,' she said. 'You have gathered the runes. The god played his trick on you even in death.'

'I have played a trick on him,' said Styliane and she drove her little knife into Tola's chest. 'You will never kill the wolf. The story will remain unfinished!' The knife stuck there and Tola sank to her knees, looking at it as if she didn't quite recognise what it was.

'Kill her!' said Styliane. The dead men pounced as the wolf struck.

58 A Hero's Death

The boats of fire hung in the air and on the sea all around the island, lighting the night. Gylfa watched as Tola grasped for the knife in her chest. The wolf tore at Styliane's dead men, their arms and legs, heads and entrails flying into the night. Spears and swords struck it uselessly, the fall of the point, the slash of a blade only serving to alert the wolf to the presence of an attacker; a second death at the teeth of a god who was the end of all magic.

This was death's kingdom, come to earth. This was Hel rising up into the realm of men, Gylfa was sure.

The wolf was a giant, the height of two men, its eyes green fire, its teeth red with gore. Loys. What a warrior, to transform himself so. The company of such heroes would guarantee Gylfa his own place in a saga. His kin would need to respect him then.

For a while he thought he was in a fever, dreaming. But the runes had been quieted by the presence of the wolf and he felt not nearly so sick.

Three dead men leaped upon the wolf but it shook them off as a dog shakes off rainwater. When they came again they were torn apart, the wolf throwing back its head to guzzle down a still-writhing arm or driving its snout into a belly to break the dead warrior in two.

The legions of Odin watched on, their fire ships bobbing on unseen currents in the dark air.

Gylfa felt bold. He had come through great trials, faced great enemies and now he was at the centre of his own story. The last of the dead men struck the floor, the wolf howling its victory song above the slithering remnants of its enemies. It was as if it stood in a boiling pot, the ground bubbling with flesh around it.

The wolf stood and took something from his mouth. The wolfstone? He held it up and looked long at it.

In the fire Gylfa saw a huge figure, a dark twisted shape like a root in the hearth. The runes inside him, so timorous in the face of the wolf, pulled and stretched. They wanted to go to him. How to let them? How could he be free of this sickness? He couldn't think.

Styliane threw something into the fire. It sparkled briefly against the light before exploding with a flash of bright flames, sharp as thorns. He saw a rune flicker in the flames and the dark god extend his hand to take it, thorns curling around his arm until it disappeared within him. Styliane approached the wolf but a great roar from the beast drove her backwards.

Other shapes moved within the flames, monstrous women, creatures of shadow, their bodies long, wavering in the heat of the fire. He wanted to let the runes go.

'This is the place,' said the wolf to Tola. 'The god is not yet here. Make the sacrifice. Defy fate. End the story.'

Tola staggered, clutching at the knife in her breast, but she raised the Moonsword.

'What happens if you die?'

'The god will go back to Hel, his bargain to the fates unfulfilled.'

'I am fate,' said Tola. 'No one, not even the gods, can escape the fate the Norns have set for them.'

'If you kill me, you can,' said the wolf. 'You are one of the sisters who spins the fate of all men. Finish spinning for me.'

Gylfa did not really understand what he was hearing but he knew that the wolf had saved him many times and that, in his presence, the runes were quiet, he was not sick. The woman had the sword ready to strike the wolf. She was a witch and had subdued him. He would repay his friend, save him.

He leapt upon Tola, driving his dagger down into her breast. For an instant before he struck, he saw her smile. Then a black

341

swirl leapt from the fire. He saw a woman, or the corruption of a woman, leather skin, fireblack spear, strike at Tola and she died. Styliane ran to the corpse, her eyes wide with delight.

'I have saved you,' said Gylfa. 'My friend and guide, I have saved you!'

The wolf threw back its head, howling to the cold night.

Voices were all around Gylfa. More of those tattered women and another that he knew. Freydis, the half-man.

'Three runes, three runes before the god will step from the fire,' shrieked the women.

'How shall I release them?' said Gylfa.

'I will show you.' It was a woman's voice. The warrior Freydis, her sword drawn.

She hacked at Gylfa, cutting a deep wound into his neck.

'You are parted,' said Freydis.

Gylfa collapsed, his hand trying to stem the flow of blood from his neck.

Desperately he drew his sword and slashed at Freydis. She stepped away from his blow and he had no strength to follow her.

He felt the runes going, sucked into the fire, and he saw the great god step from the boat, his skin smoking, his one eye mad, his spear high, renewed, ready for the fight. Above Gylfa the hag women shrieked.

The god came roaring at the wolf and the wolf went wild.

59 Life Eternal

Odin fell, his spear jabbing into the wolf's flanks, but the animal had him, its jaws about his neck.

A great music filled the air, a discordant pipe, a tormented drum. She saw images of hail, of fog, smelled the stink of animals, felt a cold wind blowing, then a blast like the breath of a furnace. The runes were all around her.

On the ground she saw the wolfstone, where the wolf had thrown it. She grabbed at it and the milling, spinning, crashing, thumping runes fell but did not touch her, as rain falls on the hull of a boat turned over for shelter.

Styliane, though, stretched out her arms, casting back her head in the runefall like a farmer welcoming rain to the drought-blighted land.

The runes entered her, Sowilo, Dagaz, Othala, while others were sucked away over the ocean like leaves blown by a storm.

Odin was dead and the wolf tore his body, ripping out entrails like silver ropes.

'My love!' Styliane fell into Freydis's arms.

Freydis held her.

'My magic is returned,' said Styliane. 'We are immortals together.'

'My magic has gone,' said Freydis. 'If you live forever it will be without me.'

'Come to the boat,' said Styliane. 'We will get away from this monster before he finishes his feast. The story is not finished. There is no one left to kill him! Come to the boat and let us speak of these things when we are safe.'

Freydis went with the lady to the longship, its sail limp in the windless dawn.

'We cannot sail this alone,' she said.

'Get in.'

Freydis did as she was bid.

Styliane gestured to the sail and a wind sprang up. She heard a rune say its name, whispered as if in the breath of a horse. Ehwaz. The travel rune.

'Go to the tiller,' said Styliane. 'Our life begins again today.'

But Freydis did not go to the tiller. She stood looking at Styliane.

'Will you not do as I say, my love?'

'I thought I could serve you in anything,' said Freydis. 'I thought I could die for you.'

'You have died and returned.'

'But my love is not selfless. A goddess looks through my eyes and she is wilful. You betrayed me. You offered me to the god in the mire. You grew your love for me like a cook grows herbs, cared for me like the shepherd the sheep he will slaughter.'

'My love was genuine.'

'Your love for yourself greater.'

'I wanted to live.'

'Without me?'

'Of course not.'

'I found I could bear death but I could not bear the parting. I found you again, I thought because of magic. No. It was destiny. We are meant to be together,' said Freydis.

'As we shall be.'

'As we shall be.'

'What do you mean to do?'

Freydis took a pace closer to Styliane.

'I would not use the runes against you, Freydis. It is right that you gave them to me. I am the master, you the servant.'

'I am no one's servant. I am a goddess.' Freydis stepped forward and the runes sprang up around Styliane. Sowilo burned with its cleansing fire.

'I will strike you down.'

'Then strike. Send me to the afterlife. Show you can live without me.'

A tongue of fire shot from the sharp S of the rune towards Freydis but the flames did not touch her. She was shielded by an invisible force.

She saw the fear in Styliane's eyes. Freydis held out her hand, showed her the wolfstone.

'It is a bane to magic,' she said.

'What will you do?'

'I will leave you beautiful,' said Freydis.

She put the wolfstone into her mouth. All Styliane's runes now raged. Fire, ice and hail drove towards Freydis but the warrior was untouched.

She put her hands around Styliane's neck. The lady tried to fight her but it was useless. Styliane was light, delicate, and had never had to lift a thing for herself. Freydis, a warrior, strangled the life from her and the runes flew up into the grey sky.

The wolf still gnawed on the body of the god.

Freydis spat out the stone.

'I would take you with me if I could,' she said to the wolf. 'Our story is over. You live on, your enemy dead, his bargain unfulfilled. You face forever alone.'

She lifted Styliane and carried her up to the burning ship. At the tiller was Célene, alongside Gylfa, proud as a lord, sitting on a wooden box, his hands on an oar. On the other side was Hals, he too ready to row along with the crew of dead men. There at the prow was Tola, smiling. In her hand was a distaff and with it she spun the dull wool she bore around her neck into a golden thread.

Freydis laid Styliane in the flames and kissed her.

'Soon you will wake and live forever with me,' she said, 'in my hall, in my lands, doing my bidding.'

'Row,' she said to the others. 'Row to the rainbow bridge and from there to my hall in the fields of Fólkvangr.'

The boat lifted from the shore, leading the fleet of burning longships behind it, floating up into the cloudy sky, beyond the clouds, to find the rainbow.

Below them the wolf howled, alone on the island, gazing out over the grey ocean, seeing nothing.